THE SWITCH

THE SWITCH

A NOVEL BY

APRIL McCLOUD

Queer Space

A REBEL SATORI IMPRINT

New Orleans & New York

Published in the United States of America by
Queer Space (A Rebel Satori Imprint)
www.rebelsatoripress.com

Cover design by Sven Davisson

To our future robot overlords.
I'm 1% bionic now so please consider me for a cushy dignitary position.
I'll gladly liaise with the humans on your behalf.

SUBJECTS AND THEMES

I strongly support upholding mental health as a priority and believe readers should have access to the ingredients from an intellectual work just as they might wish to as from an organic meal.

The Switch is a speculative fiction story about what it means to be human in a bionic world. There is fighting and general asskicking, as well as thoughtful conversations about how evolving ideas of embodiment have changed what it means to be trans or disabled. Ultimately, this work strives to balance meditative thought with action scenes, so our heroes can find their way through the darkness.

Below is a list of potentially triggering subjects and themes appearing in this work:

Body horror, Body dysmorphia, Misgendering, Murder/blood, Violence/Injuries, Drugs/Addiction, Kidnapping, Sexism

PROLOGUE

Tyler

While he knew the woman before him didn't have organic maggots growing out of holes in her shoulders, it was hard not to be creeped out by the realism of the upgrade. Intimidation was everything in The Underground and Tyler had to admit, he didn't have much by way of it himself. His own body had only a select number of upgrades—his sister had been apoplectic when he'd replaced his eye in order to get the retinal one. But not everyone could be as hyper-conservative and live without them like she did.

Sericata leaned back against the brick alley wall, eying him. "Do you want the location or not?"

His gaze was stuck on one of the maggots on her shoulder, wriggling around with far too much verisimilitude—but better not to irritate a powerful information monger.

"Let me transfer the credits—"

In a moment of stillness, Tyler heard the familiar whistling carried on the wind and an icy chill went through him.

Everyone in The Underground was being hunted by someone—Tyler had been part of it for long enough to realize that was just what you had to do to survive.

But whatever shadow was following him now was so much worse.

He'd been careful not to let anyone know where he was, he'd

hidden his tracks—

At the nervous way Sericata shifted her stance his breath caught. "You sold me out."

Her lips pressed together before she gave an unapologetic shrug. "You're easy money."

Simultaneously, all the maggots trained their attention on Tyler, and he saw the flickering red lights of the dozens of cameras.

When he saw her reaching for a gun, Tyler bolted.

A crack resounded and he pivoted enough that the bullet only grazed his shoulder. That hit still sent a hot lance of pain coursing through him, made him stumble into another alley. Her other shots made building shrapnel rain down on him as he made his escape.

Adrenaline kept his legs pumping and he wound his way out of the labyrinthine alleys, feeling hot blood trailing down his arm to his fingertips. He clutched the wound and slowed his pace so as not to attract attention, the small chirrup letting him know he'd passed The Underground's barrier and returned to one of the seediest parts of New York.

Panting painfully, he wondered not for the first time, how in the world his sister managed to run marathons. But thinking of her saddened him, because now that Sericata had betrayed him, his only option left was his last resort.

Which might be a choice he would regret more than even facing his fate.

He pushed down his emotions and tapped the middle finger of his right hand with his thumb twice to display the time in his visual field. *5:17am.* His sister would be up soon if she wasn't already. If nothing else, Naomi was predictable. Dependable.

Trustworthy.

Everything Tyler wasn't.

His throat tightened but he refused to wallow in the ocean of his regret. He was going to fix this so he could look his sister in the eyes again. Be the type of sibling she deserved.

But even as his feet carried him where he didn't want to go, he kept trying to think of any other options he might have missed. Could he ask Naomi for help?

Could she even help him this time?

His hand curled into a fist, feeling the sticky, fresh blood.

He'd already decided he couldn't do that to her again.

He swallowed dryly. But maybe—

Through the quiet early morning air, the sound of whistling reached him.

There was no choice left, was there?

Propelled by terror Tyler sprinted for several blocks before he careened around a corner into a dark alley, launching himself behind a dumpster. A smell somewhere between rotting corpse and curdled milk hovered in the air and he held his breath to keep from gagging. As he crouched a bead of sweat slid slowly between his shoulder blades. Time crawled by and he carefully let out a breath, chancing a glance around the corner of the rusty dumpster.

The lights from the street seeped into the alley, painting the wet boxes and scattered garbage a faded yellow. The pavement glistened and there was a sudden flash of movement, his muscles tightening—but it was only a cat, bounding up to him. There was a black collar embellished with ladybugs against tri-color fur and he was about to smile when he flinched, seeing the computer chips on her side where part of the artificial fur had been ripped off. As the broken robot rubbed against his leg in a natural manner, though, he was grateful to have company in his fetid prison.

He slumped back against the alley wall, letting out a breath.

"Bodies, amirite?"

The cat meowed in response, a brief flash of green visible on her computer chips.

In so many ways, his own body had always felt off. Just like a patch of missing fur, exposing that his insides were very different than what his outsides showed.

He took in a shaky breath. Maybe it was time he acknowledged that he wasn't all that against the idea of leaving his own body behind?

Hoping enough time had passed, he kissed the head of his new friend. "Wish me luck." But even as his legs shook from having crouched for so long, there was a bounce in his step as he made his way.

He glanced around cautiously before he tapped out the familiar sequence of middle finger, ring, and middle against his thumb. *Calling Naomi Gate.*

As it rang, he moved deeper into the alley, checking over his shoulder continuously. The call was mid-ring when it abruptly went to voicemail. His eyes closed in defeat. She'd declined his call. Figured.

You've reached the voicemail box of Detective Naomi Gate of the NYPD. If this is an emergency, say the word emergency to be connected with the police or if unable to speak, mark the police interface for immediate GPS assistance. For all other concerns, please leave a message after the tone and I will respond to you as soon as I am able.

He took a deep breath, but he was filled with hope for a change. "Hey, Noams. I don't blame you for ignoring my call, though I really wish you'd answered." As he came to a filthy door with a red X spray-painted across it, he paused, resting his hand beside the door. "It will probably come as no surprise to you that I've screwed up again." He turned his back to the wall, staring up at the sky that he could barely see between the buildings, wishing he could see the faint sunrise, wishing there was something to see other than smog. "And I know I've told you that I've never really felt right in my body. Which maybe explains part of why I've been such a screw up." He sucked in a brave breath. "But I'm going to fix everything, Naomi. And once I have—"

Call disconnected.

He blinked, his hands shaking as he went through the sequence to call her again.

He needed to explain what he was planning, he needed to—

Call cannot be completed.

His heart pounded. He held down his thumb to his forefinger and addressed his internal computer. "Why not?"

There is no reception.

A shiver went through his entire body. Even the diciest parts of New York City got excellent service. If he had no reception, it could mean only one thing.

The quiet of the night was punctured by the sound of whistling and chains dragging on pavement.

His predator was nearby, blocking the signal.

Acknowledging he no longer had a choice, he pivoted to the door with the X, lifting his right wrist to the identification lock. It scanned for his ID chip and the door chirruped as it unlocked. He pushed inside and slammed it closed, his heart hammering in his chest.

"You're late." Iago's voice was like gravel as he fixed the tubes of a machine. He wore a doctor's coat faded to gray, filthy with equal parts oil and blood. Rather than hair, the clear casing exposed component parts flickering like fireflies in the gray light of the room. A certified enhancement center would have grafted the man's hair back into place, so none of the upgrades would be visible.

The man's left eye was simply a pulsing red light, glowing eerily in the dark.

This was *not* one of those centers.

Tyler motioned weakly over his shoulder to the door. "I hid to lose my tail, but I think they're still close by."

The man gave a grunt as Tyler tried not to stare at the man's retinal upgrade. It hadn't been replaced with a facsimile eye that could pass in most lights as natural but with a laser, instead. "If they've found you, we have no time to lose. Get on so I can begin."

He motioned to a human shaped metal table, straps every four inches and host to a variety of stains. Tyler's eyes though shifted to take in the battered body in the table beside, this one having a dull metallic arm with numerous dents and a black tank top allowing access to open panels, lights shining beneath. Wires were hanging loosely from multiple ports, a breathing tube down the throat keeping the shell—Tyler's new body— alive.

His heart raced in terror and he began to rethink his plan. This certainly wasn't the type of body he wanted and would come with a lot of baggage. Maybe if he talked with Naomi, maybe there was another way. Maybe it didn't have to come to this, maybe—

Iago growled. "Do you want your new body or not?"

Tyler thought of his sister, thought of how hard she'd worked since their mother had died. She'd bailed him out of trouble countless times, but he knew this time he'd finally gone too far. He couldn't ask her to fix it. He had to do this himself.

He hurried onto the table before he lost his resolve. The man began methodically tightening the straps around his legs, before doing the same to his torso and arms. When he tightened the strap around his forehead, he shoved a piece of leather between his lips. At his confused frown, Iago grunted. "I can't resell the body if you destroy the teeth. They're too expensive."

Tyler stared at the ceiling as the bitter taste of dirty leather crept onto his tongue and slid down his throat. The man connected electrodes to his temples, inserted wires into the connection ports of his right arm, left leg, and at the base of his skull. He stared at the fluorescent lights, a graveyard of dead insect carcasses in the flickering light.

"Bite down. Hard." There was the whirring of a machine as it came to life and the man was suddenly in his view, red eye pulsing. "This is going to hurt."

Tyler felt the electricity course through his body and a scream boiled out of his throat for the last time.

CHAPTER 1

Naomi

The rhythmic pounding of her feet on the pavement perfectly matched the upbeat tempo of Ligeti's *Devil's Staircase*. She'd achieved all of her fastest paces while listening to epics like Wagner's *Ride of the Valkyries* or Tchaikovsky's *1812 Overture*. Other runners mocked her preference for running to classical music, but there was something primal about running to the sound of cannons.

As she crested the bridge's incline, the skyscrapers of New York City loomed in the distance. The still surface of the small lake reflected the city like a canvas painted in pinks and oranges. The tallest building in the watery image was white with sleek blue and green accents. A bird floated down to land on the CLM Tower, and ripples distorted the accents of the pale monolith. How they managed to keep the building clean was beyond her.

But then maybe the pigeons helped, since their crap was white.

The path widened and changed to dirt as she descended back into the urban greenery of Central Park. Vibrant trees lined the lane, with benches placed at standard intervals. As always, Ron was still asleep beneath his usual bench, with his cardboard shelter erected to keep out the encroaching daylight. She pulled his favorite granola bar out of her pocket and slowed down only enough to drop it on the bench without waking him.

Veering down a smaller path to the right she came to the reservoir. She tapped her thumb to her ring finger twice, and her internal computer spoke over the music.

Stopwatch engaged.

She leaned forward as she started sprinting around the reservoir path. The sun crested the horizon and sprayed the world in light. The sound of birds chirping was drowned out by heavy footfalls. Another runner shot past her, easily outpacing Naomi by two or more minutes per mile. The woman couldn't have sounded more like a cantankerous elephant even if she'd tried.

Naomi's gaze was drawn to the other woman's legs, and it was easy enough to spot the subtle dent of the port on the side of her thigh. Both of her legs were dark bronze, lacking a single blemish. Naomi rolled her yellow-brown eyes. It was beyond a shadow of a doubt that they were vanity upgrades. But since the port was on her thigh, it meant both of her legs had been replaced up to the hip. Why bother running? Though that truly made it a vanity upgrade, didn't it?

Naomi kept her sights on the woman as they rounded the bottom of the reservoir, pretending she was in a race and letting the adrenaline wash over her. She was used to trailing behind, because no matter how quick she was, she could never be as fast as the bionic ostrich before her. It was less than a minute before the woman was gone, but Naomi could see the head of the reservoir and concentrated on her end goal.

As she neared the light pole, she leaned forward, waiting until she was beside it to tap her thumb to her ring finger again.

Lap time: seven minutes, fifty-eight seconds for one point five eight miles.

She slowed to cool down, heading toward the Great Lawn. She panted, already knowing the answer wouldn't be what she wanted to hear. Her thumb and forefinger pressed together. "Pace?"

Five minutes, two seconds per mile.

Breaking the five-minute mile mark was consistently a problem. She'd done it on occasion, but never managed it intentionally. Yet, she couldn't understand what part of her training was lacking.

The canopy of trees gave way to the expansive Great Lawn. There was a group of twenty practicing tai chi, their hands and bodies a wave of calculated movements. When one of them fell out of rhythm, her eyes shot to his burnt orange shirt and shaven head.

Their eyes held and she could swear he was smiling at her—

Proximity alert.

She ducked to the left just as a blue frisbee flew inches above her head. Behind her, a man yelled an apology, but her eyes caught on the large German shepherd sprinting up beside her. The dog gave her a single glance before he put on a burst of speed and leapt into the air to catch the flying disc between his powerful jaws. As he landed gracefully and proudly met her gaze, Naomi felt a laugh bubble out of her. "Don't worry, I won't steal your frisbee." The beast turned to pad back excitedly to his owner.

Watching the man play with his pup she caught the unexpected longing growing inside of herself to have a pet of her own. Wouldn't it be nice to go running with a dog?

Not a chance. A detective's schedule hardly left time for herself, let alone a pet.

Naomi made her way to the kidney-shaped pond, going to her usual spot beside the water. Sitting down and stretching her legs out was luxurious, her muscles burning with gratitude.

Changing position, her fingertips trailed over her shins and there was the familiar contrast between the natural skin on her left to the metallic matte of the right. Unlike the bionic ostrich she'd faced earlier, she'd received her own bionic upgrade in a hospital, which was the only place that Naomi felt was appropriate for the procedure. Her accident with her brother had taken away her foot and shin, but her knee was still her own. She'd never wanted an upgrade but was certainly grateful to return to normalcy once her body healed and the implant was carefully tuned so as to be perfectly aligned with her human leg.

For whatever reason, her mind again put forward the image of the bionic ostrich's perfect legs, the smooth and painted perfection. Why was she fixating on them? Her own bionic leg was a replacement for a part of her that had been destroyed. The thought of willingly giving up her legs like that woman had was repugnant. Despite the width of Naomi's quads and the blemishes on her body, at least she didn't feel the need to try to be some waif with bionic appendages and a boob job in order to get attention.

Huffing in irritation, she was about to change position again when she nearly crushed a tiny flower. The single purple blossom was sprouting in the crevice of a rock, fighting valiantly toward the sun.

Naomi's ire melted at the sight.

Nature was really beautiful, and she felt like she never got enough of it. Maybe she should go on a retreat somewhere? Get away from all the tech, even for a couple of days. Maybe she could even turn off her interface—

Her moment of reflection was interrupted by a mechanical hum. A cleaning-bot crested a nearby rock. Like most, it was the size and shape of a thick dinner plate, but this one was silver with triangular wheels on the bottom to navigate the terrain. She was used to seeing the machines in the rest of the city, but it felt wrong somehow, to have them when surrounded by nature.

When the robot veered straight for the minuscule flower, Naomi found her eyes rolling again. "So, this is the type of day we're having, is it?"

Looking again, the robot had done its job thoroughly, as not even a single straggling root was left behind.

She launched to her feet in irritation and barely kept herself from kicking the stupid frisbee—she paused, eyes glancing over at the dog that was still playing and a grin popped onto her lips as she imagined herself tossing the cleaning bot into the eager pup's jaws. Her aural interface interrupted her fantasy. *Incoming call from Tyler Gate.*

She grimaced and held back on answering, closing her eyes to prepare herself. "Be nice, Naomi. He's your brother." She pinched the bridge of her nose. It was going to be a long day; she could tell that already. She took a calming breath, and while she could not find zen, she could try to dial back her vexation and speak civilly with her sibling.

Her fingers were about to tap to accept the call when the crack of a gunshot made her flinch.

Her head whipped toward the sound as people scattered across the lawn, into the trees. In the epicenter of the chaos stood two silhouettes, one towering over the other. She crouched to touch her bionic leg, waving her ID chip over the biometric lock. While her leg had originally been replaced in a hospital, she had grudgingly decided to have an aftermarket compartment installed in case of emergencies. Which had been an excellent decision since it had saved her ass more than once.

With a soft hiss her gun protruded from the hidden compartment. She grabbed her augmented .22 and touched her finger and thumb together on her other as she raced across the grass toward the pair. "Decline call and mark my GPS location to NYPD emergency, code tango-zero-seven-alpha."

She trained her gun on the pair as she neared. The smaller of the two was a man she recognized—the one practicing tai chi earlier who'd caught her eye. His orange robe was stained with blood from a gunshot wound on his right shoulder. She was behind the larger man, who was bigger than she'd thought from afar; he was easily over six and a half feet tall. His shoulders were like boulders, with a small arsenal of weapons protruding from them. There were at least a half dozen gun barrels exposed from his shoulder enhancements, his ripped shirt dangling down by his waist. Most of his chest was a sleek metallic finish. How had she missed someone of his size—she saw the remnants of a ripped skirt with a flowered pattern around his waist. So he'd been wearing a skirt to keep his bionic legs covered until he expanded them to full height? Clever.

And how refreshing to see the bad guys were getting more comfortable gender bending.

He screamed at the bloody man, grabbing the front of his robes. "Tell me about Sanctuary."

The bald man gave a cryptic smile. "Finding sanctuary is in the hands of every individual." His eyes flicked over to hers briefly, and the walking armory must have seen.

When the monolith of a man turned, she got her first glimpse of his bionic eyes. Both were black except for the white square outlining the computer chips; obviously her opponent had no qualms about replacing his body parts with tech. She trained her gun on him, covertly touching the switch beneath the trigger to change firing modes. Since he was definitely over the fifty percent enhancement mark and most of the upgrades were obviously illegal, regular bullets probably weren't going to do much.

"NYPD. Step away from him and power down your weapons immediately."

Quick as a cobra strike, the man spun so the injured monk was held between them, the strong bionic arm in a chokehold around the smaller man's neck. Not the best possible turn, but not the worst.

Incoming message from NYPD. Expect reinforcements in four minutes.

Time to stall.

She held the man's gaze, lifting a brow. "You have a name?"

His lip curled like a wisp of smoke and his voice was an ashtray. "You can call me Artillery."

Oh, good. She was up against a psychopathic murderer wanted in multiple countries, and seriously outgunned. Well. He was probably an egomaniac. She could use that. "Artillery? What type of name is that?"

His rasp continued. "Who do you think you are?"

"Detective Gate, NYPD." Her eyes glanced to the captive man. "Let him go now and this will be better for you."

His chuckle was like chains being dragged through broken glass. "He still hasn't told me what I need to know."

"And I won't." The bald man's voice was utterly lacking in fear. Now that she looked closely, there were barely even any lines of pain creasing his face—only a few beads of sweat falling down from his temples indicated the pain he must be in. He looked strangely serene, given the circumstance.

Incoming message from NYPD. Three minutes.

She could make it three more minutes. "You said something about Sanctuary, right? What is it, a code name, or are you really looking to save your soul?"

Artillery eyed her. "I don't have time for you." The world

seemed to move in slow motion as smoke billowed from the tip of the third gun on his right shoulder. There was a crack after she pulled the trigger on her own gun, which sparked and flared a brilliant orange ball of light toward him.

Phase Shield engaged.

The air crackled and popped, and neon blue netting made of light wrapped around her—the bullet Artillery had fired hit it and fell harmlessly away. Her Cannon Shot hit the mark though, wrapping Artillery in blue lightning. The sound of her shield fizzling away was drowned out by the crash of Artillery's body hitting the ground.

Phase Shield depleted.

There was a hiss and thud as her leg ejected the phase canister down by her foot, smoking as it rolled away. It wasn't the first time the bulletproof netting had saved her life, but she was always grateful for it.

She kept her gun trained on his body as she rushed forward. Hopefully if he came to, he wouldn't know she only had normal bullets left. After checking him, she breathed a sigh of relief that she wouldn't have to bluff. But the monk was a crumpled heap on the ground just beside him. His breathing was ragged and sounded hollow, but at least his neck hadn't been crushed when Artillery fell.

She tucked her gun into the waistband of her running shorts, crouching down beside the man. He opened his chestnut brown eyes to stare in disbelief at her. "How are you still alive?"

"Phase canister." She drew him into her lap and took off her headband, pushing it against the gunshot wound to apply pressure. The next biggest concern would be him going into shock; she kept talking to distract him. "It makes a bulletproof netting for a second. It's a good thing he was so arrogant he only shot once."

His eyes moved to the comatose man. "And him?"

"I used a Cannon Shot on him." Something was wrong. He looked worse than he should for being shot in a non-vital area. "He probably thought my gun was just a normal twenty-two, but it was a gift from one of my mother's old friends when I joined the force. Don't you know about any of these things?" His whole body seemed to shake in answer. Better to keep him talking. "What's your name?"

"Vimal." He took in a sudden, sharp breath. "The digo works as quickly as he promised."

"Digo?" Her eyes shot to the comatose form beside them and then to the wound on the man's shoulder in understanding. "He used a bullet laced with poison to try to get you to talk." And that's why he'd only shot her with one bullet. He'd been planning to poison her, too.

"Yes, but I know enough about men like him to know there never was an antidote."

She took his hand and held it tightly, watching his eyes. "You're going to be fine."

He gave her a weak smile and spoke as if he'd said the words a thousand times. "Loved ones who have long kept company will part. Wealth created with difficulty will be left behind. Consciousness, the guest, will leave the guesthouse of the body. Let go of this life." He let out a shaky breath, his body trembling. "This is the practice of Bodhisattvas."

Her eyes moved over his face. How much time did he have left? "What's Sanctuary?"

His gaze held hers and it felt as if the world slowed. "You'll know soon enough, Naomi."

Cacophony filled the area as a dozen officers raced in simultaneously from the trees, their heavy mech suits shaking the ground as they bounded into place. While this newest round was lighter and less bulky than the previous series of decommissioned military suits, they were still substantial. Even she, who boasted no more than five foot six normally, was over seven feet tall when wearing her suit. These suits were forty years old at this point though—she'd seen the newest ones on display at a military showcase last month and they were only a few inches thick.

With a metallic hiss, a suit opened and her coworker Sam was visible, stepping down to the grass. He pulled a medical kit out of a compartment on the leg of his suit and rushed to her side.

Naomi felt a crash of relief. "Help is here now, you'll be—" Vimal's eyes were open but staring at nothing. She reached up and closed them as Sam knelt opposite her, running the scanner over Vimal's body.

"I can't even restart his heart. There's too much poison."

Naomi looked at the blood on her hand. Her headband was soaked with it.

"Who was he?"

Sam ran the scanner over Vimal's forearm, pausing before he ran it over his other forearm. Then he began running it over the man's neck and head. "Huh."

"What is it?"

Her coworker shrugged. "He doesn't have a single enhancement. No ID chip, no aural interface, no GPS chip, nothing. Who doesn't at least have an aural interface, these days? I mean, do you think he carried a cell phone like a kid?"

Her brows drew together in confusion. No enhancements at all? Even she had resigned herself to the necessity of an internal computer, if only for the safety that precise GPS marking to the police brought.

Sam touched her arm. "I can take it from here, Naomi."

She didn't understand what he meant until she realized Vimal was still in her lap. She carefully lowered him to the ground, and Sam's voice was quiet. "I'll watch over him until the coroner gets here. Did you know him?"

Her head shook slowly. "No, I'd never met him before this." She laid a hand on his forehead. "Rest in peace." She shifted her weight back onto her heels and stood, taking a step away from them and staring off. What had Artillery wanted? And what was Sanctuary?

She held her thumb and pointer finger together. "What's a bodhisattva?"

Bodhisattvas: In Sanskrit, Bodhi means 'enlightened' and Sattva means 'being,' so the literal translation is 'enlightened being.' Also the term for the historical Buddha Gautama before his enlightenment. Also refers to any individuals who are destined to become a Buddha. In Mahayana Buddhism, the bodhisattva postpones the attainment of nirvana in order to alleviate the suffering of others. According to Tibetan Buddhism, being a Bodhisattva is one of the four sublime states a human can achieve in life.

She stared at the skyscrapers in the distance. He'd chanted words when faced with death. From the way he'd spoken, it sounded as if he devoutly believed the words he was speaking, so Naomi was inclined to believe it meant he was Buddhist by faith. Buddhists were historically pacifists, and the man hadn't had so much as a single enhancement on him. What type of information could he possibly have that a criminal like Artillery would want? It didn't make sense.

"Naomi…" Her coworker Amy scoffed. "Are you fucking kidding me?" Amy had opened her mech suit but stayed inside, so Naomi had to look up at her as she pointed down at the unconscious criminal. "This is Artillery!" There were another five officers in a circle, all staring at her.

Naomi looked between them. "He introduced himself. Not exactly a gentleman, but what can a lady expect from criminals these days."

Amy groaned and put a hand to her head. "Seriously, Naomi."

"What?"

"Could you at least act as if it were a big deal you took down Artillery—by yourself—while armed with nothing but your damn leg?"

That reminded her. She pulled her gun out from the waistband of her shorts and returned it to the slot in her calf. "Hey, my gun's reliable."

There was a derisive snort behind her. The officer peering over her shoulder was in a mech suit, but she'd know that snarky asshole Gerald's noises anywhere. Even his voice sounded as if he had a stick up his ass. "Well, if you'd bothered to get the retinal upgrade, you could have recorded it and we could have at least enjoyed it too."

The heat rushing through her veins was the first indicator she really was on edge. "We're not required to have one so you can shove it up your ass, Gerald!"

"Fuck you, Nao—"

"*Your behavior is not de-escalatory. Your mech has been locked until a supervisor can review your conduct.*"

Gerald groaned in frustration.

That made it much easier for her to dial back her rage inferno. "I'm heading home so I can shower."

Amy's mech took a step toward her. "You need to file paperwork. You're a witness."

"Not to mention we need to process the evidence on you."

Simon's mech was pointing at her hands.

She hated them both for being right.

CHAPTER 2

Naomi

The sun was setting when she stepped into the shadow cast by CLM Tower. It was a monolith with a pristine white façade. Blue and green accents gave it a clean, cultured mien. The 3D image screen spanned at least ten stories, the current advertisement a young woman leaning forward in mid-laugh, raven hair tumbling over her shoulder and hand pressed against a stomach covered by a sparkling azure evening gown. The bold letters beside her read: *Live Better, Dream Better, Be Better.*

Naomi rolled her eyes. Apparently, there was a new CLM model. Every inch of her visible skin was flawless, her eyes amethyst, but Naomi realized with a start the woman's irises were literally gems. When had that become a new upgrade? Apparently, the woman had opted for the double optic nerve replacement, which made Naomi shiver. The thought of losing one eye was creepy enough. She couldn't imagine giving up both.

She must have tripped a proximity sensor, because the woman's image sprung to life and gestured to the entrance below, her voice silken. *"Come inside and find out what Complete Life Management can do for you. Not only can you get upgrades and enhancements to your current body and life, we also offer the option to start over com-*

pletely. *Make your dreams a reality. Come talk with one of our life spe-cialists. And remember...*" The image changed to a close up of her face, the multifaceted gems in her irises reflecting points of light. "*Live better, dream better, be better.*" The woman winked before re-turning to stationary.

Naomi stared for a moment before she rolled her eyes again, turning to the door.

The glass doors slid open as she entered, the heat from the lobby warming her bare legs below her skirt. She squinted at the excessively brilliant white. Like the outside of the building, the lobby had accents of the same jewel-tone blues and greens. There were plush chaises interspersed between chairs in the same color scheme, all tasteful and modern. The doorman greeted her with a smile, his bleached teeth perfectly straight. "Good evening and welcome, Miss Gate. I'll let Mr. Raelyn know you've arrived."

"Thank you. Tell him not to rush." She moved away slowly, watching as the man lifted his hands and began typing on air. He swiped two fingers to the right before lowering his hands, clasping them before himself. She turned her eyes away, walking over to the long welcome counter. There were several interface stations not in use on one end. She rarely ever saw anyone in the lobby—usually any potential clients were whisked away with alarming efficiency to meet with life specialists within minutes, if not seconds.

Behind the counter, an obnoxiously picture-perfect woman stood at attention. Her copper skin was covered by a tight-fitting, white dress, crisscrossed fabric across her chest exposing her cleavage beneath. Naomi pointed to a station. "Can I borrow this interface for a moment?"

The woman's crimson lips smiled, but nothing else on her face moved. "Of course, Miss Gate."

Naomi murmured a thank you as she claimed the interface on the furthest end of the counter and waved a hand to wake it up. A screen jumped to life in the air before her, at the standard height of her eye level. Naomi paused and glanced at the woman behind the counter, who was watching a fashion model on an image screen across the room. The doorman was staring blankly at nothing; he must have the retinal upgrade, so he didn't even need an image screen. The room was so quiet that she contemplated using her aural upgrade to turn on some music.

It seemed unlikely either of them would notice her search, but she still pinched her screen, dragging it down onto the counter so she had more privacy. Beneath the screen, a keyboard of light appeared, and she touched the screen to bring up the Net. After switching on the private browsing settings, she typed in *The Sanctuary*.

Scanning through the results she turned off the GPS-enabled search prioritization. She didn't want to assume from the start that Sanctuary had anything to do with New York City. Dozens of advertisements popped up and she swiped past them. The results were all listings that seemed to be for hotels, spas, resorts, or homeless shelters. She was wading through more useless pages when she heard the ding of the elevator.

As the white doors slid open, the familiar form of Jax in a sharply cut black suit sauntered forth. His pristine white shirt highlighted his golden-brown skin the color of the desert, his dark hair short on the sides with slight curls on the top. There was a precise amount of stubble on his face, and she had often teased that he must measure it every morning to make it so uniform. He was straightening the neck of his sapphire blue tie when his amber eyes met her gaze. His lips edged up in the familiar greeting and she smiled in response.

When a woman stepped into view—her arm slipping casually into Jax's—Naomi had to actively work to control her face and keep her hands from balling into fists. It was as if she had walked out of the advertisement outside the building, her raven hair tumbling around her shoulders and the same self-satisfied expression on her lips. This pale pink evening dress was even higher up her thighs and lower-cut around her breasts. Something was very odd about her, though. Naomi couldn't immediately put her finger on it. She turned quickly to the interface, waving two fingers in an x over the screen to close it out and put it back to sleep.

The woman was giving an energetic laugh as Naomi turned to them, shifting her weight from one leg to the other and actively reminding herself to be pleasant. "Hello."

Jax drew his arm out of the woman's and turned to Naomi. He put his hands on her waist and looked straight into her eyes. "My darling. It's so good to see you." He kissed both of her cheeks.

"Good evening, Jax." Their gazes held for a moment, and she had to admit the unfettered attention soothed her irritation. But this was his job, and she should try to be pleasant. "Are you going to introduce me to your newest model?"

The woman gave a soft giggle. "You saw me outside?"

Naomi struggled to get her teeth apart. "Couldn't miss you." Across from them, a sheer white panel reflected her image beside that of the model. Naomi was shorter, wearing black flats, her legs muscular and quads much wider than the other woman's slim ones. The dress Naomi had chosen was form-fitting but not skin-tight. She liked the dress because the straps were wide enough to cover her bra straps. She was too big to either go without or find a strapless that didn't remind her of a medieval torture device. Her left breast was a size bigger than her right, and she noticed they were much less perky than the model's perfectly round, identical breasts. Naomi's brown hair was in layers around her face, her light skin splotched with a few freckles and a couple of scars where she'd needed stitches after playing too rough with her brother.

The feeling of Jax slipping an arm fully around her waist brought her attention away from the images.

He motioned to the woman. "Naomi, this is Nikola. She is also literally our newest model, the Apogee. Nikola, this is my girlfriend whom I told you about. I can hardly believe today is our one-year anniversary."

Naomi's brows drew together as she looked at Nikola. "I'm sorry, you are what model?" Her eyes fired over to Jax. "I hadn't heard about any new bionic models coming out recently." The woman giggled again. "Oh, I'm the first beta tester of the Apogee line. 97.56% bionic! Isn't that amazing? Feel my arm... I'm extra soft to the touch."

Naomi's mouth hung open in disbelief as she recoiled, finally understanding what it was about the girl that bothered her so much. She'd learned that as the percent of bionics increased in bodies, designers struggled to ensure that they weren't too perfect looking, because it easily crested into eerie. But Naomi saw Nikola's face for what it was: a cold calculation by a computer algorithm to have an acceptable number of 'attractive' imperfections.

As Nikola continued to eagerly offer her arm, Naomi found her hand moving out of disgusted curiosity—there were even slight bumps built into her skin.

The girl gave another giggle. "I don't even need to moisturize."

Over ninety-seven percent bionic? In Naomi's opinion, the

Zenith model had crossed the line when it bypassed the 60% bionic mark. She'd always been comforted by the fact that it wasn't likely they could go much further, because the bulk of the torso and brain were absolutely vital for sustaining life, procreation, and brain activities. How had they made the jump that far that quickly? She turned to Jax. "Did you get special permission from the United Humanity Federation? Because this well exceeds the standards set in the Bionic Accords—"

"Sweetheart." Even though he was smiling, she could see the irritation in the creases around his eyes. "Let's not talk politics."

She took in a breath, forcing a smile of her own and softening her tone. "Of course I'll drop it, as soon as you assure me CLM hasn't broken any laws?"

He cocked a brow. "Of course we got special permission from the United Humanity Federation. We received thirty-seven votes from the board, and do I need to remind my darling detective we only needed thirty, or would you also like to see the paperwork?"

She realized she was perhaps being overly hostile. It wasn't as if she had any reason to believe CLM was doing anything illegal, especially since the picture of the model was literally ten stories tall on the side of their building. That wasn't exactly subtle, if they were. "I'm sorry, I get carried away sometimes."

His eyes held hers and softened to match a suddenly genuine smile. "You wouldn't be a good homicide detective if you didn't, and that happens to be one of my favorite things about you." He leaned over to kiss her, and she was surprised. He wasn't normally so openly affectionate in public, let alone in the lobby of his company. "Nikola, my girlfriend and I need to be heading out for our date. If you'll excuse us."

Naomi would be lying if she said she didn't enjoy the jealousy Nikola tried to hide behind a smile. "Of course. It was nice to meet you, Naomi."

"You as well. Good luck with the beta testing." She bit back a remark about how most serious malfunctions happened within the first three versions of a new model's release.

The doorman was quick to take the arm of Nikola and lead her outside. Jax's hand went to Naomi's waist, his other touching her chin. "I do believe that you and I are supposed to be heading to our anniversary dinner." He leaned forward to whisper in her ear, his hand teasingly at her low back. "And to my penthouse for dessert afterward?"

His lips grazed her ear and she found herself resenting the flash of pleasure her body put forth—what was with her resentment? It was her anniversary, and with the horrors she saw on her job, she knew life was too short to waste ignoring simple pleasures. So, she leaned up to nip at his ear, and they shared a heated gaze before they turned to the exit together.

The door to Jax's custom Aston Martin was held open for them by his doorman. As always, she struggled with the dissonance between her lived experience as a detective and the world of wealth in which Jax resided. She usually took the subway to go back and forth from work, but as they settled into the car, he used the touchscreen in a familiar manner to type in the address for the restaurant. In some ways, though, it was comforting that they both benefited from the car ride. While most people with leg enhancements were able to walk faster than driving, Jax—quite oddly, for the CEO of the world's premier vanity upgrade company—still had all his original human parts.

The car chirruped, and with barely a noise from the electric engine, pulled away from the curb. She rested her arm beside the window. The sidewalks were filled with people leaving work, dozens of image screens showing advertisements—mostly for CLM. The city that never slept carried on no matter what, it seemed.

Yet that day, she'd caught a wanted felon, witnessed the death of a man who had no upgrades, and met a woman who was essentially a human on the cusp of turning android. Before bionics became mainstream, people had been afraid an Artificial Intelligence would be created that would destroy humanity. Naomi had always been, and likely always would be, more afraid of people than machines.

Let go of this life. She could see Vimal's dead face in her mind. When she'd left work for the day, they still hadn't been able to identify him. Where had he come from? Who was he? How could someone truly live off the grid? Did he have a family who was missing him? Maybe if she could figure out what he'd chanted, it would shed some light on the mystery.

"You've been distant." Jax's reflection shrugged. "Well, more than usual."

She struggled not to roll her eyes. "I had a strange day."

"What happened?"

She figured she'd better tell him before he found out on the news. "I was shot at this morning."

He touched her arm. "When?" Their eyes caught. "At work?"

"Before. I was stretching after my run and there was a gunshot. I went to investigate—"

"You went to investigate?" His hand drew back, his fingers curling into a fist. "Did you happen to pack your mech suit?"

"I'm a detective; of course I investigated." She shrugged. "And I had my gun. Though I should thank you for having your company figure out how to connect the phase canister to the proximity sensor on my leg. Making it automatically create a bulletproof netting saved my life."

He turned in his seat so he could face her better and lifted a finger. "Let me get this straight. While off duty and under no legal obligation to investigate without a mech suit to keep you safe, you heard a gunshot and went up to the perpetrator with your lone old gun and a single phase canister?"

She opened her mouth to snap before she paused. He was right. Sort of.

Her silence gave him an opening to continue. "Because that's all you can fit in the tiny compartment in your leg since you won't let me upgrade it and—"

"And I didn't need any more than that to take him down, so it's fine."

Their gaze held tensely until his brow lifted. "How many guns did he have?"

She sighed. "Let's not do this right now."

"No, you tell me how many guns he had. Then we'll multiply that by the number of bullets he had, and after that we'll start talking about the plasma guns and energy pistols that could have vaporized you or just blown up parts of you."

Heat rushed through her. "Well, if that happened, you'd be happy because you could replace them with vanity parts."

His teeth clenched, but he sighed before gesturing in a stopping motion with his hands, palms toward her. "That's not fair. I would be devastated if something happened to you. A phase canister is only a single use, so if someone had shot at you more than once, you'd be dead right now."

She watched him for a moment before she shrugged and looked away, her anger wilting under the heat of her shame. "I'm sorry. The man he poisoned died in my arms." When his hand touched her shoulder, she glanced over at him. "He didn't have an aural interface, nothing. Not even an ID chip. I'm conservative, and even I opted for them."

His arm slipped around her and drew her head to his shoulder. Her eyes closed as she rested against him. His voice was soft. "Were you scared?"

Her eyes opened to stare off. "I wasn't in the moment, though I guess I should have been."

"You're always so fearless."

She shook her head, straightening. "No, I mean once he told me he was Artillery, I should have been worried. I think I was still on a bit of a runner's high."

He blinked twice. "Did you say Artillery? As in The Artillery?"

She sucked in her lips, knowing where this was going. "Yes."

"You captured Artillery."

"Yes."

"This morning, by yourself, without armor."

"Yes again."

"The felon who is wanted in what, ten countries?"

"Thirteen." She smiled sweetly. "But that's beside the point."

He reached up to pinch the bridge of his nose, giving a half-hearted chuckle.

"Yes, actually, it is beside the point."

The motion of the car shifted and a glance out the window showed they'd stopped beside a gaggle of reporters. It was nothing new, but she found herself sighing, wishing they didn't have to face it at the moment.

Jax touched her chin, bringing her eyes back to his. "Let's go celebrate the fact that your human body is tougher than that bionic junker you brought down today."

That brought a flash of pride, and as their car door was opened, she found herself being drawn willingly into the spotlight.

[30]

CHAPTER 3

Naomi

Before they were even out of the car, there were a half dozen reporters calling out to them. Jax helped her to his side and rested her hand on his arm, placing his other atop hers. Naomi glanced at the gesture in surprise. He wasn't normally that protective.

"Mr. Raelyn! Is it true that you're already beta testing a new CLM model?"

"Yes, the Apogee model is the newest innovation in ultra-upgraded technology, designed to exceed the expectations of the most discerning user."

She struggled not to snicker at how he sounded like a commercial.

"And what about your race tomorrow, Miss Gate?"

It took Naomi a long moment to realize that the reporters were speaking to her. "I'm looking forward to it."

The man inched forward. "So, you'll still be competing, despite what happened in Central Park with Artillery?"

She felt the way Jax's fingers tightened subtly, but he made no other outward show of his tension. Naomi was incredibly grateful she'd brought it up on the drive. "I will. And before you ask, please direct any questions about the incident to the NYPD. I'm certain my supervisor will be delighted to hear from you."

Obviously realizing they weren't going to get any information about Artillery out of her, a new reporter quickly got her attention. "Miss Gate, is it true this is your one year anniversary?"

"Detective Gate." At the man's confusion, Jax motioned to Naomi. "Why, precisely, do you drop her hard-earned title?" Jax turned his gaze on her, his features softening. "I for one never forget for an instant how grateful I am for my darling Detective's unrelenting commitment to the truth."

It was immensely strange to be receiving such pride from him publicly when he'd been castigating her so fiercely in private not even moments before.

At a clamor of questions, Jax held up a hand. "If you'll excuse us."

"Can we have a photo, please?"

Jax gave her an apologetic smile. "Would you mind, darling?"

It was such a common occurrence, she hardly thought anything of it anymore. But Jax always seemed a hint embarrassed by it. "Not at all."

He turned to the reporters. "Isn't she wonderful?"

The New York Times requests permission for a photograph with these specific limitations and usage restrictions…

She tapped the acceptance sequence on her fingers before it could keep going. Since she didn't have an optical upgrade, her internal computer used her aural upgrade to read the entire message to her until she either accepted or declined. In the beginning, she'd actually tried listening to them, until she realized they were something like eighty minutes long. Another four requests came in from other reporters, and she accepted them all.

Your privacy settings have been updated to reflect this one-time acceptance.

When Jax moved behind her, she wasn't able to keep herself from glancing at him in surprise. His arms slipped around her waist and rested against her stomach, drawing her against him.

He gave a laugh, kissing her cheek. "Why are you so surprised?"

She tilted her head back to look at him fully, a smile creeping onto her lips as her hands rested atop his. "You're in rare form tonight."

His eyes were intense as his arms squeezed her gently. "It's a special night." And even though there were reporters who had full permission to take their photo, Jax was giving her a deep kiss before Naomi could think better of it.

She was a bit breathless as they made their way inside the restaurant. The hostess bowed her head to them. "Mr. Raelyn, Miss Gate. Welcome back to the Euphotic Zone. Your table is ready."

The floor was a dark ocean blue, shimmering with glass mosaics of jellyfish, dolphins, and other aquatic life. The tables were covered in tablecloths of various shades of aqua, pendant lights hanging from the high ceiling in tonal greens. Each light was shaped like an aquatic plant, and there were dozens of fish tanks around the room. The tanks seemed to grow straight out of the floor and were filled with colorful fish, rocks, and anemones. In the center of the room, three large fish tanks formed a circle. The hostess led them to the slight passageway between the tanks and motioned to the table hidden within.

It was covered in a cerulean tablecloth, a bucket of ice holding a bottle of champagne sparkling beside it. The light was dimmer in this private area, making fish shine more brightly in the pristine tanks glowing with sun-mimicking bulbs. Jax pushed in her chair and took the seat across from her. Her eyes went to the fish floating beside her and she felt a swell of happiness. She remembered him from their other visits—he was a gentle giant, a vibrant blue parrotfish and nearly as big as her torso. He was swimming slowly, purposefully forward before he turned away.

"Welcome back to the Euphotic Zone, Mr. Raelyn, Miss Gate.

Shall I uncork the champagne?"

Jax leaned back in his chair, lifting his menu placard. "Yes, please."

As the man began opening the bottle, Naomi rested her napkin on her lap before looking at her own menu. She already knew what she was going to order, but it seemed more polite.

There was a soft pop, and before the man went to pour, Jax waved a hand. The server returned it to the ice, clasping his hands before him. "The specials tonight are—"

"No need. We'll be ready to order shortly."

"Very good, sir." The server bowed his head before retreating.

Jax reached for the bottle of champagne, and before he could bring it to her glass she put her hand over the rim. "I have a race tomorrow. Water will be fine for me."

He paused, then filled his own glass. "I don't understand why you run in the class you do. You're limiting yourself—"

"I'm not limiting myself by running in the most human classification."

His hand rested on his glass stem, his eyes watching her. "You run in the human female, sub five percent bionic classification. You compete only against women."

She grabbed her glass of water with a smirk. "This may be a surprise to you, but I am a woman."

He rolled his eyes and looked off. "Do we need the sarcasm? I'm trying to be serious."

Her glass hit the table with a thud louder than she intended. "There's nothing wrong with competing based on gender lines."

"It's about women being seen as inferior."

She crossed her arms before her on the table. "My running classification has nothing to do with that."

He gestured with his hand. "How is it you can't see it has everything to do with it? At least if you competed in the all-gender division it would be different. You aren't inferior, so why would you let yourself be held to a lower standard?"

"It's not a lower standard, it's just a different one. Longer running times for women have nothing to do with inferiority, they're simply reality. Fact. A fully human female can't run as fast as a fully human male. Fact. Our bodies are different. It's human minds that put a judgment onto those facts."

Jax's arm lay atop the table, his hand balled into a fist. His other hand pointed to the table. "Naomi, a hundred years ago, women weren't allowed in active combat because they were seen as weaker. You wouldn't have been as welcome in the police force as you are now. It was only with the creation of mech suits that the playing field was leveled and women could no longer be denied entry into the military on grounds of gender weakness and inferiority."

Her brow rose. "Oh, are we allowed to talk politics now?"

His fist hit the table, shaking the liquid in their glasses. He seemed about to speak before he put his hand over his eyes. "You're making this so difficult."

The argument was like a broken record. Naomi wanted to believe that fundamentally, they were arguing for the same thing but from different angles. In the beginning, despite his incredible good looks, she'd been leery about going on a date with the CEO of a company she abhorred. She'd decided at the very least she could use the evening as a chance to make a case for advocating upgrades in moderation. Yet, she'd sat across from a man who'd befuddled her with his conservative number of personal upgrades and strong arguments for how bionics had paved the way for gender equality. She'd tried to see things his way, but over time she'd begun to wonder if there was a core worldview difference between them that was fundamentally unbridgeable.

Quite honestly though, she was just really sick of fighting. She tossed her napkin onto the table. "Look, accept who I am or leave me. It's that simple."

She was about to stand when his hand laid over hers. "Wait, please." His eyes rose to meet hers. "Look, all we've done today is fight, and I think it's my fault. I've had something on my mind that I need to get off my chest because I think it's causing a rift between us."

Her weight fully settled back into her chair. "I know I've been distant today and I'm sure that's not helping. It's been a strange day."

He let out a breath and took her hand in both of his. "Naomi, it's been a year. Do you remember the first time we came to this restaurant?"

She softened at the memory. "I was so nervous. I couldn't understand what I'd done to get your attention. And..." She shrugged with a playful smile. "I'd heard you were a playboy. So, I didn't really know what to expect."

His chuckle was soft. "Well, I did date many women before I met you. But not for the reason most people think."

Her head tilted at his words and he watched her eyes. "I was searching. After a date or two, I would know a woman wasn't for me. Until I met you." He glanced down. "You are fiery, passionate and willful. I can't express in words how much you mean to me and how you make everything I am burn more brightly when we're together." As he suddenly stood, her heart began racing, especially when he kept hold of her hand as he came around the table, kneeling before her and gazing up into her eyes. "Which is why I've been so on-edge lately, but I should have trusted you all along. I've needed to ask you the question of my heart and

I should have known you would never hurt me." He reached into the pocket of his suit jacket, pulling out a small box. When it opened, a brilliant diamond was reflecting light in a thousand directions from the top of a ring. He held it toward her. "So, Detective Naomi Gate. Will you marry me?"

She opened her mouth and drew in a breath. "This is…" She swallowed. "Unexpected." Their eyes met and she hesitated. She'd thought he was going to say they were done. She probably would have done it herself if he hadn't. But he'd just confessed he wanted to spend the rest of his life with her. Was there something wrong with her for not screaming yes? And her eyes searched his face nervously, looking for pain and disappointment.

In the silence, he began to chuckle nervously, his hand resting on her thigh as he let out a breath. "Not exactly the response I was hoping for—"

At the vulnerability in him, her finger lifted to his lips. His eyes rose to hers hopefully and she let out a breath. "It's not a no." Her words came out in a rush. "It's really sudden. I need some time to think, all right?"

His brow rose, a hint of mirth returning to his lips. "This is really a surprise to you? I've been thinking it for months." He squeezed her thigh tenderly, his voice softening. "Will you at least wear the ring through dinner? To see how it feels?"

She hesitated, but when she saw the emotions on his normally inscrutable face, she found herself nodding. He took the ring out of the box and slipped it onto her finger. His lips pressed to hers, and when he drew back, she noticed the server waiting patiently off to the side. The man smiled as he came forward. "Congratulations, Mr. Raelyn, Miss Gate."

Distantly, she heard herself thanking the man awkwardly before he continued. "Would you like another moment to look at the menu?"

"I'm ready to order." She sat forward eagerly, handing the man her placard. "I'd like salmon with a baked sweet potato and a hefty side of sautéed vegetables. The more colorful the better, thank you."

Jax handed his menu over as well. "I'm having the Kobe beef, rare. Mashed potatoes, and you can give me some of the colorful vegetables you'll be cooking for my lovely fiancée." His eyes met hers. "No steak for you?"

She bit back a nasty comment about how they weren't engaged yet—but then aimed for civility instead, considering she hadn't given him an answer when he'd put his heart out on his sleeve. "It's a race night."

He sighed playfully and handed his menu over. "Maybe next time."

"Very good, sir."

When the waiter was out of sight, she lifted a brow. "You've never ordered vegetables before."

He reached over to slip his fingers between hers, and the movement brought her eyes to the ring. "I'm a changed man, what can I say?" His fingers squeezed hers, his voice softening. "It looks as amazing on you as I'd hoped it would." Before she could speak, he continued. "I know, I know." Some of the vulnerability was back on his face. "You're thinking. I respect that."

She found she wanted to think about anything else. "So how was your day?"

His eyebrows went high as he sucked in a breath. "Oh, well, it was a board of directors meeting. so…"

"Ouch." Her nose scrunched in sympathy and she decided to use the opportunity to smooth over her interrogating him about his company earlier. "Aren't they happy about the start of beta testing for the Apogee model?"

"Yes, but…"

When he hesitated, she leaned forward, squeezing his hand. "What is it?"

His face looked a bit haunted. "I don't know really." He was gazing down into his glass, swirling it slowly. "I just get this sense Bradford's up to something."

"Has something changed in his behavior? Was it something he said? Or something he did or suggested?"

The smile he gave was dashing, his eyes shooting to hers. "I so enjoy when you turn on your detective mode." His playfulness seemed to ebb, though. "He's been trying to undermine my marketing campaigns for ages, despite the fact that the numbers support me. But actually, about the Apogee…"

"What about it?"

He glanced around and leaned forward, lowering his voice. "It wasn't my idea, it was his. And he's been pushing so hard for it…" He tapped his thumb against her hand. It caught her by surprise, since Jax rarely had nervous gestures. "I understand it will turn a profit, but it just seems too fast."

She had to keep herself from jumping up and screaming her agreement. "It does seem fast. The Zenith line only came out last year."

Jax shook his head. "I'm not even referring to a new model coming out, though it's fast when considering that as well."

Her brow creased. "You mean he's trying to advance the time-line for releasing the Apogee?"

"We normally spend at least a full year in beta testing for any completely new line. Even models that are simply modifications of vetted models, we spend at least six months in beta." His eyes held hers. "He wants to launch the Apogee in three."

Her eyes grew wide in fear. "Three months? That's irresponsible, especially for such a big jump in bionic percentage."

He nodded quickly. "I agree. But I'm worried the board may agree with him and honestly, I'm afraid—"

"That he's making a power play for your job?"

When his eyes met hers and he smiled, it was filled with warmth. "Naomi my dear, if you don't marry me, I will simply be ruined, because you are the perfect woman." She blushed and he kissed her ring. "And I have to say, this ring seems to be our good luck charm, because I feel as if we are back on our first date."

She smiled shyly, her eyes moving to the aquariums around them. "It's hard to believe it's been a year."

He kissed each of her knuckles. "I remember when we first came here. You ate your steak with such relish, it was like I was a voyeur to a sexual encounter."

"It was glorious. If I'd known it was a four-hundred-dollar steak, I would have savored it a bit more. But I'd run a marathon that morning and was really hungry."

He ran his thumb over her knuckles. "You ran a marathon? You never told me that. What race was it for?"

"It wasn't a race." She was trying hard not to laugh at herself. "I was nervous about our date, so I went for a run to calm my nerves. I ended up going for longer than I meant to, and I was at twenty miles at that point, so I figured I might as well go for the remaining six point two."

"Really? How do you accidentally run a marathon?"

"It was only two hours of running." She squeezed his hand. "If you're eating vegetables, maybe I can get you to run with me."

He chuckled. "Let's not go crazy." He kissed her hand again, smiling at her ring before he cocked a brow at her. "I know it's a race night, but if you aren't going to give me an answer, can we at least have dessert?"

She swatted at him, taking her hand back and drawing it into her lap. Her fingers touched the ring, even as she tried to ignore it on her hand. "You know my motto."

He leaned back in his chair, putting his hands behind his head as his elbows went out wide. "I know, I know. Nothing new on race day."

Her eyes moved over the muscles on his upper arms, visible even underneath his suit jacket. And despite how much they'd fought, she was reminded of some of his other best features. "That does mean I need to stick to all my routines, you know. It's very important for success."

He paused for a moment. "What routine are you referring to?"

She leaned forward, reaching across the table to grab his tie, letting it linger between her fingers. "The one where you take me home and I have my way with you." The edges of his lips curled at her words, and he grabbed his glass of champagne, motioning to her glass of water. "I'll drink to that, my dear." She took her glass and touched it to his with a clink.

CHAPTER 4

Dane

He couldn't believe there were actually that many people willing to be out on the streets at ass o'clock in the morning, let alone to physically exert themselves. Apparently, there were ten thousand competitors running and he guessed at least that number were also spectating. The sun was beginning to lighten the horizon and he'd been wandering around since before sunrise to scope out the area. A private security company had tight protections around the runners but he wasn't watching them. He knew his mark was somewhere in the crowd.

Fortunately, he now understood the start line process since he'd witnessed it a half dozen times. There were different running classes based on percentage of bionics and they'd released the first group hours before. Those were the highest ratios of bionic and he'd guessed they went first since they would finish the fastest. It was finally nearly time for the group of runners he was waiting for.

He wanted to get closer to the start line, but the density of bodies tripled and not even his fiercest scowl made anyone budge. It was a strange sensation for him to be ignored. Signs directed runners to wait for the race within protected runner's corrals. Despite looking like cattle behind the temporary fencing, they seemed more comfortable than Dane felt. He was beginning to feel like he was back on a Tokyo subway at the close of business day.

The spacious corral for the elite runners immediately behind the start line made Dane envious. All wore bibs lined with green, the plastic square on their shirt bearing their runner number. Many of them were stretching or jogging in place, but different movement caught his eye—a woman was doing a series of punches and kicks.

Her hair was up in a ponytail, a loose, black tank top over her bright purple sports bra. Her black shorts had neon blue up the side, which matched the accents on her shoes. She did a series of punches before a cross-face elbow strike, followed by a succession of kicks—the last of which took her off the ground, lights reflecting off the gray metal of her bionic calf as she floated through the air before landing in a crouch on the ground.

He wasn't sure he'd ever found a pair of legs that stunning before. Running probably had everything to do with that—she turned and he caught sight of her bib number, grimacing. Really? The universe hated him.

There was a chime before a voice cut through the cacophony. *"Elite runners will begin in one minute."*

He watched as all the green-bibbed runners moved to the start line, noticing Hot Legs was giving high fives to her neighboring runners. He forced himself to focus on why he was there and returned his eyes to the crowd. There were a lot of potentials, and he didn't know who to focus on. As a horn sounded, the runners rushed out and he decided he'd have better luck watching people head to the finish. He turned and halted though, when he came face to face with a little girl who could be no more than five.

She was staring at him with wide eyes, and he could see his reflection in her bright pink flower-shaped glasses.

While she was obviously living her best life sporting those

frames, he looked as if a linebacker had been hit by an old freight train. Both his arms and legs had been replaced with bionic parts, the metallic silver far from pristine. His marks had left him with tokens of their gratitude for catching them—a plasma grenade here, an energy shot there. Good old-fashioned bullets were the reason for the metal plates over most of his chest, shoulders and back, but none of it matched in color, size or quality so he tended to wear thicker shirts even in summer. His face had miraculously sustained little damage beyond dozens of scars.

Before the girl could draw a terrified breath, her mother grabbed her up, holding the child against her chest and turning her back on Dane. The girl though was still watching him cautiously and he paused, tapping the top of his right wrist. Up popped a little blue metal flower, which he plucked and held out to the girl. She took in a breath of surprise and he put one finger over his lips, before he gave her a wink. Her tiny fingers grabbed the flower and he chuckled as he started walking away. Worked every time.

He waded through the crowd and waited off to the side, watching people as they passed. Mǎ luó had to be there somewhere. From what Dane knew, the man had stolen from Baozhai and been found out easily, so he wasn't likely to be too clever. So why was this proving so hard?

And why were there so many damn people awake right now? It was a Saturday morning. He would have thought most people would have the good sense to either still be drunk or at least nursing a very serious hangover.

When he checked the time he realized he should start moving again. As he made his way toward the finish line even more people were milling around in anticipation. Ahead of him a man held the sign, *Naomi Gate, keep running for humanity*. His eyes rushed to the man's face but he instantly knew it wasn't Mǎ luó. The man's bald head and burnt orange robe were strangely out of place with his large, stylish sunglasses. His skin hinted at Asian ancestry. Dane swam his way through the sea of people until he came to the man's side.

"So, what's one of the Monkhood doing here?"

The monk gave a bright smile. "Here I came to cheer on a stranger and someone stranger comes to me. What's your name, metal man?"

"Dane. I'm not entirely metal."

"A lot of you is, though. Over fifty percent, aren't you?"

"Eh, these things happen. What's your name?" "Aung. How do you know of the Monkhood?"

"I hear a lot of things. What does your organization want with the Gate woman?"

Aung gave a toothy grin. "I'm just an individual, cheering on an athlete. That's not going to put a bounty on my head, is it?"

He raised a brow. "You know I'm a bounty hunter? Since when did you all get good intel?"

"How do you know we haven't always had it?"

He gave a grunt and looked around before glancing back at Aung. "I take it from all the fanfare Naomi Gate is a big deal."

"She's incredible. Have you ever come to a competition before?"

"No, see this is kind of early for a normal person."

Aung's brow rose. "This isn't early."

Dane grunted. "Yeah, I can't talk about early to a Buddhist monk, can I?"

"Indeed. Why precisely are you here? Or I should say, who are you here after?"

It was Dane's turn to raise a brow. Clever man. He wasn't

[45]

about to admit he was after a mark and pointed to the sign instead. "What's all this about?"

"It's about what Naomi is doing for the humanist movement."

He frowned thoughtfully, thinking back to the research he'd done the night before.

"You mean how bionics are becoming less in vogue for racing?"

Aung nodded. "When bionics first became available, they created new classifications based on what percentage of the body was bionic. Over time there were fewer and fewer people in the human classification, and it almost fell out of use entirely."

Dane's eyes scanned the crowd. "But how did she become popular though?"

"She started beating people even with vanity upgrades."

"People do enjoy an underdog winning." Dane grunted. "But with that hospital issued leg of hers, she was taking on people with power enhanced upgrades?"

"Not anything like yours, mind you. Most people can't go quite as far above normal human functioning as you appear to be able to."

"After market modifications are a lot of fun."

"Don't you mean black market?"

"Nuances. Besides." Dane flexed his metal arm playfully. "Gotta love feeling like a superhero."

"Indeed." He motioned to the road race. "But slowly, she's changing how people view their humanity."

He remembered other things he'd uncovered through his research. "But isn't she dating Jackson Raelyn, the CEO of CLM?" He shot Aung a look of disgust. "He's the king of vanity upgrades."

Aung nodded slowly. "But that makes her all the more powerful."

Dane waited for it to make sense. It didn't. "I don't follow."

The monk grinned brightly. "She's dating the man who people see as being at the head of creating what everyone perceives as perfection. What does it say about super models and bionic upgrades, if Naomi doesn't need them to be attractive to him?"

Dane harrumphed as he looked off. That was one unexpected positive outcome of dating the CEO of the vilest company on the planet.

An image screen on a nearby building changed to show Naomi's name, followed promptly by a picture of her in an evening gown, on the arm of Jackson Raelyn. Dane felt his nose bunching up in disgust. So what if he was storybook attractive and had tons of money? That couldn't possibly make up for the atrocities against body image he committed frequently in the pursuit of profit. Jackson Raelyn monetized fatphobia, ableism—anything and everything he could leverage in order to exploit the human instinct to strive by selling the belief that anything short of his company's very narrow— and frankly bland—definition of perfection was worthless.

Also, the man was undoubtedly atrocious in bed.

The image screen changed promptly to a picture of a full body shot of Naomi leaning back against a tree. In this picture, her hair was drawn into a ponytail and she was wearing running gear, her shoes bright orange. His eyes lingered over her bionic leg, appreciating that it was a hospital level upgrade. Though he wondered how her boyfriend felt about her having such a pedestrian "upgrade."

He turned to the monk. "Do you think she actually likes Jackson Raelyn?" When Aung turned and tilted his head, Dane wasn't sure where the thought came from. "I mean, she hasn't even covered her bionic leg with fake skin. She seems proud of who she is." Having watched Naomi's martial arts display at the start line, she didn't exactly strike him as the shrinking violet type.

While Dane couldn't see Aung's eyes, he was fairly certain the man was also looking at the image of Naomi. "Even the proud can fall, if they have to stand alone for too long."

Dane glanced at the image screen to see it had changed to Naomi and a young man. They both had an arm around each other and were smiling, despite the fact they were standing in a graveyard. With the similarity in their features, Dane knew the man to be her brother. Especially since they were standing beside a double grave belonging to a Jacob and Lauren Gate. Words overlaid the image. *I run to be strong for my loved ones, both those with me and those fondly remembered.*

Dane liked being a bounty hunter because he rarely second guessed his line of work. He wasn't enjoying the twinges of self-doubt he was feeling at the moment.

The cheering crowd distracted him. Apparently the first man had gone over the finish line.

"And as expected, Naomi Gate is leading the human female division and she's holding steady and strong. For not having many enhancements, this woman sure is a tank!" It took Dane a second to realize he was hearing the announcer with his ears and not his aural interface. He glanced over at Aung and figured out the noise was coming from the cell phone in his hand. It was one of the models trendy with teenagers, who weren't allowed to get an aural upgrade until it was safe for their bodies. It seemed strange to see a grown man with it though and he was drawing looks from people in the crowd who were irritated—they'd need to shut off whatever they were listening to now, after all. Aung gave a bright

smile and bowed his head in apology a few times.

Dane on the other hand, opted to give the people in the crowd a good glare and most took a step back. He turned to the monk. "Hey, turn it up." It was refreshing to hear the slight imperfection of the speaker.

"Her pace right now is five minutes and thirty-nine seconds over the last twelve miles. If she doesn't fatigue in this last mile she is on her way to breaking her personal record."

He looked at Aung. "How long is this race anyway?"

"A half marathon." Dane's confusion must have been apparent. "Thirteen point one miles."

"What, really? And she's finishing in what..." He did the math and didn't like the answer. "Just over an hour?" It seemed sacrilegious for anyone to be able to run that many miles in that short a time. "How quickly would an average bionic finish this?"

"Oh, this race is too short for most high percentage bionics because they would finish in fifteen minutes or less. They typically go for ultras or bionic ultras."

He stared at Aung blankly. "Bionic ultras?"

"Most humans can do ultras of fifty miles or more but bionic ultras start at a hundred miles." Aung smiled. "Some vanity bionics can run a sub half minute mile. So if the road were clear, a hundred miles could take them less than an hour."

Dane whistled and turned his eyes to the now large crowd. "And people think I'm a freak."

There were hundreds of people milling about, a few people holding bouquets of flowers, a few parents waiting with their children. There was one man in particular though, that Dane recognized from the start line. The man's clothes were old but his face was cleanly shaven and his hair looked recently cut. It was the bags under his eyes that caught Dane's attention though because it was usually a sign a Switch had occurred. He was up front by the barricade, so Dane was suspicious but couldn't be sure, just yet. When the image screen on the nearby building changed to show Naomi running the man became energized and was screaming along with the rest of the crowd.

Naomi raced down the center of the street, the yellow line being eaten by her shoes. Her arms swung gracefully at her sides, the racing bib attached to her chest identifying her as runner five hundred thirteen. She was alone for a solid thirty seconds before another runner turned the corner and appeared on the course behind her. Dane turned his eyes to the man, who was clapping excitedly with the crowd. As she shot toward the finish line the man cupped his hands around his mouth. "Way to go, Noams!"

A smirk curled Dane's lips. "Gotcha."

Dane heard the crowd cheering as Naomi crossed the finish line and used the distraction to push his way forward. He grabbed the man's arm and leaned forward to speak into his ear. "If you want to live, you won't make a scene. Now that I have my hand on you, I can hit you with an EMP blast. The bounty on your head is for dead or alive, so it's really up to you. I'll get paid either way."

The man's fearful eyes turned to him. "Please. Baozhai will kill me. She doesn't have mercy."

"Well, you shouldn't have stolen what you were supposed to smuggle. Now come with—"

A piercing woman's scream cut him off. Dane's gaze snapped to see the runner behind Naomi crying out in anguish. Her bionic calf was smoking and the fake skin curled in the heat, undoubtedly burning the rest of her. Dane groaned as he recognized what was about to happen and shoved the man back into Aung. "I'll give you four thousand dollars if you keep hold of him for me

[50]

until I get back."

He didn't wait for an answer and instead bounded forward and jumped the barricade. Naomi was rushing toward the screaming woman—she was in a pile just in front of the finish line. He yelled at Naomi as he hurried to the woman. "She put bitrous in her system but it malfunctioned. It's going to explode."

"Of course it is." When security officers started edging forward, Naomi yelled at them. "NYPD, get back!" She stopped beside the woman. "I have a phase canist—"

He slid to a stop. "She'd die but it'd save everyone else."

She knelt down on the opposite side of the woman. "You have another idea?"

He waved the smoke away. "Yes, hold her down." She grabbed the woman's shoulders and he enjoyed the way she shoved her down a little harder than strictly necessary. He couldn't really blame her—the woman had cheated and was paying for it now. Dane grabbed her smoking ankle and clenched his other fist, putting his energy output to max before punching straight down into her bionic knee.

His hand crushed and ripped through the fake flesh and metal, but he tried not to leave too big a dent in the pavement beneath. He tightened his hold on her ankle and yanked the leg off entirely, bits of wire and liquid oozing out of the stub left behind. "Pull her back or she'll get chemical burns."

He tossed the now flaming leg aside, reaching over to tap his forearm and sighing when the lock wouldn't open. "Really? Not now." He whacked his elbow with his fist and the compartment finally opened, exposing a small metal ball. After tipping his arm so it fell out, he tossed it toward the leg, igniting the shield a second before he heard the explosion. The strength of the blast bowed the blue netting outward, and he wasn't sure it would hold. But it collapsed in on itself and the smoke was released from the cage and curled toward the sky. He sighed with relief as he sat back on his heels before looking over at Naomi.

She looked far more attractive than she had a right to for someone who had just run that far. The sheen of sweat on her glistened and on anyone else the sweat marks on her clothes would have looked awkward. When their eyes met, Naomi unceremoniously dropped the woman on the pavement. He liked that she didn't even make the pretense of being gentle with the woman. "What was that charge you used?"

That was her most pressing question? "They're my own creation." He felt his lips curling as he stood. "I call them my mini blue balls." She put a hand over her mouth to stifle a laugh and he counted that as a win. "They have a really small diameter so it isn't as useful as a phase canister but they come in handy for things like this."

She motioned to the smoking remains of the bionic leg. "You see this often?"

He shrugged. "Occupational hazard."

She put her hands on her hips. "Who are you, exactly?"

"Dane Thayer. But if you'll excuse me, I have to—" As soon as he turned and looked into the crowd, he saw his mark was gone. He cursed under his breath, rushing to the barricade and growling at Aung, who was still hiding behind his thick shades. "You were supposed to watch him!"

"I never said I would." He gave an impish grin. "For the record, bribing a monk with money isn't exactly the best strategy." The cardboard sign was thrust into Dane's hands. "And I should be leaving. It's not time for me to meet her, yet. Good luck, Dane. You'll be needing it." The man backed into the crowd and Dane was about to lunge after him when he felt Naomi's hand on his shoulder. "Wait, who was that?"

Dane felt himself growling. "A man who had better hope I have no say in how he will be reincarnated after I kill him."

"You do realize I'm a cop, right?"

"I'm not actually going to kill him." He paused. "Hurt him possibly."

Her skeptical brow didn't lower. "Seriously, just stop implicating yourself already."

He thrust the sign into her hands. "Here, I think he would want you to have this." He imagined the cops would be coming soon and he really didn't want to be there when they were. "If you'll excuse me—"

"Did I see that he was bald and wearing a burnt orange robe?"

He paused, not knowing what he should say. The NYPD and him weren't exactly best friends, but he didn't think Naomi was the average detective either. "Yes."

She rotated the sign so she could read the words. "Are they part of some religion or cult?"

"They're part of a specific religious order. Why?"

She hesitated, her eyes searching his face.

He had no idea what was going on but there was something about her expression. "You have a question you're afraid to ask."

"I don't know if I can trust you."

He lifted a dubious brow and motioned to the woman they'd just saved. "So the whole her not being dead thing doesn't help my case any?"

He could feel her indecision before she gave a small shrug. "I saw someone with a similar description murdered yesterday."

He paused. That didn't bode well. "Look, all I feel comfortable telling you is that the Monkhood is a Buddhist order that is very secretive and they keep to themselves." He let out a breath and tried not to be unnerved by the news that one of them had been murdered. "One was killed?"

"Yes." She glanced down. "He died in my arms."

"Who killed him?"

"Artillery."

He'd been drawing breath to say he really needed to leave when her words registered. "Really? Where is he? What does he look like now?"

"He's in jail at the moment."

He groaned. "Oh, you—" He barely managed to bite off his rude remark.

Her brows shot up to the sky. "Excuse me?"

"You just arrested him? What's wrong with you? Do you have any idea how much the bounty on his head is worth?"

"Oh, I get it. You're a bounty hunter."

"You've seen through me. Now, I really need to—"

"Who are you after here?"

He watched her face, regretting he couldn't tell her the truth. He gave a half bow. "A gentleman never tells."

Her amused laugh was sweet. "Or maybe you're worried I'll arrest your mark first."

"Well, you did take out Artillery. What'd you use, a Plasma Cannon or did you have a tank?"

She shook her head slowly. "No, I had my twenty-two and a phase canister. He didn't know I could switch my gun to a Cannon Shot."

His mouth fell open. "You took him on with just a twenty-two and a phase canister?" When she nodded he barely restrained a moan. "Hot." He cleared his throat. "You're in the wrong line of work, you know. You should be a bounty hunter. You would only need to work one week a year with those guts of yours."

"I'm really happy being a detective, thank you."

"Well, if you change your mind, come find me. Now if you'll—" Distantly, he saw NYPD mech suits looming at the rear of the crowd and rounded on Naomi. "Oh shit, you've been stalling me."

Her lips curled into a playful smile. "I don't know what you're talking about."

He pointed at her and was about to say something rude but thought better of it. God, she was lucky she had such hot legs. "You're trouble." He needed to get out of there faster than he'd thought. "And while it's been a pleasure talking to you, I've lost track of my mark so—congratulations and goodbye." His hand went onto the barricade.

She grabbed his arm. "You're a witness and you need to stay—"

"Actually, I don't." The intensity of her gaze made him not want to leave. Focus, idiot. "But without your mech suit, you can't physically make me since I know the secret of your gun." He didn't want to fight her, so he took her hand and kissed the back of it. "Today was fun, though. We should do it again sometime." He used her surprise to hop the barricade and people were leaping out of his way, no doubt the leg ripping display still fresh in their thoughts. When he looked back, he saw an amused smile on Naomi's lips. He saluted before pivoting and disappearing into the crowd.

CHAPTER 5

Naomi

The user you are trying to reach cannot receive calls at this time.

She rubbed her eyes. She hadn't been able to contact her brother since he'd left her that cryptic voice message. He'd always been a screw up, but he usually answered or at least returned her calls. He knew enough to realize that if he wanted help after a bender, he'd better not have ignored her or pissed her off recently. So why weren't his calls even connecting now? She let out a sigh, not allowing her fears to build. He'd probably just forgotten to charge his interface and would call her later that day to tell her about some stupid escapade or scheme he'd gotten into and ask for help.

She rested her head on her fist, staring out the car window as the city streets went by in a blur. Her eyes flicked to the dashboard interface. Five minutes and thirty-two seconds to her destination. She wasn't sure where she was going—her chief had sent the car to pick her up from the race with the address preprogrammed and she hadn't cared to work the interface to find out. The strange part was the request for her presence had come with a high enough priority she hadn't been able to finish her reports of the incident at the race, let alone go home and shower.

The woman with the exploding leg had been taken to the hospital before Naomi had left the site and it seemed she would be fine. Naomi knew, though, that if Dane hadn't been there the woman would have been taken away in a body bag—if there were even that much of her left. She'd seen the outcome of bitrous malfunction before on several cases. On the force they referred to the aftermath as a "red water balloon." She'd always been particularly grateful for the forensic bots at those crime scenes.

The car slowed at an intersection. She was heading into the black market bionic district. She didn't work any of those cases. What was going on? As the car turned the corner, she felt the cardboard sign shift and hit her leg. *Naomi Gate, keep running for humanity.* She hadn't been able to bring herself to throw away the sign, though she wasn't entirely certain why.

Incoming call from Inari Hayashi. The call connected before she could accept it and Naomi was bombarded by techno music and turned the volume down. "Inari, Mars called. They can hear your music."

"*Ha ha, oops!*" The volume decreased to a normal level. "*Hey, so are you being stalked or something? 'Cause crazy shit is happening and it's starting to look like you're attracting freakoids. Just sayin'.*"

"Very funny. What's up? I'm inbound right now, so make it quick."

"*Oh, I know. You've got another minute forty-five before you're there. Why are you going to the BMBD anyway? We don't work those cases.*"

Naomi shook her head. She should have known Inari would hack the car's interface. Until two years prior, Inari had been known to the police only as Catatonic, a cybercriminal that always left a meme of a cat as her calling card. When Naomi caught her, the twenty-year-old girl had negotiated herself out of jail time and a criminal record, and into a job on the force in exchange for information leading to the arrest of over a dozen criminals.

Naomi let out a sigh. "I don't know; it just came through as a priority one."

"*So why didn't they call in your incredibly competent and cute partner?*"

And her last negotiation term had been partnership with Naomi.

"Oh, I don't know. Maybe it has something to do with the fact you're on desk suspension for not following protocol?"

"*Aww, but I fixed the firewall after I was done.*"

It was hard to stifle her laughter. "That firewall was around the Pentagon."

"*I didn't have time to file the paperwork! And the baddie would have gotten away if I hadn't done it!*"

"Which is probably the only reason you still have a job."

"*I even made the firewall better when I put it back up!*" She grumped sullenly.

"*I shouldn't have gotten in trouble; they should have thanked me.*"

The car chirruped. "*You have arrived at your destination.*"

Naomi sighed as the car pulled to a stop behind another police car. "Why don't you work for the FBI or CIA or something? Or at least transfer to the cybercrimes division."

There was a short pause, Inari's voice softening. "*But I like being your partner.*"

Naomi smiled. "I like you being my partner too."

"*Duh!*" All her usual surety was back in full force. "*Now let's race to see which of us can figure out why you're there first.*"

Call ended.

She took a deep breath before getting out of the car. There was an officer she didn't recognize in a mech suit directly before an alley, cordoned off by bright yellow police tape. Past the tape was Chief Sanderson, an imposing presence she barely recognized without his uniform. He was wearing jeans and a polo shirt, and his graying hair suited his dark skin. When their eyes met it felt as if a boulder grew in her stomach. She'd known him a long time but didn't know the last time she'd seen him look that serious.

"Thank you for coming, Naomi."

"It's no problem." Why was he being so formal? "What's the emergency?" She ducked under the tape and came to his side.

He turned down the alley, leading them past a rancid dumpster. "I need you to understand your presence here is a professional courtesy. I'm extending it because I know you would want to be here."

"Thank you." This was strange. "What's this about?" She frowned as they came to a stop beside a door with a red X spray-painted across the front.

"This is about your brother."

Tyler's interface wasn't just in need of charging, was it? People lost access to their ID chip when they made the Switch illegally, after all. Her eyes closed and she sucked in a shaky breath, past her fear. She was in the black market bionic district—there were only two possible outcomes. "Is he dead or did he transfer?"

She forced her eyes open to get her answer.

Her chief met her gaze. "We hope he transferred but it's being investigated as we speak."

She wiped her cheek and gave a single nod, pushing back her tears. "I'm ready."

"If you need—"

"I'm ready."

His face showed his sadness, but he pulled the door open for her.

The two steps into the darkness of the room left her blind. The hum of the machines mixed into a discordant symphony and all she could see at first was incessantly blinking lights. A hand on her arm kept her from moving forward and she looked down, her eyes beginning to adjust. There were exposed wires running along the floor beside a body she thankfully didn't recognize lying mangled in a pool of congealed blood. A bionic leg was twisted, and fluid had leaked onto the floor, a dismembered arm lying four feet away from the stump. A bionic eye still held a faded charge, the red light wavering in strength. Four legged forensic bots were swarming the body like crabs, blue lights shining beneath them as they scanned for evidence. One crawled off and moved across the floor to a table. As it made its way to the second body she flinched.

Her brother was strapped onto the table.

Dozens of wires, electrodes, and hoses ran from him. There were six forensic bots climbing over his form, which was covered with blood. Whether it had come from him or the body on the floor in front of her, she didn't know.

"Oh my God."

A hand grasped her shoulder, her chief's voice gentle. "Remember, we aren't sure whether or not he was in the body."

Her eyes closed as she fought back tears. She wiped at her cheek, looking at her chief. "When will you know?"

A door slammed open. "The transfer was complete. Now can I please call my girlfriend so she doesn't have to worr—" Jax halted mid stride. He'd come out a door from what she could only assume was a back room. "Naomi!"

She stared in surprise. "Jax?"

He rushed to her and she'd never been happier to fall into his arms.

He held her tightly, rubbing her back. His voice was almost a growl as he addressed her chief. "You brought her here?! What type of a sadistic bastard are you? Do you have any idea—"

"It's all right." She pushed back against him, squeezing his arms. She'd never seen him that angry before. "He was right. I do want to be here."

Jax sighed, meeting her gaze as fury was washed with concern.

When she looked over her shoulder at the chief, their eyes held. She'd known him almost her whole life. He'd been a friend of her mother's, after all.

He motioned to Jax. "We work closely with CLM on any black market body transfer stations we find. When I called to say this may have something to do with you, Jackson came over himself."

She found herself unexpectedly emotional at the gesture, feeling like a total fool for hesitating the night before—she had to focus. "You said the transfer was complete?"

Jax's arm stayed protectively about her waist. "Yes, I checked three times to confirm." His voice softened. "I didn't want you to have false hope. But I assumed from the moment I walked in, since the shell was hooked up to the stasis machine."

She recoiled. "Shell? That's my brother's body."

Jax's eyes searched hers. "Call it what you want, Naomi. But your brother isn't in there anymore."

Her eyes went to her brother's body, to the scar in the center of his forehead. They'd been running around outside and he'd fallen face first onto the edge of a concrete step. She'd watched as the doctor gave him stitches. Her eyes moved back to Jax. "You said he was put on stasis? So his body is okay?"

The way he paused told her everything. "No. He'll never be able to return to it because whoever killed the handler dismantled the machine."

She felt as if she'd been punched in the gut. She looked at her chief, trying to stay focused. "Were they after my brother or the handler?"

Sanderson shook his head. "We don't know. Do you have any idea why your brother would resort to this?"

Her fingers pinched the bridge of her nose. "I mean he's gotten into trouble before but this…" She looked at the lifeless form on the table. Why hadn't he asked her for—she gasped. "Oh God. When did this happen?"

Jax squeezed her waist tenderly. "He made the transfer early yesterday morning, right before six am."

Her eyes closed and she heard herself whimper. "He called me." Her eyes were burning as she looked at Jax. "I didn't answer! It was during the shooting in Central Park. He left me a voicemail." The shame was moving down her throat like magma.

Jax drew her head to his shoulder, speaking gently. "You couldn't have known."

Sanderson's voice was gentle, but firm. "We'll need a copy of the voicemail for our investigation."

She straightened and turned, wiping at her cheeks. "Chief, you have to let me—"

"Absolutely not."

"But—"

"No, Detective Gate. This is non-negotiable. Am I clear?" He held her gaze and in that moment she knew there was no argument strong enough to dissuade him. She nearly argued anyway but bit it back. "Yes, sir."

Incoming message from Inari Hayashi. I'm so sorry.

Jax cleared his throat. "I can't speak to the murder that took place here…" Her boyfriend motioned to Tyler's body. "But I can say most people don't resort to taking on a black market life except for very drastic reasons."

When she looked at Jax, she tried not to see him as the man

from last night who'd asked her to marry him, but as the head of a major corporation whose specialty was buying and selling bodies and lives. What would her brother's next move be? She suddenly wished she'd spent more of their time dating questioning Jax about every nuance he knew regarding body transferring. "But taking on a black market life would hold the same parameters as buying one through an approved channel, wouldn't it? New identification and all that?"

His head bobbed side to side. "Mostly. Except, when you buy one from CLM you get a life that's been carefully combed through to ensure the last user didn't leave you anything behind. We thoroughly check over lives and bodies before people buy them. You don't get those assurances with a black market life."

Her eyes fell to her brother's form. The forensic bots were making their way off him; apparently they were finished with their scans. Her eyes stayed on his lifeless face. "So not only are you desperate enough to leave everything you knew behind—"

"You're desperate enough not to care about the baggage you're taking on with your new life."

Even though homicide didn't do much with body transferring, she'd understood this basic principle in theory. But it was different to think about it happening to her Tyler. Her eyes burned. This couldn't be happening.

Jax took her hand, turning to her chief. "There are another three bodies back there, in stasis. I can have them tagged if you'd like to use them as bait bodies."

Sanderson gave a nod. "Let me talk to Patrick about the timing with the investigation." He gave Naomi's shoulder a squeeze before he walked past, leaving her alone with Jax.

Her throat ached. "I hadn't realized you did so much work with the police."

He squeezed her hand. "You're not the only one whose job has secrets."

They hugged again and she whispered into his ear. "I'm glad you're here."

"I came as soon as I heard." A hand cradled the back of her head. "I'm sorry you had to fear for an instant your brother was dead."

She took in a shaky breath. "Thank you for letting me know his body is just— empty." When she glanced around, no one was paying attention to them and she whispered into his ear. "What would his next move have been?"

He drew back enough to look around casually, his voice quiet. "The Switch would have taken a lot out of him. They don't exactly have the best equipment here, mostly crap from Kazakhstan and China." His nose scrunched and he shook his head, sighing as he looked off. "Sorry." He leaned in close to whisper. "Six yesterday morning, add about an hour of vomiting, three before he would be able to sit up and maybe another two before he could walk."

That sounded terrible. "That takes us to noon. Then what?"

"I doubt the handler would have infused the body with extra nutrients to make the transition easier, so he probably would have been incredibly weak and very hungry. He would have left here to eat and sleep, not necessarily in that order."

"So, he couldn't have gotten that far?"

His eyes met hers as he shook his head. "Not physically, no. But you know the circles a black market life walks in aren't the same as ours. And you still don't know if whoever killed the handler was after him or after your brother."

Incoming message from Inari Hayashi. I've done some research; I think your brother was into some serious shit. I've got a lead for you, but you're not going to like it. Call me when you have privacy.

"Naomi?"

She searched his eyes. "I'm sorry. What were you saying about black market circles?"

His voice lowered. "Any life he could have bought would have been a criminal's. So he wouldn't be able to access much mainstream. He would have had to go to The Underground."

Being a cop, she'd always been comforted by the fact technological advances helped to readily identify criminals. They could barely go into stores, banks, or public places without triggering alarms that notified the police. The Underground was the one place where criminals gathered off grid but the place itself was nomadic and hard to find. Worse though, was that advanced technology worked both ways—while criminals couldn't move freely in most areas, police couldn't get anywhere near The Underground.

And the ones who did, never returned.

She stared at her brother's body. Perhaps a part of her had always known she couldn't protect him from sliding down the dark rabbit hole, that she couldn't always save him. But he was still her little brother, and she wouldn't let him go easily.

If she wanted to find him, there was only one way.

Her chief appeared out of the back room and as he neared, she took a step to him. "Sir, I respectfully request to be assigned to undercover duty."

He shook his head. "My answer is still no."

"Look, no one knows my brother the way I do—"

"And I'm not giving you an undercover body so you can go put yourself in danger trying to find your brother. We have people in place already. Let them do their jobs. Now, if this situation makes it so you cannot continue to do your own, I'll have you suspended until this is over. Am I clear, Detective Gate?"

She paused and gave a single nod. "Crystal."

"Good." He held out a picture, enclosed within an evidence bag. "Do you recognize this?"

There was a picture of a man seated with his legs crossed, beneath a large glowing circle, like a sun. He had at least a dozen arms if not more, and each was holding a different item. There were what looked like prayer beads, a sword, a book, and other items she couldn't readily identify. Two of the hands were positioned before the chest of the being, palms against one another as the head bowed in meditation. The man was seated on a large raft made of lotus blossoms and a golden dragon swam in the sea beneath him.

She shook her head. "No, why?"

"It was in Tyler's pocket. Are you sure you've never seen it?"

"No. What is it?"

"The search says it's a bodhisattva but I'm going to have a specialist look at it. It's a Buddhist symbol. It doesn't mean anything to you?"

She felt her heart racing as she thought back to Central Park. Her eyes met her chief's. "If you would just let me go undercover, I—"

"Does it mean anything to you—yes or no, Detective Gate?"

She hesitated, watching his eyes. She hated herself for knowing her answer before she said it. "No. Nothing."

Jax took her hand, looking at her chief. "I'm done here, and I'd like to take Naomi home. I can send someone else if you'd like the bodies tagged. If you'll excuse us."

Sanderson's voice lowered. "We will find your brother, Naomi. Trust us."

She'd always put her faith in the police. Sanderson and her

mother had worked together, had helped create sweeping changes in the structure of the force through de-escalation trainings and founding a truly independent board of reviews. Being an office had always been the only thing that made sense to Naomi. But this was her brother and for the first time, she found she didn't believe they were doing enough, that they could do enough. Her mother had died while on duty after all. She couldn't lose her brother too, especially not when she could help.

She met her chief's eyes and felt her anger about to erupt like a volcano when Jax spoke, tugging her hand urgently. "Let's get out of here, sweetheart."

That jarred her enough to get her out the door, down the alley and into Jax's car before her rage overflowed and she slammed her fist into the door panel. "What do they expect me to do, just sit back and pretend like my little brother isn't in trouble?"

"It's truly unfair." Jax calmly hit the GPS button for the car. "Naomi's apartment."

"Location confirmed."

He sat back beside her, slipping an arm around her shoulders and speaking quietly. "Are you all right?"

She huffed. "No! How could my chief do this to me?" Her breaths were ragged, feeling as if they were only fueling her rage volcano. "Why couldn't he give me an undercover body? What am I supposed to do now, go buy one on the black market?"

Jax sucked in a fearful breath. "You absolutely cannot go to a black market body station. They'll only ruin your body while you're out of it. Especially considering how pristine your current body is, you'd need state of the art stasis equipment to ensure you didn't lose muscle mass, not to mention the calibration of nutrients and electrolytes for an athlete such as yourself..." Jax trailed off. "Why are you staring at me like that?"

[67]

"Jax..." Naomi swallowed, turning to him as nerves overtook her. "Can you give me a body to use? Please?"

He let out a stilted guffaw. "You want me to help you break at least a dozen laws by giving you an illegal body transfer?" He sucked in his lips, staring into her eyes. "That's..."

Disobeying a direct order at worst would get her fired or at least get her demoted. This though, was different. This was illegal and the last place any cop wanted to find themselves was either in The Underground or in jail.

What was she willing to give up for her brother? Did she believe he really was in trouble or had he just had enough of his straight and narrow big sister? She hated herself for wondering but she mostly hated her brother for not being trustworthy.

She felt her throat tighten. "Please."

He blew out a breath. "Naomi..."

Tears threatened and she looked away. "Never mind. Of course you won't help me."

"I'm hurt that you think I don't want to help you."

Bitterness at her situation crept past her lips. "Well last night you were arguing with me because I was doing my job."

"No, I wasn't, I—" He sighed heavily. "I was arguing about the fact that you put yourself in danger when you were seriously under-gunned. You know I support you being in law enforcement. I'm proud of the work you do. I just want you to be protected and I'm sorry if you running in with just a twenty-two and a canister seemed rash to me, but it did and still does. But that doesn't mean I don't support you."

Their eyes caught and he reached over hesitantly, rubbing her cheek with his thumb. His voice was soft when it came. "If we were to do this—and I'm not saying that I'm agreeing—but if we were to do this..."

Naomi's skin felt aflame. "What is it?"

Jax gave a slow, reluctant nod. "You couldn't argue with me about the body you'd be taking. I'd want you inside a body that is fully outfitted, with enough firepower to keep you safe in any situation."

She blinked, trying not to look too eager. "Of course, that seems reasonable." Going to The Underground was dangerous, after all. She glanced down at herself. "And my real body?"

"We have special stasis equipment for athletes. And I'd put it in a secure location with all the other high-value bodies, ensure no one could gain access to it."

She found herself giving an odd laugh. "High-value bodies?"

Jax though, was not laughing. "At auction, your body would be worth millions, if not a billion."

The matter of fact way that he stated it was an uncomfortable reminder that he was the CEO of a company whose commodity was the human body.

Jax gave a nod. "Another reason not to use a black market body transfer station. Your body wouldn't there upon your return."

That was a horrifying thought.

His hand rested on her thigh. "Is this something you seriously want to do?"

Her throat tightened in indecision. Maybe she should take a minute to think about it. She could lose everything, after all. "You're right. Maybe I shouldn't make a decision about it just yet."

His smile was playful when he touched her chin. "I'm sensing a theme here."

Somehow that made her laugh. "Jax."

He rested his forehead against hers. "I'm here for you, sweetheart. We'll get through this."

Her eyes closed. Dear God, she hoped so.

CHAPTER 6

Dane

The last rays of the evening sun and a gentle breeze were warming his scant amount of skin. He rested his chin on his metal fist, staring down at the chessboard. The remaining pieces were well positioned for both himself and his opponent. Felix was a good match and Dane enjoyed playing against him.

"You're killing me. I'm dying over here." Felix's eyes narrowed. "Could you hurry it up? Are you waiting for the apocalypse or something to save you? Because it's not going to."

The man sure was an acerbic curmudgeon. Dane grunted. "Shut up old man, I'm thinking."

Felix guffawed, leaning back in his wooden outdoor chair. He was bald save for a few dozen white hairs on the back of his head. His skin was speckled with age spots and he had a small white mustache and beard on his chin. His nose and ears were large enough that most people would have had them altered. While the man had never told him his age Dane was fairly certain he had been born during the Paleolithic Era.

Felix waved a hand and rolled his eyes. "Now you insult my age? Please. I'm proud of the fact I was born when your genetic ancestors were still single-celled organisms."

Dane chuckled and picked up his piece. "Queen to E2. And by your own token, it isn't an insult so you can stop feigning indignation."

"Who's fainting? You, once I decapitate your King in three moves. Rook to A1. And check, you shmuck." Felix wasn't prone to exaggeration when it mattered.

"Crap. Well, since I'm going to lose, why don't you start giving me the information I called you here for in the first place? Queen to E1. Check."

"Can't even let an old man have any fun, can you? Fine, Queen to A6. Checkmate."

"What?! You said three moves!"

"You were irritating me." He leaned back in his chair, his crafty eyes smiling. "Now, why do you care about the Monkhood so much?"

Dane lifted a brow. Sly old devil. "I heard one was killed by Artillery."

"Ah, yes, I'd heard the same thing. How exactly did they get onto his radar, I wonder?"

"Yes, how indeed. So, are all those dollars I transferred into your account going to loosen your tongue or not?"

Felix lifted his hands, palms toward the sky. "You ruin the thrill of discovery. You know this, don't you?"

"As you tell me, every time I want you to get to the point."

Felix's smile vanished. "The Monkhood is planning something, codenamed Sanctuary. It's made them a terrible enemy. Very shortly you're going to be notified about an open bounty going up for the Monkhood's hideout or for information about Sanctuary. I believe everyone in The Underground will be looking for them now."

Dane cringed. "But they're non-confrontational by nature. They're Buddhists for Christ's sake. What could they be doing that would piss off anyone that much?"

"I don't know. I assure you, if I did I'd be collecting the money

[72]

myself."

There was one other mystery to the puzzle. "Who placed the bounty?"

"That's the strangest part. No one knows. The request to have it added to the forum was sent anonymously through an encrypted relay." He gestured with his hand, off to the side. "They must have a sizable bank account, considering the amount of money the bounty is rumored to be."

Dane leaned back thoughtfully. "Must be a crime boss. Maybe Shrew?"

"She prefers to use poisons to settle her disputes." Felix shook his head. "What do you think the odds of Margay are?"

"Higher if our first thoughts were to blame someone else. You know Margay likes to mimic and cast blame on others."

"True, true. There are so many clever bastards who could be to blame for this. But I'll keep snooping, you know me." His eyes flicked up and a big grin slithered onto his face. "Though it seems as if we're done now because you have company."

Dane blinked and turned in his chair, brows shooting up at the sight of Naomi Gate. She was wearing a pair of black dress pants with a warm red shirt, covered by a black jacket. Felix stood and the devil bowed to Naomi before taking her hand and giving it a peck. "My dear lady, you are simply a vision to behold."

She smiled but Dane saw her brow rise dubiously. "Why thank you. I didn't mean to interrupt. Were you done with your game?"

"One does not continue to play chess when a woman of your radiance comes by. But I fear I am a few decades too old for you."

Dane grunted. "She may like wrinkly skin, don't assume."

Naomi was laughing and Felix flashed another smirk. "Well, I'll leave you two young kids alone." He mock whispered to Naomi. "Watch out for his Queen. He likes to take her on an endless dance all around the board—he doesn't treat her like a lady at all."

"Hey, shut it, you hoary geezer."

The man turned and waved a hand over his shoulder as he sauntered away. Naomi watched him go before turning to Dane with an amused smile. "Good friend of yours, I take it?"

He began resetting the chessboard. "The man takes after his codename." His hand paused and he continued. "For the record, you being a cop is sad because I can't talk freely around you."

She took the seat across from him, crossing her legs and resting one arm on the chair back. "I'm off duty."

"Bullshit." He finished with the last of the pawns. "Cops and bounty hunters never go off duty. You have first move."

Her brow arched before she turned to the board, moving a pawn. "Well, that's one thing we have in common."

"Hardly the only thing. But I suppose you don't really want to be associated with my kind?" His pawn moved forward.

Her bishop came out and she sat back, her hand resting on her raised leg. "I never said that." Their eyes held and she motioned with her head. "Who was he?"

Dane watched her before turning his eyes to the board, moving another pawn. If he wanted her to open up, he'd have to give a show of good faith. "The Gray Squirrel."

"Really?" She glanced over her shoulder. "The police use him on occasion but we don't usually have the budget." Her eyes returned to the board and she made another move. "I didn't expect the infamous information monger to look so normal."

"Oh, he changes appearance. Unpredictably, of course. He's had that body for a while though, seems rather fond of it. I think he's always wanted to be an old Jewish man."

[74]

"Haven't we all?"

He glanced at her curiously and couldn't get a read on whether she was being funny or not. "I don't mean to sound ungrateful but why exactly are you gracing me with your presence?"

Her hand was on a pawn and she hesitated before moving it. "My partner did some research and discovered my brother has a bounty on his head."

"Who's your partner?" He moved a pawn but when she didn't respond he looked up at her. "You're not really going to leave me hanging like that, are you?"

"It's just that I don't know if I can trust you."

He felt exactly the same way. But he was probably more adept at traversing the gray area than her. "So let's exchange information. That's what these tables are for."

"And here I thought they were for playing chess in Central Park. Silly me."

"Yes, silly you." He winked. "Now, your partner?"

"Her name is Inari." She hesitated. "But she's also gone by Catatonic."

He leaned forward. "Wait, really? I'd heard she was caught by the police, not that she worked for them."

Naomi tilted her head side to side. "Well, technically both are true. She was caught by me and then joined the force. She's quite clever."

"That's an understatement. But how did you catch her? You're homicide and I would think the cybercrimes division would have had their hands full with her."

"That's a funny story, actually."

He raised a brow. "Please don't end it there."

"Well." Her eyes went distant. "I was working the homicide of Gigabyte—the cybercriminal who was big into hacking databases and altering data?" When he gave a nod she continued. "Well, she was his friend and as I was searching for his killer, she was too. I found her accidentally."

"Accidentally?"

"I was off duty and found a warehouse Gigabyte had used. She'd been holed up there, trying to trick Gigabyte's killer into thinking he was still alive and revealing himself. She had up a ton of firewalls and misdirects for anyone with enhancements entering the warehouse—except I went in without a mech suit. If anyone else had come in she would have known immediately and been gone before they even got close. But she didn't actually think to protect against someone like me. I went in and used the old school method of finding her by following all the wires to the server room."

He moved his queen out. "How did you arrest her without a mech suit though?"

Her knight came out. "Oh, she doesn't have any enhancements. Not even an aural interface."

"Wait, nothing?"

She held his gaze meaningfully. "If you could hack into any computer, would you willingly have one implanted in your body?"

His nose scrunched up. That sounded eerily like someone he knew. "She sounds interesting. And now she's your partner? Why isn't she in the cybercrimes unit?"

"About that." Naomi let out a long sigh. "When I caught her…" She leaned forward, put one hand on her rook and the other on her king. "I didn't exactly arrest her immediately." She castled her king and cleared her throat. "But when I did, we also arrested Gigabyte's killer. He was brought to justice with a damning pile of clearly labeled evidence against him. Serving four life sentences currently."

Apparently, Naomi was a little better at navigating the gray area than he'd thought. He moved his queen again. "Good. I'm glad there was justice for Gigabyte."

"Inari was hit hard by the loss. I didn't know how she felt about me until I was informed the terms of her negotiation included becoming my partner. She still doesn't want to hear anything to the contrary." She moved her own queen out, taking one of his pawns. "Your turn."

He gave a nod, taking her bishop. "I'm going to guess since you know your brother had a bounty on his head, you want to know about who placed it on him."

"I already know Baozhai put it on him." She took his knight, leaning back and meeting his gaze. "What I want to know is what you've discovered since she hired you to go after him."

He chuckled and leaned his arms on the table, letting out a breath. "You would have good intel with Catatonic on your side. Not to mention you're a detective, so you snoop for a living."

She tilted her head in agreement. He took one of her pawns. "I claimed the job and Baozhai's henchling explained Tyler had been working as a mule for the last six or eight months. But he stole things he was supposed to smuggle. Dash and Bitrous, coincidentally—how is that woman doing, anyway?"

"She's alive, thanks to you. And in jail, thanks to me. So why were you at the race, anyway?"

He paused, his brows drawing together. "You really haven't figured it out yet?"

The way her eyes narrowed made him realize she hadn't, so he continued. "Well, you are going through a lot. If someone had changed bodies and you didn't know what they looked like, where would you go to look for them?"

"Shit." Her eyes looked off. "I'd look for him at his sister's race, of course." She sat forward, her elbows hitting the table. "Was he there? Was he all right?"

"I did see him and he looked drained but unharmed. But I lost the signal on my tracker a few hours after the race."

She shot to her feet. "What? You were tracking him? Where was he last?!"

He held up a hand. "I'll get to that. This puzzle is bigger than just your brother, though."

She seemed about to argue but sat back down.

"Right, so your brother was supposed to smuggle dash and bitrous and stole it instead. Baozhai found out and that's when I was hired."

She nodded, moving her knight and taking a pawn. "The day he switched bodies."

"Yes. Iago is one of those handlers people only go to when they're really desperate, but he does have integrity and doesn't reveal his clients. He wouldn't tell me what Tyler's new body looked like but I knew I'd have a good chance of finding him at your race, so I didn't care."

"Just so you know Iago's been murdered." He stared at her and she motioned with her hand. "Don't worry, you've already been cleared."

"What? I don't care about that. I know *I* didn't kill him. But who did?"

"We don't know. We can't figure out if they were after the handler or my brother. Well, the detectives investigating it anyway. I'm not allowed to actually participate in the investigation, but Inari keeps me updated."

He let out a breath. "Naomi, your team is thinking about this all wrong."

She lifted a dubious brow. "Enlighten me."

"Let me guess, Iago was dead and lots of machines were broken?" When she leaned back and kept staring, he continued. "Most criminals aren't exactly the most well adjusted. When they don't find what they're looking for, they get pretty violent."

"Okay, I'll give you that. But what does that have to do with this?"

"Criminal walks into a body transfer shop. He doesn't find what he was looking for and gets angry, killing the handler and breaking some machines to soothe his rage." He leaned forward, taking her other bishop. "So, what else could he have been looking for? If not your brother or Iago, what else was missing that could have been his target?"

She took in a breath. "The body my brother took."

"Exactly. Sometimes it doesn't matter if a new person has taken the body, some crime lords will pay the bounty on the body. They aren't always particular about who was inside because they feel the message is sent."

Her eyes closed. "So, you're saying my brother may be worse off."

"A black market body Switch usually comes with a lot of baggage, but this one might be worse." He moved his queen. "After seeing your brother at the race, I was able to figure out who he had been. Turns out, in a previous life he was Trigger."

"My brother would take the body of a Yakuza hit man." She sighed moving her knight. "You mentioned a tracker?"

"When I saw your brother at the race, I was able to get a tracker on him before I got distracted by the one-legged bomb wench." He moved his bishop. "I had his signal but lost him when he went to—"

"The Underground, I know." She moved her queen in re-

[79]

sponse. When he gave her a quizzical look she continued. "Jax pointed it out to me."

He watched her before looking at the board. "So, you're dating Jackson Raelyn, CEO of CLM, huh?"

"I know you're jealous." It was his turn to look at her with a raised brow but she was smirking. "I'm not sure if he's into men but if he wants you, I give you both my blessing."

He chuckled and moved his queen. "Your magnanimity is overwhelming."

"You know, Dane…" Naomi had her fingertips on her rook. "You really do like to take your queen out for a dance." The rook slid down the lane.

"Well, I am always looking for a good partner." Their eyes held before he moved his queen again, just for good measure. "Speaking of which, is that how you found me here?"

"I swear Inari could track a flea on a dog, so long as there was a computer chip somewhere on it." She used her queen to take his. "And check, by the way."

"Girl on girl, action, eh? I suppose I deserve that." He moved his king but saw only one more move left to him.

"So how much are you getting paid by Baozhai?" She moved her queen. "Check."

He paused. "Fifty thousand." He moved his king to the last viable spot.

"I'll double it and pay you half up front. You work for me now." She set down her queen. "Checkmate."

He liked that her face had a few freckles and a couple of scars, but mostly he enjoyed the intensity of her gaze. Not like he had any intention of turning her offer down but her eyes said she wouldn't take no for an answer. He paused before reaching out a single finger and tipping over his king. "I'm all yours." He held his hands up in defeat. "Though I do have to wonder where an NYPD detective got that type of money."

"Years of competition earnings. It can pay to work out." She stood and his eyes moved over her muscular form as she stretched. Up close, her legs were even sexier than what he'd seen of her at the race, and he nearly got caught staring when she turned. "But my brother will be paying me back. He's going to regret what he's done."

Dane came to his feet. "I assure you; he already does." She glanced away and her face creased with worry. He softened his voice. "There's one last thing."

"More good news about my brother?"

He let out a breath. "No, it's about the Monkhood."

She hesitated. "What about it?"

"I got information from Gray Squirrel about a new bounty that's about to be placed on the Monkhood. Apparently, they have some plan that's got them onto the radar of someone powerful in a bad way."

He barely heard her whisper. "Sanctuary."

"How do you know about that?"

She waved a hand. "The monk who I saw murdered? Artillery had been asking him about Sanctuary. But it gets worse."

He frowned. "How exactly?"

"My brother had a picture of a bodhisattva on his body when he transferred."

Dane did not often wrestle with self-doubt. Especially not where it concerned bounties and large amounts of cash. This felt like he was trying to wrestle an elephant in increased gravity. "Let me get this all straight. Not only is the Chinese smuggler Baozhai and Trigger's old boss Yurik chasing your brother, but also potentially everyone who is going after the bounty on the

Monkhood?" When she nodded he scrunched up his nose. "Has his luck always been bad?"

She sighed heavily. "Yes. That boy could find trouble in an empty paper bag." Her hand was held out to him. "You still in this?"

"Oh, fuck me." He hesitated before he took her hand, shaking it. "Yes. But I can't make any promises we'll get him back in one piece." All the digital neural receptors of his tech told his brain her hand was simultaneously soft while also hardened through battle, and he thanked the bionic gods for the replacement part that meant he was able to experience it so thoroughly.

"All I'm paying for is your expertise. And maybe a few dozen of your weapons." She took her hand back and put both hands into the pockets of her jacket. "I need to figure out what I want to do. I have one possible plan, but I don't know if it's the right one. I need time to think. Let's meet again in the morning. All right?"

He gave a slow nod. "All right. Take care of yourself." His voice quieted. "We'll find your brother."

She gave a brave smile. "I know. He can't die before I kill him, after all."

"You do realize you're a cop, don't you?"

Her feet were carrying her away. "I'm off duty."

He watched her hips swaying as she moved off, his voice quiet. "We're never really off duty." He glanced at the chessboard and his fallen king.

"Would you like a partner?"

Dane sighed, turning to the gangly android standing where Naomi had been moments before. It proudly bore a first place ribbon from a nearby high school science fair, but looked as if a soup can had bred with a toaster and a mixer.

Dave gave a snort. "Fuck off, Chess-bot."

[82]

"As you wish, sir."

CHAPTER 7

Naomi

She was seated with one leg up beside her chest and the other curled beneath her. Her chin rested on her knee and her hands were by her feet. Littered around her on the bed were trinkets she hadn't taken out of her memory box in years. She was a minimalist by nature, but these were things even she couldn't bear to part with. Her eyes lingered over a ballerina figurine her father had given her when she was a little girl. She remembered her mother's stories of him more than the man. He'd fallen to cancer just after her mother became pregnant with Tyler. After his death her mother had been brave and soldiered on, though Naomi hadn't understood how hard it must have been for her until later. At the thought of her mother, her fingers began running slowly over the folded NYPD flag of green, white, and blue.

The flag had been draped over her mother's casket during the funeral. Naomi had been eighteen and was not only suddenly an orphan but also the guardian of her fourteen- year-old brother. While the funeral had been hell, it was nothing compared to the next four years. The death of their mother seemed to have destroyed something inside Tyler and he'd transformed from a fairly normal teenager into something Naomi hadn't been equipped to deal with. He'd gone from drugs, to drinking, to gambling at breakneck velocity. She'd gotten him countless hours of therapy and he'd gotten himself endless hours of community service.

Nothing had helped until Veronica. She'd become his girl-friend shortly after his eighteenth birthday and Naomi got her first reprieve and a glimmer of hope. She'd been able to join the police force and breathe for the first time. That had lasted long enough for her to make detective. She didn't blame Veronica for leaving him. Her brother wasn't easy to live with and his down-ward spiral started again, paling the toxicity of round one.

She'd wished a thousand times that she could talk to her mother about Tyler. Her mother had always known what to say, how to handle him. As a child, Tyler had once wanted a new gaming system so badly he'd threatened to run away. She'd let him go with an easy smile, saying he wouldn't get far. He hadn't and he'd come home, apologetic and much less prone to follow-ing his rages.

Naomi rubbed the bridge of her eyes. What was she supposed to do? She'd stayed up all night searching for an answer but it was now nearly seven. Her next shift didn't start until Monday morning so if she were going to transfer bodies, she should make the most of this Sunday time before someone would notice she was gone. They wouldn't start looking for her until Tuesday, pos-sibly Wednesday. But she couldn't call in sick because her chief would know immediately she was up to something.

Her eyes fell to the memory box and she sighed. Better to put all the junk away— when she picked up the box, there was a rattling noise. Inside, there was a small, round stone, cool to the touch. It was painted a faded brown, with a pair of rabbit ears drawn on with a marker and two squiggly eyes glued onto it.

She'd been maybe ten when she'd begged her mother for a pet rabbit. Naomi now understood why her mother had said no—the life of a supervisor in the NYPD left little time for family, let alone pets. But Naomi had been a child and had simply wanted something, anything, as a pet. Tyler had come to her when she'd been crying and given her the little rock. He'd said he didn't want her to cry anymore.

Naomi wiped at her cheeks, looking at the little rabbit now resting atop her mother's flag. If something happened to Tyler… Her stomach ached with the thought that these could be the only remnants of her family if something happened to him.

Incoming visual message. Sender unknown.

She jumped off her bed, hurrying to her wall interface. "Display the message."

It showed a dark alley and she could barely see anything in the twilight. There wasn't the sound of music so much as the rumble of bass in the background. The video was bouncing, and Naomi gathered the person was recording from a visual interface. The person was walking at a brisk pace past garbage cans—then someone with a bright red eye was glaring at the camera before the recorder hurried on, more quickly than before.

The sound of chains trailing along the ground echoed in the alley and the camera ducked behind a dumpster, his breathing becoming more rapid. He glanced around the corner of the dumpster as the sound of chains neared, a soft whistle echoing in the twilight.

The visual went dark but the sound continued. Naomi had to swallow. He'd been so scared he'd closed his eyes. The whistler came closer and closer—

And then the chain and whistling began to fade. The camera's owner began to pant in fear and then looked down. There was a piece of broken glass on the pavement and it reflected a single eye. The voice whispered a plea. "Help me, Noams. Please. Help me."

The screen went blank and this time, the video was truly over.

She trembled before her fingers flew into action. *Calling Inari Hayashi.*

The user has set do not disturb—

"Override: NYPD code Alpha, Tango, Two One Six, Bravo."

There were three rings before she picked up. *"Why can't you let me sleep like a normal pers—"*

"Hack my interface, NOW."

"Whoa, okay! No need to get all grumpish, geez. I was just a little curglaffed because you woke me up suddenly and—"

"Inari, hack into my inter—"

"Already have. Sneck your trap so I can watch."

The video began playing again but halfway through computer code overlaid the image. Inari must have been scrolling through the code because it began to move, pieces of it jumping in and out of magnification. To keep herself from asking anything Naomi began pacing. The little rabbit was still sitting atop the flag, staring at her blankly.

"Okay, so this message is encoded really well but the syntax is unusual, and I may have to build a cipher in order to—"

"English."

"Right. So, it's complicated and I'm not a hundo percent sure but it looks like a real video, not spliced or anything weird." Naomi closed her eyes and Inari continued. *"But that doesn't mean this is Tyler! Just that all the back-end stuff looks legit."*

Naomi let out a long breath before opening her eyes. The rock rabbit's unseeing eyes seemed to pierce her soul and she closed her own again, taking in another deep breath. Could she live with it if something happened to him and she had done nothing to try and save him? She knew she'd already decided and hated herself for it. But what else could she possibly do? He was her brother. For better and for worse, he was the only family she had left. She hadn't been able to do anything for her mother. She wouldn't lose her brother, too.

"I need you to send a message to the bounty hunter Dane Thayer. Tell him to meet me at CLM Tow—"

"CLM TOWER?! ARE YOU INSANE!!"

Naomi cringed. She hadn't meant for Inari to figure out her plan. "I'm just going to see if Jax has any leads—"

"And also conveniently a body for you? Naomi, I'm not an idiot."

No, she certainly wasn't. Naomi's voice softened. "Inari, I have to do this. He's my brother." She whispered. "Please understand."

There was a moment of silence before Inari let out a frustrated groan. "Urgh, you're so much trouble! FINE, I'll help you." She sighed heavily. "What were you asking me before you gave me a figurative heart attack?"

Naomi was able to smile despite the circumstance. She was lucky to have as good a friend as Inari. "Tell Dane to meet me at CLM Tower. I'm heading there shortly."

"You know bounty hunters have encryption systems in place so not just anyone can send them messages, right?"

"What, so it will take you ten seconds instead of five? Just send it." She paused. "And Inari?"

"Yeah?"

"Thank you. I don't know what I'd do without you."

There was a catch in the girl's voice and Naomi knew her well enough to know Inari was trying to cheer them both up. "Probably suffer endlessly from boredom and a lack of late night Chinese takeout. Oh, and-and cookies! Let's not forget the mountains and mountains of cookies that would go uneaten."

She headed to her closet. "True, that would be a tragedy."

"Speaking of which, for waking me up at this ungodly hour and *putting me under this much stress—not to mention I need to be on my game in case you need me to code— you owe me a cookie cake from that bakery down on fifth and probably a case of energy drinks—better make it two, actually, just to be on the safe side."*

She yanked off her tank top and shorts, tossing them into the hamper. "Fine, I'll call and—"

"Oh, I've already sent in an order on your behalf. I just didn't want you to be surprised when the notification comes about the deduction from your bank account."

Naomi's leg was hovering above her pants, the other already having made its way inside. "You hacked into my bank account?"

There was a pause. *"Wait, are you really surprised?"*

Naomi tucked her shirt into her pants before zipping them up. "No, actually. But could you put up some extra blockades in apology?"

"Oh please. I added encryptions to everything about you right after we first met. I have to keep you safe from baddies. You're my partner!"

She shook her head slowly as she headed out her door. "I suppose I should be grateful you'll only break the law for cookies, now."

"Hey, cookies are life."

Incoming call from Restricted User.

"Inari, I've got another ca—"

"It's the bounty hunter. I'll patch him through."

As Naomi went downstairs, she was surprised the call hadn't gone through. When she tried to call Inari back, she found her interface still registered the call as active and chalked it up to something Inari must be doing. She'd left her apartment building, was inside a self-driving taxi, had the address to CLM Tower programmed, and the car was moving before she finally heard Dane's warm and boisterous laughter. *"That was hands down the best death threat I've ever received."*

"Who issued you a death threat?"

"Your partner. She sounds adorable. And really young. Is she even legal? Never mind, that sounded creepy."

Her brain was hurting. "Get back to the death threat part."

"Oh, she picked up the line and informed me that if I let anything happen to you she'd start my torture by hacking my bank account and making donations in my name to evangelical religious organizations and give them my GPS coordinates so they could proselytize to me while I'm working and... well a bunch of other things too, she went on for a while. But anyway, my favorite part was when she said she'd kill me by hacking my interface and forcing my appendages to do her evil bidding and have them take me out into a swamp somewhere so I could be attacked by crocodiles. I'm assuming she would make me run to the bayou first, seeing as we don't have any crocodiles in New York that I know of. But maybe she knows somebody. Either way, it's definitely the most creative death threat I've ever gotten."

"Do you get a lot of death threats?"

"Eh, you know. Occupational hazard." There was a beat. *"So why exactly am I meeting you at the Tower of Overcompensation?"*

She had to stifle a laugh. "Are you referring to CLM Tower?"

"That and Jax's small penis, yes. But seriously, what's going on?"

Thinking of her mission sobered her mood. "Short version is I've decided to go after my brother and I've found a way. But I need you with me if you're willing."

"When do I find out the long version?"

"Probably after it's happened."

"Fair enough. Will it be dangerous?"

She hesitated. "Yes."

"Good, I don't like being bored. I'll see you there shortly. Oh, and Naomi?"

[90]

"What is it?"

His voice softened. *"We will find your brother."*

She managed a smile. "Thanks, Dane. I'll see you soon."

When the call ended, she looked out the window to see she was only a couple blocks from CLM. She tapped her fingers in the familiar sequence. *Calling Jackson Raelyn.*

There wasn't even a single ring before he answered. *"Naomi? Are you all right?"*

"I'm fine." She sucked in a breath. "I've spent some time thinking and I—" Her throat caught. "I need your help."

"Anything for you. Can you come over now?"

She blinked in surprise. "I'm almost there, actually."

"Good, I'll tell them to let you into the R and D lab on floor eighty-two."

When the call ended she leaned back in her seat, looking out the window in relief that Jax seemed willing to help her. She spoke quietly to her reflection. "Tyler, you'd better be alright until I can come find you and kick your ass." When only silence answered, she sighed, closing her eyes to wait until the car drew to a stop.

The security guard opened her door. "Welcome, Miss Gate. Mr. Raelyn is expecting you."

She made her way into the pristine white lobby, the image screens shining and the hostess standing behind the counter. Her eyes slid over Naomi's form and she didn't bother to hide her derision. Naomi had never been clear whether the women at CLM despised her for her lack of upgrades or whether it was jealousy because she was with Jax. Either way, Naomi was grateful yet again she'd never felt the need to alter her own body like they had. As they neared the elevators the doorman waved his hand over the panel beside them, and the doors obediently slid open.

Once inside the elevator he gave a nod. "Mr. Raelyn will see you now." The doors closed and she was able to see her reflection in the white surface of the walls. Her eyes moved over the freckles on her face, her strong legs and her messy hair. She caught herself smiling sadly at her reflection. She was going to miss her body.

The doors opened to an expansive space with numerous workstations. Each housed projects in various stages of completion. The brightest lights were in the back corner, and she weaved her way amongst the tables toward it. She quickly realized all the projects were enhancements of some sort or another, based on the volume of appendages she passed. A pair of feminine legs were standing on a table, the thighs nowhere near to touching. Naomi glanced down at her wide quads and hated herself that she was comparing. When her eyes caught sight of an unfinished mechanical skull, she hurried along.

She had been about to call out when Jax stood from a crouch, his back to her. He stepped away from a table where a body was lying. Wires, tubes, and electrodes were stuck to the woman. Her skin was a cool sepia reddish-brown, a green tank top tucked into her cargo pants. Dark hair was braided tightly against her skull, but Naomi couldn't see the eyes because they were closed. Both her arms were obviously bionic since the shoulders had exposed compartments showing a host of weapons beneath.

She breathed a sigh of relief. Apparently she wasn't going to have to try to persuade him. "Is that body for me?"

Jax turned quickly before giving a nod. He touched a control panel on the left forearm and the weapons compartment closed. "I upgraded the weapons store. I want you to be safe." He wrapped his arms around her tightly. "Are you sure about this?"

She held him loosely, her eyes staring at the body. "My brother needs me."

He sighed with a nod. "All right. I know how you are when you make up your mind about something." When he drew back, he rested his hands on her shoulders. "I put some military level upgrades into the shell. You should have more than enough protection for any circumstance."

She blinked in surprise. "Military level upgrades?" How had he gotten those?

He waved a hand. "We do work with the military, of course. Most undercover agents both domestic and abroad use our technology. And not to mention a lot of branches of the government that I actually *can't* legally mention."

She realized then, she wasn't the only one putting herself at risk. "Jax, you could go to jail for this."

"I'm aware." His eyes held hers. "But unlike your police chief, I know you'll find a way no matter what. So, I'll take my chances with getting caught because I refuse to let you go to the black market for a body." He looked off and frowned. "Were you expecting someone?"

That was fast. "Yes, he's a bounty hunter I hired. I need him here."

Jax hesitated before he gave a nod. "Send him up." He put a hand to the back of her neck and gave her an unexpectedly deep kiss. When his hands slid over her hips she heard herself moaning, her own hands grabbing at his ass. The passion of their kiss deepened, and she had no sense of time until she heard Dane clearing his throat behind them.

When they disentangled, she cleared her throat, motioning to Dane. "Jax, this is Dane Thayer. Dane, this is Jackson Raelyn." When neither of the men immediately went to shake hands she glanced between the two, until they finally seemed to notice her.

Dane was the first to extend a metallic hand. "Dane Thayer."

Jax gave his hand a shake. "You can call me Jax. Would you like me to fix up some of those hospital grade implants before you two head out?"

"Despite popular opinion, not all of us hate our bodies." Dane took back his hand as if he'd touched fire and turned to Naomi. "Please tell me this—" He motioned to Jax and the body on the table with a single finger in a wide circle. "—is not your plan."

She raised a brow. "Do you have a better one?"

"Yes, actually. How about the one where I search for your brother through quasi-legal channels, and you do your thing as a cop and search through all your truly legal channels? In case you are unclear, my plan has you not potentially ending up in jail. You do remember jail, don't you? The place where you send all the people you arrest? Who would be really, really happy to see you should you end up there?"

She knew he was being more rational than she was. But the reality was that message had changed everything for her. There was no longer any other choice. "I've made my decision. Either you help me, or you get out of my way."

"That's my Naomi." Jax gave a small grunt as he turned to his machines. "Nothing will change her mind now."

Dane watched her for a long moment before he gave an irritable grunt. "Fine. But if you start regretting this don't expect a shoulder to cry on."

She gave a short laugh. "Wouldn't your shoulders rust if I did?"

"Please. It's a rust-resistant alloy." He gave her a wink that was delightfully charming.

Jax offered her a hand. "Come along, dear. I need to hook you in."

He led her to another table and, once she laid down, he

turned to Dane. "Start strapping her in, I need to connect the electrodes." Her boyfriend began putting cool electrode stickers onto her temples and the sides of her neck as Dane tightened the straps around her legs. Jax spoke calmly. "We'll need to put your body into stasis in order to keep it alive. Once you're out of it, I'll transport it to another floor to keep it safe. The actual Switch will not be painful so much as disorienting. I've already infused your new host body with enough nutrients that it should be an easy transfer."

Dane was working on the straps at her arms. "What about body identification?"

Jax added electrodes to the insides of her wrists. "It has a fabricated authentication. It will show up in The Underground as a low-level lackey. The body's Underground name is Sai."

Naomi glanced up at him. "How did you manage that?"

"I do a lot of work with the police, remember?" He muttered softly as he turned toward the computers. "Though not usually hiding police from the police..."

As Dane tightened the strap around her stomach his eyes rose to meet hers. He paused for a long moment before he leaned forward, tightening a strap around her forehead. When he finished, she swore he hesitated before he straightened. "You'll have to remember you aren't the police and there are places you can't go. But I'll be there to show you the way."

She tried to nod but her head was strapped in. "I'm glad."

There was a whirring of machines before Jax turned back to them. "Are you ready?"

She took in a breath and stared at the ceiling. "Yes."

He slipped a simple mouth guard past her lips and she tried to brace herself for whatever would come.

Her brother had better appreciate this.

"You will feel a slight pinch."

CHAPTER 8

Naomi

"Slight pinch, my ass!" She was grimacing in pain when the husky alto voice registered. Was that what her voice sounded like now? She tried to open her eyes but was hit with a blinding headache.

"The transfer was obviously a success." Jax quickly began to peel the electrode stickers off her temples and neck.

Dane began undoing the straps at her legs. "So how do we get out of here without being seen? Otherwise this is going to be a bit obvious."

Jax was now undoing the straps on her arms, muttering. "Then maybe you two shouldn't be seen together, since you are rather hard to miss."

Dane rolled his eyes and undid the strap around her torso. "Where we're headed is a place I'm familiar with and in case you've forgotten, a place that will kill her if they figure out who she is."

"Well, if you hadn't—"

"Jax, shut up." Her head was spinning but when the last of the straps came off she sat up anyway, fueled by irritation. "Both of you, actually." She felt hands helping her to stay seated and she slumped over. "My brother went through this?"

Jax lowered his voice. "The difference between this procedure and what your brother went through is equivalent to having an arm amputated with and without anesthetic."

Dane grunted. "I'm told it feels more like having your brain forcibly removed with an ice cream scoop."

She nearly regretted the act of turning her head to look at Dane, but the disorientation was quickly wearing off. "You've never switched bodies?"

He guffawed. "Why would I? My body is a temple."

A temple that had been remodeled a few dozen times by her reckoning. But as she looked closer, she noticed everything was at its base a hospital grade replacement. She'd thought they were all weaponized upgrades but realized the weapons were actually all after-market additions. Her brows drew together in sympathy. Whatever had happened to get him those new appendages hadn't been his choice.

Jax's hand on hers drew her attention and with his help she was able to stand.

Which was incredibly weird because she and Jax were almost the same height now. She tried to imagine she was wearing high heels and—

It was hard not to flinch when her eyes fell on her real body, still strapped down to the table where she'd been moments before the Switch. It was like watching herself in a video except it wasn't the same. It was too tangible for that and she was hit with the reality of what she'd done. The world swam and when she swayed Jax's hand steadied her. "Easy now. It'll take you a moment to get used to the interface."

She frowned until she realized he had no idea what she'd actually been feeling. But she didn't feel like correcting him and simply nodded instead. When she was standing under her own power, she looked down at her hand, balling a fist and releasing it several times. The skin appeared to move naturally and if she hadn't seen the shoulder compartments, she wouldn't even know it was a fake. That was perhaps more eerie than anything else, considering she was inside the body now.

"Don't forget you can change the power output. I know you have your leg carefully adjusted by your doctor but that's because it could destroy your organic leg if it weren't calibrated perfectly. Both the arms and legs on this body have been upgraded so they can have their output altered through your interface to above normal human output levels. It should be similar to your mech suit, though this will obviously be the most recently released operating system."

She tapped her finger twice and the display overlaid her vision. It was a more advanced and streamlined display than what she had in her mech suit. But that made sense, considering the NYPD suits were decades-old technology. She quickly browsed through the menu, trying to get her bearings. It seemed fairly straightforward and when she got to the armaments display she realized Jax had been right. It was very well armed.

When she was finished, her hand automatically went to try and lift her visor before it occurred to her she didn't have her mech suit on. Dane's voice was quiet. "You'll need to break that habit, fast." He met her gaze. "No one wears mech suits in The Underground."

"Right." But she was too busy trying to calm her revulsion. It was funny that mistaking her interface for her mech suit was what made her realize she didn't have human eyes anymore. She just needed to focus on getting to Ty and then she'd be back in her body. "Speaking of The Underground, we need to get out of here." Her eyes turned to Jax. "How do we do that?"

"Are you still nauseous?"

Her eyes narrowed. "No, why?"

"You'll see." He motioned with his head over his shoulder before turning. "This way."

She and Dane shared a glance before following Jax, and she nearly fell for lack of realizing exactly how long her new legs were. Dane grabbed her hand, as well as adding a steadying touch to her low back. His voice was gentle. "You okay?"

Seeing his metal hand within hers was a shock to her. How did he live every day with so little of his body? "I'm all right." Even so, knowing he was going to be with her through this whole mess was perhaps the only thing keeping her from total panic. His presence was oddly calming. Eyes lifting to take in Jax's back, she fought down a sigh.

Far more calming than her would-be fiancé.

Jax stopped beside the elevator and a protest halted on her lips when she saw he wasn't going to the elevator interface. He waved his hand on the wall beside it, an access panel popping forward. When he pulled the square panel open, it revealed a dark shaft lit by blue emergency lights running parallel to the elevator shaft. Naomi leaned over enough to look down into the abyss with a little shiver. "But we're eighty-two floors up." Jax grabbed a pair of harnesses from the back of the access panel door. "This emergency exit system is graded for up to a hundred and fifty-two floors. You'll be to sub-basement three in less than ten seconds."

He offered them both harnesses and when Dane met her gaze he gave a little shrug. They both took a harness and began putting them around their shoulders as she sighed. "That sounds fast."

"This system is designed to get people to safety from high floors in case of a building wide structural integrity failure. There are dozens of escape shafts throughout the building. But it does tend to leave one wishing they'd skipped on breakfast. Fortunately, your new body hasn't eaten food recently so you shouldn't vomit. Dane on the other hand—"

"I skydive."

"Fascinating. Are you both ready?"

"I'll go first." Dane stepped forward. "What do I attach to?"

Jax chuckled. "Please, we're not so primitive. It's electromagnetic. You don't strictly need the harness but it's factory recommended so you'll land heads up."

Dane glanced down the shaft. "How does it make sure we won't hit each other?"

Jax raised a brow. "Do cars hit each other on the road? We have algorithms for that. Now, are you going?" The men held each other's gaze before Dane turned around and leaned back into the shaft. He was yanked inside with a gush of air.

Naomi rushed forward to look down but caught no sight of him. Jax slipped his arms around her and his voice was soft. "Please be careful. There's a tracking beacon in your body in case you have need. It will lead me straight to you. All you have to do is activate it and I'll come with an arsenal."

Since when did he have an arsenal? "Thank you." She'd learned a great deal about him the last few days. Very little of it was comforting. Yet, when their eyes met she felt her insides fluttering. "Jax, about the ring... when I get back—"

"I'll simply be glad you get back safely with your brother."

She nodded, her heart rate slowing.

She nearly flinched.

It was someone else's heart that was slowing.

Jax's hand moved to her cheek as he leaned in to kiss her. When her chin was resting on his shoulder her eyes were drawn to the far side of the room. Her body was lying there without her, attached to machines for life support. She found it oddly comforting that Sunday was normally her rest day from training. It didn't seem to be as much of a betrayal to leave her body behind today. But she was just lying to herself, wasn't she?

She closed her eyes and focused on her brother. He was what mattered now.

Jax drew back to wave his hand over her arm. *Credentials updated.*

"I've given you access so you'll be able to activate the locks and get out of the building. My apologies, but you'll have to go via the sewer."

Her nose scrunched. "The sewer?"

"Do you want to be spotted?" He touched her wrist and a map popped up in her vision. "You'll need to crawl out an access panel and into the sewer. Then if you go down the marked passages, you'll be able to get out of a manhole cover hidden behind a dumpster. After that, you'll be on your own."

She nodded and her eyes returned to her real body. Was she doing the right thing?

Once she went down the shaft, there would be no turning back.

"And Naomi?" After their eyes met he leaned forward, his hands on her hips and his breath a whisper in her ear. "Good luck."

He kissed her once before he pushed her backward and she was sucked into the darkness.

Dane

He was on a knee hunched over, his arms resting on his other knee. While he didn't know what was keeping her, he was grateful for the time to recover.

Incoming message from Jackson Raelyn. Take care of my fiancée or I will make sure you don't live long enough to regret it.

Dane felt a rush of disgust.

Had Jax just called Naomi his fiancée?

A whoosh preceded her new body hovering above the bottom of the shaft. She hung weightless for a second before the electromagnets released her and she settled on the bottom of the shaft with a thud. She groaned and put a hand to her head. "That bastard pushed me!"

He grunted as he reached over and unhooked her harness. "Yeah, him being pushy is the only reason an intelligent woman like you would agree to something this foolish." From the daggers in her eyes he seemed to have hit a nerve and realized he was a little edgy himself. Stupid Jax. "Look, I get the desire to find your brother and all, and I'm sensing you may have some control issues—" She was about to protest when he raised a hand. "—but this isn't just some gray area of legality. You will go to jail for this, if any of your cop buddies find you."

He helped her shrug off the harness. She leaned back against the wall, closing her eyes. "I know." She sighed and put a hand to her stomach. "What is the point of this emergency shaft if you can barely walk afterward?"

"Seriously." He found his pride helped him get to his feet; he didn't want to look weak in front of her, even though he needed the wall to steady himself. "Can you walk? We should get going." And get the hell out of CLM. For good measure he turned his privacy onto the highest setting possible and told himself it was for protection and not because he didn't want another cryptic message from her fiancé. He would have been pleased if he'd never come in contact with the man. That Jax was messaging him directly was wholly unsavory.

"Let me see if this thing has an equilibrium reinforcement." She tapped her fingers a few times and was on her feet looking more at ease than she had a right to. When she went to take a step she stopped, pointing to a pile of vomit. "I thought you sky-dived?"

"I do! Well, have. From space, even." She didn't look sufficiently impressed and he shrugged. "Just once, though. Hated it, actually." Her brow stayed risen so he continued. "I had a mark who thought I wouldn't catch him. I had to prove him wrong, it's bounty hunter honor." She kept staring and he sighed. "Okay, he was worth a lot of cash. You're so judgmental."

When he tried to step, he swayed and she put her arm around his waist. "You're an idiot."

"I'm a cis-man. It's kind of a requirement."

She began leading them and since she seemed to know the way he simply followed. They had turned down a dank hallway lit only with emergency lights when she spoke. "I would have thought with as many enhancements as you have, you'd have switched bodies."

"No desire to either." He glanced over at her as they stopped beside an access panel. She waved her forearm and the light flicked from red to green. "How'd you get your leg?" He grabbed the panel door, pulling it open. "In your own body, I mean."

As the vile stench hit them, they both jumped back and covered their mouths and noses. He was suddenly grateful he'd already vomited. "What is that?"

"The sewers." She spoke from behind her hand. "This smells like a crime scene. Is there a dead body down here?"

As they crawled through the panel, he was able to see the channel where the fetid water was churning. Fortunately, there were walkways on either side so they wouldn't have to stand directly in the putrid water. He was trying to puzzle out where he recognized the smell from when it finally occurred to him. "The stench. It's coming from CLM."

She kept trudging on and with every corner they turned, the smell lessened. "Yes, yes. You think CLM stinks, very funny."

"No, though I do wish you appreciated my unintentional pun." She glanced over her shoulder at him and he motioned to the water channel. "It's the byproducts from CLM making the smell. It's the same odor you'll get around a black market enhancement center. It's basically rot and decay from all the leftover human parts and excrement from bodies in stasis." He was glad they were getting away from CLM for a number of reasons now. "Though I have to say, no black market place ever smelled that bad."

She came to a ladder and paused, glancing at him. "I guess it would have something to do with volume. CLM Tower does more business than most of their satellite stations combined." When she shimmied up the ladder he tried not to think of where she'd gotten her current body. He struggled to shake off the creepy feeling crawling down his spine and hurried after her.

They came out from under a manhole cover and he was grateful for the fresh air. When she put the cover back into place, he glanced around the dumpster blocking them from view of the street. She turned to him, her brown eyes on him. "What now?"

"Now, I lead. And you're going to have to trust me."

"That's what I'm paying you for." Ah, yes, the stereotypical hardened cop. Well. She'd either trust him or she wouldn't. He turned away, taking them out of the alley. They were several blocks away from CLM now and he was grateful to lead them further away. After walking a time in silence, he noticed she was looking down at her arms, turning her hands over and back a few times.

He remembered how strange it had been, when he'd gotten his first bionic hand. He'd thought it would feel more unreal but the neural connectors made it seem as if nothing had changed, despite the fact everything had changed—more than once, in his case. "I sometimes feel like a bionic Potato Head too."

She turned to him with her brows creased together. "A what?"

"Pota—eh, never mind. I'm guessing you aren't into Millennial Collecting?"

"Oh, you mean those people who obsessively collect hundred-plus-year-old junk and then either horde it or sell it at Antique's Gameshow—"

"Roadshow."

"Whatever."

His brow rose as he pointed to the alley on her left. "You're a real charmer, you know that?"

"So I've been told. Now will you explain why we're heading to Chinatown?"

"The Underground moves around but what you cops also don't know is that there are multiple satellite locations. Since your brother worked for Baozhai, we are going to start our search there."

They went into a Chinese herbal medicine store. The walls were covered in bottles and ointments, all under a thick layer of dust. The man behind the counter kept his eyes firmly planted on the image screen as Dane moved to an interface station, which looked to be forty years out of date. Naomi met his gaze with curiosity but didn't say anything and he appreciated she was trusting him. He waved the back of his hand in front of the reader and motioned with his eyes for her to do the same. He held his breath until the unit beeped in approval. *Credentials updated. Directions uploaded.* Out of the bottom of the unit, two thin plastic bracelets dropped out. He grabbed the one with the proper numbers, slipping it around her wrist before adding the other to his own.

She gave him a questioning glance and he shook his head once before they headed out through the back door, into another alley. *Turn right.*

When they headed right, she took in a surprised breath and whispered. "There's a line we're following."

So, she had an optical upgrade in her new body. "This is how you find The Underground. You go to an access point first, get your credentials updated so you get access, grab a bracelet, and get directions."

Turn left.

They headed down another alley. "The bracelets seem risky. If they're stolen—"

"They'll melt into the ID chip of the thief's wrist." Their eyes caught and he gave a slow nod. "Until the entire hand falls off."

She cleared her throat. "So how does it keep moving and yet no one ever runs into it?" She stopped moving as they faced the dead end of an alley. "And why does the trail end here?"

You have arrived at your destination.

He took her hand and pulled a surprised Naomi two steps forward, through the image of a wall. *Access granted.*

"Is that just a 3D projection? That doesn't seem very secure."

He kept his voice low, holding up his wrist and shaking the bracelet they'd just received from the access point. "You don't watch enough sci-fi movies."

She frowned. "What happens if someone doesn't have a bracelet?"

"You've no doubt seen homicide cases of inexplicable exsanguination?"

She gave a quiet grunt, part disgust and part acknowledgement.

The alley in fact continued for quite some distance, a few people littering the side of the alley despite it being early on a Sunday morning. There were a couple of blankets and boxes spread out with various illegal bionic parts and weapons available for sale. There was a gambling table set up by Sparrow, as usual. Each door down the alley was marked with a small flag which designated what could be found inside and there were people hovering, waiting to see if they could pick up work, be it killing, maiming or thieving. All in all, an average morning in The Underground.

"Now let's find your brother." Dane spoke quietly, caught her gaze meaningfully. "Hopefully before anyone finds out who you really are."

And they stepped forward, together.

CHAPTER 9

Naomi

She met his casual pace, fighting down her nervous energy and finding, as usual, she turned to humor. "Is this really it?" Their eyes met and her brow rose playfully. "I'm seriously underwhelmed."

His lips curled with a hint of amusement. "It's not so much a place as the services it provides."

She paused, glancing ahead. There was a man with a blanket of wares and when she looked closer her heart skipped a beat. Everything he was selling was specifically designed to take out a police mech suit. It was like cop-killer central. The seller met her gaze and she tried not to flinch. Both his eyes had been replaced with bionic ones reminiscent of fly eyes, bulging out of his eye sockets. Worse, though, was that his eyelids had been removed since blinking was no longer necessary.

Dane grabbing her ass broke her out of her horror. "See something you want for your birthday, sweetheart?" He turned to the seller, shaking his head sadly. "Her brother's locked up."

The man nodded knowingly. His voice sounded like a car crushing machine as he motioned to a box of Plasma Charges. "Buy three and I'll give you one on the house." His toothy grin showed he'd had some teeth replaced with sharp metal filings. "Special, for the cop who got your brother."

Despite her horror, she'd regained enough control of herself

[109]

to remember her cover. "That's a generous offer, I'll keep it in mind." She turned to Dane, lifting a playful brow. "Thanks, dearest."

His smile was equally as saccharine. "Anything for you, pumpkin."

They started walking and she took in a deep breath to calm herself down. When they were out of earshot, she shot him a look. "Ass grabbing a typical day on the job for you?"

He looked a hint chagrinned. "Bounty hunters don't have a reputation for being the most consent oriented. I apologize for using the trope to keep us out of trouble."

She softened, her eyes moving ahead. "It's not like it's my ass anyway."

"So whose consent should I have gotten?"

"Maybe Jax's. It's technically his company's ass."

"But you're in that body illegally."

"So this is an illegal ass maneuver?"

"Are we seriously having a meta conversation about ass ownership?"

Their eyes caught and they snickered, her gaze turning back ahead. "What happens if we don't find any word of my brother?"

"It may not be big, but The Underground's tendrils run deep. This is how we'll find him." There were a few offshoot alleys and doors, and above each were tiny flags waving in the breeze. When they reached a yellow flag with a black square surrounded by an orange circle he stopped, waving his hand on the panel beside the door. It clicked open instantly and he pulled the handle before motioning inside. "Cis-ladies first."

The room inside was far smaller than she would have imagined, long and narrow. The only space was a small walkway that led to a counter in the back. The rest of the room was filled with

cages and glass tanks on every shelf. There were dozens of different animals, from amphibians and reptiles to birds and rodents.
Something about them struck her as odd though, but she couldn't
quite put her finger on it.

"Welcome, Dane. Who's your friend?"

Directly in front of the counter, an Asian woman was sitting
atop a large glass tank covered with a long piece of wood. Her
shorts were high on her crossed legs, a book lying open on her
thighs. A long, thin pipe was hanging from her lips, a tendril of
smoke floating like incense and her long, black hair up in high
pigtails. Having grown up with a younger brother, Naomi wasn't
grossed out easily and it wasn't the woman herself that disgusted
her. It was the glass tank she was sitting upon filled with maybe
a thousand roaches all writhing and squirming, their backs shiny
as the tumbled over one another. In the silence of the room, the
sound of their legs scratching was enough to make her taste bile.

Dane bowed his head. "Shǔ, this is Sai."

When Shǔ glanced at her, Naomi hit the sequence to take a
picture out of habit. It popped up into her field of vision for approval and the woman's face was blurred beyond recognition. It
was only then she remembered she wasn't in her standard issue
police suit, which could bypass any privacy setting. That foolish mistake paired with her moment of revulsion at the entrance
to The Underground made her certain getting Dane's help had
been the right choice. Naomi gave a bow of her head and Dane
continued.

"We're trying to find a mark, Mǎ luó. He's done a Switch and
I'm sure you know how to find him."

Mǎ luó? Her brother had an Underground name? He was in
deeper than she'd suspected.

Shǔ's eyes were on Naomi. "I thought you were working for

Baozhai?"

Naomi held Shǔ's gaze and barely caught the way Dane stiffened out of the corner of her eyes before he quickly covered it with a good-natured laugh. "What? I am working for Baozhai."

Shǔ held Naomi's gaze for a moment before her eyes turned to Dane. Shǔ's fore and middle fingers elegantly grasped her pipe as smoke leaked from her nose and mouth. "Mǎ luó was here yesterday. He thought I could mistake him for Trigger. But Trigger had a swagger. Mǎ luó does not."

Naomi couldn't help herself. "Where can we find him?"

Even though it was restrained, Dane shot her a glare that told her to shut her trap.

She kept her face even, reminding herself to calm down.

Shǔ returned the pipe to her lips. "The standard price will suffice."

Dane gave a hefty sigh and held out his hand. Shǔ gave an eloquent wave of her wrist beneath his, and she turned to touch the air before her. After a moment of her pushing aside what Naomi could only assume were bank account screens, the woman gave a single nod. She pushed two fingers toward Dane and he gave a nod. "Thanks for the address. As always, it's been a pleasure, Shǔ."

The woman returned her eyes to her book, giving a dismissive wave of her hand. When they turned to the door all the animals in every cage were turned to stare at them as they left. She suppressed a shiver of fear as she realized they must be the highest quality spybots she'd ever seen.

When they hit the alley, before she could speak, he shushed her. He went at a brisk pace back the way they'd come and whispered under his breath. "Something's not right..." He stopped at a vending machine, and she was about to ask him if he was seriously thirsty at a time like this when the interface changed from offering soda brands to something she didn't recognize.

Dane grabbed her arm and waved it over the strange interface before letting out a restrained sigh that bordered on a groan. She was able to see that it was an authentication verifier—she supposed in The Underground there would be numerous instances where you wanted to be sure of who you were dealing with. But why was he checking her authentication? She gave him a questioning look and he gave her a single shake of his head, hurrying toward the barrier.

Once they were out of The Underground and back on the street, she felt she could speak again. "What happened? What address did she give you?"

He grabbed her arm and led her down a different alley. "It was a fake address. We'll be killed if we go there."

"What?! Then why—"

"Because Jax the genius made your body one of Shurikan's henchmen, which means—"

"Oh shit, Shurikan and Baozhai are blood enemies." She fell into time beside him as he started jogging. It felt good to do something familiar, even if she felt gangly in her new body. "Then why did you say you're still working for Baozhai? And why are we running?"

"The answer to both of those questions is the same." He sighed as they rounded a corner and came to a subway entrance. She gave him a quizzical glance as they dashed down the stairs. "I am still working for Baozhai because if I released the bounty, someone else might pick it up and get to him first."

It took her a moment before she cursed.

He hit the bottom of the stairs. "Right, so by now Shǔ has told Baozhai I'm doubling crossing her by working with Shurikan."

He let out a frustrated breath. "I can't believe I didn't think to check who your cover was supposed to work for. But then it was supposed to be fabricated!"

"How do you know it wasn't?"

He eyed her. "Shǔ took one look at you and knew. So either she just happened to have decided to check your authentication—"

"Or she's seen this body before." Her mind was racing. "Jax might've gotten it from the police, he works with them." Was that really the truth? She'd learn so much about Jax the last few days already and she found she didn't really want to learn more.

Dane sighed. "Whatever the reason, it doesn't help us now, does it?"

Rather than heading toward the entrance to the subway, he rushed over to a door labeled *Service Entrance.*

"What are we doing?"

Dane whacked his left shoulder, which made one of the access panels pop open. "We're getting as far away from Chinatown as we can. Hopefully before Baozhai's hit squad finds us." He took out a square metal chip, tossing it against the access panel beside the door. Upon connecting there was a quick series of chirps before the door popped open.

"Are they supposed to kill or capture us?"

"Kill you, definitely. They're probably supposed to capture me." They both rushed inside the dark hallway and the door closed behind them. "Baozhai prefers to torture or kill traitors herself, usually quite painfully and creatively. You're lucky your brother didn't piss her off as much as we probably just did." They hurried down stairs and the smell changed a moment before they hit the tunnel.

It was dank and musty, as well as having a heavy metallic

odor. Once their feet hit the gravel they started running. "Where are we going?"

Dane didn't glance back at her. "To the next station so we can get on a train. Hopefully before a train comes through."

Her eyes shifted to the light rails, which were wide and carried the subway cars at incredible speeds. She'd never thought about the potential problems associated with electromagnetic transportation before. While the escape shaft they'd used in CLM used electromagnets, those had been specifically designed to carry humans with bionic upgrades and computer-based implants. These electromagnetic rails were exponentially stronger, and she wasn't even sure what could happen to her internal computer should they get too close when they were activated. "What happens if—"

He skidded to a stop, and she halted beside him. Blocking their way were the silhouettes of four heavily armed, highly bionic men. One had a grenade launcher in place of a right arm, while another had his shoulder compartments open to expose several gun barrels. The third had what she recognized as an illegally modified Plasma Cannon and the last didn't seem that menacing until his mouth opened in a grin and she saw he'd gotten his tongue replaced with a metallic version with a serpentine splice up the center.

Right. She was going to go ahead and assume they were Baozhai's hit squad.

When she saw movement on the top of the tunnel it took a long time to comprehend that there were two women, somehow hanging upside down from the ceiling. Her brain was having trouble processing what she was seeing. "Dane, do those women have—"

"Hands for feet? Yeah."

Their "legs" were shorter than normal length, but it gave them a substantial advantage in using all four of their hands to hang from the wires and pipes running along the ceiling. When one of them bent their knees in the opposite way than the joint was supposed to go, Naomi couldn't help but flinch. Even though they were bionic parts, it looked as if that should hurt.

Dane put his hands up and took a step forward. "Hey guys, this is all a big misunderstanding. I'm heading over to see Baozhai right now and this will all be sorted out. Sorry for the confusion, but I would never double cross Baozhai because that would be really, *really* stupid."

Every one of them lifted a gun and trained it on Dane and Naomi. She lifted a brow at Dane, whispering. "Your negotiation strategy seems to be a bit lacking."

He eyed her and whispered in return. "You have a better idea?"

She paused for a moment and pulled up the interface of her body, flipping through her weapons store. Her targeting system noted the six enemies as hostiles and she made sure to mark Dane as a friendly. "Several actually." When her fingers touched, the shoulder compartments of her body popped open and missiles fired. The hit squad simultaneously opened fire on them and the tunnel was rapidly filled with explosions.She tackled Dane to the ground, anticipating that her firing system would send out shots to neutralize the incoming fire or throw up a Phase Shield when it had to in order to protect them, but she still wanted to make sure he was safe while it happened.

There was a loud pop as a green netting appeared to envelope them both and she felt her jaw drop in shock.

Phase Armor engaged.

A Phase Shield used a single phase canister connected to a

proximity sensor and was capable of stopping a seconds worth of bullets or a Cannon Shot. The Phase Armor netting around her now was stopping at least a dozen Cannon Shots, a plasma shot and a couple of grenades for good measure. The chasm of technological difference between the Phase Armor and a Phase Shield was like trying to compare a slingshot to a mech suit.

She finally understood why Jax was always going on about her being under gunned. She hadn't even had a conception of just how much she actually was under gunned and suddenly felt very naïve.

A smoke grenade launched from her shoulder into the space between them and their enemies, blocking visibility.

Phase Armor has reached zero percent. Please exert extra caution.

As the netting fell, Dane grabbed her hand and yanked her up. "What the fuck was that?!"

They ducked into an access hallway as a pair of canisters dropped out of her shoulders with a hiss. "I don't know but it was my only one." What type of body had Jax given her? Was the stuff even legal? Or was it only used by Black Ops or Navy Seals??

She glanced around the corner into the tunnel. The smoke was beginning to clear and her targeting system showed two of the men were still standing. Her system issued a warning and she ducked back into the access hallway just as a spray of bullets went past. "There are at least two left." Her forearm gun popped up and she crouched to shoot around the corner.

After she fired the first Cannon Shot, habit made her think that she'd be switching to bullets only for her targeting system to indicate she had plenty left. "Holy shit, thirteen more Cannon Shots??"

Dane was standing and shooting above her, looking down at

her in shock.

"Seriously? I have military level upgrades and I only have a max of eight."

She kept shooting, though the two targets seemed to be very adept at dodging. But then, they wouldn't be part of a hit squad if they were easy to kill. She wished they could get closer but it was too dangerous with no cover. "Yeah, but what military are yours from?"

He glanced down at her meaningfully. "No, what military are *yours* from?"

That was a harrowing point.

She kept a Cannon Shot in reserve. "I don't think we've even hit either of them!"

Dane went into one of his hamstring compartments, pulling out a smoke bomb. "We got the one on the right indirectly, he was hit hard by a big chunk of cement. I'm going in. Give me cover."

The smoke bomb gave her an idea. "I think I've got something to go with that." She tapped her fingers to release what she wanted, attaching it to his smoke bomb.

"What's that?"

"Dispersal bomb called the 'Porcupine.'"

"That sounds painful." He rolled the bombs out into the tunnel.

"If we're lucky." They were both watching as the tunnel began filling with smoke. There was a flash of light followed by an explosion. A sickening thud preceded a scream and she flinched. "Ouch."

"And that's my cue. Cover me."

"With pleasure."

He flashed her a playful look as he grabbed a second gun. "You're trouble, you know that, don't you?"

"You have no idea." She began shooting into the smoke.

He rushed out into the smoke, heading directly across the tunnel. She let off a few more rounds before she held back, not wanting to accidentally hit him. To keep their enemies from guessing though, she aimed her gun at the ground and let out several dozen rounds before she stopped, waiting to listen.

There were a mixture of grunts and the smoke cleared enough for her optical upgrade to zoom in on Dane in hand-to-hand combat with the last member of the hit squad. Dane caught the man's arm before he twisted and ripped it off at the elbow. He threw the man back into the tunnel wall and did a powerful back knuckle strike. The man slumped to the ground and his head lolled to the side.

Dane's fighting style was definitely not a formal martial arts form but it was quite effective. She wondered where he'd learned it. It was a pity the bad guy gone down that quickly—

Wait, had she really just wished a bad guy hadn't lost so she could lurk and watch a guy she hardly knew fight more? She shook her head and stood. What was she, a silly girl who—

Proximity alert.

Naomi spun around fully, frowning when she didn't see anything. Maybe something was wrong with her proximity sensor… A chill went down her spine.

She looked straight up and came eye to eye with one of the women of the hit squad, looking at Naomi from above the barrel of a gun. The other woman was wearing black and her joints were all bent in the wrong direction, so her back was to the ceiling. Her face was expressionless, and she looked like an evil opossum. The world seemed to halt for one terrifying instant before the gun fired.

While she was resigned to her fate, her body had different

plans. *Phase Shield engaged.*

With a flare of energy, a shield reflected the Cannon Shot.

Grimacing she muttered that she was grateful Jax wasn't there to be smug.

The deflection didn't hit the woman, but it did send her flying. Opossum landed in the access hallway on the exit side, between Naomi and the tunnel. Naomi felt a gush of air that could mean only one thing—a train was coming.

So, she could either head toward a moving train or fight the killer opossum who was blocking Naomi's exit.

It wasn't a hard choice, actually.

As the air stormed around her and noise harkened the train's arrival, she took in a breath and leaned backward, into the train.

While weightless she ignited the magnetism on her hands and feet, feeling both feet and her right hand connect with the metal casing of the side of the subway train. She held out her left hand. "DANE!"

His back was pressed to the side of the tunnel and his gaze lifted to her in surprise. He recovered quickly, though, and his hand reached toward hers. The train was moving so fast she was fairly certain they were going to miss one another. Then his hand was propelled forward as her magnetized hand yanked him off his feet.

While her back was to the train, Dane settled with his front to it instead. Somehow, his boisterous laugh was louder than the noise of the train. "Okay, this is actually a first for me."

"And to think you could have missed this." Their eyes held for a brief moment before she saw movement further down the train. "Third wheel is here." Apparently, the Opossum was determined to finish her job.

Dane pulled a gun out of his waistband and she put a hand

over his. "Wait, let me."

He stared at her. "What, why?"

She motioned to the glass of the train. There were a pair of teenage boys, and one was waving his hands frantically. He mouthed the words *Are you making a movie?* and Naomi waved the kid away. She turned back to Dane. "I've got a targeting system."

He sighed. "Fine, but get on my back. I'll keep us mobile."

She looked at the space between his back and the wall rushing past. It would be a tight fit but manageable. "Does the tunnel get smaller?"

"Of course it does. So let's finish this quickly."

Her arm went under his, her hand pressing into his chest. She found one of his chest plates and connected her hand to it, her feet magnetized to his calves. She took his gun, turning it over. "What model is this anyway?"

He began moving sideways, toward the back of the train. "You're seriously asking me that right now?"

"What? I'm interested. Your weapons are impressive." She took aim and waited for her targeting system to focus on their enemy. Opossum's eyes lifted and her face was stoically emotionless. Once locked on the target, Naomi pulled the trigger.

Opossum dodged and Naomi cursed. How was she doing that? Or was having hands for feet that much of an advantage?

"Hold on!"

Dane's hands released and they fell sideways. She nearly yelled at him before she heard the whoosh of the sign as it passed inches above them. Dane remagnetized his hands and they were on the side of the car, now parallel with the ground. There was the thud of a collision and Naomi felt triumphant to see Opossum had been hit. She was still attached to the side of the train car but that couldn't bode well for her physically. Naomi nudged Dane's shoulder. "Keep it up and we may live through this yet."

He chuckled and began crawling toward their target. "You know, this may be the most fun I've had with someone in a long time."

They had to dodge a shot and she aimed again at Opossum, waiting for her targeting system to lock. "You make it sound like this is a date." She fired and it appeared to hit the woman, but Naomi couldn't tell if it damaged her.

"I wish."

She looked down at him in surprise. "Oh?"

He glanced back at her. "If I'd ever had a date that was this much fun, do you think I'd still be single?"

Her lips curled into a smile as she took aim again. "You're an idiot." She fired and the woman dodged by doing a somersault on the side of the car. "Okay, that was impressive."

"Pay attention!" Dane rushed forward , and she held on more tightly. They were almost on top of Opossum as she regained her balance, and Naomi tried to knock the gun out of her hand, surprised when it didn't fall. Dane ignited a localized concussion grenade in his hand, blowing her wrist to shreds. The gun was still held by the hand as Dane threw it away. "Magnetic, remember?"

Right, that made sense. She did an elbow strike to the woman's face, wishing she could use her Cannon Shot but afraid to in such close proximity to so many civilians.

"Naomi, the tunnel!"

She lifted her eyes and felt them grow wide. The tunnel was about to get narrower. Naomi leapt off Dane, holding her breath in fear at the way the air was changing right behind her. There was an instant where she felt as if she were hovering in air, unsure whether she was going to make it back onto the train in time. Dane and Opossum passed beneath her as she felt the subway wall scrap her back—then her hands and feet were drawn forward to the metal of the subway car.

She let out a breath of relief. Opossum's back was to her and she couldn't make Dane out beyond—and she was out of range, besides. She was crawling back to them when Dane grabbed the woman's head, slamming it into the side of the subway car. While Opossum was distracted, Naomi came close enough to punch the elbow of the arm still holding Opossum onto the side of the car. The metal joint crushed and snapped, leaving the arm still attached to the side of the car as the rest of the woman began to fall.

When Opossum's head neared the electromagnetic rails, her eyes widened and she let out a scream at a decibel level that didn't seem humanly possible. Naomi now had her answer about what happened when a bionic body got too close to the electromagnetic field—and it was not pretty.

But then the compartments on Opossum's biceps and shoulders went haywire and opened to expose all her weapons. The electromagnetic field was capable of disrupting normal functioning of her weapons system?

Naomi looked into the subway car and saw a little girl, perhaps no more than six, staring at her. Without making a conscious decision, she aimed her forearm gun at the malfunctioning bionic and fired her last Cannon Shot.

Blue electric wrapped around the woman's body, short-circuiting her bionic parts and keeping the weapons from misfiring into the subway car. But it also disrupted the magnetic connection between her and Dane, and they were forcefully ejected from the side of the subway train to ricochet between the cars and the walls, until they rolled along the tunnel and came to a stop.

Dane's chuckle came from just beside her. "That was amazing! For never having had a high percentage bionic body you're really—Naomi?"

She wasn't aware of her injury until she took a breath and her stomach felt as if it were on fire. Despite her eyes being closed, her internal computer overlaid a message in her field of view as it also spoke to her. *You have sustained a critical injury. Hospitalization is recommended. Tap the appropriate sequence and your GPS coordinates will be marked for EMS.* She whimpered, trying to close her eyes more tightly so the light of the words would go away. "Dane..."

"Naomi!" He carefully rolled her onto her back and the way he cursed told her it was bad. His hands were on her cheeks. "Look at me."

She managed to open her eyes.

"Good. Hold on, I'll get you help."

She grabbed his hand, taking in a breath of fear. "Hospital, I can't..." If she went there, she'd just end up arrested and then both her and her brother would be dead. She swallowed. "Jax... he gave me a beacon if—"

Their eyes held and she knew instantly neither of them wanted to call Jax for help. There were too many questions about the body he'd given her and what had he meant about an arsenal—

"He couldn't help you now anyway. But I know someone who can." Fear crossed Dane's features briefly before he covered it with a brave smile. "Besides, you're not paying me only for my good looks, you know." He lifted her carefully into his arms and she managed to get her arm around his shoulders. "I'll get you help. Trust me." She knew for certain now, she already did.

Though, as her face buried against his neck and she closed her eyes, she hoped Dane could manage a miracle before it was too late.

Dane

He didn't know what it said about New Yorkers, that when faced with a woman bleeding in front of them, they didn't ask any questions. In this instance however, he was grateful for their lack of concern for a fellow human being. He couldn't have handled having to deal with the police right then, not to mention the fact that Naomi absolutely could not go into custody. That would be a fate worse than death for her. But that also meant no hospital, which left him only one option.

She was seated beside him on the subway but cradled against him so he could keep one arm around her with the other discreetly applying pressure to her stomach wound. What disturbed him more than anything was that Naomi didn't seem the type to willingly show weakness and she was a lump against him. His arm around her shoulders squeezed her close and he leaned closer to whisper. "Don't you quit on me. I've got a plan."

There was a silent nod into his shoulder and he restrained his sigh of concern. He glanced up to see the next stop was theirs. It was a battle to get her standing and when he looked at the seat he saw she'd left behind a small pool of blood. If she'd had a fully human body it wouldn't have been so bad. But since the human-to-bionic ratio was so small, it meant she'd lost a large percentage of her blood and very fast. They were running out of time.

He got her off the train and they stood on the platform. She could barely stand, let alone walk. He waited for the rush of air behind them to signal that the train was out of sight before he slipped his other arm under her legs, pulling her up into his arms and racing to the stairs.

When he tried to tap his fingers to place a call, it didn't register. When he looked, he saw the blood coating his hand. He wiped it on her pants before he tried again.

Calling Leon Hartwick.

There were two rings before it picked up, and Dane spoke before the other man could get a word in. "I need a body."

"*For you??*" His friend's voice was a hint nasally. "*That's a first.*"

"No, not for me, you idiot. For a friend. She's injured and I can't take her to the hospital."

"*What did you do now??*"

"No time to explain, I'll be there in three. Get the machine warmed up."

"*Okay, but you aren't going to like what I've got in stock.*" There was the sound of metal moving in the background. "*Come in the back.*"

Call ended.

He picked up the pace as much as he dared with her in his arms. Maybe once she got back into her body, he would ask her to train him to be a long distance runner. It seemed a very practical skill to have, actually. In the distance he could see the CLM building towering over the city. Her body had been really well outfitted, but that made him wonder what exactly Jax was up to, having access to that type of weaponry. He went down by the docks, slinking around a bunch of boxes and a cranky stray cat to get into the right alley. He came to a back door so rusty it seemed as if it deserved to be rusted shut. When he got there though, he waved his ID chip over the reader and it opened smoothly.

The inside was in stark contrast to the outside. Leon's laboratory was pristine and the machines were alive and whirring, at the ready. Leon turned, a long white lab coat covering his plaid pajamas. His dark hair was haphazardly in a hundred directions, and he motioned to the empty table. "Put her here." Dane set her down carefully, grateful to hear her moan in pain. That meant they still had time.

As he began strapping her in, Leon was putting electrodes on her temples methodically. "Who is she?"

"A pain in my ass."

"She wouldn't be your friend otherwise."

Dane grunted in agreement and was putting the strap around her middle. "Let's just get her into another body, shall we?"

"Do I get to keep the shell? I don't get many CLM models to play with."

"Sure, whatever." He paused. "Wait, how do you know it's a CLM model?"

"You know my line of work."

"Never mind, just get her out of it, first, and you can do whatever you want with it after."

"Excellent." Leon slipped a mouth guard past her lips and went to the interface. "Stop hovering, she's going to be fine. Now, step away. Her new body is over there, in case you're interested." He pointed to the other side of the machines.

He knew enough to get out of Leon's way when he was working. Dane stared at Naomi's current body and let out a long breath, believing completely in Leon to be able to save her. He made himself turn away and glanced around the corner out of curiosity. He understood now why Leon had said Dane wouldn't like what he had in stock. When the lights dimmed and the noise of the machines grew to a fevered pitch, Dane couldn't resist a grin. "She's going to be so pissed when she wakes up."

CHAPTER 10

Naomi

Her head felt like a watermelon that had been cleaved in half. Opening her eyes proved to be a truly horrible mistake that made the ringing in her ears worse. She knew she was moaning in pain but couldn't hear anything and her vision was fuzzy. Her throat burned and she felt her head being turned to the side just as she began vomiting. It took all she had to concentrate on breathing. A pill was forced between her lips, followed quickly by water and she had no choice but to swallow.

Her head began to clear and her ears stopped ringing. She tentatively opened her eyes to stare at a ceiling. There were exposed beams. Where was she?

Dane leaned over her. "Welcome back to the living."

Another man came to her other side, with dark hair splayed in every direction and a white lab coat over what appeared to be... plaid pajamas? He seemed somewhere in his thirties, but it was hard to pin down considering his warm brown face appeared to be in a constant scowl. He ran a small handheld device over her forehead, looking down at the screen. "The numbers are normalizing. He should be able to get up in a minute."

She blinked. "He?" When she heard the deep voice rumbling in her ears she sighed. "Seriously?"

"Hey, Leon just saved your ass by doing an emergency transfer. Least you could do is thank him."

Before she could agree, Leon was holding up his hands and shaking them. "Wait, let's not be hasty." He began taking the electrodes off her temples and neck. "The least you could do is pay me. But don't worry about that right now." He paused to give her a smile. "I'll send you a bill."

She closed her eyes and if she weren't so exhausted, she would have laughed. "Another bounty hunter?"

"What? Please. How many bounty hunters do you know who have their own body transfer laboratory?"

Dane grunted. "I have one."

"It's my lab, not yours."

Her head turned to look at Dane. "Wait, what?"

He gave a little chuckle as he started undoing the straps on her legs. "Uh, Leon this is Naomi. Naomi, this is Leon, my... roommate."

Leon muttered under his breath as he began undoing the straps on her arms. "Don't you mean landlord? It's my warehouse, you know..."

She squeezed her eyes shut. The pain was ebbing surprisingly quickly. "Okay, can we back up to the part where I was a woman?"

A touch at her shoulder made her open her eyes and she saw Dane offering her a hand. She grasped it and sat up cautiously, shocked she was feeling so focused, considering what a mess she'd been when she'd first woken up.

Dane helped her to sit up but didn't urge her any further. "When you were hurt you lost a lot of blood. Since I couldn't take you to a hospital, I brought you here. Leon did the transfer and you were unconscious for a couple of hours." Which probably explained why Dane was in clean clothes and looked freshly showered.

She frowned, looking at Leon. "How were you—" Her voice was so strange to hear as a man's. "—able to do an emergency transfer with me in that condition? I thought it was impossible if the patient's brainwaves weren't stable."

Dane sighed. "Oh no."

Leon stood up taller, grabbing the lapels of his lab coat. "Well, I'm glad you asked."

Dane shook his head sadly, looking very much like he wished she hadn't. He was offering a glass of water and giving her a look that communicated she should hate herself for what was to come. The look on Leon's face though, said he hadn't noticed his friend's response. "You see, I've been working on a recalibration of the—"

Shattering glass stopped him. Naomi had tried to take the glass of water and had disintegrated it instead. She blinked in surprise and looked at her arm, her jaw dropping. The body she was in was obviously a body builder's, with bionic arms beneath the elbows. The biceps were enormous, and she had seriously underestimated the strength of her new grip. Maybe there were some benefits of being a man. She could probably open any jar that had ever existed right now.

Before Leon could continue, she hopped to the floor, feeling an enormous amount of energy. When her feet landed, she noticed her legs were bionic below the knees but equally as beefy as the arms. Her quads were *so* wide. She ran in place a couple of steps. "I wonder what pace I could manage in this body." When she heard Dane stifling a laugh she looked up.

And kept looking up because he seemed way taller than he had a right to. She looked around and caught her reflection in a metal panel. The body was extremely built, muscles protruding from under the shirt and pants. The skin tone was umber, a dark yellow-brown with warm undertones. Despite the width and strength of the body, the one thing it did not have was height. Her real body was taller; this one had to be barely five foot.

Dane patted the top of her head. "It happens to everyone, kid."

It was rewarding that her grumbles bordered on an angry growl in this body. "Shut up." She glanced at Leon. "You were explaining how you are able to do the transfer."

As he was drawing a breath, Dane interceded. "His full name is Leon Hartwick."

She rounded on Leon in amazement. "Hartwick? Like Hartwick Technologies?" When he nodded proudly she let out a breath. "Your technology is the only viable competition for CLM." From everything she'd learned, Leon Hartwick was a reclusive genius who only appeared for scientific showcases and even then, he was labeled as eccentric...

"CLM? Oh, those ninnies. Their technology is in the dark ages and furthermore..."

She was distracted by the realization he was wearing bunny slippers.

Incoming message from Dane Thayer. If you don't want to listen to Leon all afternoon, I'd suggest you mention how hungry you are. Or mention you need to figure out how to make a dude's body pee, which is a real concern. Or will be, soon enough.

Naomi glanced over at Dane who gave her a wink before motioning toward Leon with his eyebrows.

Incoming message from Dane Thayer. Or are you actually riveted? I can't tell with those angry male eyes of yours.

She stifled a laugh and realized she was really hungry. The next time Leon stopped to take a breath she jumped on the opportunity. "Is there food somewhere?"

"Oh, yes! The Switch does cause a nutritional deficit that can be overwhelming to the senses if not dealt with in a timely—"

"You don't say?"

Leon gave a nod. "Right. Dane can show you the way. I need to keep working on the other body. I think I can still salvage it." When he turned and walked around a bank of machines, she couldn't resist taking a look at her old host. It was lying on the table, all clothes replaced by two white towels lying across her chest and waist. There were wires and hoses coming out of arms and legs, and there was an oxygen mask on the face. The gaping wound in the mid-section was an angry red but it had been sutured and the blood wiped away. There were several health care spiderbots hovering over the body that looked similar to forensic bots, but with two notable exceptions. These bots had eight legs and were wearing tiny nurse hats with a red cross on the front. Two of the bots were directly over the wound, dousing it continuously with a medicated spray.

Leon headed over to the body and one of the army of bots crawled onto his arm and then up to his shoulder, perching there. The man turned to an image screen and when he began typing, she realized he didn't have any enhancements that she could see. Dane's hand on her arm made her turn and she was careful not to step on the cleaning bot—a spiderbot wearing a hat in the shape of an upside-down old-fashioned metal pail— taking care of the shattered glass.

She walked slowly as she looked around. Leon had said they were in a warehouse and the place was gigantic. The rest of the lab was sizable and there were numerous shelving units lining the walls, secured with encrypted covers. Several worktables were littered with projects in various degrees of completion. When they came to another door Dane waved his forearm over the scanner and it slid away.

She followed behind him, wanting to regain her bearings. "So Shǔ is an information monger?"

"Yes, the best. But not the only one. We'll find someone else who will lead us to your brother. As soon as you're up to venturing out again." They passed a workroom with walls papered with schematics and blueprints. Naomi stopped in surprise.

"Leon doesn't like storing his schematics on a computer. He doesn't trust them." Dane paused. "That's not true. He likes computers more than most people he's met; it's the people behind computers he doesn't trust." He motioned with his head. "Kitchen's this way."

They took the hallway to the next door. It looked like a standard kitchen with pans hanging from a rack and a large island in the center. There were stools beside the island and she paused before awkwardly clambering her way atop it. She was so tiny, how did short people do it? When her eyes landed on the island she paused. Having spent several years living with her brother, she found it shockingly clean for the fact that two men lived there.

Dane was at the refrigerator pulling out a large bag of sliced vegetables and another she guessed was ground turkey. He grabbed a pan and put it on the cooktop, turning on the burner. As he added oil she realized she was frowning. "You're cooking?" Vegetables? She felt like she was in an alternate universe where men ate healthily and cleaned up after themselves.

He chuckled as he added the entire bag of vegetables to the pan. "What, are you going to be like Leon and tell me to eat more ramen?"

"No, no! I'm just—I'm just surprised."

He portioned out the turkey and added that as well. "Like I said, my body is a temple. I have to take care of it. Do you like peanut sauce or would you rather have a dashi sauce?"

She wasn't even sure what dashi sauce was. "Either would be great."

Once the turkey was wrapped back up, he exchanged it for a container labeled dashi from the fridge. "The vegetables will make you feel better after your Switch."

Her stomach was grumbling loudly in agreement, and she felt like her mind was racing with questions. "Back to Shǔ. Why would she give you away?"

"Eh, she's like the Switzerland of The Underground." He paused, his spatula hovering above the pan. "An evil Switzerland." He shook his head, pushing the food around in the pan. "She'll give information to anyone, and we all use her but no one trusts her."

Her leg was bouncing. "What's with all her creepy spybots?"

"Hers are the best. Another reason why people use her so often."

She leaned her head on a hand, but frowned when she heard tapping. When she looked down at her other hand on the counter she realized it was her finger tapping incessantly. She forced it to stop, but her hand began to shake with the effort.

"That's a normal reaction, it'll pass."

She stared at him. Her thoughts were racing and it was hard to focus. It felt like being caught in a tornado. "What was that pill you gave me?"

He cleared his throat and poured the dashi sauce over the vegetables. "You don't want to know."

As she stared at him, she ignored her bouncing leg. "You gave me hit of Dash, didn't you?"

"Would you rather be vomiting right now?" His eyes wouldn't meet hers; he was stirring the vegetables. "And besides, it's not like they'll find any traces of it in your cop body."

That gave her pause and she looked down at her chest, her nose scrunching up at her lack of breasts. Though this guy did have some sizeable pecks. She wondered if she could make them bounce up and down and—

Right, Dash. It was pretty potent, actually. "Why did you have that pill? Are you a junkie, do you do drugs, are you a drug dealer? Drug dealer Dane would be hard to say though. Drug dealer Dane, drug dear Dale, durg dare Duh, see, really hard to say."

He eyed her with a raised brow; his spatula paused in mid motion. "Okay, wow. I'm going to blame the stupid questions on the Dash. In answer to the intelligent questions, I have them because there's no way I'm being a nursemaid to a mark that can't move because they just finished a cheap body transfer." He gave a shrug and continued to rotate the vegetables and meat. "I give them a pill and they're fine. And as a bonus they usually care a lot less that I'm handing them over for a pile of cash. Do you want tea?"

"Yeah, I like tea, tea is great, do you have honey, I like honey." She shook her head and put a hand over her eyes.

"Just sit there quietly for a minute; I think you're being hit with the worst of it."

She concentrated on breathing for a long while, her mind's frenetic energy calming over time. Even though she didn't want to, she remembered Dash had been Tyler's drug of choice. He'd actually enjoyed this state of frenetic thoughts and frantic energy? In a sad way, she'd been getting closer to him the last few days than she'd been in a long time. But even though she didn't understand him or his choices, thinking about him right then made her stomach clench.

She lost track of time until she heard the whistle of a teakettle.

[135]

When her eyes lifted she felt less chaotic and more mellow. Dane poured water from the kettle into mugs and there were steaming bowls with forks nearby. He set a bowl and a mug before her and then grabbed the other pair himself. "Let's go somewhere Leon can't find us and talk our ears off."

When he started heading out of the room she snorted. "What happened to ladies first?"

He called back over his shoulder. "You may want to check your pants."

Her muttering sounded like an angry cat as she managed to get off the stool that felt as if it were twelve feet tall. His words made her realize she actually did need to adjust her pants and she grimaced in disgust as she did. It felt terrible to be in a body that wasn't—

A cold chill ran through her. Her brother had often said how much he didn't feel as if his body was his own, how he'd wished it could be different. She'd chalked it up to too many drugs but what if he'd been feeling intense body dysphoria his whole life and she'd just been brushing it off?

She sighed, pushing aside the thoughts. She'd try to be a better sister as soon as she found her little brother and beat him up for doing this to her. She grabbed her food and tea, hurrying after him with her short little legs.

The large living room was equipped with a pair of oversized couches and a couple of recliners, along with space for a huge image screen on the far wall. Around all this though, were books; books were piled on top of books and in the corner there was a staggering amount of old fashioned board games. She was about to ask about them when he led her to a door, turning to her. "And let's not judge, shall we?" He turned the handle before she could ask and made his way inside.

The room was probably larger than her whole apartment, which made sense considering the warehouse seemed to have no shortage of space. There was a wide bed in the center of the room, a few feet away from a large window and off to the right was an office space. The desk was neat and there were several dozen NYC maps up on the wall surrounding it. Some were color coded with gang symbols; she didn't even recognize them all. There were lists, photos and timelines interspersed. But all of this surrounded a large chalkboard with the number 406, under the printed sign *Scumbags caught to date*. She was about to ask him what she wasn't allowed to judge when she caught sight of the other side of the room.

There was a standard table and chairs but beside it were shelving units twenty feet high. There was even a ladder set up at the ready beside it. On the shelves were hundreds of... things. She had no idea what most of them were but as she moved closer she found he had meticulously labeled them. Beside some sort of horse with a well-manicured mane was the sign *My Little Pony, 2014* and next to a pair of naked creatures with neon hair pointing toward the sky was *Trolls, 1998*. There were toys labeled Ninja Turtles, Tamagotchi, Power Rangers, Avengers, Beanie Babies, and one brightly-colored yellow rodent called Pikachu. All were meticulously organized and labeled on the shelves. As she looked up she realized how truly short her body was and contemplated using the ladder before she realized she still had the tea and bowl of food in her hands.

"Did you want to eat?"

"Oh, right. Yes." She joined him at the table; she was famished. At the first bite she moaned in pleasure. "This is great."

"I'm glad you like it. Leon only eats what I cook because he would forget to eat otherwise."

She grunted. "Yeah, no one ever wants to eat vegetables with me either. But they're so good for you and they do make you feel better." She noticed how much less food he had than her. "Do you have enough?"

"I figured in that body builder body of yours, you'd need more." He sighed heavily. "But I don't need to eat much because I don't have a lot of body left to feed. One of the pitfalls of being a high-percentage bionic. And I love food."

Her fork stopped halfway to her mouth. That was tragic. "But can't you exercise and eat more that way?"

"Spoken like a runner." He shook his head sadly. "All I've really got left are core and back muscles. I work them but it's not the same."

"That's sad." She paused. "So, what was that collectible you mentioned earlier? Something about a bionic potato?"

"Oh, Potato Head? It's right over there. I actually have one of the original Mr. Potato Heads, from before they went gender neutral." He motioned with his fork and she saw a rotund potato with a snarky grin, curly mustache, and giant ears. "He has this compartment on his backside where you can store his interchangeable parts. I've been looking for the old Mrs. version for a long time but I haven't had any luck."

She tried to remember what he'd said earlier. "Oh, bionic Potato Head. I get it now. Some interchangeable bionic parts are a little uncomfortable." She shivered in disgust. "Especially the black market sex toys. That's when it started to get really weird."

"For me, it was when they started adding motors to the sex toys. I mean, I get the reasoning for wanting a second penis on your hand but replacing your actual penis with a motorized version? Just... No."

She tried to ignore how awkward a discussion of penises was, considering she now had one of her very own. She was again hit with another wave of pure discomfort at the feeling of her new body. Soothing herself with a reminder it was only temporary brought a stab of guilt—what if her brother had always had to feel that way?

They ate in silence for a while before she motioned to the wall. "So, you're a Millennium Collector, I take it?" He gave a noise of agreement and she stabbed a red pepper. "How'd you get into it?"

"My father, actually." He stared down into his tea. "He was always traveling when I was growing up. An eclectic collector, he called himself. There was always some bauble for me when he came back." He shrugged. "I guess that was his version of an apology for being a useless father. He still sends me things from time to time. Though I don't even remember the last time I saw him. So is the Dash starting to wear off finally?"

She knew a diversionary question when she heard one but let him get away with it. "Yeah, the frantic feelings are ebbing but now I feel unusually mellow." She tried to focus enough to think of a question she wanted to ask. "So Hartwick Technologies?"

Dane waved his hands. "Leon's quirky, leave it at that."

"I gathered, but I was asking more about his technology."

"Ah. Well, he's good at what he does. And he doesn't cut corners. His transfer rate is perfect, even including emergency transfers."

"That's incredible." She tried to phrase her question appropriately. "Am I remembering correctly that CLM tried to hire him at one point?"

Dane gave an evil little chuckle. "Yeah, Jax must hate Leon." He cleared his throat. "CLM had set up a huge meeting to wine and dine Leon. I came home to find him tinkering with some project and his phone had something like forty missed calls."

"Did he forget?"

He shook his head slowly. "I thought that at the time but..."

"But what?"

"Well, he played it off that night as if he'd decided not to go and forgot to tell them. But I've seen numerous interviews where he attacks CLM's methods and chastises them for bad science. Leon may be eccentric but everything he does is calculated. So I honestly think it was purposeful he didn't show that night because he wanted to make a statement. He made it loud and clear, all right."

Leon had done what she didn't think was possible with her body transfer. And he and Dane seemed to be good friends, so she may as well be honest. "You'll be pleased to know Jax does in fact hate Leon. Immensely. That's why I know a bit about Hartwick Technologies, actually. I remember the night Leon stood him up; I've never seen him so worked up. And Jax would get so pissed at anything he heard in the news about Leon, I tried to figure out why."

Dane grinned. "Good. And it makes sense, they're fundamentally different in their approaches and their worldviews, and Leon—"

There was a noise outside the window and a chirrup before a woman's voice echoed about the room. *"Barrier encroachment in sector D. Preliminary assessment is a breaking and entering is in process. Would you like me to notify the police?"*

Both of them jumped to their feet and Dane pulled a pair of guns out of his thigh. "Negative. Code Indigo, arm." He tossed her one of the guns and she found her shortness was an advantage, as it gave her a split second longer to get in position to catch it. She was able to seamlessly click off the safety as Dane motioned to the other side of the window. She put her back to the wall as he did the same and they both waited.

A human shaped silhouette blocked out the light of the afternoon sun. Naomi met Dane's gaze. He was watching the shadow and for a long moment no one moved. Dane's hand inched toward the control panel for the window and he met her eyes before he gave a nod. When he tapped the controls, the windows opened and they were flooded with light.

CHAPTER 11

Aung

His eyes were on the screen of his cell phone as he walked. The gray area symbolized the boardwalk and an orange dot with an arrow showed he was walking north. The warehouses beside him were dark blue outlines on the map and there was a single green dot blinking on the screen, inside of one of the buildings. It hadn't moved for some time, and he was getting closer. As he lifted his eyes to check the warehouse, he paused in surprise.

There was a man carrying a bucket with a fishing net half spilling out and a catch of fish in his other hand. He stared up at Aung with a confused brow. Aung glanced down at himself. He was perched high atop a fence designed to protect walkers from the ten-foot drop into the rocky shore on his left. He'd started walking on it when the fence was only a few feet tall and had been enjoying the sunshine so much he hadn't been paying attention as it grew in height. Aung supposed it was a strange sight to see a monk wandering atop a tall, chain-link fence. He gave the confused fisherman a bright grin. "Lovely weather we're having today, isn't it?"

The man raised a brow and quickly crossed to the other side of the boardwalk. Aung waved anyway. "Have a wonderful day!"

He jumped down and looked at the screen again. The green dot still hadn't moved, which meant it was definitely Aung's destination. He glanced around cautiously before he crossed the boardwalk. The sunshine disappeared behind the curve of the warehouse. The metal siding was gray and imposing, but this building looked as dilapidated as those surrounding it. He kept moving down the outside wall until he came to a large window, above a set of crates. The dot was just on the other side.

The phone slipped into his pocket, and he frowned thoughtfully. The windows were set to an opacity too dark to see inside. He pondered for a moment how to best make his way and settled on the most direct.

When his foot touched the crate, there was the squeal of a feral cat. She darted away, knocking over a trash can lid as she went. Aung sighed and called out. "I'm sorry I scared you! See me later for some fish!" He'd be shocked if they hadn't heard the ruckus from inside. Aung decided to hop straight up onto the crates and positioned himself between the sun and the window so his shadow would be cast obviously inside.

He only had to wait a few seconds before the windows opened sharply with a clatter. Dane and a very short, muscular body builder were pointing guns at him.

Aung held his hands up high. "Hello friends!"

The pair shared a glance before they slowly lowered their guns. The new man's head shook. "Do you say that to everyone holding a gun at you?"

"No." Aung jumped down between the pair, landing inside the warehouse. "Only the nice ones."

Dane sighed. "Code Indigo disarm, passcode foxtrot, bravo, six, three." He tapped the controls to close the windows again. "How did you find this place?"

A chirrup preceded a man's voice over the speaker. *"Dane, is everything all right?"*

Dane let out a breath. "Yes, Leon. Everything is fine. We have a visitor, that's all."

"You've managed to fill your quota for the month in one day."

There was another beep and Dane turned to Aung with a sigh. "Once again, how did you find this place?"

"I didn't. I found you." The pair shared another glance and Aung looked around the room, taking in a breath of surprise when he saw the shelves of collectibles.

"Pikachu?!"

"Actually, he was a hard one to pin down since—"

"What Dane meant to ask—" The shorter man had a brow raised. "—is how exactly did you find him?"

Aung clasped his hands behind his back, moving over to the shelves of collectibles. Dane had many wonderful things. "Oh, with the tracking sensor I put on him during your race, Naomi." When neither replied immediately he glanced over his shoulder with a smile. "You shouldn't be surprised. I knew if I followed Dane, I would find you eventually."

Naomi's brow rose. "Do I know you?"

"Not yet." He bowed his head. "My name is Aung. I've been to many of your races and I'm a big fan." The pair was betraying nothing on their faces, but Aung had to grin. "So how do you like being a man, Naomi?"

The body of the man Naomi now inhabited stared at him. "I am literally a woman trapped inside a man's body." She turned away to go back to the table and picked up a bowl of food. "And it doesn't help Mr. Helpful over there drugged me."

Dane rolled his eyes and gave a look that said volumes.

Aung looked skeptically at Naomi. "Taking a hit of Dash is preferable to vomiting for a couple hours, isn't it?"

Naomi's fork paused its journey to her mouth. "Since when does a Buddhist know about drugs?"

Dane's brow rose. "Especially how to use them post-Switch?"

Ah, right. They wouldn't know. Aung hadn't been away from the monastery in a while and he'd forgotten how easy conversation was with the other monks, who understood their journey and their mission. "We aren't all born Buddhists, you know." And many of the Monkhood in particular had been further away from holy than most.

Dane was still standing near him; his distrust clear in his proximity. "Uh, so tracking sensor?"

Aung nodded and motioned to Dane's arm. "May I?"

After a hesitant nod, Aung went behind the man, plucking the magnetic sensor off Dane's right tricep. It was barely larger than a ladybug. "I attached it when you threw Naomi's sibling at me." The reference made Naomi's fork pause halfway to her lips and Aung turned fully to her. "I saw your sibling at your race. I know you're searching for answers. I have a few questions though, if you don't mind."

Dane turned to him and gave a skeptical look. "You put a tracking sensor on me, followed me to my home and you expect me to let you ask us questions?"

Aung paused and shrugged. "Would you like to ask yours first? I'm certain you have them."

Naomi and Dane shared a glance and then Naomi was pointing to the chair across from her. "My brother?"

"Was at the race." Aung sat across from her.

Dane took the chair beside Naomi as he grumbled. "And you're the one who let him get away!"

Aung met Dane's glance with a raised brow. "No, I'm the one who didn't let her sibling get captured by a bounty hunter who would have given them up to Baozhai to be murdered."

Naomi looked between the two, turning back to Aung. "Okay,

good point. Was my brother involved in anything with Sanctuary?"

He shook his head. "No. That is solely the Monkhood's plan."

"What is Sanctuary?"

Aung hesitated. "Naomi, I know you want proof and I want to show it to you. I would like you to come with me to the Monkhood's monastery where I can show it to you safely."

Dane frowned. "Have you seen this place? We're incredibly safe here."

"Not as safe as you'd like to believe." His eyes slid to Naomi's male ones. "So, I suggest we get to the car my fellow Brother has waiting, because someone is trying to kill you."

"What?! Who?"

Despite how surprised Naomi was, it was the way Dane didn't look surprised that told Aung he had suspicions too. "You were thinking the same thing."

Naomi turned to Dane in disbelief. "You think someone's trying to kill me?"

There was a long silence before Dane let out a defeated sigh. "It's just too much of a coincidence, don't you think?"

She was staring at him in shock. "What?"

Dane shrugged. "Friday you were involved in a shooting in Central Park, on Saturday there was the woman's leg during the race, then everything with your brother's Switch and Iago being killed, Baozhai's hit squad…" When she stared at him he let out a breath. "Look, I'm a bounty hunter. A lot of people want me dead. And even I don't get attacked that much in a weekend."

Her eyes were staring at the table and Dane put a hand on her shoulder. "I know it's weird because it's your own life, but you work homicide. You're used to piecing it back together after there's a body. If you'd ended up dead and you were working the case, what would you think?"

Naomi's intense gaze met Aung's. "Okay. Do you know who's after me?"

"No." He took in a breath. "However, I believe it's tied to the Monkhood's problems."

Dane nodded. "That bounty placed on you all is unprecedented."

Aung did not often struggle with panic, but the bounty made them all nervous. Whoever had placed it was intent on not only finding out the information they wanted, but they'd made it worth enough money that every bounty hunter would be after them. "Yes. And they made it an open bounty, so we could be facing multiple enemies simultaneously."

Naomi looked between them. "Is that normal?"

"No, not at all." Dane slipped his fingers around a mug of tea. "If you want your target caught, you pay one person. If you want a slaughter, you send in a few bounty hunters."

Aung sighed sadly. "If you want mayhem and overkill, you put an open bounty with a rate so high everyone will go after it."

Naomi hesitated. "And this is all due to Sanctuary?"

He gave a slow nod. "Yes." He took a calming breath so the panic wouldn't overtake him. "Now, may I have a turn to ask a question?"

Sanctuary was a collective wish of the Monkhood and what had gotten them into so much trouble. However, there were differences in opinion about what the final step should be with the project. Aung believed probably more strongly than any other in the Monkhood about the benefits of Sanctuary. But he also believed the final piece of the puzzle was sitting before him, currently locked within a man's body.

Despite his faith, there was something he wanted to know,

and he needed to hear it from her before he could take the risk with what he had planned. When Naomi nodded, he spoke gently. "Would you tell me about how you lost your leg? In your birth body."

Her eyes widened before immediately narrowing. "What, why?"

"I'd like to know."

"It was an accident, my brother and I—"

"Naomi." Their gazes met and Aung continued. "I've read all the interviews. What I'm asking for is the truth, if you're willing to share."

Dane looked at her in surprise. "What does he mean?"

Naomi sighed heavily, eyeing Aung irritably. "Since you seem to know so much, why don't you enlighten me about what lie I've told?"

Aung felt a smile growing on his lips. "Well, a lie to protect a loved one isn't exactly a lie. Now is it?"

Both Dane and Naomi were eyeing him and Dane grunted. "What type of Buddhist are you?"

Aung chuckled. "One of the Monkhood." He felt a grin of pride. "We aren't your average monks."

It was a long moment before Naomi let out a breath. "Why do you care?"

It was Aung's turn to pause. "Honestly?" He shrugged. "I've been following your running career for a while. I was a fan before you became famous because of it. And the truth is, I want to know if I'm right about you." And perhaps even more deeply, in some ways Naomi reminded him of how he used to be before he'd found the Monkhood.

Her face creased with indecision before she finally shrugged and glanced at Dane. "In all my interviews I say it was an accident. That I'd been out running with my brother in a quarry when a freak rockslide dislodged a boulder that landed on my leg. My brother called the ambulance and saved me, and it brought us closer together."Dane frowned "What actually happened?"

Naomi sighed heavily. "I was eighteen and I'd just gotten custody of Tyler. It was my first semester in college, and I was already super burned out. I was studying and didn't even notice he hadn't come home and it was getting late. When he didn't answer my calls, I resorted to using the GPS tracker I'd hidden in his backpack."

Her fingers wrapped around her cup of tea. "I found him in one of those strip mines that sprouted up after they discovered Bitronium and realized it was the best metal for bionic implants." Her head shook as he continued. "Ty and his friends had somehow managed to hack the security protocols around the excavator and were playing around with it like it was a toy. The thing was huge and they were cutting into a hill as if it were nothing. The ground was shaking under me and I lost my footing. I fell into the pit and a boulder fell onto my leg."

Her eyes stared down into her tea and Dane reached over to squeeze her shoulder. "How did you get out of that?"

Naomi sucked in a shaky breath. "I'd crushed my cell phone in the fall so I couldn't call for help. Fortunately, it wasn't long before they shut off the machine and they were finally able to hear me screaming. Ty called an ambulance while his friends bolted. That was why I got the aural upgrade. I never wanted to feel stranded and helpless again."

The creases on her face showed how much pain she carried that she hadn't dealt with. Aung spoke gently. "And when EMS and the police came?"

Naomi shrugged with a sad smile. "I knew I'd lose him if we

[149]

told them the truth. So, as we were waiting for them to arrive, I made him promise me to stick to the story I made up. I nearly lost custody of him anyway." Her head shook sadly. "But maybe I should have let him go since after that was when it all went to hell."

Dane's voice softened. "What do you mean?"

"He started using drugs and alcohol to numb out. Nothing I could do helped. I've been bailing his sorry ass out of trouble for years. I guess this situation is nothing new." The first hint of anger entered her voice. "And he's the jerk responsible for my body having fake parts."

Dane smacked her shoulder and Naomi yelped in surprise. Dane pointed a finger at her. "Hey, bionic parts aren't fake. What percentage of bionic you are doesn't matter, it's about how human you are."

"Now you're getting all philosophical?" Naomi's eyebrow rose. "Fine, oh guru. Tell me—what's the most fundamental part about being human?"

"Kicking ass." In response to Naomi's dubious look, Dane gave a nod. "It's the most fundamental human thing to enjoy kicking ass, in all its forms. Be it in a race, catching a bad guy, or kicking your own ass out of a melodramatic stupor, doesn't matter. Kicking ass is the core of humanity and I believe that if more people embraced that, there would be a lot more redemption and awesome in this world."

Aung grinned. Dane's brand of humanism was wonderful. "I second your philosophy!"

Naomi's grunt was guttural. "Since when do Buddhists kick ass?"

His brow rose playfully. "Would you like to spar and find out?"

She blinked in surprise but Aung caught movement on the far side of the room. "Perhaps later. For now, I strongly suggest we get to the car that my fellow Brother has waiting, and I'll take you to the Temple so we can discuss this further in safety." He calmly turned to Naomi. "Also, may I have your fork, please?"

Naomi paused before handing over the fork.

"Thank you." Aung took the fork by the prongs and whipped it across the room, sinking it into the side of one of Dane's bookshelves. Both he and Naomi were on their feet, hands on their weapons. Aung stood and walked over to the bookshelf as Dane called to him. "I thought Buddhists were nonviolent."

"We are and I encourage a respect for all forms of life, including insects." Aung pulled the fork out of the wood and gave a nod as he walked back, a cockroach impaled on the prongs. "However..." He let the fork drop to the table, a tendril of electricity wrapping around the insect for a brief moment. "Since this is a spybot, I am not in conflict with my beliefs."

Both Naomi and Dane leaned down to look at the bug, drawing back in surprise as it began to whir slowly with the last bits of power. Aung looked between them. "Remember those people I said were trying to kill Naomi?" They met his gaze and he smiled. "Now would be an excellent time to leave."

Dane

He tapped out the sequence to access the house computer. "Code Indigo, arm and engage. Do an enhanced perimeter sweep out to two hundred feet."

"There are sixteen potential hostiles found within those parameters and—"

"Dane, if these are more of your friends—"

"Not my friends, Leon. This is an actual Code Indigo." Dane edged over to a window, lowering the opacity on the shield so he could see out. There was a man hiding behind some crates, but Dane could still see he was holding a plasma grenade launcher. These guys were serious. "So, Naomi, Aung, and I are going to hightail it out of here and I'll try to get some of them to follow us."

"*Why would you do that?*" Leon sounded affronted. "*I can't very well collect any data on Indigo if you kill them all.*"

Leon must have disconnected because the house computer continued as if it hadn't been interrupted. "*—and unless they are arms dealers, likelihood of attack is predicted at 99%.*"

Moments like those convinced Dane he was the only sane one living in his house.

Naomi was behind him. "Is it just me or is Leon…?"

"Awesome? Yes." Aung was grinning.

Or perhaps the only sane one, period.

"Okay, let's grab some weapons—"

There were a dozen or so explosions in close succession, sounding like fireworks. A split second later the walls of the warehouse vibrated. The house computer chirruped again. "*There are now ten potential hostiles.*"

He motioned with his head and started jogging to the door. "Leon's going to be pissed."

Naomi frowned at his side. "That his warehouse is being attacked?"

"No, that his first wave only killed thirty seven percent of them."

They hurried down the hallway and he stopped by the supply cabinet, waving his ID chip over the interface. It opened to show a coat closet before it rotated and the gun store came into view. Naomi took in a breath of surprise. "Is that a Winchester plasma shotgun? Can I have that?"

Dane tried to act cool and not as if that were one of the hottest things a woman had ever asked him. "Sure. You want a Glock or would you rather—"

"Do they have the Cannon Shot upgrade?" She picked one up and turned it slowly.

"Actually, they have two Cannon Shots, each."

She made a noise of appreciation. "I'll take two, then."

He handed her a second Glock and was immensely grateful she wasn't in her own body with her incredibly hot legs. Dane cleared his throat to refocus and was about to hand Aung a gun when he hesitated. "Uh, do you know what to do with one of these?"

Aung lifted his fists. "I prefer to hurt people the old-fashioned way."

"Right, more for me." He made sure all his compartments were full and added a pair of guns to his waistband, for good measure. The trap door creaked as he yanked it open, and he hurried down the spiral staircase.

The cement floor of the underground tunnel was dank, and Dane had to sidle sideways like a crab since it was so narrow. After a couple hundred feet a ladder appeared and he waved his ID chip and put in a password to get the cover to pop open. He glanced around carefully and saw no one in the protected back area of the alley. He drew a gun as he kept watch while the others ascended.

"My other Brother is this way." Aung motioned with his head.

Dane immediately looked at Naomi. "Are we going with him?"

She tapped her thumb to her mouth thoughtfully. Even in another different body from her own, Dane was starting to recognize her mannerisms. "Yes. It makes the most sense."

Dane nodded and turned to Aung. "Lead the way."

The monk wasted no time before breaking into a run. They got perhaps ten paces before gunfire started raining down on them.

Naomi was running at Dane's side. "You know, I try not to be one to judge but…" She paused briefly to fire off a shot. "How do you guys run with this stuff between your legs?"

Dane yanked her behind a dumpster as a plasma grenade flew past them. "It's probably about as hard as running with breasts." The grenade released a wave of heat.

She gave a grunt that sounded almost angry in her male body before she aimed her gun around the dumpster and fired. "Why don't we switch bodies sometime and find out what's harder?"

"You know…" He motioned with his head and they ducked down low as they edged toward the corner of the building. "I'm usually more receptive when a woman asks me to get inside her." He cocked a playful brow. "But not so much with your offer."

Her gaze was equal parts intensity and playfulness. "You're not even a little curious what being inside me would feel like?"

He pressed his lips together to hold in a moan. The tension was so palpable he almost felt lightheaded and he had to actively remind himself she was engaged.

And also probably still on a Dash high, which would explain her talking like that.

Right, that's all it was not—

"Are you two coming?"

They both looked straight up. Aung was balancing on the banister of a rusty fire escape. He leaned backward at an unnatural angle to avoid a shot, before doing a back flip onto the fire escape and hurriedly climbing upward.

Naomi blinked. "Did you see how he got up there?"

Dane saw the escape ladder was still up so Aung hadn't used that. "Are you convinced he's human? Because I'm not." Dane clasped his hands together, holding them out to her. "Put your foot in here and be prepared to get some height."

He increased the power output on his arms and tossed her into the air. He redirected power to his legs and squatted down before taking a powerful jump.

The other two were halfway across the roof when he landed. He had charged to the center of the roof when it suddenly felt as if his body were moving in slow motion. Distantly, he saw himself screeching to a halt and his arms leaned back without conscious direction on his part. His eyes grew large when he saw a missile pass within inches of his torso, where he would have been if he hadn't somehow inexplicably stopped his forward momentum exactly when he had.

The missile slammed into the next building, and he ducked with his back toward the explosion.

"Where's Naomi?!"

Dane blinked in surprise. No call had connected so where was—

His hand came up and whacked himself in the cheek. *"Pay attention! I asked you where Naomi is!!"*

He chuckled as he started running. Naomi probably hadn't thought to update her partner, seeing as she'd been drugged and all. "Hello, Inari. I take it I have you to thank for helping me dodge that missile?"

"You're only alive because I want to know where Naomi is! Why'd she disappear and is she in a different body and who are you to have access to a body transfer station anyway, are you a criminal or—"

Dane stepped off the building, falling to the ground and landing with a thud in the cement. "Oh sorry, going through a tunnel, you're breaking up." He tapped his fingers in the familiar sequence. *Calling Leon Hartwick.*

It picked up after a quarter of a ring. *"I'm busy."*

"Someone's hacking my interface."

It was rare that Dane could make Leon speechless, even for a few seconds.

"Intriguing."

Call ended.

When Dane rounded the corner, he came to the waterfront and was able to get a look back at the warehouse. Blue electric netting had been ignited around it and on each corner plasma cannons had made an appearance. The bad guys had backed away to a safe distance—they must have realized a full-frontal assault was foolhardy. This meant however, there were a half dozen or so thugs for Dane, Naomi, and Aung to face without cannon support.

"Dane, you feel like helping or just want to stand there looking pretty?"

He grinned as he caught sight of Naomi's iron man body. She was hunkered down behind a barrel, shooting at a pair of men hiding behind a dumpster.

"You think I'm pretty?" He reached for both guns from his waistband and started shooting at the two men while he rushed over to Naomi's barrel. Since it wasn't doing much more than wasting bullets, he used his thumb to switch the right gun to a Cannon Shot and aimed for the front of the dumpster. It growled angrily before it fired and hit the dumpster square on. The dumpster was thrown back and both men yelled in surprise prior to being knocked out from the impact.

"I guess you're kinda cute." Naomi lifted a thick male eyebrow at him. "Do you think I'm pretty?"

"Not gonna lie, a cis-female in a male body is an unexpected turn on."

She grunted at him and there was more gunfire. She took aim around the side of the barrel and fired off several rounds. "I was feeling pretty awkward about this body, but now you're making me daydream about becoming a gay man."

Dane knelt behind her, aiming over the top of the barrel as he fired. "Being with me certainly won't ever be boring." When he saw the man picking up a grenade launcher, Dane tapped his shin, opening the small compartment and taking out one of Leon's incendiary bullets. He slipped it into his gun. "You may want to turn away from this one." The gun fired and there was a crack of thunder and a scream as the bad guy went up in flames.

When the heat of the blast hit them, Naomi turned into his chest and he wrapped his arm around her protectively. The heat rushed over them and he noticed she wasn't shaking in fear, wasn't quivering. She was such a fighter. It was so damn sexy he could hardly stand it. He might stop caring soon that she was already taken.

Naomi looked over the barrel at the blaze and gave a curious 'huh' of surprise. "Is that one of Leon's creations?" When he replied it was, she immediately turned to him. "How much does he charge for a box of them? Oh, does he give a discount for bulk?"

He sighed internally. He wasn't sure how much longer he could stay out of trouble. "We can ask him later. Let's get out of here before they bring reinforcements."

"And where's Aung?"

They both got to their feet and started running.

In the next alley over, they found Aung fighting a woman who appeared to be regretting the experience. She reached for a gun and he knocked it aside with a kick so powerful it sent the gun flying into the ocean. The knife she grabbed out of her belt didn't slow him; he simply pivoted, grabbed her wrist, twisted her hand back toward her and the knife fell out of her grasp as she cried out in pain. When he did a palm heel punch to her chin, she collapsed to the ground unconscious.

"Aung, which way?"

The man was turning to him when he did a backbend. It was so fast Dane had barely registered the crack of the gun, but as blood welled up on Aung's bicep Dane saw Aung hadn't been fast enough. Aung fell to the ground and Naomi rushed to his side. Dane turned to the direction of the bullet, pulling the trigger as soon as he set his sights on the woman who'd fired.

Naomi had Aung on his feet, and he was waving away her concern. "This way!" When Aung began running, Dane followed close behind the two, keeping his eyes out for any stragglers.

The honking of a horn brought his eyes to the road. But catching sight of the vehicle made him swear under his breath. "No fucking way."

Waving out of the driver's window of a beat-up Volkswagen bus was a bald monk in burnt-orange robes wearing circular wire framed glasses. "Hello!" While Dane knew it must be a revival piece, he did have a moment of fear it actually was over a hundred and fifty years old. It looked rickety and terrifying and the fact the monk in the driver's seat had his hands on the steering wheel made him suddenly fear for the few remaining human parts Dane had left.

Some bad guy chose that moment to begin shooting, though, so Dane's only option was to follow Aung and Naomi and dive through the side door. The van propelled forward and he, Naomi, and Aung were thrown into a pile by the back door. The monk

[158]

driving waved a hand. "I'm Pema!"

"DRIVE!" Both he and Naomi yelled at the same moment.

While it wasn't illegal to manually drive a car, Dane had always counted himself as lucky he'd been born after the time of frequent car accidents and vehicular manslaughter. The current experience of Pema swerving about the road was not changing his mind.

"Why are you—" When the back window was shot out, he instantly understood why. "Never mind, keep driving." He and Naomi inched to the back of the van, cautiously glancing out the window. "Okay, it's just one car, two passengers. I can use one of my incendiary bullets and—"

"But you'll kill them!"

Both Naomi and he stared at Aung as if he'd spawned another head. Dane went to grab a bullet. "Yeah, kinda the idea, Aung."

They all had to duck as they were sprayed with another round of bullets. Dane was fairly certain he was going to lose his lunch soon, the way Pema was veering all over the road. He'd just dropped his bullet when he heard a gun fire twice in close succession, but this time from within the van.

There were loud pops followed by the screech of tires. Dane met Naomi's eyes and they both looked up to see Aung, aiming a gun out the window.

Dane got to his knees so he could look out the back, the car diminishing in the horizon. But even at that distance, he could see Aung had shot out two of the tires. Dane was trying to form words when Naomi beat him to it. "I thought you said you didn't know how to fire a gun?"

Aung offered the gun pommel first to Dane with a grin. "I said I prefer to fight with my fists. Which is true."

Dane took the gun dumbly, realizing with a start Aung had

[159]

stolen it from him at some point without him noticing. Aung nimbly made his way to the front, even as blood was dripping off his fingertips from the gunshot wound on his arm. When he was seated in the passenger seat beside Pema, Dane shared a dumb-founded look with Naomi. She lifted her hands in a gesture of defeat before she rushed up to the front as well. She ripped a piece of fabric from Aung's robe and was wrapping it around his arm as Dane took a seat on the floor beside her. He eyed the man curiously. "So who exactly are you?"

Aung gave a warm smile. "I'm a Brother of the Monkhood." And even as Naomi tightened the fabric around his wound and tied off the bandage, he looked unphased. As the man rested his head against the window and closed his eyes, Dane saw the first hint of human weakness.

"Where exactly are we heading?"

"To the Monkhood's Temple!" Pema gave a bright smile and Dane had to wonder if all the monks were absolutely insane.

CHAPTER 12

Lin

She was leaning back against a tree, watching a duck drift along aimlessly in the pond before her. A wide bridge arched over the water, some cattails around the perimeter. Beyond was a sprawling compound that seemed to have been plucked straight out of an anime. The rich red pillars and dark trim accented the sloping roofs, covered in gray tiles. Many white shoji screen doors had been slid open to welcome the bright afternoon. As the breeze picked up, the bells on the corners of the building added their voice. She couldn't remember the last time she'd felt so peaceful.

When the tightness in her chest started, she drew her legs up and wrapped her arms around them. She closed her eyes and felt her body rocking, trying not to either panic or let the feelings overwhelm her. She tried to do like they'd told her; see the feelings as a leaf in a river, floating away from her. As she concentrated it became a little easier to bear and she focused harder until the wave passed.

She collapsed back against the tree again, panting. She stared up at the cloud floating past, trying to calm down. While the monks were helping her, she felt totally that the responsibility for success or failure was hers alone. They were warm and welcoming, yes, but simultaneously firm and rigid. She closed her eyes again as she concentrated on breathing. She had never been so scared of failure before.

But she had to do this, and she had to do it right. She owed it to Naomi.

And maybe a small part, she owed to herself.

When she opened her eyes again there was an older bald man, wearing an orange robe with his hands clasped before him. Lin had no idea how long he'd been waiting and she didn't know his name. She'd probably met sixty monks so far. Lin slowly got to her shaky legs and gave the man a proper bow, like she'd been taught. The monk bowed his head in return. "Your sister will arrive shortly."

Lin swallowed hard. "Thank you."

The man bowed again before turning to leave. Lin looked down at her shaking hands, clasping them and squeezing hard to try to make them stop. Now that she was on her feet she hurried across the bridge and saw a reflection of herself in the water. She was wearing the orange robes of the monks, her scalp was bald, and her eyes dainty. Her body was Asian, thin and lithe, as well as being clean of drugs and a criminal record. The monks had been very kind.

A loud thud brought her attention to the dirt driveway and a beat-up Volkswagen bus making its way. While she logically knew it was only made to look old and wasn't actually that archaic, it still looked rickety. It couldn't be a particularly comfortable ride.

At the realization she was about to face her sister she was gripped by a panic that for once wasn't due to getting over her addictions. Now that the moment had come, she didn't know how she was going to explain herself let alone be able to apologize enough.

The van pulled up before the main building and Lin watched as the bounty hunter she recognized from the race made his way out. Lin instantly froze. What was Dane doing there? When the man simply ignored her, she was confused until she remembered that Dane wouldn't recognize her now. Changing bodies was complicated.

The sight of a bloody bandage on Aung's arm brought Lin out of her concern for herself. "Aung, what happened? Are you all right?"

Aung waved a hand with a good-natured laugh. "I was not as quick as I thought. Perhaps I watch too many kung fu movies."

The bounty hunter grunted. "You are a kung fu movie."

Aung took Lin a couple steps away, his eyes holding hers. "How are you adjusting to your new body?"

She let out a shaky breath. "It feels..." She didn't have words.

He squeezed her forearm, tenderly. "It takes time."

Remembering their conversations, she let herself be vulnerable. "How long did it take you?"

His eyes met hers and seeing the real understanding there warmed her. "It took exactly as long as it needed to, for me." He tenderly hooked a finger under her chin. "And it will take exactly as long as it needs to, for you." He gently bopped her nose. "Young lady."

She was warmed with gender euphoria at the acceptance and was grateful, yet again, for having a role model like Aung to show her the way.

At the voices, she saw that beside Dane there was now another monk and a short, muscular black man. Glancing into the van showed it empty.

So where was Naomi?

Catching Aung's gaze, she felt a terrible ache in her chest. She didn't want it to be true. But the monk had said her sister was coming. Too late she realized they had failed to mention in what form. "Aung, please tell me it's not true." She wasn't sure she could take any more guilt.

The body builder shifted into a subtle defensive posture that Lin instantly recognized. "What's not true?"It was her sister, wasn't it? And it was all Lin's fault. "I'm so sorry, Noams. For everything." Lin's throat burned. "I was trying to fix all my screwups, I swear."

Naomi's eyes widened. "Tyler?"

There were tears on Lin's cheek. "I-I never meant for this to happen."

She was about to rush to her sister when she held up her male hand. "Prove it's you."

Lin took in a deep breath. Even if she didn't know how to apologize, at least she'd figured out how she was going to prove her identity. "You love rabbits, but you'll never adopt one because you work too many hours. Your favorite post run food is milk mixed with cookies and cream protein powder. You hate Brussels sprouts but mom used to love them so you still try to eat them every once in a while. Your favorite binge food is ice cream sandwiches, which I always used to buy and leave in the freezer when I knew I was being an asshole but couldn't bring myself to apologize." She had to pause to fight the well of emotions. "The night mom died, you cried to yourself on the porch because you probably thought I couldn't hear you. And that's why I came to your room and said I couldn't sleep. Because I couldn't stand how sad you were. And how sad I was."

Naomi was breathing slowly, the eyes of her borrowed body glassy. When she turned to Dane, she hit his bionic arm and opened a compartment. Grabbing the gun, she pointed a gun at the center of Aung's forehead before any of them could react. "Explain yourself." Her voice hardened. "Because as of right now it's looking as if you've kidnapped my brother and I."

Lin took a step forward, waving her hands. "Please! I came here of my own free will."

Naomi the body builder didn't move. "That's convenient."

Aung was standing still with the barrel on his forehead, watching Naomi. "We need your help."

"I thought you brought me here because people were supposedly trying to kill me?"

"We have the same enemy, Naomi."

"Well, from what I can see it's looking as if you've orchestrated—"

"It's the Apogee."

Lin saw the way Naomi froze and Aung continued, more quietly. "There's something terribly wrong with the Apogee model."

Naomi paused. "What precisely?"

Aung hadn't taken his eyes off Naomi. "We believe someone on the inside of CLM added to the code. As soon as they do an operating system update, it will allow for remote access control to any Apogee body."

Dane pointed at Naomi. "See, her friend Inari can already do that."

"Just for short bouts, minor movements." Aung shook his head very slowly. "Not permanently."

Even though her features were completely different, Lin could see the ghost of her sister in the horror on Naomi's face. "Permanently?"

"I'll happily show you the code, if you'd like to step inside." Aung lifted a brow. "Lowering the gun would also be a nice touch."

There was a long pause before the gun lowered. Naomi tucked it away at her lower back. "Lead the way." The grumbly voice softened when those dark eyes met Lin's. "Stay close." The look on the man's face was one Lin had seen often enough—it meant they'd better show Naomi what she wanted to see and fast, or else they were going to regret it.

Naomi

They started up the stairs of the main building and she glanced over her shoulder. Her brother was now in the body of a wispy, bald, Asian woman. She didn't know what to make of the situation but at least she was sure she really was her brother. No amount of surveillance or data-diving could have produced the information Tyler had just told her. That she was her brother, however, was the only thing she felt certain of. "So how exactly did you get here? And into another new body?" Her throat tightened but she coughed to clear it. She couldn't let herself get emotional—Tyler might have been the reason she started this journey but something more was going on.

Tyler's voice was soft but had the same lilt. "Well actually, that's his fault." He motioned to Dane.

"Wait, me?"

At the landing before the entrance, everyone switched their shoes for slippers before going inside. Naomi followed suit purely because Tyler did.

Ty hung back until they all moved together. "Yeah. When we were at Naomi's race, you threw me back into Aung. He told me if I truly wanted to help myself, he could help me. I wasn't sure what to do but what he said made me trust him."

She watched him as they moved down a hallway. "Which was what?"

Tyler gave a sheepish grin that looked oddly right on the new feminine face. "Honestly, he told me it would be a lot of work and it would be incredibly painful. But that I could regain my pride, if I had faith." Ty shrugged with a shiver. "It sounded like something you would say, Noams, so I thought maybe it would be the right choice, for a change."

"Idiot." She touched his shoulder and noticed that he was shaking. "Are you ill?"

He shook his head. "It's all my own doing."

She fought back the emotions threatening to close up her throat. A large part of her had always hoped Tyler would take responsibility for his actions. But she'd never thought or hoped he'd have to lose his body for it to happen.

Dane turned to Aung. "You monks have a body transfer station?"

For one of the first times, Aung dropped his goofy demeanor as they stopped before a shoji door. "Those with the greatest need are often of the slightest means."

Naomi paused and looked at her brother. "You help people?"

The monk lifted a finger toward the ceiling. "Those who have been cast aside themselves cast no stones."

Dane turned to Tyler. "Does he always talk like a fortune cookie?"

Ty sighed heavily. "They all do."

Aung chuckled and she saw he was cradling his bloody arm against his side.

"You really should get that looked at."

As if on command, another monk glided down the hallway with a first aid kit hanging at his side.

"I'll have them look after me while we talk. I know you want to see proof, Naomi. I don't blame you. We didn't want to believe this when we discovered it either."

"How did you know to look at the Apogee coding, anyway? Mystical powers lead you to it?"

"What?" Aung blinked. "No, we hacked the database." He slid the door open on a room that seemed out of place here, though it would be perfectly natural in the city.

It was a large space, and the walls were traditional shoji screens keeping it very bright. There were dozens of computer workstations abuzz with the sound of technology. There were at least a dozen monks typing rapidly at computers, looking in stark contrast to the technology around them with their orange robes and bald heads. In the center of the room was a large bare table and along the floor wires were carefully organized and trailed to the server in the corner of the room. With the availability of cloud space, having a server of their own meant they were serious about privacy. What exactly did a group of monks have stored that they wanted to protect?

Dane took a step into the room, rounding on Aung. "Why do you have Leon's equipment here?"

Aung was giving his questionable chuckle as he sat at the large table in the center of the room. "Hartwick Technologies has long been a friend to us." The other monk took a seat beside him, setting the first aid kit on the table.

As the three of them stopped near the table Dane grunted. "Okay, look, as Leon's roommate I can safely say you really can't throw the word friend around where it concerns him."

The monk shrugged and lifted his good hand. "Well, then call us business partners."

Naomi shared a glance with Dane before turning back to Aung. "What do you mean by that?"

The other monk was washing the wound with antiseptic but Aung didn't even flinch. "We both have the same goal. We do a great deal of coding for him, and he provides us with the technology to keep up with him." He paused, his eyes on Dane. "We are helping him on Project Fùhuó."

Dane took in a breath and Naomi could tell that unlike her, he must know what that meant. But since he wasn't explaining, she asked. "What's Project Fùhuó?"

The man beside Aung now had a needle and thread. As he inserted it into Aung's skin, Aung began taking slow, deep breaths. She whispered to Dane. "Did you see them give him an anesthetic?"

Dane shook his head slowly. "Nope."

She grimaced. "Baddass."

He grunted. "Showoff."

"Don't be jealous."

Aung's voice quieting was the only expression of his pain. "Project Fùhuó is our joint dream—Leon, us—to realize a more humanized world." His face twinged in pain and he forced a big grin. "Perhaps Dane could continue for me while Chen finishes with my arm."

Naomi took a step forward. "Wait, if you work with Leon and you had my brother here—"

"Lin." The girl wouldn't met Naomi's gaze. "Is my preferred name." She sucked in a breath. "Along with feminine pronouns from now on."

Naomi blinked at her bro—sister? And sucked in a guilty breath that the feminine eyes wouldn't meet hers. Before, as Tyler, he had only said he felt uncomfortable in his body; Naomi wouldn't have guessed that this young woman before her was what he had meant he would have preferred. She swallowed, realizing the others were conveniently no longer looking at them. She took in the awkward stance of the girl, reaching over tentatively to squeeze Lin's shoulder, trying to make it the same movement she'd always used before. "Lin..." Her sister's eyes shot to hers in surprise and Naomi smiled. "Can we talk later? I've obviously missed a lot."

"Yeah." Lin's eyes quickly shifted back down but there was a lightness to her soft smile.

Knowing her broth—sister had been suffering for who knew how long made the fear of screwing up nearly overwhelm her—she drew in a breath. Her anxiety would simply have to take a back burner. There were other messes to deal with first. "If Leon and Lin were a part of this, why didn't you tell us that at the warehouse? We might have trusted you more quickly."

Aung's brow rose. "Just because Leon and Lin have chosen to trust us does not mean that you should trust us. I wanted you both to make your own decision."

Naomi stared in disbelief. That was so...

"Buddhists." Dane cleared his throat. "Aung's right, Project Fùhuó is Leon's big project. And big secret." Dane looked around the room. "He's trying to reverse the trend of body transferring and enhancements. He wants to give people the option of getting human body parts instead of bionic, if they wish."

Naomi felt her brows rise in disbelief. "I'm not up on my science by any stretch of the imagination but isn't that incredibly complicated?"

"I know, but this is Leon. If anyone can manage, he can." Dane looked at Aung. "You said you're coding but I don't understand how exactly you're helping him?"

"Coding for the nano-bots." Aung motioned to the computers as Chen cut the string and pulled out gauze. "His nanotechnology will change what's possible in medicine."

She glanced at the computers and back to Aung. "So, he believes his nanotechnology can attach new body parts. And you're working with him because the Monkhood wants this?"

"Yes. We want people to see there are alternatives to bionics. Or, I should say more specifically, to vanity upgrades." Chen wrapped gauze around his arm and put a simple linen sling around Aung's shoulder. When he finished, Aung thanked him before they both stood. Chen made his way out of the room and Aung turned to them. "Let me show you the Apogee coding, so you understand what's at stake." He moved to an empty computer station and began typing with his good hand.

Naomi, Dane, and Lin shared a glance before moving behind him to watch the image screen. She saw the schematic of what she recognized instantly as the Apogee model. It was horrifying to see that internally, all that was left human was the brain, lungs, heart, and a few tubes to connect them. She supposed there wasn't even a need for a body like that to eat real food—a nutrient filled liquid straight to the blood stream could supply everything the brain would need. It gave her the creeps just thinking about it.

As the schematic rotated, code overlaid the images. Her computer programming was basic at best but even she recognized the highlighted series of command codes. Once this operation system was downloaded and the right sequence of commands entered, any Apogee model could be controlled remotely. People could become trapped inside mechanical bodies with no ability to control their actions. They could become murderers and have no way to stop it.

Dane spoke quietly. "Do you think Jax knows about this?"

She paused to consider. "He doesn't do the coding himself. And there would be no reason for him to have it checked, besides. Who could believe this would be hidden this far down in a simple update?" She paused thoughtfully, remembering dinner with Jax. "He mentioned distrusting Bradford on his board of trustees. He said the Apogee was Bradford's idea and that he's the one responsible for advancing the beta testing from the standard one year down to three months."

Lin glanced at her. "But what's it matter? Not that many people could afford an Apogee."

"No, that's exactly it!" She pivoted to Lin. "The richest one percent on the planet are the only ones who could afford it."

Dane sighed. "And that also happens to be the most powerful one percent."

Lin still looked skeptical. "Wouldn't world domination with a lot of drones be easier?"

"No." Everyone turned to Naomi but she sighed. "No, because this could take over the globe without a fuss, without a single bullet. Without anyone even knowing." She had to restrain a shiver. "At least they're still in beta testing so there's only one person in an Apogee model right now." She turned to Aung, pointing to the code. "Now why don't you explain how exactly you got this?"

Aung's nose scrunched up. "Well, it wasn't given to us, if that's what you're asking."

Lin took a step back. "You guys hacked into CLM? They have the most secure firewall probably on the planet!"

The monk chuckled. "Well, they have since upgraded their firewall. Which is why we need Naomi's help."

"To do what?" Dane was motioning to the image screen. "All you've shown us so far is a time bomb embedded in an operating system that isn't even launched yet."

"We want you to spread a virus to all of humanity." Aung turned to the computer. "We—"

Naomi was appalled. "You want to kill people?!"

[172]

The monk was chuckling again. "Far from it. We want people to live again." He pushed a button and an image screen appeared, the size of the far wall. On it the word *Sanctuary* appeared, atop lines of swirling code.

She moved toward the wall, her eyes moving over the code. It was intricate and she immediately wished Inari could explain it to her.

Dane was at her side, pointing to a jumble of code. "This shuts down all machines."

Aung nodded. "Yes."

He pointed to another section. "For twenty-four hours."

"Yes."

He turned to Aung. "In the whole country."

"Perhaps you should become a Brother because you are an excellent reader of code!"

She turned to the monk, pointing to the wall. "The monk in Central Park. He was killed because of this?"

"Yes." Aung's head hung. "We started this project because we wished for people to have the chance to see the world again. To explore their humanity while disconnected from technology. Just for a while—you can see all of us are connected to it as well. But it is very important to keep it in perspective. So many people have lost their humanity."

Lin moved to the man. "But what about people in hospitals or on life support?"

"That's why the coding is so complicated. No one will be hurt by this." The image screen went blank and she turned to see him reaching for the computer. He pulled out a small rectangular piece of plastic with a chip on the front face, offering it to her. "The best place to release this is CLM Tower in New York. Their interface is the largest on the Eastern Seaboard, and we've programmed it to connect with satellites—"

"Hold on." She pointed to the chip. "So you broke into CLM's mainframe the first time in order to release this computer virus and instead you stole the Apogee schematics?"

"We hacked CLM to see if it were possible. Finding the Apogee schematics was accidental. We had actually been looking for—"

"I should arrest you. All of you."

He gave a shrug. "If you must, then you must." Their gazes held for a long moment. "We want people to take a day, just a single day, to step away from the machines and reconnect. So many people are distant from one another and we want to help people have a human connection. We monks just want to make a difference." He was still offering the chip, head tilting with a saccharine smile. "Oh, did I mention this also has a cure for the Apogee remote override coding?"

She grimaced and took the chip. "This is illegal and I'm not doing it." She held up the card, acknowledging that while in her unregistered body she wasn't exactly legally clean either. "Once I get back in my body, I'm going to notify the police. This is evidence."

"The people who are after that—" He pointed to her hand. "—are the same ones who have been after you."

"What? Why?"

"Because of what you've unwittingly become."

Lin shared a confused glance. "And what's that?"

Dane spoke quietly. "'The spokesperson for humanity.'" Naomi looked at him in confusion and he continued. "After I saw you at the race and heard Aung talk about you, I researched. There's more than one website devoted to you. A lot of people believe you're ushering in a new wave of humanism."

She waved a hand dismissively. "Inari showed me those, they're not such a big deal."

"Not to you, Noams." Lin's nose scrunched up. "But I've been to your races. You've got a lot of fans."

Naomi was at a loss and eventually looked at Aung. "Why were you so concerned before about how I lost my leg?"

He flipped his hand, palm up. "I believed that if you would take drastic steps in order to stay connected to your sibling..." He pointed to the chip. "Then you would take the chance to help us all reconnect as human beings."

She held his gaze for a long time. "And it doesn't hurt I happen to have an in at CLM, now does it?" She put the card into her back pocket. At least now she had it. She'd get it to Inari and they would sort this out together. Before Aung could say anything she continued. "Tell me why you were there when my bro—" She winced. She'd been hoping to keep her slip ups internal. "When my sister was getting her first body transfer?"

Lin turned to her. "He wasn't."

"There was a picture of a bodhisattva in your pocket."

Her sister shook her head. "If there was, I didn't put it there. And no one else was there when I transferred."

She frowned. "Someone must have come before or after the handler was killed, then."

"Iago was killed?!" Lin's skin flushed and she took a step away from Dane. "Why would you kill him?"

Dane huffed "I didn't kill him."

"But you were after me that night, that's why I had to get that bad body transfer. You'd been after me for days!"

Dane shook his head. "No, I didn't claim the bounty on you until Friday afternoon. I have a time stamp from the forum to prove it."

Naomi held up her hands. "Hold on." Her eyes moved to Lin. "So, the night you transferred, someone was chasing you. Did you see them?"

Lin shook her head. "No, they were following me and then they blocked my reception so my call dropped. That's when I jumped bodies."

Her eyes fell to the floor in thought. If Dane hadn't been after Lin, who had? The theory they'd been working under was that the person who murdered the handler had been after the body Lin had taken. But if that theory were wrong, it would mean the handler's killer had actually been after Naomi's sibling the whole time. Which also meant he may have placed the photo on—she paused. On Tyler's dead body. She glanced at Lin, feeling a strange swirl of emotions. Tyler being a dead name was accurate in more ways than one, it seemed.

She blew out a breath. Could someone have wanted Naomi to follow that clue to the Monkhood? It was possible. Artillery had killed a monk to try to get information about Sanctuary, after all. And there was a large bounty on the Monkhood now, too. The slight card in her back pocket suddenly seemed very heavy.

"Speaking of bodies..." Lin's voice was soft. "Where's yours?"

"It's safe, Jax has it."

The girl stuck out her tongue. "Are you sure he's not creeping on your body when you aren't around?"

"Ew, Ty—Lin!"

The girl eyed Naomi in a familiar fashion. "Look, I'm just saying he doesn't do anything that's not in his best interest."

The protest felt forced. "He's not a bad guy."

"But it doesn't logically mean he's a good one either."

Dane nodded. "Your sister has more sense than you do, Naomi."

"Speaking of bodies…" Aung had a grin on his lips. "Naomi, how would you like to have a pair of breasts again?"

She let out a breath of intense relief at the thought of not being stuck in that male body anymore. "Please." And Lin's hand squeezing hers made their eyes catch. The understanding in her sister's gaze made Naomi's insides burn with the desire to do the same for her unexpected sister.

CHAPTER 13

Naomi

Aung's voice came through the speaker. "The transfer is complete."

Dane began undoing her bindings. She was impressed by how much easier this transfer had been than either of the previous two. It felt like merely a few seconds of floating before they told her it was over. There was no pain and while she felt weak, she wondered if that were more a byproduct of the stress from the last few days rather than the Switch.

Dane offered a hand and helped her to a seated position, before resting a hand on her back and helping her to stand. His arm slipped around her waist to steady her and when she looked down at the hand against her waist, she realized how petite her new body was. It was perhaps the same height as her last one, but she was an Asian woman now. They'd let her see the body before she transferred this time, though it didn't feel any less surreal.

Dane's voice was quiet in her ear. "How do you feel?"

"A little disoriented." She leaned against him probably more than was strictly necessary. But his arm around her was nice. "It wasn't too bad, really."

"It shouldn't be. This is Leon's equipment."

"What do you mean?"

"All his tech is vastly superior to CLM. But since he's not really interested in dealing with people, not everyone knows it.

It was only hard on you last time because it was an emergency transfer."

Aung came out from the control room with Lin at his side. Her sister's face was strange to see. She was covered in a sheen of sweat, but her brows drew together in concern the same way they always had. "How do you feel?"

"I'm all right." Her gaze turned to Dane, who was still at her side. Despite the comfort of his hand at her waist, she drew away but then almost instantly faltered.

Lin caught her and gave a half laugh. "Maybe I can help you for a change."

She smiled as her new sister put her arm around her to steady her. Aung motioned to the door, looking at Lin. "Why don't we go outside? The fresh air will help you both."

Aung gave Lin a meaningful look and Naomi waited until Aung was a few steps ahead before whispering to her sister. "So, it's not just me thinking you look ill."

"It comes and goes in waves." She and her sister began walking together, Dane trailing. Lin looked sad as her eyes moved away. "Addiction isn't totally physiological apparently. Some of it is neurological muscle memory." They crossed the threshold and were welcomed by a gentle breeze. "They call it 'Psychological Addiction Syndrome' or PAS for short. Apparently, the only way out of it is through treatment and then it's PAST." Lin gave her a sly grin. "They think they're very clever."

Aung led them to a small bench beneath a grand old Gingko tree. "Why don't you two sit and catch up? Dane, could you possibly help me send a message to Leon?"

Dane nodded in surprise. "Of course."

As the pair trailed away and Naomi and her bro—sister were left alone, she realized Aung had done that purposefully to give

[179]

them time.

She turned to Lin and took both her sister's hands in hers. It was strange to think she'd never get to touch his other body, touch the one that shared their parents' blood. But as her eyes met the woman's before her, she hoped no longer being in that body would help Lin. She smiled, grateful they finally had a minute to themselves. "Why did you pick Lin?"

"It's my Dharma name." Naomi's face must have conveyed her confusion because Lin continued. "It means forest in Chinese." Her eyes fell in shame. "They um. Well."

She squeezed the girl's hands and Lin glanced at her cautiously before talking hurriedly. "Look, the Monkhood is great, and you can't arrest any of them and I know it probably doesn't make any sense to you because you're not afraid of anything and you've never done anything wrong but—"

"Whoa, hold on."

"No! Don't go all cop or mom on me. Just listen."

She blinked in surprise and nodded.

Lin sucked in a nervous breath, staring down at their hands. "This place, these... utterly insane people..." Their eyes met. "Most of them are like me."

Her brows shot up against her will. "What?"

She lowered her voice, inching closer to her on the bench so their knees were touching. "When I came, they had a ceremony for me. They all gathered and any who wanted to tell their story did. Everyone here... No one's had it easy. And I realized as they were telling their stories that none of them are saints and that somehow made me feel better. Like I could belong.

"Then they asked for my story. When you agree to stay here to be healed it means you become part of this community, even if you only stay for a while. You're given a new body and a Dharma name." Her eyes fell to her lap. "The name though… To pick it…" She glanced into her eyes. "They make you say your worst fears. Then they rename you in order to reclaim that fear."

She couldn't remember the last time her sister had looked that vulnerable and she found her throat catching. "What were your fears?"

Her eyes were glassy as she stared down and Naomi felt her hand shaking. She held it more tightly.

"I said I f-felt l-lost." Lin's gaze held a deep sorrow. "Like I'd been wandering my whole life, never being good enough, never amounting to anything. Never feeling like I even fit inside my own body." She took back a hand to wipe at her cheek, giving a sad laugh. "Then Aung said that the difference between being lost and being on an adventure was whether you enjoyed the scenery." Naomi reached up and wiped at another of her stray tears, sharing a weak smile as her sister sniffled. "So, they named me after a forest. Because wandering in a forest is just a hike. And forests don't need to do anything to be enough. They just need to exist."

When their eyes held, she saw all the agony and torture her sister had been keeping inside for ages. Tears leaked out of sister's eyes and her voice was broken. "I'm sorry for everything, I've always been sorry, I didn't know what to do, I—"

She cradled her new sister as she wept and held her head against her shoulder like she hadn't in years. Her own tears came silently, and she wiped them away so she wouldn't distract Ty— Lin from her catharsis. It was incredible how much had changed and how quickly. But when she compared who she was now to the Naomi on Friday—had it really only been three days since the shooting in Central Park?—she understood. It seemed like another life.

[181]

She nearly let out a snort. Three lives at this point, wasn't it?

She held her petite sister in her arms.

And her sister was starting a new life, too.

She had to clear her throat a few times to keep her emotions in check and drew back to meet her sister's eyes, wanting her to see Naomi's sincerity. "I'm so sorry I didn't understand what you needed. That I wasn't supportive of you wanting to change your body. I put too much importance on DNA and didn't make your needs a priority."

The effect of her words was obvious when Lin immediately looked away and swallowed. Naomi took her hands again, trying to change the subject to help her relax.

"Do you happen to know what Aung's name means?"

She was instantly smiling again. "'Success.'" Naomi felt stunned. Did that mean that Aung's fear before he came there had been failure? She couldn't conceive of that crazy man having self-doubt. Aung was incredible at everything she'd witnessed. But then, maybe it explained him in a powerful way too.

"Isn't Aung amazing?" Lin let out a breath. "He and Dane are like the big brothers I always wanted."

She punched Lin's shoulder. "Hey!"

She was laughing again. "You're right, I practically have a big brother already. I have you!"

Naomi was mock indignant, and they play fought for a moment until Lin grabbed her fists with a smirk. "Though technically I did have an older brother about twenty minutes ago."

Naomi blinked. Lin's lip curled playfully. "'Cause you were a dude, remember? So, uh... Yeah. You had a penis. That's cool."

Their eyes held for a moment before they both burst into a fit of laughter. Lin had a ridiculous grin on her face. "So did you have—"

"To pee?" Her face bunched up at the memory. "Once. It was kind of terrifying. Though admittedly… the whole hose concept is super convenient." She paused. "Not going to lie, I did it standing up cause, why not?"

"No, I mean did you…?" Lin seemed to be enjoying that Naomi had no idea what she was getting at. Her brow tilted playfully and then she was lifting her forearm up slowly, making a constant noise with a rising pitch.

When Naomi finally caught the meaning, she batted at her hands. "TY—LIN!!! Ew!!" She lowered her voice, though not her level of chastisement. "I did not have an erection as a dude!"

She was holding her stomach as she bawled in laughter. "Not even one?"

"I was only a guy for half a day!"

Her brow rose dubiously. "Yeah, that's enough time for like twelve erections." Naomi kept eyeing her, but Lin grinned. "Your guy body was a nugget. I mean, not his arms and legs but man he was short! Even shorter than my awesome new body!"

When their eyes caught, the mirth was instantly replaced by tension from Lin. Naomi smiled at her, taking her hand again. "I've been meaning to say you're very pretty."

Lin blushed.

Naomi squeezed her hand. "And I'm so sorry if I misgender you or use your old name. It's—"

"It's okay." She let out a long breath. "I know that this is all new for you and I just really appreciate you wanting to support me."

Naomi felt some tension leave her. She still hoped she'd only make mistakes in her head but was glad Lin didn't sound as if she'd be hurt if Naomi messed up. "Do you think this is a body you want to keep?"

The smile that bloomed was so much like the old Tyler and yet more resplendent, somehow. "Yeah." She looked down at herself. "I feel really small and feminine. I always felt big and clunky, before."

Naomi let her gaze move over the petite form and thought back to how odd it had felt to be a man. "It must be surreal to suddenly have breasts."

"Mine aren't even that big but my back muscles ache!"

"Right? Being a woman—" She frowned. "Oh God, you're going to have to deal with menstruating." She felt her brows shoot up. "Wait, do you want to have children?"

The way Lin looked down was all shyness intermingled with excitement. "Maybe." She glanced cautiously at Naomi. "Is it weird that I find that part of being a woman kind of neat?"

She'd fixated so much on her own discomfort of being in a man's body she'd forgotten that her experience was nothing like Lin's current one. Her new sister was excited to finally be in a female body and for all that came with it. She cautiously touched Lin's cheek. "It's wonderful." She went to ruffle his—her hair, only to find her bald scalp. "Are you going to grow your hair out?"

Lin bounced with excitement. "Do you think the Monks will let me? I was hoping for some really long anime hair. Maybe purple? Or blue! What do you think?"

"As soon as this is all over, I'll buy you a wig." She felt herself laughing at her sister's joy. "And this body is a much better choice than your last one." She eyed her sibling. "Way to pick a body, lil' sis. Trigger, the hit-man? I mean really, wasn't there anything else in stock?"

She waved her hands excitedly. "Oh my God, I haven't told you the best part! Guess who I got a phone call from in that body?"

She frowned. "Who?"

"Head of the Yakuza. No joke."

Her jaw dropped. "What?! What happened?"

"He was thanking me for the package Trigger sent him." She shivered. "Apparently it was somebody's hand."

"Yikes."

"I know, right?" She hesitated for a moment. "So, I can't believe the little dude you were in is the body Jax would give you. I mean, he's creepy and everything, but I wouldn't have guessed—"

"Wait, how did you know Jax gave me a body?"

Lin gave her a look that was somewhere between 'duh' and 'I'm not an idiot.' "Cause you're a cop and I really don't think any of the black market body shops would be too happy to see you? Also, you mentioned earlier your obnoxious CLM boyfriend has your body so... Logic."

She leaned back in surprise. "You think Jax is obnoxious? Why haven't you ever said anything?"

She stared in disbelief. "Because he's your boyfriend and he already hates my guts?"

"He doesn't hate—"

"You know what, it doesn't matter what he feels about me. What matters is how you feel about him and you know what?" She leaned forward, poking Naomi's shoulder. "You don't like him that much."

It was her turn to stare in disbelief.

Lin leaned back, triumphant. "Yep. You're only ever speechless when you know I'm right."

She punched her sister's leg playfully "When was the last time we hung out?"

"Your marathon race three weeks ago. Post run brunches are

the best."

The memory resurfaced of him near the finish line. Like he usually was, actually. "That's right."

"Oh, and you know who isn't normally there for your races? Your good for nothing boyfriend." She cracked her knuckles with a cackle. "I may be a fuckup but I still managed to make it, including post Switch."

She opened her mouth to draw breath and gave a soft 'huh' in surprise instead.

When their eyes met, Tyler looked positively pleased with him—herself. "Best Sister Ever Award can be handed over at any time." There was fear and vulnerability in Lin's eyes at the words. Naomi knew she couldn't imagine how hard it was for Tyler to become Lin, let alone how hard it had been for her as Tyler for so many years; especially considering she, Lin's sister, had had no idea what was going on. All the more reason Naomi needed to redouble her efforts to be supportive now that she knew.Naomi reached over to touch Lin's shoulder, holding her gaze meaningfully. "You are the best sister a girl could ask for."

There was tension as the words lingered in the air, vulnerability in Lin's eyes.

She punched her sister's leg again. "When you grow your hair out, I want first dibs on braiding it."

Lin's words were barely a whisper. "I'd love that."

Naomi had a lot of ground to make up for. But this was a start. She decided maybe she should give Lin a moment to recover. "So this is now my third borrowed body. Jax gave me a model that was pretty much all guns. Then there was nugget body builder and now this."

Their hands clasped, her sister's smile softening. "You totally body jumped. You, Noams. You're like the most strait-laced of all the strait-laced kids and now you're a bit of a baddie. It's so wicked cool."

Despite how she wanted to laugh, her eyes were moving over sister's face. "You're my family. I'd do anything for you."

"I know." Her face sobered. "That's why I left." Her head shook slowly. "I didn't want to destroy you too."

Naomi's eyes burned All the pain and misunderstandings between them seemed inconsequential now. She hadn't really believed it could end like this. She had to clear her throat to be able to speak and changed the subject to keep from crying. "Well, I wish you'd just told me that Baozhai figured out you'd stolen the drugs—"

"I didn't steal the drugs!"

Her face must have betrayed her because Lin shot to her feet. "You don't believe me!"

She stood, holding her hands palms out toward her. "Wait, listen—"

"No, *you* listen! I may be a lot of things and I'll take responsibility for them." Lin ticked things off on her hand. "I'm a drug addict. I drank too much. I was one of Baozhai's drug mules. I haven't been able to manage a relationship since Veronica because I'm numb to the world and I've abused you—the only one willing to bail me out of trouble." She pointed a finger down at the ground. "But I did not steal those drugs."

A tense silence lingered until Dane's voice broke it. "Everything okay?"

She hadn't seen him come near. When she reached for Ty—Lin drew her hands up in a gesture of peace. "It's fine, everything's fine." She began shivering violently and when Naomi reached for her sister again, Lin stepped back. "I'm fine. I just need to lie down. But let me show you to your rooms first." She turned and

Naomi had to take a deep breath to steady herself. Dane's hand on her shoulder helped her refocus and they followed Lin along the simple dirt path to one of the back buildings.

Lin led them up the few steps to the covered walkway that ran along the outside of the building. They exchanged their shoes for slippers before heading around the walkway to the side of the building and Lin slid open two shoji screen doors, the interior rooms small but large enough to house a futon and blankets atop the tatami mat floors. Beside each of the doors was a pair of matching trays, bowls of covered food waiting for them. Lin motioned to her right. "If you follow the walkway you'll find the bathroom. And you'll want to get to bed soon." When Naomi glanced at the sun that was beginning to set, her sister gave a chuckle. "Yeah, they wake you stupid early in the morning with their chanting. Buddhists."

Naomi felt her throat constrict as she tentatively held her arms up, silently asking if she wanted a hug. That her sister accepted helped to calm her nerves. They swayed in silence for a moment before they separated, and Lin gave a weak smile. "Goodnight."She and Dane replied with the same before her sister was heading around the corner and out of sight. She stared at where she'd disappeared and let out a long breath.

"Big sister doesn't know what to do with herself now that she's not needed." Dane was seated on the walkway, having pulled one of the food trays next to him.

"It's a new sensation." She decided to follow suit, sitting on the polished wooden floor and letting her leg hang over the edge. The tray had several covered bowls and she discovered rice, vegetables, fish, and a few unidentifiable items.

When she began fumbling with the chopsticks, he set his down to reach over to her. "Here, like this." His hands were gentle as he helped her hold the pair of sticks properly. "Now the real trick is to use them like a shovel."

"Here I thought it was magic."

"It is, in its own way." The way his fingers grazed hers had her heart skipping a beat. Her thoughts returned to her sister's comments about how she didn't like Jax all that much. She had to admit she'd never felt anything close to the electricity with Jax that she felt with Dane. He turned to rest his back against the partition that separated their rooms, his bowl of rice topped with several vegetables. "I'm glad you've found your sibling."

"We found him—her." She was trying to pluck a red ball of something up, to no avail. "You're the reason she found Aung and is safe right now." She dropped the ball again, feeling guilt burning her insides. "And finally in the right body for her."

Dane's voice was gentle. "First person close to you who's transitioned?"

"I had a friend in college, but..." It wasn't the same.

He nodded understandingly. "Watching it happen is wonderful and exhausting. They have to do so much self-exploration and figuring out where they want to land. It causes a lot of heartache until they can finally be themselves."

"She seems the same as the brother I knew and yet..." Naomi thought of the way Lin smiled now. "So much lighter." Her nose scrunched. "I don't want to screw this up."

"You'll probably end up misusing pronouns when you aren't thinking about it. Brains are lazy and aren't great with change. You're most likely to end up using her old name when you're doing a direct address. You should ask her what she would prefer when referring to the past. Some people honor their ability to be their authentic selves by using their preferred name and pronouns for the past. While some people honor their change by using their old name and pronouns in memory. Everyone is unique. See what your sister wants."

She felt a bit sick to her stomach, thinking about how she would undoubtedly hurt her sister's feelings. "I've already done so much wrong though. How do I start this off, in the right way?"

Dane was thoughtful for a long moment. "Maybe you could start by thinking of all the things you would want to do with a sister."

She found that brought an unexpected smile to her lips. Even as a little girl she'd always known her mother wasn't going to have more children. The thought of having a younger sister... "Maybe I could take Lin shopping?" Her eyes burned, remembering how much it had meant to her that her mother had taken her bra shopping. Maybe she could do the same thing for Lin?

While Dane returned to eating, she continued to struggle. He eyed her playfully. "Body didn't come preloaded with chopstick software?" When she glared at him, he smirked. "You want some help?"

She sighed. "Yes, please."

Deftly, his chopsticks captured one of the small red things— what she assumed was a fruit—and offered it to her lips. She met his eyes and their gazes held for a tense moment. When she finally could bear it no longer, she took in a breath and he carefully placed the item between her parted lips. As her mouth closed, he drew his chopsticks away and she felt a hint lightheaded.

Which was when sourness beyond description hit her like a wave and cascaded down her throat. She was coughing it was so potent. "What the hell was that?"

He was obviously enjoying himself. "Umeboshi. Pickled ume fruits, from Japan, though people tend to translate it as 'salt plums.'" Perhaps to mock her, he plucked one off his tray and

[190]

popped it into his mouth, biting it with abandon. "A great hang-over cure."

It took two tries to be able to swallow past the puckering of her throat. "You know what? Let's talk about you for a change. Since when do you know so much about everything Asian?"

"I lived there for a while. Southeast Asia to be specific, though I traveled a lot. Bounties don't exactly stay in one place. I always found the cultures to be very interesting, though the purpose-ful blend of China and Japan the Monkhood has accomplished here is quite interesting. Japan was probably closest to my heart though. I'd forgotten how much until seeing this place."

She was managing to shovel some food into her mouth. "Why'd you like Japan?"

"Well, for one it's a culture of introverted nerds where polite-ness is demanded by society, and you're publicly shamed for be-ing a jerk."

That did sound pretty appealing. "And?"

"I guess Asia has had a lot longer than we have to get used to living a simultaneously ancient and advanced life." He rested his half-eaten bowl of rice in his lap. "You can walk down a street and see an image screen and then a seven-hundred-year-old tem-ple. There are vending machines on the outskirts of ancient bam-boo forests. It isn't nature versus technology. It's both, together. In harmony instead of adversity."

His bionic hands were cradling his bowl of rice. She was so used to seeing the silver color of them, it hardly even occurred to her anymore they weren't human. In the beginning the sight of him had been so jarring—when had that changed?

"How did you get into bounty hunting?"

"Well, it was either bounty hunting or be a linebacker. But I don't take orders well and I like guns, so bounty hunting won out." He gave a half shrug. "I actually went to college and got a degree in security and emergency management. I did a lot of mixed martial arts there too, so it made sense. What about your style? I saw some of your moves as we've been fighting and not to mention at the starting line for the race. Or do you just do that to intimidate your competition?"

"It's a dynamic warm up, which is better before running. It's a karate and Kung Fu mixed style. I always knew I wanted to be a cop even when I was a little, so I made my mom put me into karate when I was seven or eight."

"It looks good on you."

As she set her bowl aside and turned to him, she found herself at a loss. "You aren't what I expected."

"I was thinking the same thing."

Their gazes held and then he took in a breath. "Lin's right."

She blinked. "About what?"

"Those monks are going to wake us up well before the ass crack of dawn. And if you think you can sleep through the chanting, you'd be wrong."

"When have you been around monks?"

"Oh, I stayed in a monastery for a while." He drew himself to standing. "Not as a monk, just in one where guests can stay. My room was right next to the meditation hall. For the record, never, ever let a cute little Asian grandmother convince you that the room next to the meditation hall is great. Lies."

She was on her feet and shaking her head. "You have a lot of stories, don't you?"

"I can safely say no one has ever accused me of being boring." Silence lingered before he lowered his voice. "I'm glad your sister is okay."

Her arms were around him before even she realized what she

was doing. "Thank you. She's all the family I have left."

Dane's arms slipped around her carefully. "You're welcome."

As katydids announced the approach of twilight, their embrace lingered. She was reluctant to move from the warmth of his body but when she finally did, their eyes met and they were closer than they should be. The lack of distance only made it harder to retreat and the feel of his breath highlighted their nearness.

She was leaning up toward him when he shifted away, clearing his throat. "So the futon may be less thick than you're used to but they're surprisingly comfortable. I hope you sleep well."

She blinked a few times in surprise. "Thank you. You too."

"Goodnight. Sweet dreams." He turned and slid the shoji screen door closed behind him, leaving her standing there alone.

CHAPTER 14

Aung

Crickets chirruped merrily in the background as the moon splashed light around the rock garden. His eyes were focused on the pond before him, the koi content to swim in circles. Some of their red and white bodies were thicker around than his forearm, and their long whiskers trailed behind them as they meandered. The hills and valleys of the raked sand glowed in the moonlight. The rock beneath his shins was still warm and when he caught his thoughts drifting to the ache in them, he let the thought float away and returned to his breath.

One. Two. Three.

When he heard a board creak he held his breath, waiting. There was the slight sound of another step, soft and hesitant. The tension drained out of his shoulders and he returned to his breathing, beginning again.

One. Two.

He heard the rustle of her clothes as she settled into position beside him and slowly, her breath fell into rhythm with his own.

Three. Four.

They shared the music of the crickets, the playful circles of the koi, and the caress of the wind upon their faces.

When the time was right, he reached down for the small wooden stick and gently struck the small bell three times to chime that meditation was at an end. He set down the stick and twisted to her, holding his good hand up, palm facing her. "Could you help me?"

Her eyes narrowed in curiosity and Aung gave a grin. "I have to clap, it's tradition. But if I do, Sifu will be upset because I could hurt my arm."

She smiled in understanding and her hand clapped his before they both twisted forward once more. He drew his hands together and bowed his head, as she did the same.

He was the first to stand and she groaned, before she began rubbing her legs. "How long were we meditating for?"

His eyes glanced at the moon. "Maybe half an hour. I'm not surprised you ache. Your mind and body must be conditioned before sitting in meditation for long periods." He hopped off the rock, landing amidst the carefully tended sand. When Naomi gasped, he chuckled. "Come now, haven't you always wanted to destroy the lines? Doesn't all that perfection just make you want to play in the sand like a child?"

A dubious brow rose. "Is this a trick question?"

In response, he swept his foot around him in a wide circle. He carefully placed a half circle below his two footprints and then jumped above his creation, motioning with his arms. "The sand is happy to see you!" Naomi's eyes moved between him and his sand smiley face slowly. He gave a nod. "Now you try. I insist."

There was a long pause before her foot landed hesitantly in the sand. She stepped down and barely moved, like she was afraid of committing sacrilege. "But the garden is so beautiful."

"Have you ever seen a mandala?"

"It's the colored sand thing, isn't it?"

"Yes." He pointed at the sand to her left. "Play there while I explain it to you."

"Play?" Her face was dubious. "Like do what?"

"Draw a picture. I'd like to see an animal."

"Pretty bossy for a monk, aren't you?" Her brow was furrowed and only when he began emphatically pointing at the sand did she finally budge. She slowly knelt down and began awkwardly moving her hand in the sand. He moved behind her, watching. "There are more universal truths than most humans would like to believe. The problem is that most truths can seem very inconvenient, and people spend a great deal of their time trying to deny them, instead of embracing them."

She glanced over her shoulder at him, skeptically. "How did we go from explaining a mandala to pontificating about universal truths?"

He pointed at the sand. "Keep playing."

Her mouth scrunched to the side as she turned back to the sand, quickly wiping away what she'd already done. He knelt in the sand beside her, watching her try again. After a few quick strokes she was about to wipe it away when he stopped her hand. Her eyes met his and he bowed his head slightly. "Silence your inner critic. Let yourself be like a child and enjoy without judgment."

Their gazes held for a long moment before she turned back to the sand, running her fingers through it slowly. When a hint of a smile finally touched her lips, Aung couldn't help but wonder when the last time was she'd let herself play.

"The complexity of the mandala and the number of monks who work on it dictates how long it takes to complete. Most take at least days, others can take a week or more. It's a beautiful process. We create an outline and then add each layer of colored sand very carefully. It takes years to become proficient and even then there are levels of mastery."

"What level are you?"

"Epic grand master supreme. Obviously." He grinned playfully, shaking his head before he continued. "When the mandala is complete, we have a ceremony to celebrate the beautiful creation. Then we pour the sand into a container and go to the nearest body of running water—"

"Wait, what?! You do all that work and then you—"

"Destroy it?" He smiled. "Yes."

She sat back on her heels, staring at him. "But… Why?"

His eyes turned to the sand before her. She'd drawn the crude outline of a rabbit, whiskers askew and ears floppy. He motioned to the drawing. "Would keeping this intact, exactly as it is now, make the experience of creation more valuable to you? Does clinging to things like youth, beauty, or perfection make people truly happy? Or does it just distract people from their fears?"

Her eyes fell in thought. He continued. "People spend most of their lives trying to deny the single most honest and eternal fact of life. Can you guess it?"

Her eyes lifted to his. "That everything changes?"

"Yes. But go deeper."

There was a thoughtful pause. "Well, that everything ends."

"If you really think about it, that everything ends is the very essence of change. This is the heart of the Principle of Impermanence. Rather than be frightened by change and death, we embrace it as the natural order of life. While others try to deny this fact, we Buddhists meditate on mortality."

"You meditate on death? That's so… morbid."

Aung held out his hand eight inches above the ground. "Imagine a little dog, about this big. He likes to bite your ankles and you ignore him, hoping that he will stop. All day, all night, he tries to bite you. You continue to ignore him but what do you think would happen if you could never sleep because he is always there, nipping at you?"

"I'd be exhausted. That sounds terrible."

"It is, but so many people do just that. This dog is your fears and ignoring him will not make him go away."

"But what can you do?"

He smiled, pantomiming bringing the dog into his lap. "Face the dog. Accept the dog. Instead of ignoring your fears, take them along with you on your journey. You will have energy to expend on enjoying your life rather than trying to hide for fear of the simple truth that it will end one day. Contemplating death isn't morbid; it makes you live each moment to the fullest."

Her brows rose as she turned to look down at her sand rabbit. "There's more to life than living in the moment."

"You misunderstand me. I am not talking about drunken revelry or debauchery, though those too can have their moments."

She gave him a sideways glance "Since when do you drink?"

"I was not always as pious as I am now." He cleared his throat. "Living in the moment is how we can truly appreciate life. Too often, we are lost inside our heads, time traveling. We think about the things in our past that dissatisfy us and the things in our future that may never come to be. We so rarely are in the present moment. But if you can be in the moment while being in love, you are living. If you can be in the moment while ironing, you are living."

Her eyes met his and he picked up a handful of sand, letting it slip through his fingers slowly. "Life is not about days but about the moments we live in those days. If you live more of your moments fully, authentically, and passionately, then you will be left with a life that has more meaning when you get to the end." He opened his hand as the last grains of sand slipped away and there was a small mountain of sand beneath.

A long moment of silence settled over them before she reached out toward the sand rabbit. He stopped her hand and she looked at him quizzically. "After all that, aren't I supposed to let it go?"

"Yes, but you must honor it first."

"Buddhists." She sat back, crossing her arms over her chest. "Thanks for being a mutated version of a rabbit."

"What did Mr. Rabbit teach you?"

"What? Nothing."

"Come now."

She sighed dramatically and rolled her eyes again. "Fine. I learned about impermanence."

"No, what did you learn from Mr. Rabbit."

"I learned…" Her hands fell to her lap and she began inter-weaving her fingers slowly, her eyes falling. "I learned that when I think of childhood, I always think of my —of Lin and I, playing when we were little. And…" Her eyes rose to look at the sand. "And whenever I think of an animal, I always think of a rabbit because of the rock bunny she made me." There was a pause before she spoke, and her voice was catching. "And I wish I could go back to those days of being her older sister, because I'm scared I'll always have to act like a mom."

Aung put his good arm around her and she sniffled, wiping at her eyes. He spoke gently. "You've been hiding from your fears for a very long time."

She took in a shaky breath, reaching out to run her hand through the image of the rabbit. "Thinking of my fears as a little dog I can hug somehow makes them less terrifying."

"It will take time but you are on the path now. Embracing your fears takes away their power. Don't forget that."

Her lips were finally smiling. "I don't know how you monks do it. You don't seem real with all your wisdom and not to mention all the kung fu."

"An excellent idea, Naomi! We shall lift your spirits with an experiment in martial arts mindfulness." He stood quickly, motioning for her to stand as well.

"Is giving up contractions part of enlightenment, as well? Because you talk like a fortune cookie."

A grin was his only response. At the edge of the garden was a bamboo pole with an apple waiting atop it. "I'd been planning to do this after my meditation anyway."

The top of the pole came to Naomi's solar plexus and she eyed him dubiously. "You work up an appetite while meditating?"

He chuckled and took a step back. "Do a spinning wheel kick and aim for the apple. If your attention wavers even in the slightest while performing the move, you could underestimate and hit the pole. And in the spirit of full disclosure, that hurts. Immensely."

There was a look of concern on her face. "I don't know if this is such a good idea."

He waved a hand. "It's brilliant, let's try. The worst that can happen is you need another new body."

She eyed him. "You should be a comedian, you're hilarious."

He grinned. "I often tell the other monks that as well!"

When she groaned her eyes he chuckled, waiting for her to ready herself. After a moment she took a stance before the pole, her right leg farther back and her hips twisted so her back was angled toward him. She took several deep breaths, and he could see the moment that her focus heightened and her muscles tensed in commitment to the motion. As she spun, her back leg whipped up and around, rising and then narrowly missing the pole before it connected with the apple. He snatched the apple out of the air and gave a cheer. "Nice execution! Now, if you lean forward on the launch and twist your hips further so your back is more toward the post, it will let your leg mechanics do more of the work. You'll find you have more power."

She tilted her head thoughtfully. "You know, I think that's what my grand master has been trying to say for years but I never really understood it. Could you demonstrate? Spinning kicks have always been my nemeses."

He hesitated and rested the apple on the top of the pole. "Can I tell you a secret?"

"Of course."

He set up before the pole, his stance wide and his back angled toward the pole. His arms were in guard position but he let them hang loosely. "There are several versions of how Shaolin monks came to know martial arts. But my favorite is that there was once a monastery filled with decadent monks who lazed about all day, accomplishing nothing and living off the kindness of the people. A Buddhist from India came and was appalled at the state of things. He forced all the monks into a training regime in order to reform their bodies and minds into worthy vessels for the Buddha's message."

"Really? Wait, but what's the secret?"

"Well, it's a two-fold secret, really. First, I rather like the idea I come from a lineage of monks who were indolent and appalling. Because if those torpid miscreants could be successful, anyone can."

She laughed. "What's the second part?"

"Oh, well in honor of that, whenever I do this…" He focused on drawing in a breath, twisting his hips and carefully leaning. He waited until the very last moment to pull his leg up, letting it explode with power as it connected with the apple. The fruit disintegrated instantly and the spray of apple shrapnel floated in the air before descending into the nearby bushes.

He stood with a grin. "I always secretly call it lazy bastard's applesauce."

CHAPTER 15

Dane

"Dane? Are you awake?"

Her voice through the rice paper door barely qualified as a whisper; it was hardly even a breath. He could tell she was being careful so it would only reach him if he were already awake. Of course he hadn't been able to fall asleep, not after she'd nearly kissed him. It'd taken all his strength to walk away and he'd been the most surprised of anyone to find his morality that unshakable. But he wasn't sure he was up for testing it again in the middle of the—

The floorboards creaked and he saw her silhouette go from crouching to standing.

He bolted up in his futon. "Naomi?" He was such a weakling. But then, he argued with himself that he didn't technically know for certain it was her; it's not like he knew her new voice yet so—

"Did I wake you?"

He knelt on his futon and reached over to slide the shoji screen door aside. "No, I was awake."

She was seated on the covered walkway now, her leg hanging off the edge into the garden and the other drawn beneath her. Her face was more relaxed than he'd ever seen her, in any body. He carefully crawled out onto the walkway with her, the crisp night air a shock to his skin. Before reached back to grab the duvet before closing the door. "I forgot how much colder it gets at

[203]

night in the country."

Her eyes were looking off at the moon above the trees. "There's no concrete to store the heat. This is more natural, I think." Even with her features being a different ethnicity, the look of intensity on her face was still the same.

"Why are you still up?"

"Aung." She gave a strange laugh. "He's mad and inspiring and…" She shrugged. "And…"

He waited for a long moment to see if she would continue. "And?"

"And I'm going to adopt a rabbit when I get home." She shook her head before staring down into her lap. "I realized how much of my life I haven't really been present for. I've been sacrificing and pushing through, waiting for the payoff at the end of the rainbow." A hand went over her eyes. "But I see now, I've been missing out on everything. There is no payoff and I was just going to end up wondering where all the time went." She let out a long breath and stared out at the garden again. "I did the body transferring because I wanted to find my sibling. But maybe what I really needed to find was myself."

He rubbed his hand over her back slowly, watching the intensity of her features. "You're being too hard on yourself. We're all trying to find ourselves and anyone who says they know themselves is a probably trying to sell you a self-help product." When she laughed he caught himself wanting to kiss her and drew his hand back with a sigh. It figured he would fall for an amazing— and engaged—woman.

She eyed him. "What's wrong?"

"Nothing."

"Dane."

He shook his head. "Don't think you can use your cop voice

on me."

Her voice softened. "I'm off duty."

His eyes moved over her face. "Cops and bounty hunters are never off duty." And her smile at his words was almost too much. When the tension became unbearable, he forced his eyes away. Her head rested against his shoulder but he didn't look. Instead, he moved his arm to put the blanket around her as well and she sidled up to him. Against his better judgment his arm settled around her. He closed his eyes and tried not to read too much into it.

He caught himself wondering what her real body would feel like against him. He knew thinking like that was stupid. It wasn't enough that her legs in her body were spectacular but seeing her martial arts-ing with them could possibly be the death of him. Not to mention if she started talking about guns or if he started thinking about how she'd nearly kissed him earlier or—

Fuck it all. Why did she have to be engaged? And to Jackson-I'm-an-entitled-self-absorbed-rich-sochiopath-Raelyn no less?

"So how did you become a bounty hunter?"

Hallelujah, a distraction. "Eh, it was either—"

"'Bounty hunting or be a linebacker?'"

He loved that she had such a great bullshit-o-meter.

Her fingertip tapped his metal quad. "Yeah, you used that line already today so try again."

Did she also have to be funny, in a saucy minx sort of way?

He was so unaccustomed to getting close to people he didn't know whether or not he wanted to proceed, let alone how. He was used to the closest person in his life being Leon. And Leon, well... even when they did talk, Leon didn't exactly poke and prod in the emotion department.

Probably why they got along so well, come to think of it.

In the silence, her fingertips were running along his quad, from his metal knee to the hem of his shorts. "What I really don't get about you is that you're a contradiction."

He rested his head against hers, staring into the garden. "No, I'm not. If anything I'm too blunt and honest."

"Exactly, you shouldn't have contradictions. So why is it you say that your body is a temple—and you actually treat it like one in that you exercise it and feed it well—yet you've lost a lot of it. How exactly did that happen?"

He tried not to sigh loudly. She was such a cop. "That ties into the 'how I became a bounty hunter' question."

It was a moment before she spoke again. "I'm sorry, I didn't mean to get too personal. I'm like a bloodhound with mysteries—" Her hand was moving off his thigh and he grabbed it with his free hand before he thought better of it.

He looked at her human hand lying within his metal one. "My bionic parts aren't the only things I've had replaced." He closed his eyes. "My lungs aren't my own either."

Even without seeing her face, he could sense her confusion. "Artificial lungs aren't that—"

"Not artificial. They're someone else's." The silence lingered and he lowered his voice, realizing he should start from the beginning. "I was born with a genetic defect where my lungs weren't growing right. The older I got, the weaker I got. My mom was a nurse and a single parent, but it worked out since I spent a lot of time in the hospital. It basically came down to the fact that I needed new lungs before puberty or I wasn't going to make it. I was wearing size twelve or thirteen shoes at that point, so it was obvious I was going to go through one hell of a growth spurt, but no one knew when. It also put the doctors in a bind because they couldn't put artificial lungs in me for the same reason. If they put in a size that would fit then, I could still die from them being too small before they could get me a larger pair. And that aside, the operation is hell and you're lucky if you survive it once. You'd need the devil's luck to survive it twice."

She let out a breath. "So what happened?"

He ran his thumb along her knuckles. "A healthy boy about my age died in an accident and my name was highest on the list. I was rushed to the hospital and had the operation. Which is actually how I lost my right hand."

She straightened and turned to him. "What?! Why would you lose your hand if they're replacing your lungs?"

He grunted. "Yeah, that was my first question when I woke up too. Well. First one I wrote down since I had a ventilator down my throat." He nearly flinched at the pity he thought he saw in her widening eyes. "Look, for the record, this isn't a sob story or anything. It's just that it freaks most people out. People can handle mechanical parts. Tell them you've got someone else's lungs and they think you're Frankenstein's monster."

The way her face softened assuaged any subconscious fears he had that she'd look at him precisely that way. "Since we're putting things on the record, I would totally take a new foot and calf in my body if someone would donate one."

"Oh, don't get me started on how much I wish that were a possibility. I'd totally patchwork myself up if I could get new limbs. I love my bionic parts, but I at least wish I could get back the arm I lost during surgery." At her glance her felt the need to lighten the tension. "And with more organic parts I could eat more cookies in a day." At her snicker, he lifted his arm that had previously been around her shoulders. "Also, for the record, my side is mostly skin and it's getting pretty cold without you against it."

He enjoyed the hint of surprise and pleasure she tried to hide.

"Well, we can't let that happen." When she was resting against his side this time though, her arm went around his waist and her fingertips slipped beneath his shirt, to slowly caress his bare flesh. His head felt as if it were swimming.

"You were explaining how in the world a double lung transplant cost you a hand."

"Ah, yes." But how was he supposed to focus with her touching him? "Well, for the operation they hook you up to a machine that keeps you alive. Since its priority is lift support, circulating blood to all appendages isn't. The actual operation is like half a day and basically, some of my fingers had cellular death. Which spread to my hand." He shrugged gently and she reached up to touch his right hand on her shoulder. "I was in the hospital for six months just to recover from the surgery. I felt like I was going insane. I could barely get out of bed for the first two months. So, since I had a lot of time to think and after I got over all the self-pity—which I hate to admit took quite a while—I decided on things I wanted to do in life."

"Such as?"

"Before I'd gotten my new lungs, I'd been really freaked out by the idea of them. After I started rehab I was able to breathe for what felt like the first time in my life. And I guess a part of me was really glad that the boy who donated them was able to live on in me. I decided I'd take care of my body, no matter what, in honor of him. I was without a doubt the most health-conscious teenage boy that has ever existed. Though, a part of me does lament that I didn't spend my highest metabolic days eating milkshakes and cheeseburgers."

She snickered. "When did your growth spurt happen?"

"A year or a year and a half after I got out of rehab. Which also plays a part in why I'm a bounty hunter."

"What, why?"

"Because I got the shit beat out of me. Constantly."

She went to move and he gave a melodramatic mock sigh. "My side could freeze and it would be absolutely tragic if I got frostbite and lost it."

She settled more closely against him. "Here I thought you said this wasn't a sob story?"

He was glad she was close. "I got beat up because I was scrawny and weak. But mostly because of the damn hook they gave me instead of a hand."

"A hook?!"

"Yeah. Apparently, insurance wouldn't spring for bionic anything for a minor who was still growing so…" He rolled his eyes. "I got a fucking hook for a hand. And—this may come as a shock to you—I had enough pride to prefer being called Captain Hook over any variation of Stumpy. So, I got the shit beaten out of me regularly a bunch of times until I sprouted as predicted. That aligned with me figuring out how to use my hook in a fight and I started beating the shit out of all the bullies. Which, I'm not going to lie, has been an addiction ever since."

There was a long pause and her words were as much a statement as a question.

"You're the reason that Leon's developing Project Fùhuó."

"You're so fucking sexy." He definitely should not have said that aloud and he saw her lips parting so he spoke quickly. "And by that, I mean yes." He cleared his throat. "Since I'm on antiretroviral drugs and will be—"

"When do you take them?"

"Every day." He headed off her next question. "Leon made me an internal dispersal system where I put in a months worth of drugs and it gives them to me at intervals. Way easier method to deal with the dozen prescriptions I take."

"You'll be on those for the rest of your life?"

"Yes, which is the only reason I could be eligible for a body part transplant. They already know my body will accept new human parts and that I don't have reactions with the drugs." He sighed. "Except, to get a new arm, I'd have to go back on that good for nothing life support machine."

She squeezed his hand in understanding. "And they don't think you'd live through it."

"Nope." He ran his thumb over her knuckle, staring at their hands. He remembered how despondent he'd been when he'd originally lost his hand but how much better he'd felt about himself ever since he'd gotten his first implant. But he particularly loved that, in that moment, he could feel her. "And that, in summary, is why the medical community so readily embraced bionics and why technology for transplants hasn't advanced much in the last hundred years. In bionics' defense though, I have to admit I do like all the compartments for storing things."

"Right! I love not having to carry a purse in order to have my gun."

She was unfairly sexy.

He coughed to cover. "So how did you come to terms with being disabled?"

"I'm not disabled."

"You aren't hiding your leg." He drew back enough to take in her quizzical expression. "You could have opted to get it covered. But you're choosing to be visibly disabled."

"I've never thought of it that way. I always just felt that since my bionic leg worked, I was all better." Her lips pressed together, thoughtfully. "What's it like for you being invisibly disabled?" At his lack of an answer, she scoffed. "What? You've chosen a career that makes it seem as if all this—" She gestured to his limbs. "Was on purpose."

"That's a fair point." He stared off. "I suppose it's easier now that I don't have to remember to take pills every few hours. Constantly staring down the pills that are keeping you alive takes its toll." When he heard her drawing breath, he interrupted before she could say anything. "Don't be an ableist prick and say I'm not disabled or that I should change bodies. I am who I am because of my body, not in spite of its... quirks."

Her voice was gentle. "I was going to say I'm not sure disabled is the right label for me."

He gave a quiet grunt. "Spoken like someone with an accidental disability."

At her questioning gaze, he stared off. "I'm not like you. You had a before and an after—" He cut his hand through the air. "A moment where normalcy was lost, where everything changed." He motioned to his chest. "Everything about me that makes me disabled is a part of me, at a genetic level. It wasn't something that happened to me; it is me." He let out a slow breath. "Sure, my life can be made easier with bionics and tech, but my disability can't be 'fixed' with an 'upgrade.' Which also means, it's always been a part of me and always will be." The derision in his voice made him sigh; he didn't like being on that particular soap box. "At least the rare disease community is supportive."

"I didn't mean to be ableist, but I'm sorry that I was." She paused. "I guess I've honestly never thought of myself as disabled."

"Bionics are ubiquitous; the definition of disability has gotten a little murky. And there are levels of disability and they're fluid, you know?" He glanced at her. "Like some days are harder than others physically or emotionally. Sometimes years." He felt a heaviness in his chest, remembering the times when even breathing was an insurmountable challenge. While he was grateful for his string of good days in recent years, he was wholly aware of the threat that it could change at any moment. But he gave a shrug, only able to move forward and live every day with uncertainty. "My life now is a lot easier than it used to be. Living with someone who is better than most doctors has its perks."

"He seems to take good care of you. How did you and Leon meet?"

"Someone was dumb enough to put a bounty on him. And he was still naïve and he used to shut down socially a lot more"

"Wait, wait, wait. Are you—"

"Saying that he used to be more standoffish than he is now? Yes." A cricket began to serenade them nearby. "But anyway, the bounty hunter forums weren't as well managed as they are now so more than one person could accidentally go after a standard bounty if it didn't update quickly enough. I found Leon at the same time that someone else did. The guy was going to kill Leon, even though the bounty called for him alive. My overly developed sense of justice made me attack the guy, without realizing he had an incendiary bomb on him."

"How did you survive??"

"Leon, of course." He felt the memory of lying there on the ground, his legs having just been blown off. He'd known he was going into shock and Leon had come up to him, not at all perturbed by the blood and gore but simply looking completely flummoxed that someone he didn't know would protect him. Though Dane hadn't understood that until well later. "Leon had said he was going to transfer me and I begged him not to. I think he was really confused but I passed out from the pain and woke up in his laboratory. I'd needed a lot of work and he'd done it all himself. He questioned me about why I would rather die than transfer. And I told him the truth."

Her fingers interlaced with his. "And knowing Leon, he then made it his personal quest to try to reunite you with human body parts."

"Yep. And the saving his life thing is why he hired me as his personal body guard."

"Slash roommate?"

"Slash roommate."

Normally in the warehouse, he could hear the waves of the ocean as he lay in bed. The gentle sound of crickets intermingled with her breathing was far better.

Her voice was soft. "Are you still cold?"

That was a subtle offer if he'd ever heard one. And he wasn't strong enough to deny it. "I mean, I'm probably not going to get frostbite but..."

Her hand unclasped from his and she wrapped both arms around him fully. "Better safe than sorry."

Her head pressed to his chest and he closed his eyes, enveloping her tightly in the blanket.

Incoming call from Inari Hayashi.

Before he could accept or decline, the call connected. *"Where's Naomi and why hasn't she called me since you arrived at the Monkhood?"*

He paused at the sound of Inari's voice, tapping his fingers in the sequence on Naomi's arm to mute. "Uh, so your partner is calling and wants to know why you haven't contacted her."

"Don't mute me, that's rude!"

"Also, she's pissed."

"Shit. Yeah, I forget to call her." Naomi sighed and buried her face against his chest. "Tell her I'm out dancing."

He tapped his fingers. "Naomi said to tell you she's out dancing."

There was a dramatic sigh on the other end. *"Well tell her that Jax knows she's not in the body he gave her anymore and he's worried. Though, I would be more than happy to call him back and tell him you are obviously taking good care of her, seeing as it's three in the morning and you two are awake, sooo—"*

"Whoa, that's okay. Don't tell Jax anything." Lord, he'd actually managed to forget about her good for nothing fiancé for a hot second. "Tell him she's fine. Okay?"

Inari gave a loud sigh. *"Maybe if I tell Jax she was a dude, he'll finally leave her alone. Stupid cockalorum."* There was a pause. *"PS Don't tell her I hate her boyfriend, it's just twattle."* There was a shorter pause. *"So, were you guys actually—"*

"Goodnight, Inari." He tapped the sequence to cut the call. He took in a breath to cover his unease. "She's a good friend. High energy, but dependable."

"That's Inari for you." She paused before giving him a little squeeze. "You've been through a lot. Thank you for sharing."

His brow furrowed. "Don't you even want to know that your fiancé is worried about you?"

She sat bolt upright, eyes narrowing. "Who told you he's my fiancé?"

The alarm in her face and shoulders surprised him. "Uh, Jax did."

Her eyes rolled in a high arc before she stared off. "That shortarse." She took a deep breath and he could see her visibly trying to contain her rage. "For the record, he and I are not engaged."

He felt like his eyebrows might get stuck in surprise mode. "No?"

"NO." She huffed. "We were at dinner on Friday night and I

had opened my mouth to break up with him when he proposed to me."

He cleared his throat, trying to be nonchalant and not like she'd just completely changed the trajectory of his hopes. "What did you say?"

She looked off in the opposite direction. "I thought to myself, 'wow, he's convinced we should get married? Maybe I should rethink this whole breakup thing because maybe it's just me not wanting to commit.' So I asked for time to think about it." Her hands curled into fists. "And then the jerk is putting the ring on my hand anyway and telling me to 'see how it feels.'" She rolled her eyes again. "That act alone has convinced me I was right in wanting to break up with him in the first place. He's such an arrogant prick. I don't even know why I was with him."

"Was the sex good or something?"

"Yeah, like numb below the waist good." She whacked his stomach playfully. "Come on. I hate CLM but I thought he was different." She gave a defeated shrug. "Or maybe I just wanted him to be different. Either way, I spent most of my time either arguing with him or listening to him talk about his company's plastic abominations."

"Bionic Barbies?"

"What?"

He chuckled as he shook his head. "Never mind." He hesitated as he watched her, afraid to get his hopes up. "You're breaking up with him?"

"Absolutely."

Thank God. "Good. So, I won't have any guilt about doing this." He put both his hands on her cheeks and leaned in, pressing his lips hungrily to hers. When her hands pushed him backward, he found himself on his back with her seamlessly transitioning to straddling him without breaking their kiss. The intensity when he could finally touch her was even better than what the sexual tension had promised.

Her hands pulled at his shirt and when their lips parted, her voice was breathless. "Is this just because you have a thing for Asian girls?"

"No, I have a thing for you." He groaned as his hands went beneath her shirt. "I don't even care what body you're in. Hell, you were even pretty sexy as a dude and while I've had some fun, I usually like my sausages to be worn by women."

"You're unbelievable." She kissed the parts of his chest that weren't bionic, sending a powerful shiver down his spine. As her lips trailed down to his stomach she glanced up at him, full of passion. "So, where is your human flesh located?"

He smirked. "Let's get inside so you can find out."

CHAPTER 16

Naomi

It had been a surprise to wake cradled in Dane's arms but a pleasant one for a change. As promised, they'd been awoken at the ass crack of dawn by chanting, though they'd managed to fall back asleep. She'd awoken again a while before but hadn't particularly cared, since lying there beside him was incredibly comfortable and she was using the time to think. There were still so many unanswered questions.

Her eyes caught sight of her pants and out of the pocket poked the corner of the card Aung had given her the day before. She reached out carefully, pulling the thin piece of plastic out and looking at the chip embedded in the surface. What had she gotten herself into?

The movement must have roused Dane as he grumbled, burying his face in her hair. "Good morning."

She carefully slipped the card back into her pocket. "Morning. How did you sleep?"

"Great. You?"

"Really well." She turned onto her back, looking at his face. "Was you thinking Jax was my fiancé really the only thing keeping you away?"

"Oh yeah." He nodded, lifting a hand and making a chopping motion. "The line exists precisely between boyfriend and fiancé. Boyfriend—meh, fair game. Fiancé—going there makes me a home wrecker." He ran a hand back through her hair. "Despite what you may think I do have some morals."

"I'm glad you clarified because I was starting to wonder." He leaned down to kiss her, but when his hand rested on her stomach she took in a breath of realization. "Oh shit."

He drew back. "What's wrong?"

She stared at him. "I don't even know if this body has birth control."

He shrugged. "Eh, there's a black market for that."

"I know about black market babies, I'm not totally—"

"I meant for pregnant bodies." When she stared at him, he continued. "Come on, some guys have philias that make them want to wear diapers. Other dudes want to be a pregnant chick. Body transfer stations make all sorts of fetish dreams come true."

She grimaced. "Honestly, that wasn't something I needed to know."

He eyed her. "You really should get out of the homicide unit every once in a while. And also, maybe not be so quick to judge?"

"Fair." When she sat up, he beat her to standing and offered her a hand. "Though I think I'll stick to the terrible ways that people kill one another. It seems to be less confusing than the rest of it."

"I'm just saying Gravidophilia is sweeping the nation, you should—"

"You don't know when to stop, do you?"

"Not my strong suit, no." He gave an impish grin as he turned away. "I'm sure the monks planned ahead, don't fret." As they went to put their clothes back on her eyes caught on Dane's back. There were metal plates interspersed with skin that was marred with scars.

Despite the fact she knew better she couldn't help but compare him to Jax and the cold perfection of the Apogee model. By all accounts, Jax was textbook gorgeous, even without any enhancements designed for it. The Apogee model was the scientific pinnacle of flawless skin and faultless body proportion; every inch was engineered to be appealing and attractive. Whenever she'd compared herself to any of the CLM models, she'd always felt as if she'd fallen short.

But Dane's imperfections had an unparalleled beauty to them. Every inch of him told a story, of some experience survived or some death narrowly escaped. While he may not have many human parts left, those parts spoke volumes. He could have easily chosen to get a body that wasn't actively trying to kill him, but he loved his body and his bionics, in tandem. While her own leg was sorely missed its absence was a part of her story, too. And even though Jax had spent the past year trying to convince her that everyone on the planet would rather destroy all evidence of imperfection, here was a man who proudly displayed who he was.

It was about time she stopped feeling inferior and started doing the same.

"Thank you, Dane."

He was pulling his shirt over his head. "I've been told I'm great, but I don't really think I need to be thanked."

She punched him in the stomach. "Idiot."

His smile bordered on a proud grin.

After she slid the door to the room open, she froze in place. It took a moment for her to realize it was her sister's new body that was sitting on the covered landing, barely five feet from her. When Lin turned, their eyes met, and she felt her cheeks burn a bright red like they hadn't since she was a teenager.

Dane clapped a hand on Naomi's shoulder as he passed. "Morning Lin. Is the bathroom this way?"

"Yep." She pointed around the corner. "Fourth sliding door. It has a little image of a toilet above it."

"Thanks." He took the corner and there was a beat, before he poked his head back. "Not to be awkward or anything but I may have slept with your sister. Just throwing it out there." As if he knew Naomi wanted to chuck something at him, his head quickly ducked out of sight.

She sat down on the floor beside her sister, legs dangling off the edge as well. There was a long silence before she heard something between a snort and a cough, and then Lin was giving a deep belly laugh. Even with a new body, she still sounded like a jerk. Naomi got her arm around her neck and had her sister in a headlock before she could escape. "Repent!"

She flailed unsuccessfully, though Lin was laughing, and it hardly seemed like she was trying at all. Eventually she leaned against her as she grasped her sides. "You win, you win!"

She released her sister but Lin stayed leaning against her, wrapping her arms around her middle. Naomi's head rested against Lin's and she stared off into the garden. The sun was shining on the fiery leaves of a Japanese maple and gave them a volcanic glow. She held her little sister for a time in silence. She'd missed her.

"You know, Dane is a good guy."

That was probably one of the last things she'd expected Lin to say. "You don't even know him."

She sat up, eyeing her. "Come on, Noams. Of course he's a good guy. He saved that girl at the race."

"So?"

"So?!" She gave Naomi her best 'dumbest sister ever' look. "If you remember, he threw me away in order to do it."

Now she was beginning to feel like the dumbest sister ever.

"And?"

"And I was his bounty, remember? He was literally throwing money away to go save someone he didn't know. To save you, too."

She blushed and immediately looked away with a noncommittal shrug. "It wasn't to save me."

"You're so dense! He had a thing for you. And you were being a total fizgig and flirting with him too."

She hooked some hair behind her ear. "Were you watching or something?"

She chuckled. "Well, yeah. I waited to make sure you were okay and then I went to the meeting place Aung told me about." She gave a shrug. "I guess I should really thank Dane because otherwise I wouldn't have—"

"Hold on. You went with the monks right after the race? What about Sunday?"

There was a pause as she watched her. "I've been here since the race, yeah."

She turned to face her fully. "What about that message you sent me? Early Sunday morning?"

She shook her head. "I never sent you any message."

There was a moment of silence before a crack of thunder and the world around them caught fire.

Aung

A thick silence lingered over the large room.

"Aung, please repeat yourself."

Aung was on his knees, hands resting on his thighs as he held the gaze of the grand master. There were five total on the dais besides the grand master, all in meditation stance with their legs drawn beneath them. While Aung didn't care what the other four thought, he did not want to disappoint Sifu. Even so, there was nothing Aung would change even if he could. "I have given Naomi Gate the Sanctuary protocol."

Silence returned before Master Shen's nasally voice broke it. "How dare you do this without consulting the board for permission—"

The grand master raised a hand and even Master Shen was silenced. Aung had to fight to keep the man's gaze—those brown eyes that usually held such kindness now were unreadable. "Tell me why."

Aung took in a slow breath before he leaned forward, touching his hands to the ground and lowering his forehead in submission. "Sifu, I believe this to be the right course of action—"

"And that was not for you to decide."

Aung grimaced, grateful his head was bowed. "I'm aware."

"Yet, you did it anyway."

"Yes. I did." He did not straighten, too afraid of a reproachful glance.

"Explain yourself."

His heart was beating an unsteady rhythm. "Because—" He sat up to meet Sifu's gaze. He took a deep breath and decided on the simple truth. "Because I believe in her the way you once believed in me."

Their gazes held and Aung swore he saw the man's lip twinge upward. There was the sound of paper ripping and they all turned to look at the screen door, which now held a simple slice through the paper, sunlight pouring through. The sound of beating wings lifted their eyes to a dragonfly hovering above the grandmaster. When the man drew breath to speak, the words were drowned by the crack of an explosion and the concussion sent Aung flying backward through a shoji screen door.

A wave of heat rushed over him first, followed by a loud ringing in his ears. He pushed pieces of wood off himself as he struggled to a seated position and stared in disbelief. In the shape of a perfect circle, a huge piece of the ceiling was gone. There were flames lining the ring of destruction and when his eyes fell to the floor, he saw that most of the floor was now either charred or vaporized. The circle had ended perhaps half a foot in front of where he'd been kneeling.

No, not a circle—a globe. And at the very center had been the dragonfly.

A spybot turned bomb. He swallowed as he stared at where the dais had been moments before. There was nothing but ash left of any of the masters who had been seated there.

Past the ringing in his ears, he could hear more bombs detonating across the compound. The sound of rice paper ripping brought his eyes up to five dragonflies flitting about the room. Aung slowly came to his feet, grimacing as he looked at the now reopened wound on his arm. He grabbed a piece of broken wood just in case and all the dragonflies turned at the same moment, moving together into a crescent formation. Aung held a hand out toward them. "I know someone is listening. You're making a mistake."

The dragonflies continued hovering, and he wondered if that was a good sign or not. "We don't have what you're looking for." When the robotic insects all snapped into a diamond formation, he took that as a less than auspicious sign. "Right." He turned and began running down the hallway, hearing the tiny machines whizzing behind him. At the sound of a pitch increase he leapt into another room, rolling just as the crack of an explosion ignited behind him.

This time he was more prepared for the shock of the impact and used it to his advantage, getting onto his feet and jumping as it hit him. His arms came up to shield him as he flew through two rice paper doors. He crashed to the ground and glanced up, to see there were still four spybots following him.

One of them was dive-bombing him. His hand reacted without thought. He was still clutching the piece of wood when it connected with the dragonfly. There was a pop as the wood snapped but the bot's momentum was reversed. It was heading away from him when he saw the flash of light and felt the rumble in his chest as it exploded. He started to roll away and the concussion soon assisted, rocking him across the dirt. He came to a stop only when he hit a boulder in the Zen garden.

He groaned in pain as he touched his head, feeling the blood before he saw it. The world swayed as he forced his way to his feet, remembering there were still three left.

The remaining three had him surrounded. They were equidistant around him, in a pyramid but back twenty feet. He distantly saw brothers running to assist others, the main building he'd just left a fiery ruin. There was no telling how many more of the flying bombs were on the compound but he was certain that these three needed to be contained.

He was grateful for all the years of martial arts training, especially with group fighting. While these bots weren't humans, he imagined the same rules would apply. When surrounded and outnumbered, the best course was to even the odds. He took in a deep breath and let it out slowly, finding his center. Then he ran straight toward the bot in front of him.

The bot's reaction was to rush at him, which was exactly what he'd hoped for. He let himself slide underneath the bot, his feet burning as the rocks and dirt ripped open his skin. His foot came up to wheel around, connecting with the back of the bot and propelling it forward. As his back hit the ground with a thud, he saw the bot collide with another. They exploded and he was only four feet out of range. Aung felt the force of the blast more than he heard it—he wasn't sure he had ear drums left.

Two down meant there was still one left. He glanced around but didn't see the last one and while he couldn't be sure it wasn't whirring, he didn't feel anything moving in the air. He got to his knees and sat back on his heels in exhaustion. Maybe the explosion had gotten all three, not just two.

When he went to use the rock beside him as leverage to help him stand, he realized just how wrong he was.

The dragonfly sat there, inches away from his hand. Now that he was this close, he could see the mechanical parts glowing a fierce ruby behind the eyes. The clever bot had likely been calculating how to fight him and had learned from the mistakes of the others. When he saw the flash of white, he closed his eyes, knowing there was nothing he could do but accept that his time had come.

Dane

"Watch your three o'clock!" There was a bot making an aerial dive for Pema's head. He'd found the man as the fighting started and they'd been standing their ground in the garden since. With a flick of the wrist, a rock careened through the air and lodged in the dragonfly. Dane jumped at Pema, taking them both over a boulder and into the pond. He felt the blast and opened his eyes to see the flames shooting across the surface of the water above them. They waited until the flames passed before coming back above the surface.

Dane was checking for more bots when he saw Aung on the far side of the garden. Three bots had him surrounded and Dane hurried out of the water. "Aung's over there. He's got three around him and—why is he running straight toward one?!?"

Pema called out as they ran together. "It evens the odds, makes it one against one."

Dane watched the drama unfold almost in slow motion as Aung slid underneath the dragonfly like someone sliding home in baseball. Dane suddenly understood what Pema meant. If Aung tried to escape between two of the bots, they would have both converged on him at the same moment; by going straight at one and facing it head on, it would take the other two double the time to get to him. Even if it made sense geometrically, it was still insane.

Aung's foot flipped up to connect with the bot and Dane realized it was going to hit another bot and ignite. He grabbed Pema and forced them both into a crouch, shielding them with the metal plating on his back. As the tsunami of heat rushed past, he was grateful yet again for his bionic parts saving his ass.

When they looked, he could see that Aung was having trouble getting up. How many of those flying bombs had he taken out by himself? The sight of a dragonfly landing on the rock beside Aung made Dane take in a breath of fear. "It's too close."

Pema was calling out Aung's name. Dane was too busy trying to get the blasted compartment on his arm open to worry about that. If Aung were going to live, there was only one chance. "Come ON!" He whacked his arm and the lid popped open. He took out the cartridge and slid it into his gun, taking aim as Aung finally caught sight of the dragonfly. While Aung's face showed he had resigned himself and a flash came from the dragonfly, Dane defied fate and pulled the trigger.

When the expected blast didn't come, he breathed a sigh of relief. Aung was looking around in confusion and Dane thought it was perhaps the most human he'd ever seemed. Pema ran to Aung and Dane let his eyes scan the surroundings as he tapped his fingers. "Do a heat scan of the area. Then do a motion scan. I want to know how many of those bots are left."

Affirmative. There was a slight pause and Dane started jogging to Aung. *There are no bots remaining.*

"Good riddance." Dane stopped beside Aung and Pema, as Aung found his way to his feet. There was blood oozing from a wound on his head as well as several cuts on his arms and legs. There were brush and heat burns on his arms and right cheek, and it looked as if both his feet were bleeding. It was a marvel the man was upright. "You okay, Aung?"

"WHAT?!"

Pema recoiled from Aung's yell. "I don't think he can hear."

Dane looked between the two. "It's probably only temporary from all the blasts."

He heard a pair of voices calling his name and was about to run to them when a hand stopped him. After turning back, he saw it was a smiling Aung. "Tell Naomi I need to see her." Aung's hearing definitely was not working, as he was still talking far too loudly but no longer yelling. Dane slowly mouthed *'how did you know it was Naomi?'* and the man gave a weak chuckle. "Your eyes showed your affection."

Dane muttered several things he was grateful Aung wasn't able to hear. He turned away to call out to Naomi and her sister. They came at a jog and he was grateful to see they appeared to only be bruised and battered. Fighting against those bots could have been far worse for a pair of unarmed humans without any upgrades. Naomi gave him a once over before her eyes turned to

Aung. "Are you all right?"

Aung gave a chuckle and a nod. "Yes, yes. I'm alive thanks to Dane's jello gun."

Dane chuckled and turned his eyes to the remnants of the spybot, encased in a hunter green substance that actually did hold a remarkable similarity to jello. It was translucent enough the dragonfly was visible—except it was held static in the midst of exploding. The wings were several inches away from the body, which had snapped in half with the force. The explosive material hidden within was immobilized and the power flagged to only a swirl of smoke.

Lin leaned forward. "Zaft! It gives a whole new meaning to jello shots."

Naomi turned to Dane. "How did you do that?"

"Leon's creation. He'll be pleased to know it worked so well, we've only—" There was movement on the far side of the compound. Someone entered one of the buildings and Dane was certain it wasn't a monk—unless they had suddenly started wearing black and carrying guns. "We've got company." He tapped his fingers, pulling up his computer. "Why didn't you tell me there were hostiles around?"

Your search parameters indicated you were only interested in bots.

"I hate you. You know that, don't you?"

You have informed me 367 times.

Few things were worse than computer logic. "How many are there?"

It paused. *There are ninety-seven humans present on this compound.*

Right. The computer couldn't identify which were monks and which weren't. How could he figure it out? "How many have an identification chip?"

Twenty-one, including yourself.

Bingo. He turned to the others. "There are twenty intruders." He tapped his fingers again. "Set proximity alert of ninety feet for any humans with ID chips."

Affirmative.

Someone must have communicated the situation to Aung because he motioned and called out. "There's an escape route in a cave. This way!" He turned and they all rushed after him. They passed into the edge of the forest and Dane was starting to feel relieved when his computer chimed in. *Proximity alert, southwest, two hostiles.*

"There are—"

Proximity alert, northwest, three hostiles.

He cursed and looked at Aung. "How far?"

The man pointed at a cave that was tucked into a hillside. *Proximity alert, north, two hostiles.* That meant they were surrounded on three sides, but they were nearly to the cave. He and Naomi were in the lead, Lin and Pema behind, and Aung lagging.

"Stop!" There were pairs of men on either side of them, guns trained on their group. Four guns and five targets didn't have good survival odds. They were maybe ten feet from the cave's entrance. Dane lifted his hands and saw the others do the same.

Aung glanced over his shoulder at them, his voice quiet for the first time. "They want Sanctuary." His eyes met Naomi's. "They're after you."

Naomi turned her gaze forward and even though her face was virtually expressionless, Dane could still see her fear.

"Naomi Gate, come forward."

Dane saw her hesitate before her foot lifted. But she was too late.

"I'm right here." Lin had already taken three steps forward,

[229]

away from the cave and to the center of the group of men with guns. "Let the others go. It's me you want."

The men holding the guns hesitated, sharing a glance. One took a step forward, holding the gun to the side of Lin's skull. "Prove it."

When Naomi went to move, Dane grabbed her hand to stop her. When their eyes met, there was a battle of wills but he just kept shaking his head as slightly as he could manage. He could see the fear in her eyes, but she eventually turned her eyes back to her sister.

"Naomi Gate, NYPD, badge Alpha Seven Six Six Nine, hire date—"

"Something that's not public information."

Lin shrugged. "I'd tell you my bra size but it's not like it matches this body."

Dane had to admit Lin was doing a good imitation of a snarky Naomi. More soldiers came through the woods, adding to the number. Now that they were closer, he realized they were all bionics, and they seemed too perfect. The one in charge paused for a long moment before he gave a nod. "Let's take them all back to the Tower. He'll know whether you're telling the truth."

The Tower?

It couldn't be.

Aung took a single step forward, his voice loud once more. "Attached to your loved ones, you're stirred up like water."

All the guns trained on him, and Pema took a step forward beside him. "Hating your enemies you burn like fire."

Aung turned in a circle slowly and when he met Dane's glance, he motioned with his eyes into the cave behind them. Dane gave a slight nod before squeezing Naomi's hand and inching backward as Aung made a sweeping gesture with his arms. "In the darkness of confusion, you forget what to adopt and discard."

Pema followed suit and fell to his knees before Lin. "Give up your homeland."

Aung knelt beside him and both monks chanted the last words. "This is the practice of Bodhisattvas."

The soldiers exchanged glances and two of them lowered their guns so they could grab the monks. "Get up, freaks."

He and Naomi had taken enough steps backward that they were at the mouth of the cave. On Naomi's left was an inconspicuous button built into the wall, only visible from this angle. Two of the soldiers turned to them, lifting their guns. "Come on out. It's time for a little ride."

But at the crack like thunder from a jet flying low overhead, everyone turned their eyes skyward. Dark spots in the sky began to grow larger with frightening rapidity. When the thrusters were hit into reverse to slow their descent, it sounded like a pack of wolves were growling. *"The bounty is ours."* A dozen heavily armed bounty hunters hit the ground with thuds.

The threat of the open bounty had finally caught up with the Monkhood. Dane had no idea how many bounty hunters were incoming but it was enough to make even the group that had attacked them nervous.

The sound of gunfire rang out but before Dane could even duck, a thick metal door slammed closed in front of them. The noise of the battle was muted and they were alone, safe behind the protected door sealing in the cave. There was total darkness for a moment before a dull red emergency light switched on. He turned to Naomi, seeing a tear slip down her cheek, her hand still on the button.

She wiped at her cheek and turned away. Beside the button a compartment had opened to expose a stack of money, transit tickets, and a folded map. She cleared her throat as she unfolded it. "It looks like this leads to the train station. We can get back to the city that way."

He was almost afraid to confirm his fears. "Those men, are they—"

"Apogee models? Yes." She stuffed the money into her pocket. "Apparently the beta testing is over."

He put a hand on her shoulder. "They'll be fine."

"They won't be killed. At least because our enemies can't be sure they aren't me. And those bounty hunters won't be able to beat the Apogees." Her eyes met his and they were both thinking of the first body she'd had, and the overwhelming firepower of it. It hadn't even been an Apogee. "We'll be seeing them at the Tower." Now he knew her plan was what he feared; they were heading to the only building anyone referred to as the Tower in New York City.

CLM would be their battleground.

She took the emergency light out of the wall compartment and started down into the darkness.

CHAPTER 17

Naomi

Outside the train's window, the landscape was changing. There were fewer trees and more buildings. The rusty fire escapes in the poorest part of town were perhaps the best barometer of their growing proximity to the city. Her eyes refocused on the reflection of her face in the window. It was the face of a woman she didn't know. There were soft curves around her eyes highlighting Asian heritage but drooping under the weight of despondence. If Naomi had seen a woman looking like this, she would have immediately sat down beside her, taken her hand and asked her what was going on.

Because obviously, something was terribly wrong.

Attached to your loved ones, you're stirred up like water.

She didn't want to think about whether or not her sister was still alive. Closing the door to the cavern had been one of the hardest things she'd ever done. But seeing the swarm of Apogee models—this was no longer just a mission to rescue her sister. This was something bigger than both of them.

Hating your enemies you burn like fire.

But who was their enemy? What did she actually know about their situation? She needed to think her way out of this. It was a case, just like any other. That made her mind stop racing and focus on the evidence she had.

She knew it was someone within CLM—wait, that wasn't entirely accurate. Just because the coding was within a CLM model didn't necessarily mean it had originated there. Maybe it wasn't something as simple as a corporate takeover. She had seen first-hand how efficient the Apogee model was in a firefight. This could be far worse than a corporate take over—someone could be building an army. It could be anyone.

No. She knew better than to speculate. The closest proximity to a crime was the first place to start searching. Everyone in CLM had to be a suspect in her mind until she could prove otherwise. While she didn't enjoy the logic that led her to identify her ex-boyfriend as a prime suspect, she wasn't about to ignore it even though she saw more evidence to exonerate him than to condemn him.

When the train entered a tunnel she glanced over at Dane, a row up and across the aisle. Jax wasn't exactly her ex yet though, was he?

In the darkness of confusion, you forget what to adopt and discard.

Since coming out of the cavern she and Dane hadn't spoken because they hadn't deemed it worth the risk. Better to arrive at the station as two strangers and draw less attention. Her eyes moved over his profile; his eyes were closed, his jaw set. He was resting for whatever lay ahead. He reminded her a little of Aung, in that moment.

Give up your homeland.

Give up your homeland? What did that even *mean*?

She let out a frustrated breath, resting her head back and trying to calm down.

She missed Aung. Something about that crazy monk had helped her to feel less confused and more certain about what she needed to do. Even if she hadn't agreed with him about his plan for releasing Sanctuary and darkening the country, she'd admired it. Now she just felt lost.

What she knew for certain was that she was heading to CLM for a number of reasons: for her sister, for others, and for herself. Now all she really needed was to figure out how she was going to do it. It was obvious they were up against something terrible, and she needed help. Besides Dane, there was only one person whose moral compass she knew could be trusted. Right. Her first step was to contact—

The train lurched and Naomi grabbed the seat in front of her. Dane was still sitting with his head back, his hands clasped over his stomach. His finger was tapping out a beat and she wondered if he were listening to music. Wasn't he being a little too cavalier about the situation? He couldn't actually be asleep, could he?

"Please pardon the interruption. This train will be making an unscheduled stop at the next station. All passengers must exit to the platform. Another train will be along shortly to take you to your final destination. We apologize for the inconvenience."

Naomi sat up straighter so she could look at the other passengers. There were another two in their car, and she saw several heads in the car ahead of them. The train crawled to a halt in the station. Naomi saw the others in their car stand and was on her feet herself before she noticed that Dane hadn't moved. As the other two walked to the platform she was following behind them when Dane spoke. "Don't bother." The doors clamped shut in front of her face and the train shot forward, tossing Naomi ungracefully back into a seat. "This is a trap for us."

She rubbed the back of her head and muttered. "Couldn't you have warned me?"

He tilted his head sideways, opening a single eye. "Where's the fun in that?" When his gaze returned forward, she stood and took the empty seat beside him.

He silently slipped his arm around her shoulders and she was cradled against his side. The rush of the tunnel filled the silence before she could find words. "This isn't your fight."

"While I am wholly confident you can win your own battles..." His hand rubbed her shoulder slowly. "I never pass up an opportunity to kick a lot of ass or watch a hot woman do the ass kicking. So, I think I'll stay."

Her head rose and their lips met.

When the train began to slow, he handed her a gun before getting another for himself. They both got to their feet and waited beside separate exit doors. She held his gaze and he gave her a single nod as the station came into view.

The platform held ten men who looked eerily similar to the ones they had evaded back at the Monkhood. When she examined their faces more closely, she realized why they looked so similar—they were literally the same three men, over and over again. There must not have been time to customize them and these probably hadn't been sold to anyone. It was not only highly irregular it was also illegal. Creating an endless number of bodies that looked identical was not in anyone's best interest and all the governments in the world had unanimously agreed to forbid that long before the technology even existed, just in case. She realized these models before her could mean only one thing.

Whatever the end play was for the Apogee code, whatever the plan was—the timeline was being advanced. That was the only reason for taking such a dangerous shortcut that would most certainly get the person caught. There were too many identical men at the station before her. It couldn't go unnoticed, could it?

All of them had guns trained on her and Dane as the train doors slid open.

She shared a glance with Dane before they stepped forward

onto the platform, the doors of the train sliding closed behind them. They were facing nearly ten advanced bionic models. She was armed with only with a lone gun and Dane's ammo had to be getting low.

Simultaneously in all ten models, gun barrels popped up from their shoulder compartments, tripling the gun total of their enemies. She stared in disbelief before she glanced over at Dane, catching his eye. There was absolutely no way out of the situation that she could fathom so she put her hands up and stepped out from her hiding spot, onto the platform. At least if they took her to CLM she would be inside the building.

As soon as her foot landed on the platform, the station was cast into darkness as all the lights were cut. A whoosh of energy preceded bolts of bright yellow electricity wrapping around the ten Apogees, and Naomi was able to see their outline in ghostly color in the darkness. They all screamed and twitched before the lightning cut off as quickly as it had started, and Naomi heard the thud of bodies hitting the floor. A smell hit her shortly after, something smoke and tangy; like an electrical burn. What had happened?

A quiet hum announced the return of the lights. All of the soldiers were crumpled on the floor, wisps of smoke rising from their bodies. She glanced at Dane in surprise and hurried over to the closest Apogee, nudging him with her foot. He was un-responsive but she saw he was still breathing. A part of her had been hoping that it wasn't actually an Apogee but just a really well made android. No such luck.

"Let's not tempt fate, come on!" Dane grabbed her hand and yanked her into a run after him. They were up the stairs and as they neared a service door it popped open an inch.

"What is it with you and going into service areas?"

Dane grunted as he yanked the door fully open. "Not my idea, this time."

She was about to ask what he meant when she saw someone wearing familiar toucan-colored sneakers inside the service corridor. "INARI!" Naomi wrapped her arms around her partner, feeling suddenly as if all were right with the world again.

Dane closed the door behind them and let out a breath of relief. "Thanks for knocking them out. We would have been captured for sure."

He hadn't been surprised by her appearance. "You knew." It clicked then, Dane's fingers tapping on the train. "You were texting her!"

"Zaft and duh." Inari's tone made Naomi feel every year of their age difference, and not in a particularly flattering way. "You think I wouldn't be monitoring you? Puh-lease."

Naomi paused and promptly punched Dane in the stomach. "That's for not telling me everything would be fine!"

He grimaced. "And here I foolishly thought you hadn't been paying that close attention last night to know where to punch and avoid all my metal plates."

Inari made a playful noise. "In a borrowed body? You're such a slag, Naomi." Naomi's cheeks burned a bright red as Inari looked her up and down. "Speaking of your body, you are positively nugatory in that one."

Naomi looked up at Inari, blinking in surprise as the height difference registered. The current body of the Asian girl was really tiny. "Well, I think I'm an inch taller than that body builder guy I was in before. But I'm getting used to the lowered center of gravity, it's actually kind of nice." Inari though, was the same as always with her multicolored hair up in four pigtails. She had on her toucan sneakers, black and white striped tights and a short blue skirt. Her pink t-shirt had a skull and cross-bones on the chest, the purple jacket sporting a large patch of a black cat on her chest.

Inari's eyes were bright green gold with a cat-like slit instead of a normal pupil. While she had no upgrades whatsoever, she did like modifications. But she went the route teenagers had to before they were eligible for upgrades; she simply wore contacts. "You're still a nugget." She patted Naomia on the head with a smile. "But I could get used to this."

Naomi eyed her.

"Now, I know your sister is in danger but I have an important question." Inari gave a serious nod. "What type of bitch is she? Because I want to plan an epic post-rescue shopping trip for her to get her started on her new wardrobe."

Naomi snorted. "Let's rescue her, first. Where are we going, exactly?"

"Oh, Leon is waiting in the safe room—"

It was Dane's turn to interrupt her. "Leon?"

Inari gave an uncharacteristic giggle. "Yeah." She cleared her throat before promptly spinning on her heels and heading down the hall. "He's the one who cut the power and rerouted the energy so I could use it to take down the baddies. Did you know he uses a portable computer server too? Only he uses a roller case for his, which I think is actually genius because it lets him use it as a chair too."

Since Inari hacked so much and so often, she did not trust the Net or anything that was hard wired. Whenever she had to leave her apartment—albeit, rarely—she would take her server back-pack with her so that she could access anything, anywhere. It was the main reason she had been impossible to capture. She had outfitted it with an independent power supply and enough computing power that she could take down the stock market from a coffee shop.

Dane trailed behind Inari, at Naomi's side. "How did you get in touch with Leon?"

When they came to an intersection, Inari turned to their left. "Oh, you know. He was trying to stop me from hacking into your interface, so I put up a firewall around him and then he tried to use a latent cipher encryption on me, which meant I—"

Both Naomi and Dane spoke. "English."

"We tried to destroy each other virtually." She gave a wistful sigh. "We virtually succeeded, too." She and Dane shared a glance before Inari continued. "But it was a stalemate and then he invited me over to look at his server and let me tell you—"Dane waved a hand. "I really hope that's a euphemism for sex, because otherwise I'm a little uncomfortable."

"What?" Inari stopped beside a door, blushing a bit. "No, I mean, he's nice and maybe I do think he's snoutfair and all but I mean unless he's said something that would be really awkward to even think about unless he did say something so has he said something about me? Maybe?"

Dane rubbed his face with his hands. "Unbelievable." He drew his hands down just enough to look at Inari. "I thought Leon was asexual. Sure, I thought he might breed someday, but via a test tube with donations of genetic material from an unknown origin."

"Oh, don't say that!" Inari gave a little giggle again. "I mean, I haven't been thinking about names for our children or anything weird. That would be totally awkward and I'm not that much of a hugger-mugger." She paused. "So, I mean, *has* he said anything to you—"

Naomi shook her head. "Lead the way, lovebird. You're embarrassing yourself."

Inari's cheeks blushed red and she waved a keycard over the access panel beside the door and it popped open with a hiss.

The room was cramped to begin with but after adding four bodies Naomi was glad her current body was petite. There was a long, metal workbench in the center and the walls were lined with a maze of wires and pipes. She stood across from Inari and Leon, a wall of computers on the workbench further separating them. It didn't help that Naomi could barely see over the electronics.

Inari's tower housed her mobile server, which could link up to a satellite. While it had never been confirmed, Naomi had the distinct impression that Inari had hijacked her own personal satellite from god only knew which government. There was a battery pack, an image screen and an old style physical keyboard, since she wasn't a fan of light boards. The backpack was sitting beside it, covered with her various patches in support of humanitarian efforts in several countries and protection of animals. She'd often used her computer skills to further a variety of causes before she'd joined the force. Though, Naomi wondered suddenly if she still was and just wasn't getting caught.

Dane was the last one in and stopped at the threshold, staring at Leon. "What happened to you?"

Leon was behind his own computer system, also clicking on a physical keyboard. "You're being unspecific. Clarify your question."

Dane grumbled. "Your clothes."

When Leon paused, he looked down at himself as if in surprise. Naomi leaned around the table so she could see what he was wearing. On the only other occasion she'd seen him, he'd been wearing white lab coat over plaid flannel pajamas and bunny slippers. Now he was wearing a tweed jacket complete with dark green elbow patches, a blue bow tie over an orange button down shirt, and pinstriped pants. His shoes were conspicuously still bunny slippers and she saw a few of his spiderbots milling about, one positioned on Leon's shoulder. This time, the bots were wearing little green military berets.

Leon gave a shrug. "I can't very well wear my lab coat outside the lab. People might get the wrong idea and think I'm a medical doctor."

Dane smacked his forehead with a groan and shook his head. "Never mind. A lot has happened and we—"

"We know. We've been—"

Dane interrupted his roommate. "*We?*"

Naomi was fairly certain Leon was blushing. "Yes, Inari and I have been working closely—"

Naomi grinned. "I bet you two have." Leon lifted a brow at Naomi's comment before he hit a single button on his keyboard. The strike brought up a projected image in the air above the table, of a body that Naomi recognized. "That's the body Jax gave me."

"Yes." Leon's eyes moved to her. "Now, do you want to hear about the kill switch or not?"

CHAPTER 18

Dane

"Kill switch?!" Naomi seemed about ready to leap over the workbench. "What do you mean, kill switch?"

Leon hit another series of buttons and code overlaid the image of the body. "Remote access weapon control was written into the code. There was a password that, if uploaded, would have ignited one of the grenades. Very subtle. Lesser coders than myself would have overlooked it." He turned to Inari with a shy smile. "And you, of course."

Dane couldn't actually believe what he was seeing. The number of times that he'd seen Leon dress up could be counted on one hand. Even when he'd gone to an awards banquet in Leon's honor, the man had worn jeans. Now, not only was he dressed up but Leon had just complimented someone, other than himself. There was no doubt.

Leon was smitten.

Even the idea of Apogee models being unleashed on the world to do unspeakable horrors was less wild to him than the idea of Leon having a crush.

Naomi held up a hand. "Is that in all models? Or just mine?"

Inari's nose scrunched up. "Just yours and we—"

Dane moved forward. "Can you tell who added the code?"

"That's the thing. We can't." Inari let out a sigh. "But the password was *Sanctuary*."

Dane looked at Naomi. Her eyes were down, and he could tell she was trying to think it through. There was one terrible conclusion that they both had to draw at this point. "We have to consider the one responsible may be—"

"Way ahead of you." She pulled out the plastic chip, handing it to Inari. "Speaking of Sanctuary, I need you to look at this and tell me what it does. I want to know if what Aung told me was the truth."

Inari took the chip card and turned to her computer. As she began punching in numbers, Leon stared at the code in the air above them. "Inari, do you see—"

"Forget that, look at this."

He leaned in and when the image screen brightened, their faces took on an eerie glow. Leon's eyes widened. "Where did you get this?"

"The monks." Naomi watched them. "What is it?"

"It's intricate and..." Leon trailed off.

"Beautiful." Inari breathed out the word like a sigh.

Dane leaned over to whisper to Naomi. "They're already finishing each other's sentences."

She lifted a brow at him but returned her eyes to the pair. "That's supposed to be the cure for the Apogee coding that allows remote access control."

Inari's fingers began flying over her keyboard. "Yes, but it's more than that. It'll also shut off all machines for twenty-four hours. In the entire country."

The code flashed to life in the air between them and Leon pointed to a section as it scrolled by. "There are numerous sub-protocols as well. It won't affect any machines that are coded for medical purposes. Or anything that aids in accessibility. It's actually well executed."

Inari gave an unexpected giggle. "That could be fun! Ooo, could we build a fort and tell ghost stories, Naomi?"

Naomi stared at her friend in surprise. "I would have thought you of all people would hate the idea of machines shutting down."

"No way! I'm sick of people being obsessed with their upgrades; it'd be nice to be unplugged for a little while. OMG Leon, do you think it'll be like those blackouts back in the day where everyone plays soccer in the streets?"

He was apparently still absorbed in the code. "I can't believe a bunch of backwater monks could write something like this."

Inari's hand lifted off the keyboard to smack his arm before seamlessly returning to her typing. "Don't be jealous."

Dane and Naomi shared a glance and when he went to speak, she simply put up a hand for silence. She blew out a breath through puffed cheeks and grimaced before she held out a hand to her partner. "Inari, I need your cell phone."

"Why?"

She let out a long sigh. "I need to call Jax. Everything is pointing to him being the one behind all this."

Inari scoffed. "Jax?! That guy would need a serious cerebral upgrade before he could accomplish anything on this scale." When Naomi didn't budge, there was a long pause before Inari begrudgingly handed over her phone. "Fine. But how is calling him going to change anything?"

"It isn't. But I'm assuming he'll want to trade my sister for the Sanctuary program, and we can record his offer to take to the police. That way at least he's more likely to get an appropriate sentence when we take him to court. So please record the call, okay?"

As she dialed the number Dane shook his head slowly. At least as a bounty hunter he didn't have to worry about evidence and whether the person could get away with their crime if something wasn't recorded properly.

She set the phone down atop Inari's server, putting her fingers to her mouth for silence. The connection rang a few times before it picked up, but the voice was not the smooth, even voice Dane was expecting. *"Who is this and how did you get this number?"*

Naomi took a step back in surprise. Jax sounded like a wounded animal. "Jax, it's Naomi."

There was a long pause. *"Prove it."*

The look on Naomi's face said she'd forgotten she was in a borrowed body. "My race day routine—"

"Something no one else would know."

Dane kept himself from looking at her as her voice lowered. "On our first date, I devoured a steak because I'd accidentally run a marathon that morning, to soothe my nerves. I told you that story on our last date when you proposed."

Inari caught Dane's eyes and mouthed, *proposed*? Dane just shook his head and tried not to look revolted at the prospect.

"Naomi." Jax let out a breath. *"Where are you? The world has gone mad since you left."*

"What do you mean?"

Rather than a response, the line was filled with noise. There was an alarm klaxon blaring at a regular interval, along with an arrhythmic pounding. Jax must have switched his aural interface from private to public, and that cacophony was happening around him.

No wonder he sounded on edge.

Dane had only ever heard him sound arrogant and triumphant. Now, he just sounded defeated. *"They're trying to take over CLM."*

Dane spoke before he realized. "Who, exactly?"

There was a sigh, the klaxons still ringing in the background. *"Oh, we aren't alone? I shouldn't be surprised. Who else is with you?"*

Naomi looked at Leon and held up a finger. "We have Inari with us as well." Leon gave a single nod in appreciation.

"What about your brother? Did you find him?" There was what sounded like genuine concern in Jax's voice.

Dane saw the way Naomi hesitated. "We did, but the others have been kidnapped by Apogee models."

"Oh no." He sighed. *"I'm so sorry. But this explains so much."*

"What's going on?"

"It started when I found out Bradford was trying to steal your body."

Naomi flinched, fear on her face but she kept it out of her voice. "Steal my body?"

"I told you before, high percentage human athletes are an incredibly rare commodity. It's worth more than an Apogee on the black market."

Naomi's hands were covering her mouth so Dane spoke up. "Did Bradford manage to steal it?"

"No, I hid it in plain sight downstairs and password protected it. Even if he did find it, it would take him a while to be able to do anything to it."

Naomi had regained her voice. "What could he possibly need the money for?"

"It's not about the money; you're a cop, you'd be a liability to his plan. Bradford must be responsible for what happened with your brother, too. He's insane, Naomi. He somehow managed to sneak code into the Apogee model operation system update so they can be controlled remotely. He wants to use them to control the world market. Possibly even the world, I don't really know."

"How did he manage that?"

"There's a cluster of coders he bribed. They hid it from everyone

[247]

else. *Once they push out the update, there won't be anything we can do. We have to stop them before it happens. I know there's a countdown to when it's supposed to be released but I haven't been able to find it.*" The klaxons suddenly stopped and Jax swore under his breath. "*I don't have much time left.*"

Dane caught the surprise on Naomi's face. "Jax, they wouldn't kill you—"

"*Oh, Naomi. Don't you get it? If they get their hands on me, they won't have to.*" An icy shiver went down Dane's spine before Jax continued. "*Inari, do you think you can get ahold of the Monkhood? I have intel that says they've developed a counter virus.*"

Inari met Naomi's gaze before she nodded, and Inari spoke. "I've already got the program."

"*Thank God. Maybe our luck is changing. Can you hack the firewall and launch it now?*"

Inari blinked in surprise, looking between everyone. "No, I'm sorry, I—"

"*It's all right, Inari. We'll go with Plan B then. Dane, do you remember the way you two got out of here the first time?*"

He wasn't going to forget that smell anytime soon. "Yes. But how do we get up the emergency exit shaft?"

"*The old-fashioned way; I hung a rope ladder. I figured the less tech you use getting in the less likely they will be to notice you. You'll end up on one of the lower-level research and development floors. You'll need to make your way to the Apogee R&D floor to launch it but I left you everything you'll need at workstation A27.*"

Naomi took in a breath. "Do you know where he's going to take you or—"

There was a screeching sound, like metal being forcibly ripped in half. The silence that followed was eerie and Jax's voice came as a whisper. "*Naomi?*"

Dane saw she had to swallow before she spoke. "Yes, Jax?"

"*If the worst happens...*" He paused. "*I wanted to say I'm truly sorry I never got to hear your answer to my question.*"

There was a loud explosion and even Dane took a step away as the phone vibrated from the noise. Several voices were shouting and there was the sound of a struggle, and punches landing between curses being uttered. Jax's next words morphed into a terrible scream before the connection was lost.

In the silence that followed, no one made eye contact. Dane stared at the phone in disbelief. Five minutes earlier, their number one suspect had been Jax. Now it looked as if they had all nearly believed one of the best framing jobs of all time.

Leon was the first to break the silence—or more accurately, Leon's keyboard was. In the air above them code flashed to life. The cursor flew through the code before a section of it was highlighted and then the numbers 1:20:19 flashed brightly over it all.

Then 1:20:18... 1:20:17...

Dane frowned. "What's that?"

Leon sighed. "I can only assume it's the countdown he mentioned. It was buried in the kill switch code."

"I think I've seen that code before..." Inari began typing on her computer and a video image overlaid the time image before it dissolved into code. "It's here too."

Naomi pointed above them. "Was that—"

"Hidden in the code of the video message we *thought* your sister sent you."

Naomi hesitated. "How come you didn't see that before?"

Leon shook his head. "It doesn't look like anything until you realize it's redirecting. It looked strange to me but I wouldn't have known if he hadn't said something about a countdown."

Dane took in a breath, grimacing. "Okay look, I hate being

the one to say this but..." He met Naomi's eyes. "Are we really buying the 'Jax is being framed' line? He could have faked that whole call."

He'd been afraid Naomi's response would be emotional but he should have known better. Her eyes showed her fear and unease but her words were logical. "Either way, it doesn't matter because we have to go and at least we have a way into CLM now."

Inari took a step back. "You can't go there!"

Naomi shrugged with a breath. "If that countdown is to be believed, we have just over an hour to fix this mess. What about the Sanctuary program?"

Keyboard typing preceded Leon's words. "In the time we have left, there's no way to separate out the Apogee code fix and the code that turns off machines. I've started debugging the program to ensure that it won't inadvertently hurt anyone."

Dane watched him. "How long will that take?"

"Just over an hour."

Inari watched her partner. "You don't actually mean to use it, do you? Shouldn't we, you know, call the police? A.K.A. our coworkers?"

Naomi turned to Inari. "And how long would it take the cybercrimes unit to debug the program?"

When Inari didn't answer, Leon gave a grunt. "Probably a day or longer."

"As I thought." Naomi sighed. "The only thing I can't figure out is why anyone would embed the countdown in a place we could find it."

Dane glanced at her. "Unless they wanted it to be found."

"Exactly. What if—"

Incoming message from Restricted User. Bring the Sanctuary program to the Tower or Tyler Gate will die. You have until the countdown

[250]

finishes.

Dane stood bolt upright, interrupting Naomi to turn to Leon. "Hack my incoming message, now."

When the shit hit the fan, Leon was steadfast and predictable. His fingers moved over the keyboard with the artistry of a concert pianist and within seconds the message was hovering in the air above them. Naomi took in a sharp breath at the words and Inari whispered under her breath. "Curglaff."

"It appears you have your answer, Naomi." Leon's voice was even. "They wanted you to know."

Dane shook his head slowly before looking at her. "How do we do this?"

Her hands were clenched into fists, her knuckles pressing down on the top of the worktable. She stared up at the message in the air above them. He knew she was cunning and determined, but for the first time he saw her eyes looking deadly. Any bad guy who got in her way was going to regret it.

"We break into CLM and launch Sanctuary before the countdown hits zero." Her eyes turned to Leon and Inari. "We'll need your help."

Inari grabbed her backpack, stuffing in her keyboard. "Zaft, way ahead of you."

Dane had a moment of confusion when Leon didn't argue with Inari packing up her things. Instead, the man grabbed one of his guinea-pig-sized spiderbots. "Yes, the best formation is with my heading back to the warehouse where I have the most server power. Inari will provide on-site support and you two will need this."

He touched the bottom of the bot and the military beret was pulled inside the machine, but surprisingly there was no replacement hat. The whole of the spider took on a black color, an oval of dark gray surrounding the two cameras for eyes. Dane took it and frowned as the spider crawled up to his shoulder. "Why isn't she wearing a hat?"

Leon gave him a look that perfectly communicated that Dane should feel like an ass for needing to ask. "She's in stealth mode."

"Oh, right." Dane glanced at the robot on his shoulder. It did look like a little ninja.

Inari hiked her pack onto her back, putting the straps onto her shoulders before connecting the chest and waist straps. She turned to Leon and was suddenly up on her toes, giving his cheek a quick peck. "Good luck."

She blushed profusely as Leon did the same. He recovered quickly though. "You as well." They paused before Leon leaned halfway down to her, tilting his head awkwardly as she went in the same direction. They both tried to turn the other way, until Inari grabbed his face and pressed her lips to his. Leon didn't seem to know what to do with his hands and left them at his sides as he kissed her.

Dane turned to Naomi and motioned his head toward the door. She nodded vigorously and they were both in the hallway with the door closed behind them.

He slumped back against a wall. "I never thought I'd see the day Leon kissed a girl." He glanced at Naomi. "Are you upset?"

"Not at all." She had a tender smile on her lips. "Honestly, Inari's dates don't tend to go well. She starts talking servers and they go to the bathroom and don't come back. They seem really sweet together."In the silence that followed, he saw the worry creasing her face and rested a hand on her shoulder, softening his voice. "Aung, Pema, and Lin will be all right." He paused and felt he needed to address what else had happened. "And Jax too."

Naomi leaned back against the wall, her voice turning distant. "That wasn't how I expected the call to go."

"Me either."

The silence that followed was so uncomfortable that he was grateful when the door opened again.

Leon cleared his throat, his roller case looking unassuming but filled with more technological power than most universities. "Yes, well. Good luck." He gave a single nod and headed down the hallway away from them. Inari had a bright grin on her face, whispering. "Let's go kick some CLM butt because I want to start daydreaming about the nerdiest wedding of all time!" She gave a single giggle before she skipped down the hall in the opposite direction.

CHAPTER 19

Naomi

She wasn't sure how it was possible, but the smell in the sewer was actually worse. This time, though, they'd brought gas masks for the journey—otherwise she was certain they wouldn't have made it. But the smell had unexpectedly snaked up into the emergency exit shaft and they were all suffering. Balancing on the rope ladder, she pushed open the exit door carefully, looking around to make sure they were alone.

"Not to rush you or anything, but…" Inari sounded green. "I'm going to make paunch art in a few seconds if you don't hurry."

Naomi didn't see anyone and hurried up out of the shaft, offering a hand to Inari.

"If you have to puke on Dane, I'm sure he'll understand."

Inari huddled on the floor, breathing deeply before Dane landed beside her.

"Speak for yourself."

Naomi looked around the room with a frown. "Which workstation did he say?"

Leon's spiderbot was perched on her shoulder still in stealth mode when the sound of pounding came from it and then a recording of Jax's voice: *"You'll need to make your way to the Apogee R&D floor to launch Sanctuary, but I left you everything you'll need at workstation A27."*

The recording promptly stopped and Naomi scrunched up her nose, her ear ringing from the proximity. "Was that necessary?"

The spiderbot turned, its eye cameras focusing on her. *"You ask for the information and then criticize me for providing it promptly?"*

Naomi took a deep breath. Well. He wasn't wrong. "Right, so workstation A27." The workstation nearest to them was labeled B10. Each station held a workbench, tools, manuals and projects in various states of development. There was an unfinished man's face, half metal, half covered with artificial skin. The artificial eye had an iris in the shape of a bullseye.

As they came to the end of the B section the aisle continued but there were now only workstations on the left. On the other side of the aisle were stasis pods, which looked equal parts spaceship and coffin—only the face was visible through a small rectangle of glass. The first workstation they found was A39 and they all hurried their steps past the nameless faces. That the eyes were closed just made her feel even more as if they were walking through a tomb.

Workstation A27 was unassuming and had a project in half completion, like all the others. Thankfully, it was just an incomplete bionic forearm, hand gripped in a tight fist around a red ball. Inari sat down promptly in the chair, spinning around and looking at the area. She stopped her momentum at the interface and waved her hand to wake it up before she began typing on the light keyboard.

It was a quick moment before she spoke. "There's nothing special on here that I see." Inari sat back, frowning. "But I guess that makes sense. Maybe he didn't want to leave an electronic trail, all things considered?"

Both Naomi and Dane looked around for a moment, before

they frowned at one another. Dane said what she was thinking. "We're missing something."

"I know, but what?"

All three of them were looking around in the space, but there wasn't much to take in. There were schematics but Inari was already looking at those, and Dane went to help her. As much as Jax infuriated her, he was a clever man and everything he did was deliberate. If he had to hide something, how would he do it? There was something Jax had said that was itching in her mind. "Leon, please play the recording of Jax's phone call. The part about where he hid my body."

There was a brief pause before the recording came out of the bot on her shoulder. Her own voice was first. *"Wait, so did he manage to steal it?"*

There was a pounding in the background before Jax spoke. *"No, I hid it in plain sight downstairs and password protected it."*

Hidden in plain sight. That was Jax's way, wasn't it? Her eyes immediately went to the bionic arm, grasping a red ball. She went to lift it and her muscles protested. It was far too heavy; bionic arms were designed to be no heavier than their human counterparts and this felt like a cement brick. The spiderbot sidled down to the fist and beneath the spider's body there was a slow flash of light as it scanned the object. The hand suddenly unclenched and the ball hit the table with a thud. Now that the ball was gone, the arm was a much more reasonable weight.

Inari and Dane turned to look at the ball. It gave another thud as it hit the floor and then rolled into the aisle. Naomi lifted a brow. "Is that you, Leon, or...?"

"The ball is controlled via its own programming."

The bionic hand gave her a thumbs up before pointing toward the ball, which was rolling away from them now. She shared a

[256]

glance with the other two before Dane shrugged. "I've followed weirder."

They were making their way when Leon's voice came from spiderbot. *"It's not very sophisticated but I suppose that's the point. There's an ID chip in the bionic arm which I'm guessing has been keyed to any doors you'll need."*

The ball made a sharp right turn between a pair of stasis pods and up to an elevator. She held her breath and waved the bionic arm in front of the sensor. There was a quiet beep before the elevator beeped.

Inari's voice trailed behind. "Naomi..."

The door to the elevator opened and the ball rolled inside. "Inari, we don't have time, we—"

Dane's grabbed her arm urgently. "You need to see this."

When she finally saw what Inari was staring at, she felt her stomach clench in surprise.

Even though she hadn't seen her own face for days, it felt as if it had been years. The square of glass only showed her face, the rest of her body was blocked by metal. The glass was fogged due to the temperature and humidity regulation inside. But it absolutely was her face, waiting past the glass of the stasis pod.

Inari turned to her. "Is it safe to take it back?"

Dane blew out a breath. "Is it safe to leave it?"

The girl's nose scrunched up. "That's true. First rule of breakup is get your stuff back."

Naomi stared at her face and felt a wave of sickness. Jax had said Bradford wanted to sell her body. But even worse was the thought that if she did die in that place, she wanted to be inside her own body. She understood now. The pain in her stomach— she was homesick.

She turned to the spiderbot, still perched on her arm. "Leon,

[257]

can you switch me over? Or will I be too sick to—"

He harrumphed. *"I can manage, even with these machines from the antediluvian era. I'll need Inari to work the interface for me; we'll do some tweaking to ensure you aren't a mess. Could you, darling?"*

Inari was only too happy to scoop up the spider before moving over to the transfer station. "Come on, Naomi! It won't take Leon and I long to break the password protection."

Dane's hand slipped into hers, his voice softening. "Are you sure this is a good idea?"

She turned to him and paused for a long moment before deciding on total honesty. "I don't know. But I don't want to leave it here and lose this chance."

He hesitated but let out a breath. "All right. I'll strap you in."

He helped her to lie down on the transfer station before working the straps along her arms and legs. He had just finished with all the electrodes when he heard a triumphant squeal from Inari. "Got it!"

Leon's voice was hesitant. *"Naomi, the levels coming from your body seem strange."*

"Is something wrong with it?"

"Quite the opposite. The readings are statistically too ideal."

Dane frowned. "Well, is it safe to do the transfer?"

"Strictly speaking, yes. However, I'd like to—"

"This way!" The others turned to the sound of voices. Naomi could only guess they were coming from guards who were about to find them.

"Just do it."

Dane held out a mouth guard for her and she bit down as the machine growled to life in the background. Leon's voice was even. *"For the record, I am against this."*

But before Naomi could form a rebuttal through her mouth

[258]

guard, the world went black.

Dane

He rushed over to the pod with her body in it, watching as the inside glowed brightly before dimming. The pod opened with a hiss, the top lifting up and away. He heard the deep intake of breath from her and relief washed over him. "Naomi..." The relief was cut asunder when her eyes opened. They were still the same shade of light brown, only now gem encrusted and made out of citrine. "Holy shit." Please let them have just given her a double optic nerve upgrade and not let her be an Apo—

"Dane!" Inari shifted backward nervously.

There were five guards, two male, two female, and one sporting a they/them pronoun patch on their black CLM security uniform. By the looks of it, the weapons in their hands were dual-purpose Tasers or Stunning Blast Guns.

He took a step in front of Inari, keeping his voice low. "We've got a bigger problem. You check on Naomi, I'll deal with these guys."

He heard Inari's startled gasp and knew his first suspicion had been accurate; Naomi was an Apogee.

The woman at the head of the other four guards met his gaze. "This is a restricted area. You all need to come with us, immediately."

He lifted both his hands with an easy smile. "Absolutely, but first..." He flicked his pointer finger at the ceiling as he closed his eyes, seeing the bright flash of light from behind the safety of his eyelids.

With a flick of his wrist a small metal disc came into his other hand, which he flung at the larger male guard while simultane-

[259]

ously rushing the female commander in front of him. In his peripheral vision he saw the male guard wrapped in blue electrical ropes before he dropped to the ground, unconscious. He was on the female commander and was about to wrench the gun from her hands when she regained hold of it. He yanked her toward his chest instead and used her as a shield, aiming her gun at another guard. He got the gun to fire but it missed the target, and the commander did a backwards headbutt right into his face.

Dane stumbled back with a groan and heard several shots fire before it occurred to him that he wasn't either in pain or a lump on the floor.

Naomi, still in Apogee form, was in a defensive position between him and the guards. A lightning-fast spinning roundhouse kick dispatched two of the guards' guns. He didn't know when she'd done it, but the commander was already out cold. Naomi rushed the nonbinary guard and Dane whacked a compartment on his thigh, a gun popping up. He shot and stunned his guard just as Naomi finished hers.

He turned to Inari, pointing back at Naomi. "Not that I'm not grateful she's basically a tank, but why isn't she back in the other bod..." He sighed at the look on Inari's face. "You can't get her out of it?"

The spiderbot on Inari's shoulder crackled with Leon's obviously frustrated voice. *"There's a constantly renewingencryption. I've started the process to crack it but it will take hours, at least."*

Dane growled in frustration. "When did they even have time to render it??"

"It's all right, Dane. We should have known it was a trap." Naomi was over by the body she'd just left behind, pulling items out of the pockets. From her profile, despite how she was trying to hide it, he could see the way she was biting her lower lip. This was probably Naomi's worst fear, after all.

Her Apogee body was the same height as her real one, the same brown hair to her shoulders. The black tank top and shorts were skintight, and even though she'd been fighting, her hair looked as if she'd walked out of a stylist's chair. Her skin now was beauty-industry flawless; there wasn't a single blemish or freckle that wasn't clearly designed to be there to add 'attractiveness.' When he looked closer, he saw a host of the other 'enhancements.' Her eyelashes were thick and curled, her lips were puffier and seemed an unnatural shade of pink, her breasts were probably at least a size larger, and there wasn't a single extraneous hair on her body.

He understood now why they'd mistaken it for her real one at first glance—it was the same proportions and colors as the original, but this one had an eeriness that made his skin crawl. It was as if someone had touched up a photo of Naomi. But even all the photos he'd seen of her in magazines had never looked like this and his insides burned at the unfairness of it all. Whoever had sculpted this warped rendition of her had also felt the need to push her to some unrealistic standard of beauty that diminished the things that had made him enjoy her so much in the first place. Scars, freckles, the width of her quads—without them, there was something lost in the mechanical duplicate.

Naomi caught him watching her as she put the last of her things into her new pockets. "Take a picture if you like it so much."

He opened his mouth to correct her when a deep voice boomed around them.

"I see you've found my gift."

He shared a glance with Inari while Naomi sighed. "Bradford. Let's talk face to face about your return policy."

"Does a king meet with those who infiltrate his castle? You are welcome to come and find me, if you wish. But I assure you, it will not change anything."

Dane met Naomi's eyes and despite the gems, he could still see the fire of her anger burning there. "Where are you, Bradford?"

"You'd better hurry if you hope to find me in time. By my count, you have... Oh, thirteen minutes remaining until every Apogee is under my control. And I do mean every Apogee."

Naomi called out a few more times to Bradford without a response. Dane spoke quietly to her and Inari. "That was cryptic. Why was he going on about every Apogee being under his control?"

Inari almost squeaked. "Because of Naomi, of course!"

Naomi waved a hand dismissively. "It wasn't about me." She pressed her fist against her lips thoughtfully and Dane recognized the mannerism he'd seen her display in so many different bodies. Naomi's hand fell with a heavy sigh. "No, it has to be about Jax."

Dane's brow furrowed. "Why would—" And then it dawned on him. If you wanted to control a company without a fuss, turn the CEO into a literal puppet. It would be the quietest corporate takeover in history. As his eyes met Naomi's though, he knew she was sharing the same unease that he felt. Threats aside, it was a far worse realization that their number one suspect was looking increasingly as if he really had been framed all along.

There was the sound of typing from an interface as the spiderbot worked. *"Yes, villainy and betrayal and blah, blah, blah. This is why precisely why I work alone."* Leon's voice dead-panned from the spiderbot, while a three-dimensional building array popped up in front of them. *"Now, would you like to know where Jax is so you can rescue him?"*

Naomi

The elevator door opened, and she started running onto the floor, fueled by her tumultuous thoughts. As much as it had troubled her at first, she'd settled on Jax being her number one suspect. Now that it was beginning to look as if he'd been framed, she was having trouble separating her personal guilt from her occupational concern. She didn't regret sleeping with Dane, but she ardently wished she could go back to feeling totally guilt free. Not that she wished Jax were the bad guy, of course. But she'd be thrilled if he'd go back to simply being a jerk.

Now that she thought about it though, the thing that actually bothered her most was the fact that running was zero effort.

"Naomi! Slow down!"

She stopped to glance back at Dane and Inari, almost on the other end of the production floor. Her heart sank and she knew there was no doubt she could probably break all of her best times. But what would be the point?

And what would she do if she were stuck inside that body forever?

Her heart raced in fear and at least that felt human.

When something bumped her foot, she looked down to see the little red ball. It was following her or perhaps more correctly, the disembodied bionic arm she still carried. The arm had an ID chip that opened doors, but she was still unclear on what the purpose of the ball was. She could hear the others nearing and turned her back on her friends to take the last few strides over to the stasis pod.

Beneath the small window she could see Jax's sleeping face.

His chin had a perfect amount of stubble and she realized he hardly looked any different, even as an Apogee. She was hit with a wave of familiarity so strong she could barely stand it. She set the dismembered arm on the nearby control panel and distantly registered the spiderbot slipping off her arm onto the interface. There was a loud hiss as the stasis pod began to open.

Jax's eyes opened to reveal irises made of dark brown smoky quartz. Naomi couldn't make herself move, until she heard him whimpering.

"Jax?"

Only his eyes turned to look at her and his lips barely moved. "Help. Can't. Move."

She turned to the spiderbot. "What's wrong?"

Two of the spiderbot's legs were holding it up while the other six moved rapidly over the keys. *"His power output has been decreased to less than one percent."*

Naomi tried not to think about what it would be like to be trapped inside a body that could be controlled in such a way. If she'd had a stomach anymore, she was fairly certain she would have been sick to it.

"It's fixed."

Jax took in a breath and lifted a hand. She helped him sit up and was shocked when he wrapped his other arm around her middle. His head pressed against her chest and his voice softened. "I'm so glad to see you."

Instinctively, she rested her free hand on the back of his head to comfort him. "I'm glad you're all right." He'd never once in all their time of dating been that vulnerable with her. Previously, it would have been refreshing but now she tried to ignore the fact that Dane and Inari were right behind her. "We need to—"

"Of course, I just..." He stood and his hand went to her cheek.

He went to kiss her, but before she knew what was happening, she'd turned away. He drew back in surprise. "Naomi, what's—" His eyes flicked between everyone and when they met Naomi's again, she looked down in shame. He cleared his throat, stepping away from her and releasing her hand as if it were on fire. "Right. Now's not the time." He turned quickly to the dismembered arm, pushing several spots until a couple of compartments opened up.

When he found a small gun and pair of phase canisters, Dane grunted in his surprise. "Those were in there, too?"

Jax muttered, though loudly enough for everyone to hear. "I suppose you were too busy to check." He pulled out an ID chip before adding it to his own arm, his voice distracted. "How long do we have left?"

Inari answered quickly. "Nineteen minutes."

Jax looked at Inari. "Do you have the Sanctuary program?"

Naomi hesitated briefly before nodding. "Yes."

"Good." He closed the compartment on his arm.

"Do you have a way to find the others?"

"Not yet."

Naomi pushed away all the awkwardness and confusion, focusing on the mission that would hopefully lead to her sister as well. "So, what's the plan?"

As Jax bent down to grab the red ball from the floor, she couldn't help but notice the tight-fitting black shorts and matching short-sleeved shirt that were similar to her own. His body had always been amazing and while not much had actually been altered, it was enough for her to miss the real him. And that made her hate herself a little bit, considering.

Jax offered her a phase canister as his eyes met hers. "We take back my company and make Bradford pay."

CHAPTER 20

Dane

The man was unbelievable. While Dane had not doubted it before, he was now certain Jax was a total egomaniac. "Could you maybe add to that plan finding Naomi's human body and getting her out of this creepy atrocity? Because in case you hadn't noticed, she's stuck inside one of your abominations now." Jax's jeweled eyes met his gaze, and it was hard for Dane to unclench his jaw enough to growl. "Or are you so twisted that you actually prefer her this way?"

Jax held his gaze for a moment but was infuriatingly unflappable. "Forgive me for not being surprised that Bradford would lay a trap like this. But do tell—" He turned to Naomi. "How exactly did you end up trapped in there, my dear?"

Naomi's voice was soft. "We went past it downstairs. I thought it was my body and I asked to be transferred over."

Jax touched her upper arm in sympathy. "Where was it?"

"Just past the workstation you sent us to."

His hand dropped in surprise. "Right beside the elevator?"

Dane's brow furrowed. "Yes, why?"

Jax looked away and Naomi grabbed his arm. "What is it?"

He swallowed. "That's where I left your body. I'd hoped you'd find it." In the eerie silence that followed, he left the rest unspoken. Jax turned to Naomi, putting a hand against her cheek. "We will find your body." Jax gave Dane a sideways glance before taking his hand back. "But we obviously need to launch Sanctuary first seeing as we can't get you out of this model even if we were to find it."

Dane's ire lessened, though only slightly. That actually was a valid point.

Inari was on Naomi's other side. "How did you know about the encryption that limits body transferring?"

"He did the same to me." Jax rolled his eyes. "Bradford has always enjoyed monologuing. I was almost grateful when he locked me inside the stasis pod." He let out a breath, moving over to the control panel. "Speaking of Bradford, we should figure out where he is."

Leon's voice came out of the spiderbot on Inari's shoulder. *"Apogee R&D floor, level one hundred and one."*

Jax turned with a frown. "What is that?"

Under no circumstances did Dane ever admit he had a connection to Leon Hartwick. The man had a lot of idiosyncrasies that made Dane nuts—but his desire for utter secrecy was not one of them. It made sense considering the number of people who would be happy to either steal Leon's ideas or kidnap Leon himself. Further though, Dane simply did not trust Jax and it wasn't only due to his feelings for Naomi. Dane caught Inari's gaze and the girl reached up to touch the bot on her shoulder. "One of my pet projects. A spybot with an enhanced AI."

Jax made a noise of appreciation before turning. "If we get out of this alive, remind me to offer you a very lucrative job here."

Dane shared a knowing look with Inari, and spiderbot gave a tiny bob of its head before they all turned to follow Jax.

Naomi was already walking at Jax's side and Dane felt sick to his stomach seeing the pair. They looked like all the unrealistic expectations of perfection that were constantly being shoved down people's throats. It was as if they'd walked out of an advertisement for a gym or—no. Worse than that. Advertisements for gyms or health spas at least offered the pretense of helping you become healthy. The pair before him reminded him of something far more insidious.

CLM's advertisements preyed on the fear that not only were you not good enough, but that you could never become good enough—unless you joined CLM and either got a new body, a new life, or preferably, both. To Dane, their singular purpose had always been to convince people that the only way to happiness was through trying to reach a bar of perfection—a bar that was, of course, constantly rising. It had always seemed to Dane like the company got off on the Sisyphean torture.

His eyes rose to Jax as they waited beside an elevator. Or maybe it was just the CEO who enjoyed cruelty?

Jax put a hand on Naomi's forearm, his voice soft. "I know being in this body is hard on you."

Her eyes glanced up at him and she gave a single nod. "At least the probability that my actual body is unharmed is high."

Jax returned a sad smile. "And you look like yourself and not one of those other Apogee models." The way Jax's hand slid down her arm to hold her hand made it very hard on Dane to resist reaching out and crushing the man's metal skull like a can. "I hope you know you're a vision of perfection to me."

When the elevator opened and they all moved inside, Dane purposefully turned his back on them and rolled his eyes at Jax's drivel. Naomi gave a polite and quiet thank you and Dane tried not to read too much—or at all—into it.

He had to wonder though. Did it make him a bad person for wishing Jax would die in the hopefully soon to be ensuing firefight?

Naomi

They stepped out of the elevators, and she found it a betrayal of her new body that the hairs on the back of her neck didn't stand up straight. It was a giant production floor with a wide aisle down the center and a variety of different cordoned off workspaces. Some of them were as large as a room, and there were dozens of slabs that had bodies lying supine in their midst. This, though, was not the creepiest part. Along various walls were compartments, filled with Apogee models in assorted states of completion.

Some were naked, though most were wearing shorts and either tank tops or short sleeved shirts. There were ones without arms or legs, or in various states of having their permanent skin attached or coloring sprayed over the paper white 'skin.' The chest was exposed on one to show the mechanical parts inside; another's eyes had yet to be added and were sitting on the table before it, seeming to stare at her despite their disembodied state. Most were entirely lacking hair, but a few were also missing a scalp; the top half of the head was completely gone, apparently in the final stages of waiting for a human brain to complete their transformation from puppet to something that would somehow, defying reason, resemble a human.

Naomi couldn't help but look down at her arm, turning her hand over slowly. What was she now that she was one of them? Was she even a human anymore? Whose brain, heart and lungs was she even using right now? Despite how she'd tried not to think it, she was terrified they might be her own. Jax had said her body was incredibly valuable intact, so she had to believe that it was somewhere safe. She wasn't sure she could go on if she didn't.

"I see you've accepted my invitation." They were in the center of the production floor when Bradford's voice jarred her out of her thoughts. "And you brought another guest." He stepped out from behind a dividing wall, with four Apogee guards surrounding him, more identical duplicates of the models they'd faced at the train station and monastery. Bradford's hair was dark brown with streaks of gray—though in true CLM fashion, they appeared intentional in order to make him seem more regal. She'd always thought his face was unnaturally smooth for his age on the other occasions she'd seen him at CLM functions. His suit was pressed and he clasped his hands behind his back as he came to a stop. "Welcome, CEO Raelyn. How nice of you to come."

Jax lifted a brow in obvious annoyance. "Well, you cleared my calendar once you put me in stasis so I didn't really have anything else planned."

Naomi stayed at Jax's side, watching Bradford. "What do you hope to gain from this?"

Bradford's eyes slid to Naomi, and he lifted his hands palm up. "Isn't world domination enough for you?"

She worked to keep her laugh to herself. That sounded like a line from a script in a bad movie. "So, there's no way I can talk you out of it?" The four Apogee guards beside him lifted their guns and trained them on her group. "I'll take that as a no."

Bradford took a single step behind his line of guards and they closed rank before him. "That would be correct. It was nice knowing you all. Please try not to hurt any of the merchandise in this room on your way to your death."

She was going to enjoy arresting him.

"Hey Bradford?" Jax lifted the red ball in his hand, turning it slowly. "You really should have thought better about trying to steal my company." He squeezed the ball and flicked his wrist, tossing it straight toward the guards.

All four guards began shooting, but the ball morphed into large red netting that caught and absorbed their bullets with flashes of light. Naomi was already using the opportunity to turn back to Inari, as she reached into a compartment for the phase canister Jax had given her earlier. "Hide!" Inari needed no encouragement and was already halfway to a workspace before Naomi activated the canister and threw it at the guard on her right. The blue electricity raced around his form and the man immediately went down like a puppet whose strings had been cut.

Jax had taken out another of the guards with his canister. It was obvious Bradford saw the writing on the wall since he began backing away. As he went to turn and run, Naomi left Dane and Jax to the last two guards and raced after him.

She caught up to him in six paces, just as he was rounding on her with a gun. She didn't want to admit it, but her Apogee body was lightning fast and she grabbed the gun without thought, increasing her power output and crushing it.

His eyes met hers and she decked him in the chin, before she realized she probably should've turned her power level down. He fell to the ground, and she checked his pulse, grateful to find it still going strong. Hopefully he wasn't concussed but she'd have him checked later. She reached behind her back for her electromagnetic cuffs, only to realize she didn't have them. Being an Apogee felt eerily as if she were back in a mech suit. Over her shoulder, she saw Jax and Dane had taken care of the guards and were currently using some sort of electrical wiring to tie them together. She dragged Bradford over to them, dropping him unceremoniously at Jax's feet. "I don't have my cuffs."

Jax hit a button on the binding wire and it began to glow a fierce orange around all the guards. Inari appeared from behind a dividing wall as Jax handed Naomi a similar wiring device. "Use this, it'll hold him."

"But what is it?"

"The Seals use it. Trust me, it'll hold them. I need to see if I can stop that countdown." He rushed over to a workstation, calling to Inari as he passed. "Care to help me, Inari?"

Inari blinked in surprise and hurried over with him.

Naomi bent down beside Bradford, wrapping the wires around him and frowning to herself as she worked. Something wasn't right.

Dane knelt beside her and whispered. "Is it just me or was that too easy?"

So it hadn't just been her that had noticed. Something else was bothering her though and she wasn't entirely certain what. She very nearly asked him to scan Bradford when she realized she had the capability herself.

Accessing the scanner produced an overlay in her field of vision. It showed Bradford's vital statistics atop his form. As she examined them in turn, she finally understood what Leon had meant about the statistics being 'too perfect' when they'd first encountered her 'body.' Now that she was seeing them for herself, it could mean only one thing.

Bradford was an Apogee.

She rapidly tapped her fingers against her leg. *Bradford's an Apogee.* She sent Dane another text once she could get her mind to stop swirling as rapidly. *We have to at least consider that he was being controlled, even though the update hasn't theoretically been pushed out.* She met his gaze meaningfully, motioning over her shoulder to Jax. *I would mark my GPS coordinates or call the NYPD, but I don't trust my current body and who knows what redundancies and firewalls CLM has.* She set the electrical wiring around Bradford to active.

"Naomi?" She had to cover her flinch as she looked over her shoulder at Jax, typing at an interface. "I've cleared the jamming that was stopping outgoing calls. Why don't you call your chief and get him over here? Preferably with a lot of backup, just in case. And maybe if we work it right we can keep you and your partner from getting fired or arrested, too." Jax kept typing, talking distractedly. "Inari, we need to clear the code so we can launch Sanctuary. He left a lot of interference." Inari was at his side, typing away.

When Naomi met Dane's eyes this time she saw as much confusion in him as she felt herself. With everything she had uncovered that exonerated Jax, why were there still lingering doubts? In the end, she wanted someone else on the force to do a thorough investigation and assure her that he had indeed been framed and had not been responsible for any of this mess.

She hadn't wanted to call the NYPD before because Jax would have overheard. Now that he'd given her an excuse though, she didn't waste any time and was grateful when her boss picked up his private line. *"How did you get this number?"*

"It's me, Naomi."

"Naomi! Where the hell have you been?"

"Long story. You need to come to CLM. Bring back up, I think we may have the situation contained but Jax isn't sure and frankly, neither am I."

"CLM? Do I need to call in the National Guard or just skip straight to the Army?"

He was joking but she was tempted to take him up on it. Despite everything, she felt herself cracking a smile. "An update for the Apogee models had hidden coding that would allow permanent remote access. Bradford appears to have been behind it and we have him in custody." She hesitated before continuing, trying to carefully convey the complexity of the situation to her chief without also letting Jax know she was suspicious. "Though of course, it warrants a thorough investigation, seeing as it appears that Bradford was trying to frame Jax."

"*That's a mess.*" Her chief was silent for a long moment. "*I'll get ahold of cybercrimes as well.*"

"Good. I'll see you soon."

"*And Naomi?*"

"Yes, sir?"

"*I'm glad you're safe.*"

Call ended.

She heard Jax curse loudly behind her. "Who has Sanctuary? We've got less than five minutes before his program launches, we need to run it." Jax's gaze turned to Inari and the girl just shook her head. His quartz eyes turned to Naomi. "You have it, right?"

She hesitated and wasn't entirely certain why. The truth was she didn't have any hard evidence that pointed to him being a suspect. At best she had some murky evidence that could simultaneously show him as being at fault or having been framed—and actually, she had more evidence in support of the framing, seeing as Bradford had admitted to guilt in front of her, a police officer, no less.

So why when he asked for the Sanctuary program did she hesitate?

Hurt moved over his features and he stepped away from the interface, lifting both his hands. "Fine. If you trust me so little, put it in yourself."

She should trust him—if he were somehow the one behind the Apogee coding, the last thing he would want was for the Sanctuary program to be launched. So why didn't she?

His arms crossed over his chest. "Unless you have some desire to allow others the ability to take control of us both?"

She sucked in a breath. It couldn't be Jax. He was an Apogee too and had as much to lose by the program launching as she did—and unlike Bradford, he was actively trying to get Sanctuary launched before the countdown was finished.

She sighed as a cloak of guilt descended over her. "Jax, I'm sorry, I—"

"Naomi." He watched her for a moment before he gave a sad smile. "I'm the one who wants to marry a cop. I can't very well be upset when you're doing your job well."

She ignored her discomfort and pulled the card out of her pocket, the small chip staring at her. She was about to offer it to him when he screamed her name.

A gunshot echoed and before she knew what was happening Jax had tackled her. She felt the heat of the Cannon Shot as it grazed her arm but her Apogee nerve endings didn't register any pain. They landed on the ground in a heap and Jax had a gun in his hand and fired at Bradford.

The man's head exploded from the impact, the dividing wall behind him a neuropathic map of a different sort, as bits of brain matter and blood covered it. Bradford's shoulder compartment revealed a gun barrel pointed at them.

She sat back on her elbows in shock as Dane and Inari rushed to her side. Jax's hand was on her cheek. "Naomi?! Are you hurt?"

It took her a moment to assess herself and she was surprised to find the Sanctuary card still in her hand. "I'm all right."

He helped her to stand. "Maybe you're starting to see I'm not actually that overprotective of you. People are always trying to shoot at you, after all."

A wave of guilt moved through her, and she was grateful that she couldn't get sick seeing as she didn't have a stomach. "Maybe you do have a valid point." And maybe she'd been a little too hard on Jax, all this time.

Her eyes glanced at Dane in apology, and she moved over to the interface.

Jax's arm went around her waist. "Let's launch the program and put this whole mess behind us."

Naomi took a deep breath and pressed the chip to the reader, hitting the button beside it to activate the program.

The computer chirruped and Jax hit a few buttons on the interface. "Good, it was accepted. I'm glad that worked. Does she always cut everything this close, Inari?"

Naomi's eyes shot over to Inari and Dane, and they both glanced between each other, her, and then up at the lights. If Sanctuary had run, the lights should have turned off. Naomi kept her cringe to herself. Maybe it was just a mistake… She caught her partner's eyes and motioned to the interface.

Inari bit her lip for a second before she smiled. "Um, yeah, actually. She really likes suspense. So, hey, can I just check something really quickly?" She pointed to the interface. "Uh, to make sure that… the cybercrimes unit doesn't have any trouble when they get here?"

Jax met her gaze and motioned to the interface. "Of course. Is something wrong?"

Inari smiled brightly. "No, I'm just not used to being around all the action bits, and I'm actually supposed to be on desk suspension right now, so my being here probably isn't going to go over super well so I'm hoping that if I smooth things over for everybody then—okay Naomi you can stop giving me that look I'll stop talking and start working."

Naomi realized her partner was more on the ball than she was. Naomi would normally have been giving her a look by that point in a monologue. She lifted a brow and tried to look playful. "Get a move on, nerdlette."

Jax squeezed his arm around her waist, and she forced herself to think. She didn't have any EMP Discs to knock Jax out. How long ago had she called the police?

She needed to calm down and wait for confirmation from Inari.

"Maybe we should go upstairs to the penthouse while we wait for the police to get here?" Jax shifted to address Dane. "Naomi particularly loves the view of the city from my hot tub."

She ignored Jax's deliberate attempt to goad Dane. "It won't be long before the police get here."

Jax gave a short laugh. "Naomi, we're a hundred and one flights up. With the Tower Protocol, it'll take them at least twenty minutes if not half an hour to get here."

She struggled not to wince. After hostages were taken custody at Willis Tower twenty years prior, the first responders who'd tried to get to them in the elevator were killed when the shafts were bombed. Now part of standard practice required all police to take the stairs until the elevator shafts had been cleared of explosives. But that meant she and her friends had a lot of time before any help was coming, especially since CLM did not have an accessible roof.

She turned toward Jax so she could see over his shoulder and meet Inari's gaze. The girl's terrified face told her everything she needed to know. It figured that her gut was right the one time she would have been okay with it being wrong. Would she even be able to restrain him or knock him out? Or had he thought that far ahead? If help wasn't coming for a while, it was better to try play along for now and hope he didn't figure out that they knew who was really behind everything.

Naomi put a hand on Jax's chest and smiled. "Why don't you head up? Inari and I will start getting the crime scene ready."

His hand laid over hers. "I'm not leaving you."

She leaned up to kiss him. "We won't be long, honest."

Jax held her gaze and touched a finger to the bottom of her chin. "What gave me away, my darling?"

Well. Might as well stall. "The lights didn't turn off." She took stock of all their positions. Dane and Inari weren't within reach of Jax. Naomi's hand was on his chest and her other hand was free. She'd only get one chance, so she needed to wait for a good moment.

His brow lifted and he shifted just enough so he could access the interface, while keeping his arm around her. Just as she went to punch him, Jax spoke. "Attack me and your brother dies."

Her hand stopped a half-inch from Jax's sternum and both Dane and Inari edged away too. Naomi's heart raced in fear. At least she knew her sister was still alive. The code for the Sanctuary protocol appeared in the air before them and Jax let out a breath. "It wasn't enough that the monks had to write a fix for my Apogee override code, but they had to go and muck it up by adding this?" He shook his head in disapproval before turning to her. "Did I do anything else to give myself away?"

Since she had his attention she decided to stay focused and keep it. "You weren't surprised I was an Apogee."

"Guilty." He shrugged. "When launching a plan like this it's harder than you'd think to keep track of what you are and are not supposed to know. What else?"

She frowned. It was almost as if he were enjoying this. "Bradford's an Apogee."

"Ah, so you did scan him. I wasn't sure if you would, but I couldn't be sure if it would matter even if you had. Why did that

[278]

make you suspicious?"

He was enjoying this, wasn't he? "Because Inari and Leon haven't had any upgrades precisely because they don't trust machines, seeing as they are well aware of how vulnerable they make people. So why would Bradford switch into an Apogee model that could be remotely hacked if he'd created the hack, unless there was some purpose? You being in an Apogee took suspicion off you. Bradford wasn't obviously an Apogee, so it makes more sense he wasn't in it by choice."

When the grin spread on his lips, she realized something had gone terribly wrong. "Ah, good. So, my dear friend Leon is involved?"

She closed her eyes. What a foolish mistake.

"If you use the word friend again when referring to myself or any of my actual friends, I will personally ensure that the only view you have of your penthouse is from the sidewalk after your brain matter is splattered upon it."

Naomi's eyebrows shot up. Leon was curmudgeonly and grumpish to be sure, but his words were a severe escalation to open hostility. She met Dane's glance and saw that he was equally as surprised. Jax leaned back against the interface, his arms wrapping tightly around Naomi's waist and pulling her back into him. "Now, now, Leon, that's not very nice. I'm sad to see you didn't join your friends on this adventure. When I ensured Dane would pick up Baozhai's bounty on Naomi's brother, I'd been hoping you'd come play with us. But then, you do love to hide behind your keyboard."

Dane's jaw dropped. "This was all to get to Leon?"

"No, but if I'd gotten my hands on him, it would have been a bonus. No, the whole point of this was—well, I can't say much with Leon listening in, now can I?" He picked his gun off the control panel, aimed it and shot the spiderbot off Inari's shoulder at point blank range.

Inari screamed and jumped away, covering her ear with both hands. Naomi couldn't move out of Jax's hold and she stared at the pile of spiderbot remains, still smoking with a single leg twitching. Dane got Inari to stop bouncing and checked her ear, which was uninjured but no doubt ringing from the proximity to the shot. Jax motioned with the gun as he spoke. "The whole point of this was Naomi, which is why I wanted to know how I made you suspicious of me. But fortunately for me, you confirmed that I did everything right."

She frowned, glancing back at him as much as she was able. What did he mean, he'd done everything right—oh, no. "You wanted me to exonerate you?"

"I figured if I made it look as if I were being framed, then it would mean I didn't have to try so hard to perfectly hide what I was doing. It really took a lot of the stress out of all this and made it a lot easier to deal with dating a cop." He brushed her hair back slowly with the barrel of his gun. "But you will look so lovely on the witness stand, testifying in my defense."

She tried to stay calm. He'd just made her call the police in, saying that Bradford was the bad guy. Well, best to keep stalling until the cavalry arrived and she could explain it to them later. "So, our whole relationship was a lie?"

"Well, yes, obviously. That goes without saying." He leaned forward though, running his nose along her jawline. "Though honestly, I needed you for several reasons." He straightened with a sigh. "The most pressing of which was leading me to the Monkhood and being so kind as to hand deliver me the Sanctuary program. Speaking of which… I'll be needing this for evidence." He slipped the card into his pocket.

She flinched when she saw the plastic disappear. "We made copies."

He shook his head. "It doesn't matter. Now that we input it, I've created a program to catch Sanctuary and treat it as a virus. So, unless you entirely rewrite the code, it won't matter. I simply needed you to bring it here so it would work." His eyes trailed along her face. "Thank you for making my life easier. Now I can publicly redouble my security efforts while in actuality, my override protocol still exists." He squeezed her back against him and kissed her neck with a moan, the gun pressing against her stomach.

Jax was utterly insane. She forced down her panic and tried to think. It didn't make sense to her, if for no other reason than the timeline didn't match up. "But we've been dating a year, and the Monkhood only recently found the override code."

"Oh, well, the original reason I started all of this…" He gave a dark chuckle. "That you'll learn in a moment." The panel beside him began to beep and he reached over to hit a button. She gave him a curious look and his eyes moved over her face. "The countdown's finished. But don't worry; it hardly matters. I've been able to control any Apogee since before the first one was rendered. I orchestrated the countdown to get you here on my schedule. Speaking of which, I could talk forever about my genius plan, but we are on a strict timeline here."

He pushed her toward Dane and Inari, making them frown in surprise. He was still leaning against the panel and pushed a series of buttons. There was a succession of beeps before the sound of metal moving from the far end of the room. Jax crossed his arms loosely over his chest, the gun dangling carelessly in his hand. Behind him rows of identical male Apogees appeared, walking in two single-file lines. All had skintight black tank tops and shorts, over mahogany skin. Their dark hair was cut close to their skull and they stopped just past Jax, perfectly in sync and eerily waiting.

Jax waved his gun as he spoke. "Thirteen Apogee models, all controlled with separate AI systems, each one slightly different. You're going to help me with live human combat testing, so that I can decipher which one is the best for future software updates that I need to push out."

Naomi felt her jaw clenching. "I won't do anything to help you."

"No?" He gave a smile, a brow cocked. "I was hoping you'd say that." He pushed a button and the Apogee in the back of the line exploded.

Dane pulled both her and Inari behind him, shielding them from the worst of the heat. When she lifted her eyes to look in horror, the other twelve Apogees were still standing motionless, as if nothing had happened.

Jax leaned back against the interface panel, his arms crossed casually over his chest when he lifted his finger. "You know, I probably should have led with the fact that Tyler and those two monks are inside three of the bodies."

Her heart raced in fear. Her eyes took in the pile of rubble that had previously been an Apogee. Her sister, Aung and Pema were trapped inside those things? "What about the rest of them?"

"My Apogee coders." He gave a saccharine smile. "Delegation is so important as a CEO." His eyes narrowed. "Will you help me now?"

It was all she could do to keep herself from reaching out and choking the smugness right out of his features.

"Statistically speaking…" Jax tilted his head to the other side. "You only have a one in four chance of killing the wrong one."

He lifted his hand, fingertips in snap position. "Good luck." He snapped his fingers and the Apogees charged.

CHAPTER 21

Dane

For one horrifying second, the world seemed to stand still. Then the Apogees advanced and the three of them jumped backward in fear, Naomi calling out. "Any bright ideas?"

He whacked his forearm with a fist and twisted his arm so the four discs would fall out into his other hand. After taking a deep breath he pretended he was skipping rocks on the shore. As a disc connected with an Apogee it was wrapped in blue electricity before it crashed to the ground. Only one missed its target but that still brought the enemy total down to nine. "How's that?"

Inari's eyes had gone wide with fear, and he grabbed her by the waist, throwing her over his shoulder, caveman-style.

Inari flailed at his back. "Let me go, I can totally—"

He dodged a plasma shot that narrowly missed them and Inari squealed.

"Never mind! Get me out of here, I'm a techy, I'm not cut out for battle!!"

Dane hurried backward and motioned to his bicep that was currently blocked by her head, buried beneath her hands. "Inari, pop that compartment."

She slapped it with the palm of her hand and pulled out a gun. "I should really tell you that despite my status as an officer of the law, they've given me special dispensation for my lack of accuracy—"

"Not for you! For Naomi!"

"Oh, right!"

She tossed it to Naomi, who sprinted forward to catch it before ducking into a workstation across the aisle. "I'll distract them. Get her somewhere safe!"

The sound of shots firing echoed as he rushed into the maze of workspaces. He dashed around a few corners before he unceremoniously dumped her onto the ground. "Can you get ahold of Leon—"

"Way ahead of you."

She'd already opened her backpack and a spiderbot emerged, but this one wearing a Napoleonic hat. *"You didn't honestly think I'd send you with only one, did you?"*

He breathed a sigh of relief. If Leon and Inari were working together, they could sort this out. She removed her image screen and keyboard from her pack and he looked at the spiderbot. "Can you figure out where her sister and the others are?"

"No, I already tried. And before you ask, I can't hack Jax. That was the first thing I tried because I really want to blow him up. But his encryption changes to a random ninety-eight digit code every thirty seconds."

Of course it couldn't be that simple. "So, what can you do?" He was itching to get back to Naomi.

"Rewrite a new code for the Apogee override. That's our only option, unless you can manage to incapacitate them all, Jax included."

"And even if you do, he may have other redundancies in place, so the rewrite code is probably more—" Inari squealed and pointed at the unfinished Apogee in the compartment beside Dane. "AH! Did that thing just move?!"

It definitely had not moved. "Inari—"

She started typing. "Okay, okay, but what do you want from

me, I'm a techy, I'm creeped out by these freaky quockerwodg-ers..." Her eyes went wide and a smile spread on her face. "That's it! Quockerwodgers!!" She started typing at lightning speed.

Dane shared a glance with the spiderbot before the bot turned to Inari. "*Darling, what are you—oh, you mad genius.*"

Inari gave an evil giggle. "New plan. I help you, while Leon starts rewriting."

Dane glanced toward the sound of the fighting. "So what do I do?"

"Stall them!!" Both Inari and Leon yelled at the same time.

They were such a weird pair. "For how long?"

"*Anywhere between twenty minutes to several days.*"

Dane grimaced and wished he hadn't asked, jumping to his feet. "What's a quocker-whatever?"

Inari's eyes didn't move from the screen. "A wooden puppet, controlled by strings. Now stall already!"

His brow was still furrowed in confusion as he rushed away, taking the corners until he neared the main aisle. He saw the herd of Apogees on the far end, congregating around a workstation. There were only eight that he could see—one seemed to have been added to the unconscious body total.

"A little help would be nice!"

A gun fired and Naomi tumbled out from behind a worksta-tion, sliding flat on her back and shooting Apogees in the knees as she passed. Two merely stumbled and Dane charged forward to help. One of the Apogees crouched and took a flying leap fifteen feet into the air toward Naomi. Dane screamed Naomi's name, but the Apogee twisted in mid-flight and landed before Dane. He swallowed as he stared the robot down and brought his hands up to defend—only to find it aiming next to him and giving a pow-erful upper cut to an Apogee he hadn't even seen lurking at his side. The first model gave out a decidedly adorable giggle. *"This is just like a video game!"*

Dane recognized Inari's voice. "Oh, Quocker-whatever. I get it." He pulled a gun out of his quad compartment, setting it to taser. "Inari, can you hack more of them?"

Her Apogee landed a powerful punch. *"No, most of the AIs have already learned how to defend against this now. But one is better than none!"*

Dane slid to a stop beside Naomi, offering her a hand. "I thought your partner said she wasn't any good at fighting."

She took hold of his hand and used it as leverage to yank herself up with an upward kick to the Apogee nearest her. "She only works so she can afford to go to the arcade."

Inari's Apogee was fighting a distance from them and Dane put his back to Naomi's, so they could face the five Apogees who were ringing them now. "Kids these days." One Apogee went to raise a gun and Dane shot it out of his hand. "Just so you know, our great plan is to stall so Leon can rewrite the override protocol."

She grunted as she kicked one of the Apogees before her. "No chance he can hack Jax?"

He activated his shoulder cannon, the Plasma Blast just missing its target. "Come on, that'd be too easy."

"DUCK!" Inari yelled and they both crouched as a workstation table flew over their heads.

Naomi threw out her leg in a wide sweep, hurtling one Apogee to the ground. She was able to swing her hand through its knee, ripping the leg off with a flourish and offering it to Dane. "But I so would have enjoyed watching that asshole dance the polka."

"The polka, eh?" He took the leg, using it to strike the next one in his face. It barely bent, but it was still pretty satisfying. "What are these things even made of?"

"I'm thinking they're at least part wolverine."

He glanced at her. "Did you just make an X-Men joke?"

She hooked her arm in his and used it to roll herself up and over his back, kicking one of the Apogees that got too close. "A what?"

When one of them landed a punch, he grimaced but pivoted so he could grab the arm. Before he could manage to take a swing at the elbow, it had hit him in the chest, back into Naomi. "You probably haven't seen the old ones, but what about the reboot that came out this summer?"

"Let's get out of this alive and I'll watch them all." When she kicked an Apogee it caught her foot and tossed her to the ground with a thud.

He jumped over her and rushed the Apogee before it could attack her, shoving it back into another and the pair clattered to the ground. "You know, we're losing."

"Yeah, I know." She was on her feet again. "Trying not to kill them is way harder than it seems."

"And we're running out of ammo." They'd been fighting pretty much nonstop since they'd left the warehouse. Even Dane couldn't carry enough for what they'd been up against. "Let's split up, keep them from ganging up."

She gave a devilish smirk. "I bet I take on more than you."

"Game on."

As their eyes locked, he knew she was doing exactly what he was—putting on a brave face when in reality, neither of them believed they were going to live through this.

But before he could say or do anything else, they both turned and separated, to face the Apogees alone.

Aung

At first, it had seemed as if he were dreaming that he was a robotic man. He saw himself moving but had no control—there had been others, all identical, and he'd been sure then that he was deeply asleep inside his bed at the monastery.

Except that he remembered quite vividly that he'd watched Sifu and the other masters die, right before his eyes. Even that though, had not been enough to convince him that he was awake yet somehow inexplicably unable to control his own body.

But he'd seen Naomi and Dane. Naomi was herself and yet she wasn't.

Something was very wrong, but he couldn't figure out what.

When he saw Naomi sweep one of his copies to the floor and rip off the mechanical leg, he felt a whirlwind of understanding. He *was* a robotic man—only, it *wasn't* a dream.

Which meant he was caught inside an Apogee model at that moment and was being forced to fight his friends.

Dane and Naomi split up and ran in opposite directions—his legs followed Naomi. She threw objects back at him, but his robotic self merely brushed them aside, unperturbed and losing no ground in his chase. Aung wished he could call to her; tell her that it was him. But mostly, he wished he could stop his body from attacking her.

He willed himself to be calm, willed himself to do what he always did when chaos threatened to encircle him; he focused on his breath. Even though this was a robotic body, it still had a pair of lungs that hungered to be filled with life-giving air. He focused his mind on the sensation of that air within him, on how it felt to hold that connection to the world for the briefest of moments before releasing it.

One. Two. Three.

He felt the world slowing, felt the sensation of all existence heightened with laser beam clarity down to the only moment that truly mattered, the only one that could be experienced; the present.

Four. Five. Six.

When his fingers began to tingle he ignored it, focusing only on the breath.

Seven. Eight.

His legs stumbled and he let himself fall to the ground, pretending the movement was simply a stray thought and ignoring it.

Nine.

He collapsed onto his hands, feeling a grin spread onto his lips.

He never had managed to make it all the way to ten.

Naomi

She was doing everything she could to deal with the Apogee before her. Jax hadn't been exaggerating when he'd said the AIs were all different. Some were smarter and this one in particular was learning a lot faster than the others. It also now appeared to be directing the second Apogee that was following her. It was bad enough being attacked by one of the monsters at a time. She wasn't certain she could survive them teaming up on her.

Her block was slow to counter, and the strike collided with enough force to throw her through a dividing wall. When she finally stopped moving, she had to blink a few times to get her bearings. Could an Apogee body get a concussion?

She dragged herself to her feet, the pair of Apogees facing her on the other side of the dividing wall, staring her down through the new hole.

And that was when the Apogee on her right fell to its knees.

If it had been a human, she would have thought it was some sort of ploy to confuse her and make her drop her guard. But an AI wouldn't do that, no matter how clever, would it? She turned her sights instead on the other one, taking a breath as she realized she'd been distracted long enough to miss it launching toward her.

It landed atop her, and both its hands clamped around her neck as they tumbled to the floor. She managed to wedge her hands between its wrists but that only kept it from completely crushing her throat; it didn't give her enough leverage to free herself. The machine had positioned itself perfectly above her so that she couldn't fight back and panic was quickly setting in. Its fingers were too strong to yank and she doubted it would care as much as a human would even if she ripped one off. If she couldn't get free, then it was going to crush the only human pieces she had and she was terrified she was going to die in that metal can instead of her body—

The Apogee atop her was ripped away, violently. Her eyes shifted to take in another Apogee finishing a flawless and powerful spinning wheel kick. The force sent the choke-happy Apogee crashing into a nearby workbench.

Naomi sat up slowly, leaning back on her hands. There were only a handful of people she'd ever witnessed perform a spinning wheel kick with that much skill. But there was simply no way it could be possible. "Aung?"

The Apogee face, which had been so cold and lifeless, came to life with a broad grin. "You shouldn't be so surprised to see me."

"But... How?" She got to her feet, hurrying to him and trying to contain her shock. "How did you manage to get control of the Apogee?"

The easy shrug was so like him. "All I did was meditate my way out."

Of course he had. "But—"

Aung leaned backward at an unreal angle to avoid the fist of the other Apogee he'd just tossed aside. Apparently, it had regrouped and added Aung to its list of targets. She thrust her right knee to the sky in order to launch herself off the ground, rotating her hips and landing a roundhouse kick to its face. The Apogee model hardly seemed to notice.

Aung was still grinning as he did a series of punches. "Naomi, let me fight him!"

She hesitated. "You seem as if you're having fun."

"I've always wanted an out of body experience!" His fists came together in a mountain punch, and when he hit the Apogee in the solar plexus, it was thrown back fifteen feet.

"We don't know where my sister and Pema are so don't do any permanent damage!" She had to admit the Apogee was having trouble with Aung. But his fighting style would be new data for it and Aung's fighting was unreal. She ran back to the others, seeing Dane was fighting two by himself. "Aung got control of his Apogee!"

Dane threw a screwdriver at one of the Apogees nearest him. "Inari's got short-circuited, so that evens out." He threw a gun to her. "Go end this."

She caught the gun, hesitant to leave him. "You need help?"

"This is total cake, what are you talking about?" He was promptly punched in the gut and groaned in pain. "Okay, more like Brussels sprouts, but whatever. Now, go, already! You're distracting." He yanked one Apogee by the arm, tossing it into the second.

She turned away and texted Inari as she ran. *Aung found a way to control his Apogee.*

Incoming message from Inari Hayashi. WHAT??! How did he do that?!?!

No idea. Are you close to being done with the rewrite?

Incoming message from Inari Hayashi. If by close, you mean not at all, then yes. Very.

As she neared the interface where she'd left Jax earlier she slowed, putting her back to the dividing wall. *Should I go after Jax?*

Incoming message from Inari Hayashi. I mean, everyone is still trapped inside those Apogees and we don't know if he's plotted anything else nasty. I don't know if it's a good idea. He could have herds of vampires or something!

She lifted a brow. *You've been reading too many of those comics.*

She didn't like the idea of facing Jax but she also didn't like the idea of stalling being their only option. And he was bound to notice none of them were dead and his evil Apogees were dwindling in number. Jax being free to roam and make their lives more complicated wasn't in their best interest. She suspected his Apogee body was made of a stronger material than the others they'd been fighting, which meant shooting it would do little. Destroying one computer interface wouldn't help, as there were a multitude of others. That left her with distraction as her only viable option.

Peeking around the corner, she saw Jax at the interface where he'd been earlier, typing and moving information around on the image screen. She carefully pushed away from the wall and crept up behind him, putting the barrel of her gun to the back of his skull. She'd never had a moment where she'd wished so strongly she weren't a cop and could pull the trigger with a bullet that would kill him. "I'm done with this crap. You're under arrest and I'm going to enjoy telling the world about who you really are."

Jax chuckled, seemingly unperturbed by the proximity of her a gun. "Oh, my darling. I'm not going to jail." His smile incensed her. "But I'm enjoying myself too much." The absolute confidence he was displaying made her falter. Was there more to his plan? "You see, you won't be telling anyone about what's really happened."

Her eyes narrowed. "I'd be dead before I'd lie for you."

"I could kill you." He turned just enough so their eyes met. "But you're so pretty now." Their gazes held and she saw his finger press a button. When she went to tell him to stop, she found her lips wouldn't move. He let out a long sigh of relief. "Especially now that I can finally shut you up."

Naomi's arm moved against her will, lowering to her side. She willed herself to pull the trigger, to make the gun work. But her body stubbornly refused to follow direction. Out of her peripheral vision she saw Dane come around the corner and stop in surprise.

"Naomi…" Dane's voice was nervous. "What are you doing?"

A large image screen popped to life in the air behind Jax, showing a perfectly coifed woman in a power suit sitting behind a wide desk. "Breaking news tonight in the love life of playboy billionaire and CEO of CLM, Jackson Raelyn and NYPD detective, Naomi Gate." A photo was juxtaposed beside the anchor and Naomi remembered it being taken. Jax was behind her, his hands pressed to her stomach and his lips against hers. They'd been heading into their anniversary dinner. The whole screen switched to a video. Naomi recognized the table and the aquarium in the background; it was the Euphotic Zone and Jax was kneeling before her, holding open a ring case. "So, Naomi Gate. Will you marry me?" Even though she remembered she'd asked for time to think, in the video it moved seamlessly to her nodding. He put the ring on her finger before leaning up to give her a deep kiss, them both looking every bit the excited newly engaged couple.

The picture paused and held on the image of their kiss.

She remembered the waiter who had been watching them. He must have been the one recording and then someone had edited it perfectly. Jax clearly had staged it all, from having the reporters there to having the waiter watching with an illegal optical upgrade that could bypass privacy settings. It explained why Jax had been so emphatic about her wearing that stupid—

Jax reached over to take her left hand and turned it palm up, running a finger along her wrist. A small compartment popped open and she took in a breath of fear as she saw him pull out the ring. "I believe I've given you enough time to think, so I'll ask again. Will you marry me, Naomi?"

Her mouth answered despite her brain screaming for the words not to come out. "Yes, of course, my dear." He slipped the ring around her finger and his lips were pressing to hers as he wrapped her in his arms.

Dane

His eyes were moving between the frozen image of the newly engaged Jax and Naomi on the screen to the real life drama of them kissing before him. Naomi had said that he'd pressured her to wear the ring, hadn't she? That she'd asked for time to think and hadn't given him an answer.

But in the video she'd clearly answered yes and now—

Oh God. What if it had all been a lie? His mind reeled, thinking of all the things that could've been either lucky coincidences or utterly planned on her part. Even everything with her sister could have been a hoax and now she was smiling at Jax and wearing his ring and what if she'd been on his side the whole time—

Wait. Apogee, remember? Right. While he hadn't known her that long, he knew that Naomi loved eating vegetables, running, and living on the straight and narrow. There was no way someone who freaked out at being given a hit of Dash would be involved in any illegal CLM bullshit. Not to mention, since he'd spent the night with her, he couldn't believe she was into Jax. So, until he had reason to believe otherwise—admittedly, perhaps flying in the face of reason—he decided it was more believable that she was under Jax's evil mind control.

Which posed a serious problem. He needed time to think. "So Jax. Is it true you can't get it up unless it's detachable? Let's be honest. Are you actually more interested in toasters than women?"

Jax chuckled as he turned, his arm around Naomi's waist. "For your information, I personally participated in extensive product testing to ensure that every inch of her is utterly perfect."

"Ew." His nose scrunched up. "Please tell me that's a euphemism for making some sort of portable vagina and not that you were banging all the freaky mannequins up here."

"You JERK!" Inari's small form ran out of hiding, pointing straight at Jax. "I knew it!!!" Dane had to wrap his arms around her waist to keep her from launching herself at the man. Even then, she was flailing enough that she came off the ground. "You were cheating on her with that gross Apogee model from the image screen outside!?!"

Jax gave a nonchalant shrug in answer.

[296]

It was nice the man was every bit the asshole Dane had always assumed. But not only was his guilt for having slept with someone else's girlfriend gone, he felt pretty good about it. He shook his head. "All this aside, why the hell are you enslaving her now?"

"Oh, I expect Apogee sales will go through the roof. I mean, after all…" Jax looked pleased with himself. "You didn't think I made her famous because I liked her, did you?"

The Apogee model that was currently housing Aung was now standing at Dane's other side. "You wanted her to become a symbol for humanity."

"Of course, once she—" Jax faltered only momentarily at one of his Apogees talking back to him. "Once she becomes my Apogee bride, everyone will see what real perfection is."

So, this had been Jax's true end game all along. Dane frowned as he tried to think it through. Aung had found websites dedicated to Naomi, and how she was changing people's perceptions of bionics. Jax had probably planted those and obviously orchestrated their romance. Aung had said that by her dating Jax, it threw into question the reason to get bionic upgrades if someone like Naomi was good enough for him.

Conversely though, if Naomi suddenly became heavily bionic with vanity upgrades—

"You made her an icon for humanity specifically so you could get her into a bionic body and destroy your opposition?"

"Genius marketing plan, isn't it?" He gave an incorrigible smirk.

There was a computerized trill before a voice broke through. "Mr. Raelyn, the NYPD SWAT team is here."

Dane felt a thrill of relief for only a split second before he realized that Jax looked far too pleased by that news. Though, Jax did manage to make his voice sound afraid.

"Please, send them up quickly."

Naomi's facial expression didn't change but her words sounded fearful. "Tell them to hurry! The bounty hunter I hired has turned on me and he's trying to kill us!"

"You're incredible. I mean, I've dealt with a lot of scum bags in my day but you..." Dane let out a chortle. "You are hands down the sickest fucker I've ever met."

"I'll take that as a compliment from someone like you." His eyes turned to Naomi and he ran a finger over her lips. "Now, while I do enjoy my work being appreciated, the reality is, it would be very inconvenient for you all to still be alive when the police get up here, so... Let me introduce you to the true capabilities of a full strength and militarized Apogee. Naomi..." He stepped away from her and glanced at Dane with a terrible smile. "Kill them."

CHAPTER 22

Dane

Naomi gave a frosty smile, devoid of warmth. "My pleasure."

The arm holding her gun lifted lightning fast and it was all he could do to tackle Inari and get them both out of the way behind the walls of a workstation. As the heat of the blast washed over them he looked at the girl. "Go code. Fast." She gave a hurried nod and crawled around a corner. Dane turned back in time to stare in shock at the sight of Aung rushing toward Naomi and her gun.

Aung grabbed her wrist and yanked her arm toward the ceiling while simultaneously sweeping his leg behind her and kicking the back of her knee so she fell to the ground. Before Aung could take control of the gun though she launched up at him, and the weapon ricocheted across the room into a distant work area. As they continued to engage in hand-to-hand combat, their arms and legs were moving so fast Dane could hardly follow. The terrifying thing was that despite what he would have expected, Aung appeared to be losing ground. The only thing he could figure was that Jax was somehow to blame.

Jax whistled to himself as he typed at the interface. Well, if Jax was the puppet master it was clear Dane's target should be the man behind the curtain.

Even though Aung wasn't gaining ground, it meant Naomi was occupied and that was enough. Dane rushed across the aisle, pulling one of his last guns—scratch that, his last gun—out of his bicep compartment. That just meant he had better make it count. He looked around the corner, took aim and was about to pull the trigger—

When he felt his arm get ripped off at the shoulder.

Naomi dropped his arm to the floor with a thud and he was splashed with chemicals. The contact burns felt like his skin was on fire, eating through his shirt. When she lifted a hand to bring a hammerfist down on his skull, he managed to slam his other hand into her side, igniting a low-level current that incapacitated her long enough for him to increase the power to his legs and race away.

He ducked into a workstation and wove his way into a secluded area, hiding beneath a large desk to catch his breath as the pain from the burns started to ease. How the fuck was he supposed to fight a military grade Barbie? And more challengingly, not hurt her in the process? He'd used up all his EMP discs, which—come to think of it— had probably been Jax's plan all along when he'd set those Apogee models on them earlier.

As much as he hated the man, he was really fucking clever as a villain.

Jax's plan aside, Dane was intent that his chaotic good group would somehow still win the day. He texted his wildcard. *I'm in serious shit out here, help me.*

Incoming message from Leon Hartwick. I can only do one thing at a time. Stall.

I hate you. You know that, don't you?

Incoming message from Leon Hartwick. I'm aware.

Dane leaned his head back and closed his eyes. Distantly, he could hear Naomi fighting again and assumed Aung had found his way back to his feet.

He tried to think of any situations where things had seemed bleaker. Even that time in Costa Rica was a breeze compared to this clusterfuck.

Even his humor failed him, which made his heart truly sink. The reality was he probably wasn't going to live to help Naomi get back into her body. He'd been looking forward to having her teach him to be a long-distance runner. He knew it was silly seeing as he didn't have quads but the truth was, despite all his protestations to the contrary, no one had ever made him feel as human as she did.

What were they going to do?

There was a whirring sound as if a can opener had mated with a percolator, and Dane opened his eyes to see the unfinished Apogees in the compartments against the wall were now moving.

Incoming message from Leon Hartwick. But since I don't want you to die, here's something. Apogees can't fully function without a person inside, but I've coded them to wander around and provide a distraction. Now stall so Inari and I can fix this mess.

Dane felt a grin spreading across his lips as the Apogee army began filing away. *I take everything back. You're the best and I owe you.*

Incoming message from Leon Hartwick. You do enjoy wasting time telling me things I already know.

He stood and glanced around the workstation for anything he could use as a weapon. Fortunately, someone had left behind a stack of smoke bombs. He put them into a quad compartment and then grabbed a really big wrench, because why not? Hopefully now, even if he couldn't save the day, he could at least stall long enough so the tech geniuses could.

Aung

His body flew through the air before slamming into a wall.

Naomi was still on the far side of the room as she'd thrown him quite a distance. He hurried to get his arms untangled from the metal—he'd caved it in with the force of his impact—but she was already on him. He was barely able to duck and shove his leg out in a wide sweep, bringing her to the floor. While he had control of his new body, it did not have power settings as high as hers. He felt like a swallow trying to fight a mountain.

He rushed away, calling to her. "Naomi, I know you can hear me. I want to talk to you. The real you, not the monster that's controlling you." He ducked into a work area. "You can find your way out, if you believe."

A ball landed near his feet and a loud hiss preceded smoke gushing out of all sides. The hand at his back made him turn quickly into a defensive posture, but it was Dane—or he should call him one-armed Dane, now.

Incoming message from Dane Thayer. Distract her for me.

Aung nodded and kept calling out to Naomi, working his way deep into the smoke. "Do you remember what Pema and I chanted, when you escaped in the cave?" He carefully began moving, sweeping his feet in wide arcs before setting them down. He was grateful he'd spent so much time practicing night fighting, since the same principles also applied to fighting-in-thick-smoke-against-your-friend-who-is-being-controlled-remotely-while-inside-a-robotic-body combat. "That chant, I think it's very applicable to our situation right now. But why don't I let you decide?"

There was the noise of fighting and flashes of light amidst the smoke, and something metallic was ripped apart before silence settled over them again. Aung ran into something and jumped backward, surprised when he saw the unfinished Apogee marching forward—it was missing the top of its skull and one eye was hanging out of its socket, attached by a wire. He watched until it disappeared in the smoke.

He did another sweep fully around, searching with his hands in wide arcs along with his feet. "Attached to your loved ones, you're stirred up like water." As soon as he spoke, he quickly shifted to another area, so that his voice would not give away his position. "Hating your enemies you burn like fire." Maybe he could find Jax in this, find a way to free her. "In the darkness of confusion, you forget what to adopt and discard."

He was stopped in the center of the aisle when his searching hand found purchase and he knew instantly it wasn't one of the soulless Apogees. His voice softened as he met her cold, lifeless eyes. "Give up your homeland." And despite how quick he was, he wasn't fast enough to get his hand away before she ripped it off.

Naomi

Aung's Apogee disappeared into the smoke and she distantly felt herself dropping his dismembered hand to the floor. Another of the empty Apogees came into view and her hands dispatched it with cold efficiency, leaving it in two piles on the floor, ripped clean in half at the waist.

It was a nightmare. It was worse than total paralysis because she was forced to bear silent witness to the atrocities her shell was committing. She wouldn't let herself call it her body because it wasn't; it was a shell—a prison—in which she was powerless against the programming. She wanted to believe she could break through like Aung had. But every second that passed, every instant she had to watch her shell ripping them apart made her realize that she was not a super powerful monk and there was no way she was going to be able to free herself like he had.

Attached to your loved ones, you're stirred up like water.

The room was full of smoke but bodies scattered on the floor periodically came in and out of her view. Which of the machines lying there housed her sister? She realized now at the monastery, Aung had been doing more than just helping her sister—he'd been helping them to reconnect as siblings. She wanted to adopt a cat or a rabbit, anything really, and spend hours with her sister, playing like they used to. They hadn't played since they were children—since she'd been trying too hard to be a mother. She desperately wanted a second chance to be a big sister again.

Hating your enemies you burn like fire.

How could Jax do this to her? It wasn't just the money for him. His entire plan had been designed to strike down those who loved their humanness and replace it with cold, bionic perfection. He wanted the world to be filled with lifeless machines.

In the darkness of confusion, you forget what to adopt and discard.

But machines weren't all bad. Leon and Inari clung to their human parts, yes, but they adored machines. Their passion for computers had brought them together and given them a common ground of understanding—one that let a pair of two awkward loners come together and find a human connection.

Give up your homeland.

While Naomi could never truly understand what it had been like for Lin when she'd been Tyler, she imagined it must have felt like being trapped. Seeing the way Lin had given a resplendent smile while talking about feeling aligned with her new body... her sister had found her truest self through technology.

Give up your homeland.

And then there was Dane. His human parts had nearly killed him and yet, he loved his body—his human and bionic parts, equally. He believed in a fundamental humanness that was somehow stronger than anything she'd ever believed in. The eyes of her body lifted to set their sights on him and she saw he was missing an arm. What had she done? Terror gripped her further as she saw her body's arm lift, and a gun barrel popped out of her forearm and fired.

Give up your homeland.

Despair was crushing her. What could she do? Feeling anguish without tears welling up, without the tightness in her chest… it felt more terrible somehow. She didn't want to die a machine. She wanted to at least be in her body and—homesick. She was homesick.

Give up your homeland.

But she was never getting her body back, was she?

Give up your homeland.

Dane had been hit but he was still standing, still fighting. He really was amazing. No matter what percentage of bionic he became, he would still be just as insufferably human.

Give up your homeland.

Dane. Of course. She felt the surprise almost as a physical sensation. She knew what her homeland was now—what it had always been.

Give up your homeland.

Her body. Her temple. Her home.

Give up your homeland.

Distantly, she felt fingertips and let her rage form her hand into a fist.

Give up your homeland.

She didn't need her body.

Because no matter what, no matter where she ended up or whatever happened...

Nothing and no one could take away her humanity.

Dane

He was exhausted. Beyond it, actually. Even with Aung at his side fighting Naomi they hadn't made a dent in her, figuratively or literally. All they'd managed was to rip off some of the fake skin from her right thigh, and one of her shoulder compartments was wedged open. When she'd been in control of her body she must not have had access to the highest levels of power output that her body was capable of. Even Dane's aftermarket military upgrades couldn't compare and Aung, while an Apogee, was so damaged that it hardly made a difference.

Quite simply, they were going to die.

When he slammed into a workstation he was spun end over end before landing on his face. He groaned and tried to stand, but found his right leg bent at an unreal angle. Now he couldn't even run away. He backed up as much as he could but saw her leap and there was nothing he could do to avoid her. She landed atop him and lifted her fist, and he resigned himself to the fact that it was over.

When the metal crunched in his ear he flinched in surprise to find her fist directly beside his head. He looked up into her eyes in shock. "Inari?"

The way her eyebrow tilted playfully told him before she could. "No." She pressed her lips to his, giving him without a doubt the most heated and passionate kiss he'd ever experienced. When their lips parted he stared into her eyes and he could almost swear they were her own again and not gem-encrusted forgeries.

"Sorry, there's not time for more but we need to keep the element of surprise. My apologies..." She picked him up off the floor and while he was still reeling she hurtled him across the room like a football. He had a moment of weightlessness before he began to descend, trying to figure out why in the world she'd tossed him—

Oh, well, if his trajectory was taking him there, he might as well make it worthwhile.

Aung

He watched in shock as Naomi picked up Dane as if he weighed nothing and threw him across the room. While still in midflight, Dane twisted and landed with both legs aimed at the center of Jax's back. As the pair crashed through the interface, there were sparks of light and flares of protest from the machinery as it was shredded. Naomi called back to Aung, nearly there herself. "I'll need your help!"

Aung snapped out of his haze to rush over, though not nearly as fast as Naomi. Dane tumbled out of the rubble and came to a stop against a wall. One of his legs had been snapped off at the knee while the other was twisted back on itself. He wasn't even sure Dane was still conscious, but Aung did see that he was still breathing.

Naomi crouched and launched herself up high, coming down onto the rubble where Jax had been moments before. Aung heard a scuffle and was about to rush to her aid when his arms were grabbed from behind. A dozen unfinished Apogees crowded him. Dane had said they were acting as a distraction and previously they'd just been walking around aimlessly.

Now though, they were swarming him and before he could react, they grabbed his legs, lifting him from the ground. For every hand he got off his body, another two took its place. They weren't incredibly strong, but their numbers made it impossible for him to get free—he felt them starting to pull at his feet, yanking off a toe.

And he knew it wouldn't be too long before he was literally pulled apart.

Naomi

Jax hadn't been prepared for her attack, but he'd rallied faster than she'd hoped. Even though when they'd dated he'd never shown any interest in her martial arts, he now seemed to be far better than she was. Inexplicably, even better than Aung.

She faked a low punch to his chest and her hand snapped back up to his face. He somehow blocked it, grabbing her hand. How was he doing that? His kick came out of nowhere and she was flipped over fully before she landed face first on the ground, sliding to a stop.

"Did you know your brother was working as a mule for Baozhai?"

She got to her elbows and saw his foot aiming toward her. She was able to roll out of the way as his foot slammed into the ground where she'd just been. Naomi jumped to her feet and took quick steps backward. "Yes."

They exchanged a series of punches and when he slammed a fist into her chest the breath was knocked out of her and all she could do was cough. Jax grabbed her hair, staring down into her eyes. "Did he tell you that he stole one of the packages he was supposed to deliver?"

She was able to get a breath. "She said she didn't steal it." She tried to kick him in the groin, but his other hand caught her leg, tossing her back onto a table. How was he beating her? How did he know everything she was going to do before even she did?

"Is Tyler trans? He should have said something! I could have gotten him a body."

She blinked at Jax, but he grabbed her ankles, yanking her toward him. He gave a terrible chuckle. "Please, I love taking money off trans people. They're one of our most profitable demographics." Jax grabbed both her wrists, his body crushing her into the table. "You know, for once, your good for nothing brother was telling the truth about those drugs." His voice lowered. "He didn't steal them."

She struggled to process his words past her anger at the misgendering of her sister, her hands pinned above her head and his face inches from hers. "How do you know?"

He leaned down to whisper into her ear. "Because I did."

His warm breath in her ear and the way he was pressing himself between her thighs made her feel defiled. "You did?" Why couldn't she get any leverage? She felt weaker with every instant.

Jax's breath was in her ear. "Did you know his drug of choice is Dash? A few free hits and I was his best friend."

Her brows drew together in confusion until it dawned on her. "That body you gave me…"

His eyes met hers. "Hardly the only criminal body I've created."

Jax was the reason her sister had been forced into a dangerous Switch. Jax was the reason Lin had been terrified and nearly died in an attempt to fix a problem she hadn't actually caused. And, insult to injury, Jax's twisted smirk conveyed that he was clearly enjoying misgendering her sister. Naomi felt a surge of rage and wrapped her legs around Jax, and for a split second, she saw the sick, warped lust in his eyes. She took that opportunity to headbutt him and used her leverage to toss him to the side in his moment of surprise. She hopped to her feet and backed away from him. "Why are you telling me this now?"

Jax chuckled darkly, shaking his head as he watched her. "Because I want you to know how wonderful it was to hunt your pathetic excuse for a little brother. You should have seen the way he ran to that shop to get his new body. Oh, Naomi." There was a vile smile on his lips. "It was such a thrill."

Her throat ached, thinking about what it had been like for Lin. "Don't talk about my sister that way! You're disgusting."

"This is what we do at CLM. I'm just cleaning up your life." His eyes moved over every inch of her body slowly before they returned to hers. "Because it's mine now."

She was fairly certain she could have walked down the streets of New York naked and not felt even half as violated as she did right then.

Taking in his stance change, she frowned. He hadn't studied martial arts, how was he—but she seemed to be moving in slow motion and his foot connected with her stomach before she could stop it. She flew through the air, slamming into a wall and slowly slumping to the ground. As she got her bearings she was more terrified than hurt. Had he just done a spinning wheel kick?

Jax's chuckle echoed, and the residual smoke seemed to part for him. "Those AIs worked better than I'd imagined."

He'd taken all the data from the twelve Apogee AIs, compiled it and launched the program within her. But then, he'd taken the data from her and compiled it for himself? Which meant he had the collective fighting skills of her, Dane and Aung.

His fingers tapped out a sequence and her legs buckled. She

landed on her knees, Jax towering over her. His backfist strike was so fast she couldn't get a block up in time. Her body felt unnaturally heavy. She was on the floor and could barely hold herself up on her elbows.

He got to a single knee beside her, brushing a hand through her hair tenderly. "Poor thing. You're so weak." He sat back on his heel. "Tell me, how did you and the other one override my programming? Was it Leon?"

She looked up at him, her eyes narrowing. "We meditated our way out."

Jax yanked her up by the hair and she felt as if she were a rag doll. "I made you what you are. Now how did you break the code?"

Despite the fact she knew it was suicide, she decided watching him unhinge was worth it. She lowered her voice and enunciated every syllable. "We med-i-ta-ted."

His free hand went to her throat and he was kneeling on both legs now, crushing her against the wall. "I liked you so much better when I could shut you up." She could barely lift her hands to fight him. It dawned on her he must have turned her power down that much. Over his shoulder she caught sight of Aung being pulled apart by the unfinished Apogees that Jax must have somehow gotten ahold of. There was a sick feeling at the acknowledgement that no help was coming. It had been a long shot that Leon and Inari could rewrite the entire code in time.

Their gamble had failed.

Jax ran his nose along her cheek before growling into her ear. "At least I can have a copy of you now that will behave better than you ever did."

Well, if she couldn't physically fight him she could at least piss him off. "Speaking of better than..." She smiled sweetly.

"Dane's better in bed than you ever were."

"Well, Nikola isn't thrilled with your looks, but she'll be fine inhabiting that body since I trimmed down your thighs."

"Hopefully you gave yourself a choice upgrade or she'll be just as dissatisfied as I was." He yanked her forward and slammed her hard into the wall. She heard as much as felt the metal bending around her and it was enough to knock the breath from her lungs. She felt like a toy and despondency overwhelmed her. As her insides ached, she closed her eyes and wished she could say goodbye.

Incoming message from Dane Thayer. I thought you might need a hand.

She felt pressure against her leg and saw a dismembered silver bionic hand poking her urgently. It pressed something into her palm and as she recognized the shape of the item, she felt her soul lift with hope. She lifted her eyes to meet Jax's terrible gaze, his hand drawn back in a fist. "Say goodbye, Naomi."

"Go to hell, Jax." As his fist was coming toward her, she put all she had left into lifting her hand to his side, not believing she could possibly make it in time. She cringed as Jax's fist was about to hit her face—but her hand reached his side first and the EMP disc activated to wrap Jax in blue lightning. As the light ebbed, their eyes caught. The surprise was apparent in his before he slumped to the ground, unconscious.

She took in a shaky breath, slumping back against the wall. Her throat hurt as she swallowed but at least she was still alive.

And that was when the lights went out.

She shouted into the darkness. "Seriously?!"

There was a thunderous crash and when the emergency lights flicked on, she saw the unfinished Apogees that had been attacking Aung had fallen to the ground like broken puppets. Naomi was prepared for a struggle to get herself to standing but was pleasantly surprised to find her power level had normalized. She could only assume Leon and Inari were responsible. She hurried over to check on Aung, finding that most of the skin of his arms had been removed to show the mechanical parts beneath. His legs were completely detached but he let out a sigh of relief at seeing her. "Naomi, you're safe."

She hugged him tightly, letting out a shaky breath. "Thank you." She wasn't sure whether an Apogee could cry, but she knew she'd find a way even if it couldn't. "I heard you, when I was locked away. I heard you and you were right and—"

"And you found your way home."

She drew back to smile at him. "You're crazy."

He grinned like the chaos wizard he was. "Maybe just a little." She leaned him against the pile of broken Apogees so he could sit upright and he motioned with his head. "Go to Dane. I think he was surprised to join the circus and be part of an aerial display." She felt bashful as she backed up, promising to come back in a moment. When she came upon Dane she found her heart aching.

He was slumped against a wall and looking even worse than earlier. Now one leg was completely gone and the other twisted and inoperable. A quick scan revealed he also had a pair of broken ribs, a broken collarbone and would likely need a few more plates to add to his collection. Kneeling before him she helped him to sit up. "Where'd you find that EMP disc?"

"Under this table. I missed one of the Apogees earlier." He gave a weak chuckle. "Lucky I wasn't able to move or I might've missed it."

There were numerous cuts and bruises he'd gained throughout the battle, one above his eye issuing a river of blood down to his chin. She wiped it away carefully. "You're a mess."

"Well, you're actually looking a lot better." Her brow rose dubiously and Dane smiled. "You look more human."

Their eyes held in silence.

He lowered his voice. "What happened when you were locked inside there?"

Distantly, she heard the metal door screeching open and the police calling out their presence.

"I realized something." Her hand rose to touch his cheek and he leaned into it, still watching her. "You were right." She sat down beside him, putting an arm around him and drawing his head against her shoulder. "The most fundamental part of being human *is* kicking ass."

Dane

"We will be contacting you if we need further information."

He cringed at the promise in the officer's tone. "Great." At the woman's pointed look he cleared his throat. "I mean, of course, ma'am." The woman had grilled him non-stop for at least a couple of hours on the events of the last few days. He felt validated for all the previous times he'd avoided questioning by the police. At least Leon's spiderbot had come and provided him some quality first aid; otherwise the interview would have been far more painful.

He rested his head against the wall to wait, seeing as he was almost totally immobile now. There was a tap on his side and he looked down to see his dismembered hand had found its way back to him. It reattached to his wrist and he was about to use it to message Naomi when he caught sight of her.

She was talking with a group of officers and her eyes found his. He adored the reserved smile she gave and was grateful when she headed toward him.

Until he remembered he couldn't stand.

She crouched before him with a lifted brow. "Ready to get out of here?"

"Yeah, just get me a shopping cart and I'll be good to go."

She snickered and offered her arms with a questioning brow.

He grumbled angrily. "No fucking way are you carrying me! I have cis-male dignity!!"

Their eyes held, her arms still outstretched. He muttered, slipping his only remaining limb around her shoulders, since she seemed intent on disgracing him.

She stood with him far too easily. "I think you'll survive, somehow."

He looked over her shoulder and muttered into her ear as they made their way across the floor. "You've single-handedly destroyed my cis-manhood."

"Really?" She whispered in his ear. "And here I was hoping you'd prove your manhood to me later."

That assuaged his ego just enough.

In the hallway Naomi settled him onto a gurney beside Aung. The man's Apogee body had taken a beating during the fight and he was also lacking in mobility. "It looks as though we've won." Aung glanced at Naomi. "Though how were we able to launch Sanctuary?"

Inari sighed loudly. "Geez, you don't need to be so grumpish, I was only suggesting—"

"Thank you, Detective Hayashi. We will take it from here." The officer who was walking Inari out of the room promptly turned and left her at the threshold.

Inari crossed her arms over her chest and scowled at the man as he disappeared. "You'd think since he's with cybercrimes he'd want to know that his encryption settings were faulty—"

"There, there, dear. Not everyone's genius is understood during their time." The spiderbot on Inari's shoulder gave her cheek a gentle nuzzle.

Naomi turned to her partner. "So. How did you and Leon do it?"

"It was due to you and Aung, actually."

Dane glanced between the two in surprise as Inari continued. "We weren't making much progress with trying to recode by hand. It was too time consuming and trying to make it substantially different from the first Sanctuary code wasn't working."

The spider shifted. *"It wasn't until Naomi found her way out that we thought to look at the coding in your bodies to see how you'd done it."*

Dane's head was spinning. "What do you mean, see how they'd done it?"

Inari shrugged. "The human brain is really just an awesome computer—or I suppose more accurately, a computer is just trying to be as great as a human brain. So, when those two took over their bodies they basically rewrote the code. Copying that was better and faster than us physically writing it."

Aung raised his arm, seemingly oblivious to the fact that he was missing his hand. "But why are the lights still out?"

"We'd been editing the original Sanctuary protocol. Once we added the coding from Aung and Naomi it was faster to just edit the rest before launching it."

Naomi shifted her weight to one side. "Wait, so you had to change something in the lights out part of the code also to get past Jax's protections, didn't you?"

The girl gave a giggle that bordered on a squeal. "We left the lights on in places like cat cafes, libraries, arcades. Ooo, and vending machines!" Naomi was lifting a brow at her friend and Inari giggled again, punching the sky. "Places that exemplify humanity!"

Spiderbot gave a slight cough, turning on Inari's shoulder to more fully face her.

"And perhaps places that you would like to go on a date in the next twenty-four hours?"

Inari cupped spiderbot in her hands and spun around once. "Yes, of course!"

Dane rubbed his eyes as he chuckled.

When everyone went silent, he lifted his hand to see a new officer standing in the doorway, with an Apogee model that looked just like Aung's beside him. Naomi took a step forward. "Lin?"

They rushed together and embraced. Dane was grateful to see Lin's Apogee hadn't sustained any noticeable damage in the fighting and wondered if she'd been one of the three Apogees he'd taken down at the beginning of the fight.

Naomi was still hugging her sister as she looked at the officer. "What about Pema?"

The man shook his head. "The other Apogees we've woken are all coders here at CLM."

In the silence that followed, the officer lowered his voice. "Naomi, we've got the whole building to search too. He could have tons of people locked up here."

Dane looked at Aung. They were all thinking about the thirteenth Apogee, that Jax had blown up before the fighting began. Aung gave a sad smile. "If Pema is no longer of this world, I know that he is at peace. But we will miss him." Dane squeezed Aung's arm though because he looked like he needed it.

The officer excused himself and Lin straightened, putting a hand on Naomi's cheek. "Is your human body okay?"

Naomi gave a sad smile and a shrug. "I don't know. We'll find out as soon as the police know. No matter what though, we'll be okay." She put a hand on her sister's male cheek, frowning. "Are you okay? I'm sorry you're stuck again in a body that's wrong for you."

Lin gave an uncomfortable shrug. "Hopefully they'll find my body soon."

"I've found a female body we can transfer you into as soon as you get to my warehouse."

Inari sucked in a breath. "And you can borrow some of my dresses until we can get your new wardrobe figured out!" "I'd like that." A smile warmed Lin's lips as she looked around at everyone. "But what happened?"

Naomi glanced at each person in turn. "We kicked a lot of ass as a team."

Dane took in the motley friends that surrounded him. Aung, the humanist monk who had been unperturbed to find himself locked inside of a machine. Lin, the younger sister who was still trying to make amends for her choices. Inari, an extraordinary hacker who was a loyal and steadfast friend. Leon, who strangely seemed more human in spiderbot form than he did sometimes in person.

And Naomi.

When she smiled at him, he realized he couldn't even put into words what she was. But that was oddly fitting, somehow.

Lin let out a sigh. "Figures I missed all the action."

"Don't worry, I recorded it."

Inari lifted spiderbot up high. "Spidercam!"

They all shared a cathartic laugh and Naomi put an arm around her sister's shoulders. When they turned to look out the window Dane's eyes followed her gaze. It was strange to see the nighttime city so darkened on the horizon. Even so, there were small pockets of light, places where Inari and Leon had left the lights on.

Little bastions of humanity amidst the darkness.

EPILOGUE

Naomi

She was down in a squat, the large support beam suspended on her shoulder. She waited for the other three monks to get situated before she heard the call for them to stand and they lifted the beam in unison. Her quads were burning painfully, and she delighted in every twinge and angry blaze.

It had taken the police three days to find her body. It had been in a one of CLM's warehouses down by the harbor. Apparently, Jax hadn't been exaggerating when he'd said her body was worth a lot of money. He'd found a buyer in China and Naomi was pleased to know her body was worth more than any model CLM had ever created. And she was never going to leave it, ever again.

"You should go easy on your body. It was in stasis for nearly a week and you've only been in it for a few days."

She ignored Dane. "I'm busy and you're distracting."

He was now standing on a new pair of bionic legs, but his right arm was in a sling. "How come I'm listening to doctor's orders and you aren't?"

The support beam was locked into place and she breathed a sigh of relief when she stepped out from under it. She hated to admit it but he was probably right that she needed to go a bit easier. "I'm just getting reacquainted with my body. You haven't had a human arm in a really long time." Her hand carefully reached out to touch the hand in the sling. The skin tone was similar to his own and when her fingers touched his, he curled them around hers carefully.

He shivered, his voice softening. "It's surreal."

After the fight at CLM Tower, they'd all gone back to Leon's laboratory so he could care for them. He'd been able to transfer Aung and Lin back into their bodies late the next day, and Naomi later that week. But he and Inari had immediately started repairing Dane. They'd started by giving him some strongly outfitted legs but before they'd gotten to his arm, Leon had had a breakthrough in Project Fùhuó. With Aung's and Inari's help they'd found a way to code the nanobots to make the procedure safer and less invasive. Dane had agreed to become the first test subject and the operation had gone flawlessly.

She leaned down to kiss his fingertips. "I still can't believe it worked."

"It won't be for everyone because of the anti-retroviral drugs but... I wonder, if in time, that can be figured out too." He met her gaze. "It's nice to have the option out there."

"Naomi! The surprise is finished!!"

She turned to her sister's voice, seeing her over by a short enclosure wrapped in chicken wire. She was back in the Asian body she'd been given by the Monkhood and was still wearing the burnt orange robes. Her insufferable grin was all her own, though. "Look!"

She pointed into the enclosure and Naomi took in a breath of surprise. "A rabbit house?" There were four fluffy bunnies huddled together in a corner. There was a large wooden box with a small ramp in the back, a small circular hole marking the entrance. Lin opened the little gate in the chicken wire fencing, bending down to grab a brown and white spotted rabbit with floppy ears. She handed it to Naomi, and she cradled the precious thing with a bright smile.

Lin's grin was broad. "Aung said we have a lot of animals on the compound and he thought having a rabbit enclosure would be a great addition."

Of course he would. The sly fox. "I'm glad, Lin."

Her sister had picked up a rabbit of her own. "You can come visit them anytime." She rubbed the fur between its ears. " And-and me."

She hesitated, her eyes lifting. "What?"

Her gaze wouldn't meet Naomi's. "I'm going to stay here, Noams. It's where I belong."

"Oh." Her legs felt weak, and she had to swallow. "I'm happy for you, of course, I just thought—"

"That I'd move in with you and we'd start fighting again?" She gave a sad smile, finally looking at her. "I'm happy here. I finally feel like the person I've always wanted to be. I just didn't know how to do it."

Dane grunted. "And if you fuck up, there are lots of people who can kick your ass back into gear."

Lin grinned. "Exactly!"

She wanted to laugh and she was happy for her sister. It just hurt, too. "I'm glad, little sis." She gave Lin a one-armed hug, the rabbits cuddled between them. And somehow, that fact made her feel less sad.

"Speaking of what's next." Dane lifted a brow. "When are you going to finally tell us about your chief's decision regarding your punishment?"

Naomi took in a deep breath, returning her bunny to the confines of the pen. She turned to Dane and glanced at Lin. "I'm on a one-year unpaid suspension."

"Me too!" Inari was walking down the steps of the nearby

building, Leon trailing at her side. He was wearing an eclectic suit and had upgraded his bunny slippers to loafers with a cat face design on the top.

Dane's brow rose. "But what did you do?"

She sucked in a breath through her teeth. "Uh, might've maybe had something to do with something I borrowed without asking during our epic Apogee battle."

When no one else did, Dane finally asked. "Which was what?"

"Um... Maybe a CIA satellite?" She cringed. "Or two?" This pause was shorter. "I mean, if I ever had time I'd ask permission but I did check and nothing was happening in Turkmenistan, soooo—"

"Regardless." Leon grunted in annoyance. "Suspension is ridiculous, considering without you the police wouldn't have even been aware the Apogee override existed, let alone found a fix for it."

Naomi gave a nod. "Which is pretty much the only reason we aren't in jail."

Leon put an arm around Inari's shoulders as she muttered. "They never care about all my good reasons and I'm tired of them expecting me to be grateful that they haven't put me in prison. I mean, we were awesome! Totally RPG-esque. I was the mage and Leon was the medic and you guys were the fighters. We're a great team!"

"Which leads me to my next question." Naomi felt herself blushing, clearing her throat and turning to Dane. "Since Inari and I don't have jobs, we were wondering if you'd like some help with bounty hunting?"

Dane's eyes showed his surprise and it was Leon's turn to clear his throat. "You are going to need some help paying your medical bills, after all."

Inari whacked the back of his head. "You're not charging your roommate to experiment on him."

Leon looked at Inari, his face full of hurt but when she kissed his nose he melted like butter. Dane met her gaze and was thoughtful for a long moment. "On one condition."

It was her turn to be surprised. "What's that?"

"We start a new scum-bags-captured counter. As a team."

She smiled in return. "As long as Jax is number one."

She could see in his eyes that they were agreed.

Out the building behind Leon and Inari, Aung appeared. At his side meandering casually down the stairs was someone she recognized. The dark skinned, well-toned body builder had enormous quads and biceps, but his forearms and lower legs were bionic below the joints. He was a formidable presence, perhaps especially because he was shorter than five feet.

Aung grinned. "Naomi! Meet my good friend Gabriel Scott."

She was still in shock as the little man took her hand and kissed the back of it. "My dear lady, you are simply a vision to behold."

The cadence and mannerisms were oddly familiar.

Aung motioned to Gabriel. "He finished his checkup with Leon, and he and I were just catching up."

She stared at the man. "You know, in another life, I was a body builder too."

He seemed amused. "Were you?"

"Yes, in a body almost…" She paused. "Well, exactly like that one."

Gabriel's eyes sparkled playfully. "Ah, well, in a previous life I was an old Jewish man. It's funny how the world works, isn't it?"

She felt her jaw dropping. Gabriel Scott. *Of course.* GS for Gray

Squirrel.

The man stretched his arms out above him. "And I've heard rumors that..." He checked an old watch that looked oddly appropriate on his silver bionic wrist. "Yes, right about now someone should be waking up to a new life as a Jewish grandfather." He grinned at her. "It's funny. One day, you think you're young and perfect, and the next... You wake up and you're an old coot."

She stared in disbelief. He couldn't possibly be referring to Jax, could he?

Dane chuckled beside her. "You're such a devil. How did you manage?"

The man shrugged, his eyes moving to Inari. "Well, Catatonic knows better than most that the police will make a lot of concessions for certain pieces of information."

Inari giggled and rushed up the stairs, dragging Leon behind her. "I'm going to hack their cameras so I can watch Jax waking up!"

Gabriel chuckled and bowed his head to Naomi. "It's been a pleasure, my dear." He winked before he moved past them and Naomi could only turn to watch him go in stunned silence.

Lin came to her side, letting out a long whistle. "Wow. Remind me never to piss him off."

Naomi frowned and glanced at Aung. "Wait, when you say you two were catching up, what precisely were you talking about?"

Aung gave a devious grin and waved a hand. "Oh, just about things from another life." He cleared his throat and looked at Lin. "Why don't you come help me, Lin? I believe there's a chicken coop that needs mending."

Her sister squeezed Naomi's arm as she passed, and Naomi caught Aung's smile before the pair turned and walked away together. Lin really did belong there now, didn't she?

Dane put his bionic arm about her waist. "Do you think in another life Aung used to be an information monger or a crime boss?"

She shook her head slowly. "I can't even begin to speculate."

He squeezed her waist. "Being here will do your sister good."

"I know." She paused. "But I'm going to miss her."

He touched her chin tenderly, before he raised a brow. "Or are you just worried she's going to become a better martial artist than you?"

She feigned indignation. "She's my little sister. She'll never be better than me."

Dane chuckled before he kissed her. His eyes searched hers. "So, what now?"

"I'm thinking first we should go watch Jax wake up."

"Naturally. And afterward?"

"How about we revisit our humanity?" She tilted her head thoughtfully before giving a single nod. "In bed."

He gave a sage nod. "I thought you'd never ask."

ACKNOWLEDGEMENTS

There are endless people to acknowledge for helping this book come to fruition.

A big thank you to Rebel Satori Press and my editor, Joseph Campbell, for publishing my debut novel. I am proud to be part of the Queer Space author family.

Thanks to my beta readers and writer friends who let me bounce ideas off them. Sean, Dave, Aprille, Shauna, and Casey, I love that you think nothing of going down nerd-schema rabbit holes or talking about writing craft.

To my Grand Master and my Zen center: I'll probably never perfect my spinning wheel kick or ever stop struggling with meditation, but my soul is comforted by both.

To my long-time writing group, my deepest gratitude for putting up with my zany novels and giving me inspiration to write, because I looked forward to you reading and giving feedback. Ashley, Anne, Chris, and JoAnn, you all are absolute legends.

To my alpha reader and zesty bestie, Elise Scott, there truly are no words for how much you have uplifted me. From helping me with grammar to discussions on therapeutic methodology or emotional sensitivity, you always help me to be better. I would not be the writer or the person I am without you.

But since this is all so vulnerable, let me give a shout out to my cat, Inari. You couldn't care less that I created a character based off you, but you were integral to my getting my work done by lying atop me and not letting me move for hours on end.

Lastly, thank you, dear reader, for reading! I hope to see you again, in many more books to come.

Cheers,

April McCloud

www.ingramcontent.com/pod-product-compliance
Lightning Source LLC
Chambersburg PA
CBHW022210010726
47493CB00002B/503